About t

Elle James spent twenty years in South Texas, ranching horses, cattle, goats, ostriches and emus. A former IT professional, Elle now writes full-time, penning intrigues and paranormal adventures that keep her readers on the edge of their seats. Now living in northwest Arkansas, she isn't wrangling cattle, she's at her computer, she's snow-skiing, travelling, or riding her ATV, dreaming up new stories.

Bewitched

May 2023
Seduced by the Enemy

June 2023
I Put a Spell on You

June 2023
A Hex Gone Wrong

Bewitched:
A Hex
Gone Wrong

ELLE JAMES

MILLS & BOON

First Published in Great Britain 2023
by Mills & Boon, an imprint of HarperCollins*Publishers* Ltd,
1 London Bridge Street, London, SE1 9GF

www.harpercollins.co.uk

HarperCollins*Publishers*
Macken House, 39/40 Mayor Street Upper,
Dublin 1, D01 C9W8, Ireland

Bewitched: A Hex Gone Wrong © 2023 Harlequin Enterprises ULC.

The Witch's Initiation © 2012 Mary Jernigan
Possessing the Witch © 2015 Mary Jernigan

ISBN: 978-0-263-31937-8

MIX
Paper | Supporting
responsible forestry
FSC™ C007454

This book is produced from independently certified FSC™ paper
to ensure responsible forest management.

For more information visit: www.harpercollins.co.uk/green

Printed and Bound in the UK using 100% Renewable Electricity
at CPI Group (UK) Ltd, Croydon, CR0 4YY

THE WITCH'S INITIATION

To my sister, who is my greatest cheerleader, who always has my back and who challenged me to take the journey on this exciting road to publication. Sisters rule!

Chapter 1

Movement in the shadows caught her attention.

Aurai Chattox strained to see what lurked in the dark. It wasn't something or someone hiding, but wispy shapes growing and creeping steadily closer to the circle of girls gathered around the candles. Had someone lit a smoke bomb? Were there girls or guys hiding among the rosebushes producing the special effects for this weird show?

When she sniffed, all she smelled was the scent of pine and roses and something she couldn't quite define. A pungent, decayed smell, almost imperceptible, buried beneath that of the more powerful aromas of the roses and natural vegetation.

As the dark, shadowy tendrils drifted closer, goose bumps rose on Aurai's skin. She fingered the pentagram at her neck and closed her eyes, drawing on the forces within, the strength of her sisters, the knowledge of the light and her own inner connection with the air, the wind and atmospheric conditions.

She'd made a promise to herself not to use her craft. She wanted to stand on her own as a mortal, not a witch. But something stirred deep inside—call it premonition, call it a portent of evil. If she gave it a nudge, perhaps it would go away.

Aurai lifted her hands by her sides, just enough to stir the air around her. Just a little, not enough to scare the other sorority initiates standing in the circle, their eyes wide, bodies trembling. But maybe enough to dispel the shadowy mist creeping in around them.

A light breeze blew in from the west.

When the West wind blows o'er thee, departed spirits restless be.

A tremor shook Aurai from neck to knees as the breeze kicked up, lifting the tendrils of her hair around her face. Softly, at first, tickling her skin with the strands like the gentle touch of a lover's hand. The stroke was deceptively soothing, and Aurai opened her eyes. Her hood slipped backward, exposing her head to the night air.

Wind was her friend, her lover, her power, the one force within that always gave her comfort and foretold of change to come. Until now.

The gentle breeze intensified, mixing with the inky shadows to lift her hair away from her scalp, slapping it against her face. White-blond locks acted as whips stinging her open eyes.

She squinted against the onslaught and raised her hands to block the battering strands.

Tall pines, which a moment before had stood stately and stoic at the four corners of the garden, swayed like erotic lovers in the throes of passion, twisting and undulating like naked bodies.

Something was terribly wrong.

Her gift of wind should have been a gentle influence to cleanse the air of the encroaching black shadows around the circle of pledges. Instead, it became a force unto itself, gaining in power and magnitude until the girls fought to remain standing.

Her roommate, Rachel, dropped to her knees, blocking her face against flying debris. "What's happening?"

"I don't know," Aurai called out. Branches broke from the trees and pummeled the small gathering of females, drawing blood, scraping and bruising delicate skin.

Thorny rose stems tore at her legs and battered her face and neck. Aurai closed her eyes again, feeling for the ornate pentagram at her neck. The solid piece of silver given to her by her mother. Each of her sisters had a matching pendant, blessed with a protection spell. She called on the spell now.

Unwanted spirits I call thee
I call thee into the light
Guardian spirits I call thee
I call thee to the fight

The spell had no effect on the wind raging around her. The black, inky shadows swept in, twisting her cape around her body until she couldn't move.

"Aurai!" Rachel reached out to her. "Aurai!"

Aurai tried to lift her hand to capture Rachel's, but both arms were trapped at her sides, her cape plastered to her limbs and body like a mummy's death shroud.

Her feet left the ground and her body twirled through the air, faster and faster, caught in a funnel of leaves, rose petals, thorny branches and black, shadowy fingers.

For a moment, Aurai thought she saw the face of a man in the swirling, black wind. The face transformed into a hideous creature with two heads, one with the teeth of a raging lion. Both heads had the soulless, black gaping eyes of a demon.

As the force lifted her above the girls' heads, she gripped her pentagram and cried out, "Sisters, come to me!"

The world spun in a vacuum, lifting her higher still. Then the bottom dropped out of the dark cloud, the earth opened and the wind sucked her down, into a black abyss deep below the surface of the mossy garden soil.

Chapter 2

Sisters, come to me!

Deme Chattox's hands shook as she held the paper cup of green tea, letting the warmth permeate her skin. She'd been chilled since arriving in Chicago. Having left her cushy private investigative business in the balmy breezes of St. Croix and flying overnight to get here, she hadn't had a chance to acclimate. Hell, she hadn't had a chance to breathe.

A nit in the scheme of things, considering her baby sister was missing. Deme could stand to be a little cold. She could only guess at the horrors Aurai faced. For her sister to reach out in the middle of the night and across great distances with enough force to knock Deme out of her bed, she had to be in serious trouble.

She downed the last of the tea and crushed the cup between her fingers. Deme and her sisters would find her if it was the last thing they did. She just hoped they found her before anything really bad happened to the youngest sister of the five of them. For now, her heart told her that her little sister was still alive.

Now where the hell was that detective?

She glanced around the student commons, searching every face for the one that looked most like an undercover cop. Her sister Brigid had given the detective a description of Deme, but she didn't have a name or description of him, and he was already ten minutes late.

The girls at the table next to her leaned close, their expressions nervous. "Did they find her yet?" one asked.

Deme blocked out the extraneous noises of the large cafeteria-style room in order to hear every word spoken by the college girls. That's why she'd come to this campus as a nontraditional student. Not because she wanted to improve her lot in life through a college degree. She already had a BS, an MS and a private investigator license. She'd enrolled as one of the students only to get inside and learn the truth about her sister's disappearance.

"No, they haven't found her," a blonde responded, her blue gaze darting around the nearby tables, briefly pausing on Deme.

Deme's attention remained on the entrance as she used her peripheral vision to study the girls beside her.

The blonde's glance moved on. "I bet the Gamma Omegas know what happened to her. Hell, they probably kidnapped her as part of the hazing."

A brunette snorted. "I don't think any of them are smart enough to get away with it."

The group of six giggled, their fingers pressed to their lips, their glances taking in the room.

The blonde sipped from her soda before asking, "Did the police interview you yesterday?"

"No," the brunette answered. "What about you?"

"No. They seem to be concentrating on the staff and the sorority. I hear the G.O.s were performing their initiation ceremony in the garden when the girl disappeared. I mean, like really, how can you lose a fully grown college student in a garden? That's just random, if you ask me."

Deme wondered the same, and then her attention was distracted by a gray-haired man stepping through the glass entrance doors. He could be a college professor... or maybe an undercover detective.

With the patience of a Yorkshire terrier dying to be unleashed, Deme tapped her plastic spoon on the laminate tabletop. The man stopped at the coffee urn, filled a cup, paid and weaved his way through the tables. He didn't stop until he came to a table in the far corner by the floor-to-ceiling windows overlooking a garden. He never once looked her way.

Damn. Either he wasn't her detective or he was playing hard to get. A man like that would fit right in. No one would ever suspect a guy who looked the image of a college professor of being an undercover cop.

For several long moments, Deme stared at the man by the window. She cleared her mind and focused on him, trying to read into his thoughts. Her sister Selene was much better at reading minds than she was. It wasn't Deme's talent. Give her dirt and plants, and she could whip up a tempting spell with her knack for all things relating to the goddess of earth. Reading minds? Nah. Not her bailiwick. Still, who was he and what was he doing here? Did he have anything to do with her sister?

The man stopped sipping his coffee, a frown pressing his silvery-gray brows together. Was he feeling her probe?

Excited that maybe for once her mind probing might work, Deme concentrated harder. *Who are you? Did you take my sister? Who are you?*

A thin, bookish, young man carrying a tray with coffee and a Danish passed by, stopped and spoke to the professor. At first it all looked like any student stopping to say a word to his instructor. Until the gray-haired man lurched to his feet and shoved the younger man's tray into his chest, toppling the coffee cup. The boy yelled and dropped the tray, pulling his sweater away from his chest, cursing as scalding liquid burned his skin.

The older man hurried from the room, pushing people out of his way as he went.

Deme half stood, torn between helping the guy with the soaked sweater and chasing after the man who'd blown a gasket. A student commons worker beat her to the younger man with a handful of napkins. Meanwhile, the gray-haired gentleman had already left.

She sank into her chair and stared through the glass doors at the back of the retreating professor. What the hell was that all about?

The young man walked by her table talking to the employee, his brow wrinkled in a frown. "I don't know what set him off. All I said was 'How's it going?' Then he yelled, 'No, I didn't, and none of your effing business' and slammed my tray into me." He lifted his sweater away from his skin and flapped it. "That coffee was hot."

"Wonder what came over Professor Dane. He's never blown up like that before."

"It's like he was possessed or something. Did you see his face? Even his eyes didn't look right."

They moved out of range and Deme sat back in her seat. Was the gray-haired Professor Dane feeling the pressure of a missing student? Was he responsible for Aurai's disappearance? Had Deme's probing pushed him over the edge?

She'd never been successful at probing before, so why should it work now? And why in such a way as to cause a violent reaction?

Her chest tightened. Not known for her patience, Deme could feel the blood boiling inside her. She wanted to follow the professor and shake the truth out of him. If Brigid hadn't insisted on this detective, who came highly recommended by the Chicago police as the best undercover operative on the force, Deme wouldn't have waited ten minutes past their scheduled time for him. She could have conducted her own search and interviews. She had shoved her chair back and leaned forward to stand when the glass doors opened again.

Deme sat back in her chair, her mouth falling open. *No way.*

He strode in as if he owned the place. Every female gaze riveted on his incredibly broad shoulders encased in a black leather jacket. Black jeans caressed his thick, muscled thighs and tight ass, moving with him like a second skin.

His black hair hung to his shoulders in loose waves, and he carried a helmet in one hand. Pausing for a moment, he removed sunglasses and stared around the room.

Deme held her breath. When rich, brown eyes collided with hers, her heart skipped several beats then made up for the loss by hammering a staccato against her ribs. She'd never reacted to a man so instantly or with such impact. For a moment she couldn't breathe, and then every nerve ending lit up like the Fourth of July.

No way.

No way this biker bad boy could play an under-cover role at a school. The Chicago police might as well have hung a red flag on him, announcing him as the superhero who would magically reveal the location of their missing sister by waving his incredible magne-tism around a room full of women.

He set out across the floor headed straight for her.

A familiar heat flashed over her, filling her chest and crawling up her neck into her cheeks. Worse still, the heat raged south into her belly and lower, sending searing liquid flames into places that hadn't been lit in a long time. Not since the last time she'd seen him.

Damn! Why him? Why now?

As his boots ate the distance, a slight smile tipped the corner of his lips, as though he knew the secret and he was going to enjoy every bit of it.

When he stopped in front of her chair, he held out a hand.

Deme stared at it a moment, her mind refusing to en-gage, her voice completely choked in her throat. She'd never been this off balance in the presence of a man, no matter how good-looking, except this one. The inten-sity consumed her. Without even thinking it through, she dropped the mutilated cup on the table and laid her hand in his.

Instead of shaking it, he yanked her to her feet and into his arms.

As her chest crashed into his, shock and the whoosh of air escaping her lungs kept her from crying out. Her lips parted in a gasp just in time for his to descend and claim them.

One hand cupped her ass and pulled her pelvis against the natural bulge behind his zipper. The other circled her neck and threaded through her long, auburn hair.

Firm, sensuous lips plundered her startled ones, his tongue delving deep, pushing past her teeth to taste her and drink his fill.

Where their bodies touched, her skin was on fire. Deme squirmed, constrained by the clothing she wore, longing for her naked skin to melt into his.

Long, loud sighs from the young girls at the table beside her brought Deme out of the trance the man's sheer allure had thrown her into. She pulled back, fighting to mask the shock in her eyes. How could she have fallen into his arms—his kiss—without so much as a mew of protest? What had come over her? She never acted so mindlessly. She'd fallen for this macho bullshit before, and what had it bought her?

Heartburn and heartache.

The blue-eyed blonde coed sighed again. "I wish someone would kiss me like that."

"Hi, sweetheart." The man caressed the back of Deme's neck again before he dragged his fingers over her shoulder and downward to capture her hand in his.

Deme tried to pull free, struggling to come up with words to voice her anger at his flagrant attack on her senses. Anger at herself for responding so willingly. By the goddess, she was here to save her sister, not to crawl into a man's skin.

"Want to find a quieter spot?" His look was like liquid chocolate, melting into her pores. With a flick of his eyes, he indicated the girls drooling at the table next to them. More sighs rose from the hormonal young ladies.

"The table by the window." Deme cringed. Was that her voice, that reedy squeak?

Without releasing her hand, he led her to the table at the far corner of the student commons with a lovely view of a rose garden. A table near to where the professor had exploded in a fit of rage.

As she walked like a docile dog behind him, Deme let the anger build. Righteous anger beat mindless lust any day of the week. She'd been in one too many relationships where a man had tried to take charge of her life. Okay, so only one doomed relationship—the relationship she'd had with this man. Besides, her purpose for being at Colyer-Fenton was to find her missing sister, not get all weak in the knees over a cop too sexy to blend in.

With his empty hand, he pulled out a seat and dragged her into it.

Deme sat down hard, her lips drawn into a tight line.

He leaned over her, pressing his lips to her ear. "Try to look a little less like you swallowed a lemon." Then he slid his mouth down her jawline and claimed hers in a brief kiss.

Rendered speechless yet again, Deme sat with her mouth open and nothing coming out. *How'd he do that?*

He pulled out a chair, flipped it around and straddled it like a Harley, his brows hiked into the hair dangling like temptation over his forehead. "Deme Chattox. You never did tell me what Deme means. We can talk about that later. We have business to discuss." He lifted one of her hands and threaded his fingers through hers.

With her lips still tingling from his kiss and the warmth of his fingers on hers stirring up those old feelings of lust all over again, Deme finally pulled herself together. Yanking her hand free, she hid it in her lap.

She leaned forward, her head turned away from the others in the union still watching them. "Is this a joke?" She stared around the room, hoping she'd find some sadistic huckster ready to spring out and tell her she'd been punked. When no one did, she sat on her hands to keep them from shaking in front of him...Cal Black, her former fiancé, lover and her own personal nemesis. "How the hell did you end up on this case?"

He smiled, the act an unaffected thing of beauty. His dark chocolate eyes twinkled and his full, kissable lips stretched over straight, white teeth, a stark contrast to his coal-black hair. She'd fallen for that look once before. "You're my cover, sweetheart." He ran his fingers down her cheek and touched a finger to her swollen lips. "To you, I'm the detective the Chicago police assigned to this case. But to everyone else, I'm your boyfriend until we find your sister."

Cal almost laughed out loud as Deme Chattox's mouth opened then closed before she gathered enough steam to blast him. He had his cover as a maintenance man nailed shut, having spent the past half hour with the Human Resources Department of the small college, charming everyone from the secretary to the woman who ultimately hired him. She'd explained it was only a temporary position until they could find another, more permanent replacement for their previous maintenance man.

He'd asked what happened to the man, but no one knew. He didn't show up for work three weeks ago and hadn't been back. No call, no resignation. Just disappeared. Unfortunately, he didn't have a worried family calling to report him missing.

Cal didn't like that. That made two disappearances in the past three weeks from the same campus. He didn't believe in coincidence and placed a call to Martin Warner, the detective in charge of the case back at headquarters. Was the missing maintenance man responsible for Aurai Chattox's disappearance? If not, was the same perp responsible for both the missing persons?

Now, sitting across the table from Deme Chattox, he drank his fill of the woman who'd managed to turn his world upside down in just the four short weeks they'd known each other. He hadn't even realized she had sisters. She'd never told him. Apparently Deme was the oldest of the Chattox sisters. He wondered if Aurai was anywhere near as beautiful. It was hard to tell from the photograph he'd been given.

Deme's long, auburn hair fell in loose waves around her shoulders and all the way down to her waist. A man could get lost in all that glorious hair. Her deep green eyes sparkled in the fluorescent lights. Lights that normally made everyone else look ill made her pale skin seem only more ethereal. Beautiful women were natural targets for demented kidnappers and killers. "You don't look anything like your sister, do you?"

"Not even close." She pushed her hair behind her ear and sat up straighter. "I'm the redheaded Amazon of the family. Aurai's the pale blonde, petite sister." Her brows furrowed. "Now what's this about being my boyfriend? I don't need a boyfriend."

His lips pressed together in a thin line. "Maybe not to you and me, but for everyone else on campus we need to be convincing." He tipped his head up. "Come here and give me a kiss."

Deme shook her head. "I can't work with you. I work alone." She leaned over the table toward him, the swell of her breasts visible above the figure-hugging, low-cut sweater she wore.

As if a hand had reached out and cranked up the thermostat, the air in the room heated. Cal resisted the urge to tug at his black T-shirt or shrug out of his jacket. As perspiration eased from his skin and his pants tightened uncomfortably, he frowned. He was *not* getting bothered by this woman with enough attitude to overwhelm most men, no matter how sexy she was in that skin-tight sweater.

He made it a strict habit to separate business from pleasure. No matter how pleasurable he had found her in the past. Despite the warnings going off in his head to refuse the assignment and run the other direction, Cal couldn't stop his body's reaction to her nearness. Certain parts refused to forget what it felt like to lie naked against her, to bury himself deep inside her warmth. "I need a cover so that we can talk and not raise suspicion. If you want my help finding your sister, you're stuck with me as a boyfriend."

She opened her mouth and closed it before words could spew forth. Then she leaned across the wooden tabletop and rested her hand on his, squeezing harder than typical for a lover's affectionate grip. "Understand this. I'm only tolerating you because I want to find my sister. So, don't get in my way." She tipped her head to the side and gave him a saccharine-sweet smile. "Am I clear?"

"Crystal." He turned his hand over and captured hers before she could withdraw. "I'm here to do my job. Either help me or go home. Understood, sweetheart?" His words were spoken in a deep, rich timbre, the tone soft

and modulated like a caress. But the steely strength between the lines could not be missed.

Her luscious lips thinned. "Look, you're too pretty.
Working undercover requires a detective who can blend
in. Sorry, you don't blend. Do they have any other
agents they can send?"

"No, I'm it. Besides, I'm the best." He grinned,
knowing it would set her off and added another jab,
"So you really think I'm pretty?"

Deme sighed and resigned herself to having biker
boy as her connection to the police force. "Look, if
we're stuck with each other, let's just keep in mind what
we're after. We're here to find my sister."

"Naturally. Now, are you going to play nice and be
my cover, or not?"

That frown was back, crinkling the bridge of her
nose. "Okay, but don't get any ideas. You're not my
type."

"You made that abundantly clear last time we met."
With her hand still in his, he stood, bringing her to her
feet. Then he tugged her hard enough to throw her off
balance. The only place she could go was smack against
his chest, again. "Besides, you're not my type, either."
He pushed her hair behind her ear, thumbing her earlobe in a tender caress. "At least do a better job of fak-
ing that you like me."

The rigid line of Deme's spine slowly relaxed until
she melted against him, her hands clutching the fabric of his shirt instead of pushing him away. One hand
slid around his backside, where it found its way into
the pocket of his jeans. Using a surprising amount of
strength, she slammed him hard against her, his cock
nudging firmly against her pelvis. At the same time, she
reached up with the other hand and slipped it around

the back of his neck, tangling in his hair. Steady pressure brought his mouth closer to her lips until they were only a breath away.

She leaned close to his ear. "As your girlfriend, do I make you hot?"

Did she make him hot? At the warmth of her breath in his ear, Cal's cock jerked beneath his zipper and his hands clenched around her arms. He wanted her. Wanted to plunge his tongue into her mouth. He wanted to get naked and have hot, juicy sex with her. His body remembered hers in ways that would make a virgin squirm.

Her lips dragged along his jawline until they reached his. For a moment she hovered over him, and then she pressed in for the finale, slanting her mouth over his, thrusting her tongue deep inside to slide across his. Her hips ground against his, teasing his engorged member, converting it to granite.

As quickly as it began, it ended and she stepped out of his arms and reach. Her brows rose and she smiled. "I can fake it with the best of them."

For a moment, Cal breathed in and out. The teasing look in her eyes was enough to bring Cal back to his senses and stir him up all at once. Forcing a light tone into a voice he was sure would crack, he said, "That's more like it. I'll see you tonight. Your room." With that, he left, inwardly cursing his momentary loss of control. Deme Chattox was a prop to get his job done. A prop, damn it. Anything they might have had in the past was just that…in the past. He was in charge of the inside investigation.

Once outdoors, he slipped his helmet over his head and fastened the buckle. As he slid onto the seat of his Harley, he could imagine sliding into Deme. He kicked the starter and the engine roared to life, rumbling beneath his still-hard cock. Oh, yeah, Deme Chattox was a hell of a ride. But that wasn't the point.

From the moment he'd stepped into the student commons, he'd been drawn to her. Irresistibly. He'd had no intention of making her agree to be his girlfriend in order to provide himself additional cover for his investigation. Hell, he'd half convinced himself he could do the job without her help altogether. She could go home for all he cared.

Then what the hell had come over him? The idea was for Deme to help his investigation by infiltrating the Gamma Omegas, but at this point, Cal feared her presence would only distract him, in more ways than one.

He'd better get his mind in the game instead of on the sexy redhead he'd wanted to toss across the nearest table and make love to in front of God and everybody.

Chapter 3

Deme dumped her backpack on the narrow bed tucked against the wall in the tiny dorm room, the echo of her sister's cry reverberating through her. Having met with Detective Cal Black hadn't set her mind at ease, not when her lips still burned from his kiss. If anything, her meeting with the cop had left her more shaken than she cared to admit. Her overwhelming attraction to him couldn't be natural. Not after their breakup over a year ago. Something wasn't right.

Her aversion to the man had a basis. Every time she was near Cal, she couldn't think straight, couldn't focus, couldn't even claim every thought coming from her head was her own. He infiltrated her mind, body and life in a way that left her off balance, her world in a perpetual tilt. She'd kept her relationship with Cal separate from her sisters, and her special "talents" secret from

Cal. How would he react if he'd known about her propensity for magic? Would he think her a freak or crazy?

Torn between the rampant lust raging through her body and her sacred duty to protect her family, Deme avoided his questions, dodging his desire to know more about her personal life. When he'd pushed to know more, she dumped his ass and moved as far away from Chicago as possible to avoid him and his overpowering magnetism. Once bitten by the lust bug, twice hesitant to make a repeat performance.

From the start of their relationship, he'd been clear... He was dedicated to his job protecting the good citizens of Chicago. Nothing and no one would get in the way of his work. He took his responsibilities seriously. He demanded as much passion in his work. And he demanded full disclosure from the people he let into his world. Namely her.

Cal Black was exactly the kind of man Deme didn't need in her life, even if he was there to help her find Aurai.

She crossed to the one small, dingy window and set the ceramic pot containing her beloved angelica root in the meager sun, distorted by the aging glass. The plant drooped, the colors appearing dull in the dreary environment. Deme empathized with how the plant felt. She, too, needed the light to flourish and chase away the emptiness. She touched the fragile stems and they seemed to brighten and reach upward. A ghost of a smile curved Deme's lips.

"The girls are usually pretty good about obeying curfew. I'm sure you'll have no troubles keeping tabs on them." Dr. Diane Masterson entered the room behind her and gave the space an appraising glance. "It's not much, but I hope you'll be comfortable."

"Thank you." Deme faced the college president. "I'm sure I will."

"I'm so glad you chose our school to complete your degree. We needed an older student as a resident assistant. If nothing else, the girls will have a mentor, someone to look up to. You should have no troubles catching up with the coursework." She paused, her eyes narrowing slightly. "Miss Jones, tell me again why it was you decided on Colyer-Fenton College and to start three weeks into the semester."

"I was out of the country visiting a sick relative. I chose Colyer-Fenton because the campus suits me. Quaint and quiet."

"Oh, yes, yes, of course. And that's what we are, quaint and quiet." Dr. Masterson glanced back over her shoulder as if to search the hallway for anyone who could refute her lie.

Deme found it odd that the college president personally escorted her to her room instead of one of the administrative employees in charge of housing.

"If you need anything, just ask one of the girls. They can show you where things are. I'd better go. I have a meeting with my staff in five minutes." The older woman backed out of the room, closing the door behind her.

A meeting, ha! The Chicago police detective in charge of finding Aurai had interviews with the staff scheduled throughout the afternoon. Her Harley-riding sister, Brigid, had met the officer in charge of the case and he'd informed her of the steps they were taking to find their sister, including a thorough interrogation of each campus employee and a number of the over six thousand students.

As far as Deme was concerned, it wasn't enough.

She stared around the stark confines of the room deemed the resident assistant's quarters for the Gamma Omega sorority dorm. She'd had to pull some major strings to land in this one. But this is where she needed to be in order to discover the whereabouts of her youngest sister.

Deme unlocked the window and pushed it upward. A cool blast of fall air blew in, stirring the stale air. She had the best view of all the rooms in the dorm. Maybe it was a perk for being R.A. Located on the shortest side of the building, the room overlooked a fenced courtyard garden. The majority of the dorm rooms stretched out and away from the courtyard.

Deme inhaled the scent of the pines growing close to her window and the sweet fragrance of roses. Ivy clung to the brick walls just below her window, the leafy green vines filling Deme with a sense of calm. The roses in the garden below were in the full bloom of late summer, early fall. Before long, frost would claim the plants and lay them dormant for the chilly winter months.

They would find Aurai before then. She was their sister, the fifth point of the pentagram. They were a unit. Together they were as one. Deme's fingers wrapped around the ornate silver pentagram hanging by a delicate silver chain at her throat. They couldn't fail.

Water dripped from the faucet in the single sink against the wall. Deme moved across the room and twisted the handle to make it quit, but no amount of tightening the handle stopped the slow, steady dripping. She'd have to get maintenance to fix it or she'd be up all night counting each drop.

A light knock at the door echoed against the plain white walls. Before Deme could call out for the person to come in, the familiar willowy, sandy blonde with bright sea-green eyes slipped through the door.

Deme hurriedly closed the gap between them and hugged her sister tightly against her chest. "Oh, Gina. I can't believe this is happening."

Aegina Chattox squeezed her around her middle and then pushed her far enough away to look her in the eye. "Me, either. I'm just glad you and I got in without anyone knowing who we really are."

"Did you have any troubles selling yourself as the aquarium cleaner?"

"None whatsoever. And the aquariums are in atrocious condition in the central library. I should have several days' work on my hands and lots of opportunities to snoop around."

"Let's hope it doesn't take long to find Aurai."

Gina hugged her again. "I'm glad you're home."

Deme nodded. "Me, too."

Without so much as a knock, the door burst open and another one of her sisters entered. Selene, wearing a flowing white skirt, with her long, rich, chocolate-brown hair tied up in a bright colored scarf, entered, stepping into Deme's arms. Tears trembled on her thick lashes, blurring her deep brown eyes. "Where could she be?"

Deme fought the lump in her throat. "I don't know, but between the four of us, we will find her." She patted her second-youngest sister on her back and set her away. "What do you know so far?"

"We met with Brigid off campus and she filled us in."

Gina drifted toward the window and peered down into the garden. "Supposedly, she disappeared during a sorority hazing ceremony. None of the girls know what happened. Or at least they're not talking." She wrapped her arms around her stomach. "How could someone vanish in a crowd of people and no one see it?" She turned back, a frown marring her smooth, tanned forehead. "They know something."

Footsteps in the hallway made the three women fall silent. When the steps continued on, Deme relaxed but she spoke in quiet tones. "No one knows we're related. Brigid was the only one of us to openly meet with the detectives in charge of the investigation and the school officials as Aurai's sister. She can continue to be our contact with the external investigation. I met with the undercover detective. He'll pretend to be my boyfriend so that we can pass information."

Both Gina's and Selene's brows rose. "Boyfriend?"

"His idea, definitely not mine."

"I'm impressed already," Selene said.

Deme glared at her sisters. "Don't get any ideas."

Gina touched her sister's arm. "You can't let that last guy you dated affect every relationship, Deme. What was his name, anyway? You never did tell any of us."

"Yeah, why all the secrecy?" Selene added.

Deme shrugged. "No reason. Besides, it didn't last."

Gina slid a glance sideways at Selene. "Still evading the question."

"No kidding." Selene addressed Deme. "Well, you shouldn't let him taint your feelings for the other men in the world. There are some nice ones out there to choose from."

Deme closed her eyes and drew in a deep breath, guilt pressuring her. She really should fess up to her sisters. She'd never kept secrets from them, with the exception of her relationship with Cal.

For the first time in the year she'd been away from

him, she could actually think of him without choking up. Leaving him had been about the hardest thing she'd ever done. She couldn't begin to contemplate how she'd feel after leaving him a second time. As best she could, she would remain aloof…an overwhelming challenge in the presence of the man's alpha-male sex appeal and bad-boy biker persona. "The undercover detective's name is Cal."

"Nice, strong name. What does he look like?" Gina's eyebrows disappeared into her sandy-blond bangs.

"Does it matter?"

"Of course!" both sisters agreed as one.

"He's your typical eye candy with dark hair and dark eyes." And muscular legs and arms that could wrap around her and carry her to places she'd never been. That flash of heat she'd experienced in the cafeteria returned in force. "Not my type," she lied.

Selene's brows drew together. "Since you're not interested, perhaps I could provide his cover."

Deme held up a hand. "We've already established our so-called relationship in public. Otherwise I'd let you."

"Point made." Gina grinned. "In the meantime, loosen up, sis."

"I'm not here to find a man. I'm here to find Aurai."

Selene wrapped her arm around Deme and hugged her tight. "That dude you dated really did a number on you, didn't he?"

"Let me at him," Gina said. "Any man who makes my oldest sister a basket case for a year deserves to be infested with the fleas of a thousand camels." She pulled a pen and notebook from her hobo bag and jotted down a note to herself. "I'll come up with a potion that'll give him webbed feet."

Deme's lips twitched. "Although I like the image, you can't do that. Cursing someone is delving into dark powers."

Gina's lips twisted. "I'd only do it once. And it would be well worth the risk if it makes the man as miserable as he made you."

Deme turned away. The image of Cal with webbed feet almost brought a smile to her face. Not that her sister could conjure webbed feet. Their powers didn't work like that. But wait until her sisters saw Cal Black. They'd never give her a moment's rest with their sisterly teasing. Even the thought of the tall, dark cop made Deme's body burn. "We all have our covers established. We need to maintain our anonymity in order to gain the trust of the other girls. We want answers, and the sooner the better."

"All I know is that it's been two days. Two days too long." Selene winced and pressed fingers to the bridge of her nose.

Deme laid a hand on her shoulder. "Are you all right?"

She breathed in and out for a moment before answering. "There's a dark aura surrounding this campus. I sensed it as soon as I came through the gates. It feels like someone trying to push into my mind."

"Do you think you should let that someone in? Maybe he or she can tell you what happened."

"I tried, but so far there's like this wall blocking them."

"Them? As in more than one?" Deme asked.

Selene's fingers moved from the bridge of her nose to her temples, where she massaged the skin, her eyes squeezed shut. "I think so."

Still staring out the window, Gina asked, "Think it

would help if we get together tonight to cast a circle and call them forth?"

Deme had sensed the darkness, too, but Selene had a better connection with the metaphysical world than any of them. She'd even had conversations with the dead. On more than one occasion, her ability to sense trouble had saved their butts. When Selene perceived a disturbance in the spiritual balance, invariably she was right. It was her gift, as knowledge and connection to the earth was Deme's and Selene's was water. Brigid connected with fire, and Aurai, sweet Aurai's gift was her ability to influence and communicate with the wind and air currents.

"Let's wait and see what happens and what we can learn from the students and staff on campus," Deme said.

"Brigid said the Gamma Omegas' sorority initiation ceremony was conducted in a garden." Gina turned back to the others. "Do you suppose it was this one?"

Selene walked toward the window, her face paling as she neared the opening. When she reached the windowsill, she wavered, her body swaying. She clutched the raised window and pulled it down, pressing her forehead against the glass. "Something happened here. I can't tell exactly what, but it wasn't good."

Deme's lips tightened. "Then that's where we start our search. Gina, see if you can find any history on the college in the library. Past students, old newspaper articles, anything. Selene, you'll be a member of the faculty. Check out the other professors and staff for anything concerning Aurai's disappearance, the garden and the sorority. I'll work on the girls in the sorority."

"We need to maintain our distance in front of others." Gina looped an arm around Selene and led her away from the window. "Hanging out together will blow our cover. If there is a kidnapper lurking on campus, we can't let him know we're sisters. When we meet again, it needs to be away from campus."

Deme nodded. "Agreed. I'll get close to Aurai's roommate. I think she's in this building." Deme flipped through the roster Dr. Masterson had given her of students living in the dormitory. "There she is—Rachel Taylor. Brigid said she was one of the girls initiated into the sorority that night."

Selene gripped her arm, her clutch pinching Deme's skin. "You aren't going to try to pledge the sorority, are you?"

"I don't think it's possible." Deme loosened Selene's grip and patted her hand. "Don't worry. I can take care of myself."

"I know you can. But promise me you won't join the sorority. It's too dangerous." How she just seemed to know things was a mystery to all the sisters, but they didn't ignore her when she gave them warnings.

"I promise. Pledge week is over and they've done their initiation. New members have already been inducted. I'll be on the periphery since I'm the R.A." Deme glanced at Selene. "Are you sure you're going to be all right?"

She smiled, her dull, green eyes brightening. "With my sisters around me, I'll be fine. Speaking of which, where's Brigid now?"

"She's working with the detective on the police investigation." Gina closed the window and twisted the latch before she crossed to the others. "We'll see her around campus as they conduct their interviews. However, everyone will know she's Aurai's sister. They won't know who we are, if we're careful."

"Then come on, we need to part ways and get this investigation under way." Deme held out her hands. Gina took one and Selene the other until their hands closed the ring.

Without her other two sisters, Deme sensed how incomplete the circle was. She closed her eyes and began, her sisters joining in.

"Feel the power
Free our hearts
Find our way
Be the one
With the strength of the earth
With the rising of the wind
With the calm of the water
With the intensity of fire
With the freedom of spirit
The goddess is within us
She is power
We are her
We are one
Blessed Be."

As each word passed their lips, the air in the room grew thicker until breathing became more difficult. A funny odor filled the room, similar to the scent of decaying vegetation. A scratching sound penetrated Deme's concentration. Selene's hand squeezed hers in a death grip.

"Do you feel them?" Selene asked. "They're screaming. Can you hear them?"

Deme opened her eyes and stared around the room. The lights seemed dimmer, and the sunlight that had a moment before shone through the window had disappeared behind a cloud. The scratching sound she'd heard was English ivy rubbing against the window.

She didn't remember it being that high before. Had she missed it?

The water dripping in the sink had become a thin, steady flow. Gina dropped Selene's and Deme's hands and reached for the handle on the sink. "What's with this faucet?" She twisted the handle and nothing happened.

"I can hear them, but I can't understand what they're saying." Selene clutched her head between her hands and swayed. "They're so loud. I can't shut them out." Her hands dropped to her sides and her troubled gaze searched the room until she found the door. "I have to leave."

Deme wrapped her arm around Selene's waist. "Go. Get off campus."

"I'll go for now, but we need to meet tonight. I want to know who they are and why they're fighting to get in my head."

"This damned faucet isn't working." Gina slammed her hand against the handle.

"Leave it." Deme herded her brown-haired sister toward the door. "Selene needs to get out of here."

Gina jiggled the handle again. "Give me a second. I think I can get this thing—" The handle flew off and water gushed from where it had been, shooting in a four-foot radius around the room.

"Damn, what the hell's wrong with this place?" Gina slipped on the floor and dropped to her knees, reaching beneath the sink for the shutoff valve.

"I have to go." Selene staggered toward the door, her eyes squinting and her forehead lined with pain.

Deme opened the door and glanced out into the hallway. "You can go now. The hallway's clear." When

Selene passed her, she gave her sister's arm a squeeze. "Be careful."

As she closed the door behind Selene, Deme turned to the scratching at the window. The vines now choked out the little bit of light. A chill that had nothing to do with being wet or cold shivered across Deme's skin.

Gina turned the shutoff valve, and the geyser of water slowed to a trickle and finally stopped. She straightened, soaked to the skin, and shook some of the water from her arms. "What just happened?"

"I don't know, but you'd better go before the Gamma Omega girls come looking for all the commotion." Deme checked the hallway and held the door for her sister. "See you tonight. Be safe."

Once her sisters were gone, Deme closed the door and leaned her back against it, staring at the wreck of her room.

She wasn't Selene, but she'd felt it, too. As they'd stood in the circle, the air in the room changed as if drawing on their power.

Standing in a puddle of water, the lights dim and the window blocked by ivy, Deme knew with certainty they were dealing with more than just a kidnapper. Aurai was in a lot more trouble than they'd originally thought.

Chapter 4

After Cal left campus, he returned to the Chicago Police Special Investigations Division. Lead investigator Lieutenant Martin Warner had requested his presence. Cal hoped he'd fill him in on the rest of the details he'd left out in the hurried initial briefing that morning.

Cal passed the front desk, waving at the sergeant who manned the telephone. He wove his way through the office cubicles to the rear of the building, where the Special Investigations Team had set up a war room.

Having been on the team all of four hours and twenty-seven minutes, Cal didn't know anyone but the lieutenant who'd briefed him earlier that morning.

When Cal entered the war room, Marty had his back to the door. He stood with his feet braced wide and his chin resting in his hand, staring at a white board with a thick black horizontal line stretched across the surface. Taped in one corner was a preprinted map of the

Colyer-Fenton College campus. Beside the lieutenant, a woman dressed in black leather with long, ink-black hair hanging down to her waist leaned against the edge of the table, her arms crossed over her chest. "Has to be connected," she said, her voice husky, yet smooth, like milk chocolate-covered gravel.

Marty, as he'd asked Cal to call him, nodded. "Every one of the incidents occurred either on campus or were performed by people who are related to Colyer-Fenton."

Cal cleared his throat.

Marty spun and faced him. The woman beside him turned more slowly. When she saw who was standing there, her lips curled up on the sides in a devilish smile. "Ah, our detective has arrived."

Cal's eyes narrowed. He couldn't remember meeting this woman, but there was something familiar about her. "I'm sorry, I haven't had the pleasure." He stuck out his hand. "Cal Black."

When she took his hand, an odd burst of heat streamed from her hand to his, shooting like an adrenaline burst up his arm and into his chest.

He pulled his hand back quicker than normal, his palm still tingling. "And you are?"

"Brigid." Her smile grew wider.

Marty clapped Brigid on the back. "Brigid is one of the team."

"How long have you been on the force?"

"Counting today?" She checked her watch. "Approximately four hours."

Cal's gaze shot from her to Marty.

Marty sighed. "It's a long story, but suffice it to say, she's been working with the Chicago Police Department for almost a year and demonstrated her...uh...expertise.

Mostly with arson investigations, but we have reason to believe she could be of assistance on this team."

Cal frowned. "Does she understand the risks of working on the Chicago police force?"

Brigid crossed her arms over her chest, her black leather vest creaking, the black nail polish on her fingertips shining. "I can take care of myself, if that's what you're asking."

"Do you have a license to carry a weapon?"

"No."

"Do you even know how to shoot?"

"No." She glanced at Marty.

"She's not a trained police officer, Cal." Marty grinned. "But she has talents that could come in handy on this case and others we've seen like it."

Not until she stared up at him, forcing him to look directly into her eyes, did he realize how intensely blue hers were.

Cal nodded, not entirely sold on Brigid's so-called talents, but willing to give the lieutenant the benefit of the doubt. "Maybe you can explain to me what exactly the Special Investigations Team does?"

"Yeah." Brigid sat on the conference table and crossed her legs Indian fashion. "Tell him what we're up against."

"That's just it." Marty shook his head. "We don't know what we're up against. We've taken a select few of Chicago's finest from the police force and a couple detectives like you and a few trusted civilians we've worked with in the past…"

Brigid shot a frown at the lieutenant.

The man's lips twisted. "Okay, one trusted civilian… to form this team."

Brigid's frown smoothed.

The lieutenant stared hard into Cal's eyes. "We get all the cases no one knows what to do with, the ones that don't make sense, and we try to make sense out of them."

Brigid snorted in a very unladylike manner, yet in keeping with the black leather, bad-ass persona she'd adopted. "What the lieutenant is trying to say, but isn't quite nailing, is that we will be investigating the cases involving paranormal activities. Incidents that defy the norm. The quirky, weird, bizarre, uncanny and downright strange occurrences that usually get shoved under the radar because they make people feel too uncomfortable to address."

"What are you talking about? I thought I was investigating the disappearance of a girl." Cal reminded himself this girl wasn't just any girl. She was his ex-girlfriend's sister.

"And you are," Marty assured him. "First and foremost, we want to retrieve the missing girl and reunite her with her family." The lieutenant stared over at Brigid. "While I have both of you here alone, I need to know something."

"Know what?" Cal demanded.

"I need to know that your connections with the victim's family members will not get in your way of performing a thorough investigation."

"What connection?" Cal's heart beat faster, but he played dumb to the lieutenant's question. What did Marty know about his relationship with Deme Chattox?

The lieutenant shook his head. "We conduct a thorough investigation of all our team members, security check, background check down to what vet you take your dog to."

"I don't have a dog," Cal stated flatly.

"Well, we knew you had a thing going with Deme Chattox, the victim's oldest sister."

Brigid's eyes narrowed. "Were you doing my sister? Tsk, tsk. And here I thought we'd have a shot at making things happen."

"Sister?" Cal glanced from Brigid back to Marty. "What do you mean, *sister*?"

"Our missing girl, Aurai Chattox, has four sisters."

Brigid gave him a little wave with the tips of her fingers. "Brigid Chattox, Deme's younger sister. She didn't tell you about us, did she?" She tapped her chin with her fingertip. "I wonder why."

Cal wondered, too. Seems like when you're sleeping with someone, they'd tell you all their secrets. Family shouldn't be a secret. But not Deme. From the get-go, their passion singed any other thoughts from his head. When he finally got around to asking, she'd gone. Completely out of his life. There one day, gone the next.

"One of the reasons I brought you in on this case was because I knew you had dealings with Deme Chattox and probably knew a little about her and her family. When Brigid told me what the Chattox sisters had planned, I knew I needed one of Chicago's best detectives on the inside."

Brigid shook her head, her lips twisting. "He didn't trust us to do it on our own."

"Damn it, Brigid!" Marty pounded his fist on the conference table so hard, even the ubercalm Brigid bounced, her eyes widening.

Marty's lips pressed into a thin line, his face beet-red and getting redder by the second. "We've already lost one young woman to whoever or whatever kidnapped her. I don't want to lose four more."

Brigid uncurled her legs and pushed off the table, standing tall. "She's not gone for good. We just can't find her." Her jaw tightened. "But we will, I have no doubt. I only told you because I wasn't going to refuse a little help."

"And rightfully so. A missing girl on a campus is not something to take lightly. The police need to be just as involved in returning the girl to her family as bringing the perpetrator to justice." He aimed the remarks at Brigid, then he turned to face Cal. "Back to my original question. Is your relationship with Deme Chattox going to cause you any difficulties?"

"I don't have a problem keeping on track." Heat rose in Cal's belly as he recalled the feeling of Deme's lips on his. She could be a major distraction, but he refused to let her. Their "thing" had ended a year ago.

Brigid's hand brushed his, ever so lightly and briefly, the heat burning a path across his nerve endings. "Yeah, and you didn't want to kiss her, but you did," she whispered to him, low enough only he could hear.

"Huh?" Cal jerked away from the woman. How'd she know?

Brigid's lips twitched. "You heard me. Play nice with my sister. She had a nasty time of it with a man almost a year ago and hasn't dated since. If I'd known who it was, I might have been tempted to inflict some bodily harm on him."

Cal almost laughed out loud. The petite woman with the long, black hair didn't look as if she could harm a fly, much less a full-grown man. Besides, she had her facts all wrong.

A year ago placed Deme with him. He had to be the man Brigid was talking about. But Deme hadn't had a nasty time of it. More like she'd given *him* a nasty time. As soon as he'd asked her to marry him, she'd left. Talk about cold feet.

It wasn't as if he'd meant it—he'd blurted it out immediately following the most mind-blowing sex he'd ever had. Hell, they'd spent every night for a month in his bed, in his apartment. It must have seemed like a natural progression for her to marry him and move in permanently.

He'd waited two days, thinking maybe she'd been thrown off balance by his proposal.

Those two days had been the longest he'd ever experienced. When he'd gone by her apartment in downtown Chicago, she'd moved out. Nothing left but an empty roll of box tape.

Apparently Deme hadn't told her sisters any more about him than she had told him about them. Why all the secrecy? If she didn't want to be a part of his life, all she had to do was say so. Moving away had been extreme.

When Marty had told him about Deme's involvement in the case, his first instinct was to walk away. Getting answers to why she left was one of the reasons he'd agreed.

In the back of his mind, the need for a little payback had spurred him into action. Thus his kiss in the student commons. And if he wasn't mistaken, Deme Chattox was not immune to him…unfortunately, not any more than he was immune to her.

"Very well, then." Marty turned toward the white board hanging on the wall. "Let me fill you in on what's been happening on or around campus. Maybe you'll understand why the Special Investigations Team is working this case."

Brigid shot a narrow-eyed glance at Cal before turning her attention to the board as if to say, *I'm watching you.*

Cal could have laughed out loud, but the lieutenant was talking.

He pointed to a time line on the board with a tick mark near the start of the line. "Two weeks ago, a male student attacked a female student while she was walking through the campus. She'd never talked to him, he'd never expressed any interest in her. Up until the attack, he'd been a model student, making good grades, working toward a prelaw undergrad degree. Clean record, no criminal history. Nothing. Out of the blue, he attacks a girl."

"So? Doesn't it happen every day?"

Marty nodded. "You'd think. But when questioned, he broke down in tears claiming it was as if he had no control over his actions. One minute he was worried about his economics test, the next he'd jumped a girl and practically raped her before a member of the faculty came along and pulled him off."

"Again...so?" Cal had seen rapists claim temporary insanity too many times to believe. If a man could rape a woman, he had to have something wrong with him and needed to be taken off the streets.

"At first, it looked like a cut-and-dried case of attempted rape...but then it happened again." Marty shot a glance over his shoulder at Cal and Brigid before he pointed at the second hash mark. "Two days after the first incident, another boy attempted rape."

"Same one?"

"No, a different boy. Same thing. He was a model student, premed degree. On his way to the library when he lost it and tried to rape a girl."

"Power of suggestion?" Cal offered.

"You mean because news got around the other boy wanted to get in on the action?" Marty shook his head. "That's what I thought at first. The university didn't let the information out about the previous attempted rape for fear the parents would yank their kids midsemester. That and we had their rapist."

"Is there any connection between the two guys? Are they in the same fraternity? Do they live in the same dorm? Involved in a hazing event or something?" Cal asked.

Marty shook his head. "We checked into all that. Again, one of the students is prelaw, the other premed. Neither has joined a frat house. One lives on campus and the other in an apartment nearby. As far as both are concerned, they didn't even know each other existed until these events occurred."

"Where did the attempted rapes happen?" Brigid stared at the campus map, her gaze so intense her blue eyes appeared steel-gray.

Sweat popped out on Cal's forehead. "Is it me, or is it getting hot in here?"

The lieutenant tugged at the tie around his neck, loosening it, a bead of perspiration sliding down the side of his head. "It's getting hot." He stared across at Brigid. "Do you mind?"

She flushed, a weak smile crossing her lips. "Sorry." Then her smile disappeared, she clasped the medallion hanging around her neck and closed her eyes.

Within a few seconds, the room temperature dropped enough that Cal could tell a marked difference. He looked around for who might have adjusted the room's temperature. When he located the thermostat, nobody stood near it. The only occupants of the room were the three of them.

His gaze returned to Brigid, who clutched at the medallion, her eyes blinking open. She met his gaze with quirked lips and raised eyebrows.

"The Chattox girl disappeared here." Marty poked the time line, smearing the black hash mark identified with a date and the letters *AC* for Aurai Chattox.

Cal lifted the dry erase marker and added a dark slash before all the hash marks three weeks prior to the girl's disappearance.

The lieutenant's brow rose. "What's that for?"

"One missing maintenance man. I spoke with HR this morning. I'm their new maintenance man as of today. The prior guy never showed up for work three weeks ago. Since he had only been on the job for a couple of months, they assumed he'd just quit. They didn't have any emergency numbers to contact next of kin, and he didn't return their calls."

Marty's brows pulled together into a V. "And they didn't file a missing persons report?"

"No family to miss him." Cal shrugged. "Think he might be our kidnapper?"

Brigid shook her head, her gaze fixed on the board though she appeared lost in thought. "I don't think so, but we should add him to our list of people to find."

"Two other incidents happened off campus involving a professor and a student," Marty continued. "Both separate, but somewhat the same. A female student who'd been part of the sorority Aurai was pledging tried to commit suicide by slashing her wrists," Marty said.

Cal sucked in a breath. "How is she?"

"She'll live, but she's in the hospital, recovering from blood loss and she's under psychiatric observation."

"The professor?"

"Ran her car into the Chicago River."

"Accident?"

"No, she'd left a suicide note at her apartment. Her sister found it."

"And her prognosis?"

"Dead." Marty pointed at the time line where two more marks broke the line, one before Aurai's disappearance, one after. "Her car was found this morning by a bicyclist."

Marty faced Cal. "Your job is to work the school staff, ask questions, get answers. Your connection to the sorority will be Deme Chattox. I expect you to pass information to her and gather it from her on a regular basis. Brigid will be working with the rest of the team on the outside of campus, questioning other victims' families and acquaintances."

"When will I meet the other team members?" Cal asked.

Marty smiled. "Soon enough. For now, get inside the campus and find out what the hell's going on."

"Will do." Cal stood tall, all but saluting his superior. "And thanks for your confidence in my abilities."

"Don't thank me. Prove you deserve it." Marty started to turn away but stopped. His voice lowered, and he pinned Cal with an intense stare. "And Cal, be open-minded about the strange and unexplainable. There's been some really weird stuff going on you probably aren't aware of."

Cal's gut tightened at the tone of Marty's voice, a chill rippling across his skin. "Yes, sir." As he turned to leave, he caught a glimpse of Brigid fingering the medallion she wore around her neck. The metal was shaped into a star with five points inside a circle. He'd seen a similar one, but where?

As Cal left the war room, Brigid fell in step beside him, her fingers still wrapped around the metal.

An image of Deme lying nude in his bed flashed through his mind. When they made love, she'd taken off everything but the medallion—a pentagram just like the one Brigid wore. She'd said it was a gift from her mother and she never removed it.

When Cal stopped to face Brigid, she looked up at him, her brows rising up into her black hair.

Cal reached out and touched the pentagram at Brigid's neck. "Does your medallion have meaning?"

Brigid's lips curled upward. "Deme didn't tell you?"

"Tell me what?" He had a feeling Deme had kept a lot more than her family from him, and the anger at being kept in the dark rose to the surface and boiled there.

"It's a pentagram. The sign associated with the Wiccan."

He had an open mind when it came to people of different religious persuasions. To each his own as long as it didn't interfere with others' beliefs.

But he also believed that everything had a logical explanation. Magic and what some would call woo-woo was just superstitious bullshit some people used to scare and control others. The lieutenant had said the Special Investigations Team, or SPIT, as Cal had shortened it, was responsible for taking on the cases that didn't have an obvious explanation. It was up to them to find it. But logic could be found in every situation.

He nodded toward the pendant. "Does it represent your religion? Your faith?"

"Most definitely." Brigid held the pentagram out in front of her to the end of the chain. "You see, our mother was a witch."

Chapter 5

After Deme cleaned the water from her dorm room floor, she set out to find Rachel, Aurai's roommate. She'd scanned the roster she'd been given as the resident assistant and found her listed on the same floor several doors down from where Deme's room was located.

Girls ducked in and out of rooms, wafts of perfume or hair spray filling the air with each passing. The cloying scents overwhelmed Deme. She didn't use scented candles in her apartment or in her rituals, preferring the natural odors the earth gave off. The sharp aroma of pine sap, the earthiness of decaying leaves or the extravagant natural fragrance of roses blooming, in her mind, could not be duplicated.

On every door she passed, the Greek letters for gamma and omega hung. Some of the rooms had the girls' names hanging on cute signs. The more young women she saw, the more surreal the experience became. Each girl seemed perfect. Thick, beautiful hair, perfectly coifed, figures a model would die for and skin as smooth and blemish-free as a newborn babe's.

Where were the late teens with acne scars? What happened to bad hair days and the few extra pounds the sedentary life of a college coed generated?

Perhaps Rachel was a thorn among the roses of the sorority sisters. Deme had received text messages from her sister describing her first impressions of her dorm room and her roommate. Aurai had given Deme the impression that Rachel was a plump young woman with frizzy hair and thick glasses, her face riddled with pockmarks from a bad case of acne.

After all the Barbie look-alikes, Deme could appreciate a real girl with curves and flaws. She'd be more human, more approachable than the other residents of the Gamma Omega dormitory.

Deme paused in front of the room her sister had occupied up until forty-eight hours ago. Her chest tightened, her hand shaking as she reached out to knock. Deep in the back of her mind, Deme desperately hoped Aurai would open the door and hug her, telling her the cry for help was all in her imagination and that everything was fine.

Her eyes stinging, Deme blinked. And if wishes were horses… She tapped her knuckles on the hard wooden door and waited, refusing to hold her breath. No matter what she told herself about wishing things better, she couldn't slow her heartbeat. As she waited, her blood slammed through her veins, pounding against her eardrums.

"Just a minute!" a voice called out from inside.

After what seemed a very long time, but in fact had been only a matter of seconds, the door swung open.

A dark-haired beauty peered out, her eyes widening when she saw Deme. "Oh." Her gaze darted to each side of where Deme stood. "Can I help you?"

"Hi, I'm Deme Jones, the new R.A. for the dorm." She stuck out her hand. "Are you Rachel?"

Rachel nodded, taking Deme's hand in a limp grip, her dark, shiny hair falling into her smooth-skinned face. She had her purse slung over her shoulder and appeared to be on her way out.

Deme frowned. This girl was not what she'd expected. From Aurai's texts, she'd conjured an image of a shy girl with self-esteem issues because of a less than perfect body and face.

This young woman was like so many others in the building, beautiful and too perfect for her comfort. Deme touched her own chin, conscious of the scar there from the time she dove into a creek as a preteen and hit the bottom. The mouthful of rocks had been the least of her worries at the time—the scar a constant reminder to look before you dive into unknown waters.

Deme swallowed hard to keep from choking on her next words. Words she fought hard to keep natural. "I hear your roommate bailed on you."

Rachel's elegantly arched brows drew downward into a frown. "What did you hear?"

"Only that she bailed. Do you want me to find another girl to share your room?" It cost Deme to offer. More than anything she wanted to find her sister, but she didn't want the girls of the dorm to know that was her real reason for being there.

"No!" Rachel reached out to touch Deme, her hand shaking, a pained twist in dark brows. "Aurai will be back. I just know it. She probably just got homesick or something and went home for a few days. She'll be back, I tell you." Her hand fell to her side, her voice fading. "She has to come back."

"Rachel?" A male voice called out behind Deme. "Is that you?" The voice belonged to a tall, gangly young man, more typical of what Deme expected from a college student. His hair hung too long around his ears, the excess flesh around his cheeks and middle gave him a big teddy-bear look.

Rachel's smile widened and her chin dipped. "Hi, Mike."

For a beautiful girl, she lacked the confidence that came with a perfect complexion and figure. No, Rachel didn't resemble the outward picture Aurai had painted. Not in the slightest sense. But the way she acted around the boy displayed a hint of the crippling shyness Deme had expected.

"Um...can we talk later?" Rachel looked up at Deme, who stood at least a head taller than the girl. Rachel's expression begged for release.

"Sure. Just wanted to introduce myself and get to know some of the girls in the dorm."

"I promise I'll come by later. It's just..." She blushed and shot a shy glance at the boy. "I have to go."

The young man stood as though transfixed, his jaw drooping. "Rachel?" He didn't seem to recognize the girl in front of him.

"Yeah, Mike, it's me." She hooked his arm and led him away from Deme.

"What happened to you?" Mike was saying as Rachel dragged him down the hall.

"Sorority science project?" she quipped, laughing shakily, her voice fading as she stepped through the door leading to the stairwell.

Sorority science project? Deme shook her head and

took out the ring of keys she'd been entrusted with as the resident assistant. She waited until the hallway emptied and jammed the key into the lock. She unlocked and opened the door, darting in as one of the doors on the floor squeaked open.

Her heart racing, Deme shut the door and stood with her back to it.

The room was nothing to write home about. Two twin-size beds, two utility dressers and two closets comprised the major assets. The dormitory was old enough that the bathroom was down the hall and shared by the entire floor. Deme had passed it on the way to Aurai's room. A cleaning schedule had been worked out and posted on the bulletin board beside the entrance.

One bed had a soft pink comforter with a giant black-and-white-dots pattern spread across its surface. Leaning against the wall were three pillows in the black, pink and white of the coverlet. Not something Aurai would have chosen in a million years. It had to be Rachel's bed.

As Deme glanced around the room, her stomach knotted. The other bed had a midnight-blue coverlet with gold stars, silver moons and white clouds sprinkled across it. So typical of Aurai. Always the dramatic one, playing up her heritage as a witch in subtle ways without actually confessing to those around her. While she'd dreamed of blending in with regular people, she was drawn to the mystical and magical in ways only her sisters understood.

Her eyes blurring, Deme continued her perusal, her gaze landing on a picture frame perched on the dresser beside the pink bed. A dark-haired, nondescript girl stood between two adults, equally nondescript, presumably her parents.

Deme lifted the frame and stared down at the photograph. Scrawled in flowing cursive were the words *We love you, Rachel. Mom and Dad.* Upon closer inspection, the girl in the picture was everything Aurai had described, chubby, pockmarked, frizzy-haired and slumping like a shy girl.

How could a person change so much in so short a time? As if she'd transformed overnight. Deme removed her cell phone from her back pocket and snapped a picture of the photograph. She'd show her sisters and get their opinion. No amount of makeup could cover pockmarks that deep. And the Rachel she'd met in the hallway didn't have a single blemish. Could there be two Rachels with the same last name?

Deme replaced the picture frame and examined the contents of the dresser. Beside the frame was an ornate blue bottle with a very small amount of liquid inside.

Careful so as not to spill it, Deme pulled the glass stopper out of the top and sniffed. An acrid aroma wafted up in her face and stung the insides of her nostrils. She quickly jammed the stopper back on the bottle, snorting to get the stench out of her system.

She held the bottle up, looking for a label where it had none. What the heck was it? Was it medicine? It had to be something strong. Even now, her sinuses pinched in protest, her head aching from the residual stench. She shook her head to clear a sudden dizzy feeling then set the bottle on the dresser and continued her search. For what, she wasn't certain. Any clue as to her sister's whereabouts would be nice. She wasn't so sure it could be found in her roommate's belongings.

The first drawer inside Rachel's dresser contained a myriad of hair accessories, facial cleansers, acne medication and perfume bottles. Typical toiletries for a female exiting her teens. The acne creams were in keeping with the girl in the picture.

The remaining drawers contained clothing befitting the conservative lifestyle of a shy, withdrawn girl of larger proportions than the Rachel who'd left the room a few minutes earlier.

Books, a backpack and more clothing were the contents of Rachel's little closet. Nothing that gave a hint to her part in Aurai's disappearance, except perhaps the black robe hanging as far to the back as possible, almost hidden by a pale blue formal. Deme snapped a picture of the robe, unsure of its purpose in a coed's closet. Especially a freshman so far from potential graduation. And the robe had a hood. Not typical of graduation gowns.

Having avoided her sister's belongings, Deme finally turned to her side of the small room. Throughout her investigation of Rachel's things, she'd felt her sister's presence in her belongings. Everything Aurai touched left a residual aura of the youngest Chattox sibling.

The photograph on her dresser was a picture taken several years ago when all five sisters had been home at the same time. Her mother had been alive and snapped the picture, capturing the essence of each girl in one still image. Deme stood tallest in the center, her red hair glinting copper in the sunshine, loose and wavy around her shoulders, her face serious, as befitting the oldest daughter.

Selene stood on one side of Deme, her dark brown hair piled high on her head, her brown-black eyes fathomless, a secret smile playing on her lips. On Deme's other side, Gina had her arm around Deme and Brigid, her willowy body clothed in light blues and greens, her sandy-blond hair a sharp contrast to Brigid's coal-black mane and bold, black, Goth attire. Gina's smile was gentle, like a day at the beaches she loved. Brigid, on the other hand, stood with a cocky tilt to her head, her eyebrows arched as if to challenge anyone to say anything even slightly offbeat.

Beside Selene, Aurai stood with a happy, innocent grin, her pale blond hair lifted by her blessed wind. She couldn't have been more than twelve in the picture, her body lean and boyish. She hadn't yet blossomed into the beautiful young woman who'd gone off to college full of dreams of the future. She hadn't come into her talents, verging on puberty and all the responsibility of the adult Chattox women.

A simpler time for Aurai.

Deme squeezed her eyes shut and pressed the picture to her chest, fighting back the tears. She hadn't cried since her mother died right after Aurai's high school graduation.

On the island of St. Croix, Deme hadn't been there to say goodbye to her dear mother. She'd run away from her life in Chicago, away from her feelings for Cal Black. Deme had spent the better part of a year trying to forget that, because she was who she was, she couldn't have a normal relationship with a man. Especially a man like Cal who saw only the black and white, the good and bad. Shades of gray would disturb him. Hell, her shades of gray would disturb most men. Why bother trying?

Fiona Chattox had been their rock. Deme hadn't known her father long when he'd disappeared from their lives. She'd been the tender age of six. Her mother told the girls he'd died, but Deme never believed it, certain that her father would return some day and tell them he'd been spirited away by some unknown force and held captive all those years. Why else would he leave his beautiful wife and five daughters?

Deme opened her eyes and stared around the room Aurai had made her second home. She might not have her parents to fend for her, but Deme would be damned if her youngest sibling disappeared forever like her father. She'd find her. And when she did, she'd make whoever had taken her pay.

She couldn't bring herself to let go of the picture. Instead she slipped it from its frame and tucked it beneath her shirt, sticking the frame inside the dresser drawer.

With one quick last look, she opened the door and stepped out into the hallway. When she turned toward the R.A.'s room, she came face-to-face with a girl with golden-blond hair and pale blue eyes, her complexion so perfect she could have been a model for a cosmetics company.

The blonde's eyes narrowed. "Who are you and what were you doing in Rachel's room?"

Taken aback and feeling like a thief, Deme clutched her middle to keep the picture from falling from beneath her shirt. She forced a smile and straightened, throwing her shoulders back. She still had to look up at the young woman, who was just a bit taller than Deme's five feet nine inches. "I'm Deme Jones, the new R.A. And you are?"

"Zoe Adams. President of the Gamma Omegas." Her eyes narrowed into slits. "When did we get a new R.A.? Why wasn't I informed?"

Deme's fingers tightened into fists as she struggled to resist the urge to punch this princess right in the face and make a mess of her perfectly upturned nose. "Perhaps the college president didn't feel it necessary to consult you before hiring me."

"We'll see about that." She crossed her arms over her chest. "You didn't answer my question. What were you doing in Rachel's room?"

"If I'm not mistaken, which I rarely am, you are rude and the room is not only Rachel's but Aurai Chattox's, as well. I was inside looking to see if our missing girl has returned. Since she hasn't, I was looking for her emergency data."

"And you don't have that on file?"

Caught. Deme didn't let the Amazon flap her. Instead she smiled. "I have emergency data for everyone but her. As president of the Gamma Omegas, you don't happen to have her emergency data, do you?" Deme tipped her head, allowing a smug smile to turn up the corners of her lips.

Zoe's lips remained firmly pressed, her eyes narrowing even more. "She's not a Gamma Omega. She just lives here. And don't unpack your bags. Things are likely to change."

Deme met her stare for stare. "Count on it." Before Zoe could come up with a retort, Deme spun on her heels and left the younger girl standing there, her mouth open.

As she rounded the corner, a hand reached out and snagged her arm, pulling her through an open doorway.

Once she was inside the dorm room, the door closed behind her.

Deme rounded on the girl, and gasped. This new girl was almost a clone of Zoe. The same tall stature, golden-blond hair and model-perfect figure. If not for the eye color, Deme might not have recognized a difference.

When Deme opened her mouth to demand an explanation for her pulling her inside her room, she stopped.

The blonde pressed a finger to her lips and leaned her ear against the door.

Deme let her fingers rest against the wall, feeling every vibration down to those of footsteps resounding in the corridor.

When the vibrations faded, she focused her attention on the girl, whose gray eyes were wide, her hands shaking. "You can't let Zoe know we talked."

"I don't even know your name."

"Shelby. Shelby Cramer."

"Why all the secrecy? Why didn't you just talk to me in the corridor?"

Shelby shook her head, her face pale. "Zoe can't know."

"Why? Will she boot you out of the sorority?"

The girl nodded slowly, her eyes narrowing. "Something like that."

"So, spill. What's so important you can't say it in front of the sorority prez?"

Shelby's hands twisted together and she couldn't meet Deme's eyes. "It's just...well..." She sighed and let her hands fall to her sides. "Just be careful, will you? Zoe can be a real force to be reckoned with when she decides she doesn't like you."

Deme smiled. "I can handle Zoe. Question is, can you?"

Shelby's eyes swam with unshed tears. "No."

A knock sounded on Shelby's door and her eyes rounded. "You have to hide," she whispered, grabbing Deme's arm and hauling her with surprising strength toward the closet.

Because the girl was obviously petrified of being discovered harboring the new R.A., Deme allowed her to shove her into the closet and close the door.

The door to the room squeaked open.

"Shelby, have you seen the new R.A.?" Zoe asked.

"No," Shelby's voice quavered.

"Just remember, part of initiation into the Gamma Omegas is your vow of silence."

"I remember," Shelby said, her voice so soft Deme wouldn't have heard if sounds didn't echo so well off the linoleum tiles.

"Now that you're one of us, you don't want to go back, do you?"

For a second, Shelby hesitated, then she answered, "No, of course not. Who would?"

"Exactly. No one wants to go back. Nobody can."

Silence followed.

"Well, if you see the R.A., let me know what she says and does."

"I will," Shelby responded.

The door squeaked open and closed again. The room was silent except for the soft vibrations Deme could feel through her shoes, vibrations caused by bare feet on hard floors. The closet door opened.

Deme blinked as she stepped from the dark closet into the brightly lit room. "What was all that about?" she added softly.

Shelby shook her head. "Nothing. It was a mistake to bring you in here."

"No, it wasn't. You obviously had something you wanted to tell me."

"No. It's not important. You have to go now." She gathered her toothbrush and a hand towel and opened the door, peering out into the hall.

"Shelby, you can trust me. I'd never tell Zoe anything you told me in confidence."

"I have nothing to say." She held the door and motioned for Deme to leave. Once Deme stepped out into the corridor, Shelby followed and closed the door behind them, then hurried toward the bathroom.

Deme retraced her footsteps to the R.A.'s room, wondering what had just happened, determined to get a background check on Zoe Adams. If anyone was crazy enough to make off with a coed, Zoe would be top of her list.

Back at the campus, Cal parked his motorcycle outside the Gamma Omega dorm. Despite his determination to remain focused on the case, he couldn't help the way his pulse raced at the thought of seeing Deme again. He called himself all kinds of fool for letting her influence him in any way.

She was like an accident. A hit-and-run ready for a repeat performance where he was concerned. Only this time he'd be ready. He wouldn't let her leave him scratching his head, wondering what the heck he'd said or done wrong.

He took the steps in the stairwell two at a time to the second floor, where Brigid said Deme's room was. He'd told her he'd be there at six o'clock to fill her in on what he'd learned that day and vice versa.

Question was, would she be there? Now that she knew she'd be working this case with him, would she bother to show up?

Since the missing person was her sister, Cal figured she would. Deme struck him as someone dedicated to her family, even if she wasn't dedicated to her lover.

Outside the door marked R.A., he raised his fist to knock.

"Don't bother, I'm here." Deme's voice caught him off guard, sending a wave of heat through his body.

When he turned, he couldn't stop the way his groin tightened at the way she looked.

Her red hair fell in loose waves around her shoulders, and the V of her button-down cotton blouse exposed the rounded swells of her breasts. Breasts he'd tasted, massaged and caressed long into the nights they'd shared.

Damn, this assignment was going to be a lot harder than he'd anticipated. Tamping down his libido, he stepped to the side as she pulled a ring of keys from her pocket and opened the door.

She walked in without looking back, holding the door just long enough for him to step through.

Once inside, she shut the door and walked several steps away, putting as much distance between them as the tiny room allowed. She leaned against the windowsill overlooking a garden and asked, "What have you found out?"

In the hallway, she'd been a turn-on. Inside the tight confines of the R.A.'s small room, her nearness sparked a lot more flames than even Cal could predict. He tugged the zipper of his leather jacket down, opening it to let in cooler air. Anything to lessen the heat rising inside. "There have been more incidents than just your sister's disappearance."

Deme's eyebrows rose. Her gaze captured his. "What kind of incidents?"

"Two cases of attempted rape, two cases of attempted suicide and one other missing person besides your sister." He glanced around the room. "Could you turn the thermostat down? It's hellacious hot in here." He stripped his jacket from his shoulders and slung it over a chair.

Her gaze shifted from his eyes downward over his shoulders and chest, the heat in the room rising the lower she went. "I haven't touched the thermostat. It was on seventy when I left the room a while ago." She crossed to the device on the wall beside him and studied the box. "Still seventy. Must be you." Her eyes slid sideways.

"No, I think it's you." Cal didn't know what came over him. All he knew was that he had to have his hands on her. He grabbed Deme and pulled her into his arms, crushing her against his chest.

"What do you think you're doing?" Her hands rested flat against his chest, barely applying any pressure as though she was torn between dragging him close or pushing him away. "We don't have to pretend in here. There's no one watching."

"Who's pretending?" His hands slipped lower, circling her hips, slamming her against the hard ridge of his erection. "Can't you feel it?"

She nodded, her eyes glazed, her tongue sweeping across her lips. Her hands slipped up his back, beneath his shirt, her fingernails digging into his skin.

The sharp pricks of pain only flamed his desire, flushing his senses with a need so powerful he couldn't hold back.

His fingers found the hem of her shirt. Instead of working the buttons loose or slipping it up over her head, he ripped it up the front, buttons flying everywhere.

"That'll cost you." Deme pulled his shirt up over his head and flung it to the corner. She bent to take one of his hard, brown nipples between her teeth and nipped, hard.

Cal jerked back and slapped her bottom. "Two can play rough."

In a flurry of motion, they stripped each other bare,

hands roaming over naked skin. Cal lifted her, wrapping her legs around his waist, walking her backward until her naked back pressed against the window choked on the outside in ivy. "Miss me much?" he murmured as he trailed kisses and nips along her jawline and down the length of her throat. He tongued the pulse beating frantically at the base of her neck.

"No." Her fingernails dug into his back, piercing skin, drawing blood. "I can't miss you. We have no future together." Her head leaned back against the glass, her breasts pressing against him.

"Who said I want a future with you now?" He shoved her up high enough to take a nipple into his mouth, biting down hard enough to elicit a gasp. Wicked satisfaction spread through him with the flame of desire. He wanted to cause her pain. Wanted to see her suffer as she'd made him suffer with her disappearance. "Is that why you left? You couldn't picture a future with me?"

"I had good reasons to leave." She sucked in a deep breath, her head lifting, her green-eyed gaze capturing his as her hands slid up to cup his face. "For the life of me I can't remember one of them now." She kissed him, her tongue thrusting into his mouth, taking his in a desperate tangle.

He lowered her over his cock, penetrating her in a hard, punishing thrust. Anger and desire merged to become a living, breathing entity within him, taking over his actions, destroying his self-control. He couldn't stop himself from taking her, even if she'd said no.

His thrusts increased, until the glass in the window rattled.

Deme's legs clamped hard around his waist, her body arching against his, taking him in as deeply as he could go until she cried out loud. Her body tensed around him as he slammed into her once more.

Just as he climaxed, he had enough sense to lift her off him at the last minute before he shot his seed into her womb.

Anger and desire still burned in his veins, but he didn't have the strength to act on them. He let Deme slide down him until her feet touched the floor. His arms remained around her waist, his palms cupping her buttocks. Guilt flowed through him as he realized he couldn't have stopped himself. If Deme had said no, he'd have raped her anyway. "What the hell just happened?"

Chapter 6

Deme stood with her back to the window, the thoughts in her head spinning like so much debris in an F5 tornado. The air in the room was thick, hard to breathe. "I don't know. Just don't let it happen again." She pushed away from Cal and gathered her clothes.

Cal shoved a hand through his hair, standing it on end. "You weren't fighting me."

"Fine. *I* won't let it happen again," she reassured him, her lips firmly pressed into a line, even as her body tingled with awareness of his nakedness standing within reach. Inside, her blood raced through every organ, vein and the furthest reaches of her body, burning a path downward to her core. She ached with need and she still wanted him. Damn him! She turned away, gathering her clothing. "This isn't about you and me."

"I know. It's about finding your sister."

Deme faced him, pressing her jeans to her chest.

"That's right. This is about finding Aurai. It can only be about finding Aurai."

"Message heard. It's not as if I'm asking you to marry me. I learned my lesson. So don't feel like you have to disappear again."

That barb hit dead center and guilt burned in her gut. She drew herself up to her full five feet nine inches and faced him. "I had to leave. There are things you don't know about me. Things you wouldn't understand."

"You didn't give me a chance to understand. You didn't give me a chance to get to know you." Cal grabbed his jeans and slipped his legs into them, dragging them up his body. "I didn't even know you had sisters. Seems like something a lover should know about the woman he's sleeping with. The woman he proposes to."

Deme couldn't respond. She wanted to stop him getting dressed—wanted to drag his jeans down and take him into her again. Wave upon wave of desire slammed into her like a freight train.

Her mouth watered with the need to taste every inch of his body, to lick, bite and rake her fingers over him in penalizing thoroughness. Her tongue swept across her lips to moisten their sudden dryness.

Scratching at the window penetrated the fog of desire encroaching on her ability to think.

She turned to discover that what she'd originally thought was English ivy growing outside her window was a dark brown tangle of vines whose thorns scratched against the glass, tapping...tapping...as if to gain entrance.

"What's with the vine?" Cal walked to the window and shoved it open. When he reached out to push the vine away, he yelped, pulling his hand back. A drop of blood oozed from where a thorn had gouged his thumb.

Deme grabbed a box of tissues and hurried to his side. "Let me see."

He held out his hand. "It's nothing, just a prick."

"You're bleeding." She pressed a tissue to the wound, absorbing the blood. As she stood so close, inhaling the musky scent of their lovemaking, she made a decision. "Maybe it's time you know a little more about me." Deme let go of his hand and took a step back. She closed her eyes, gathering her inner strength, summoning her ability to feel nature, to influence it. She breathed in and out, the air unusually thick.

She entered a fog of internal awareness, blocking out the room she stood in, the man she'd made love to and the desperation with which she sought her sister, only for a moment.

"Goddess of earth
I call to thee
Guide me now
Set me free
We are one
You with me
Grant me power
Blessed Be."

With her senses she reached out to the thorny vine, wrapping her mind around it, sending soothing thoughts, pushing it toward the ground, away from her window on the second story of the dormitory. A strange tension filled the room, as though her calming influence had run up against a wall, blocking her attempt to communicate with the vine.

Deme pushed against the wall, gently at first. The more it pushed back, the harder she concentrated. So wrapped was she in the inner battle, she lost track of time, forgot where she was until a voice penetrated her consciousness.

"Deme!" Strong arms scooped beneath her knees, lifting her up off her feet.

Her eyes opened and she stared into Cal's anxious face. "Why did you stop me?"

He raced for the door. "I don't know what's happening, or what you were doing, but you aren't safe in here."

Dragged from the fog of her connection to the goddess, Deme struggled to focus on the dorm room. A sickly aroma of decay filled her nostrils, gagging her with its intensity.

As her vision cleared, she saw what Cal was talking about. The thorny vine that a moment ago had been outside her window had draped itself down over the sill and slithered across the floor like a deadly serpent aiming for the two of them.

She shook her head, her arms circling his neck, her pulse racing. "But that can't be."

"I don't get it either, but we have to get out of here."

"No!" She stopped him, forcing him to drop her to her feet. "I can't go out into the hall like this." She motioned to her nakedness.

He hesitated only a moment, then pushed her behind him. "Stand back." Cal grabbed the comforter from the bed beside him and advanced on the vine.

Deme watched in horror as the vine lashed out, the thorns raking across Cal's legs, penetrating the denim, ripping into his skin.

"Cal!" She rushed toward him.

"Stay back!" With the blanket wrapped around his hands, he grabbed the thorny vine and wrestled it toward the window. He twisted and grunted, attempting to keep the vine from wrapping around his legs and arms.

As he neared the window, he shoved the vine, comforter and all, through and slammed the window down.

A bend in the vine stopped the window from closing completely, allowing the leaves to slip through the crack.

Cal leaned his weight into pressing the window downward. "Get something to shove it through!" he yelled.

Deme's gaze searched the room for something to use to poke the vine through the narrow slit. She grabbed a number two pencil and raced toward Cal.

Without thinking, she shoved the pencil at the vine, pushing it back through the opening. The window slammed down on the sill, the leaves retreating at the last moment to the other side.

Cal twisted the lock and leaned his back against the wall, breathing hard. Then his gaze captured Deme's. "I think you have some explaining to do."

Cal slipped his shirt over his head and tugged it down across his chest. What had just happened completely defied explanation. Never in his life had he had a vine attack him. It was as if the plant had come alive, intent on causing them harm. Surely he had imagined it.

The pain in his shin and thumb where jagged thorns had torn his skin reminded him it wasn't in his mind. He wasn't going crazy. And the sudden urge to ravage Deme's body that had taken him over was beyond any anger he might have felt at being ditched. He truly couldn't have stopped if she'd said no.

As Deme pulled on her jeans and a T-shirt, her gaze never left the window and the vine tapping against it. "I don't understand."

Residual anger simmered beneath the surface as he waited for her to finish dressing. He fought to remain in control, refusing to give in to baser instincts of a moment ago. "I don't know what's happening, but we can't talk in here."

"I agree." She straightened from slipping on her shoes, tugged the strap of her purse over her shoulder and met him at the door. "We need to get out of here." A chill chose that moment to track down her spine. She shivered as he opened the door for her, casting one last glance at the thorny vine pressing against the glass.

In the hallway, Zoe Adams stood with her back to the wall, her arms crossed over her chest. "Having troubles?"

Blood rushed into Deme's face as she thought of the violent sex she and Cal had just experienced behind the R.A. room door, probably breaking a few dozen rules. Despite her guilt, Deme managed to frown at the girl. "No troubles. Can I help you?"

"You can help by leaving." Zoe's lips twitched at the corners and she stared so hard at Deme, it was if a shaft of heat burned into her head.

"You're not scaring me, Zoe." Despite her tough words, Deme's hand raised to press against the bridge of her nose, applying pressure to the sudden headache.

Zoe flipped her hair over her shoulder and pushed off the wall. Without another word, she strode down the hall, her feet crossing over each other like a runway model's, her hips swaying perfectly.

"Did you feel that?" Deme shook her head, the pain easing slowly.

"Feel what?"

Maybe she was imagining it. Deme shrugged.

"Nothing. Let's go to the student commons. Maybe we can talk there."

Deme couldn't leave the dorm fast enough. The farther away from her room she got, the better she felt. When she stepped out into the cool evening air, she stopped just outside the dorm entrance and breathed in, absorbing the scents and aura of the surrounding trees.

Cal stood silently beside her, his brows set in what appeared to be a permanent V.

"By the goddess...this is better." She stood for a long time sucking in light, fresh air, filling her lungs, cleansing her aura of the darkness that had invaded her in her room. When she felt closer to normal again she turned to Cal. "Something is not right about that room."

"You're telling me." Cal hooked her arm and steered her toward the student commons. "Now that we're out of there, we have some catching up to do. I want to know everything you haven't told me." He squeezed her arm tight enough it got her attention. "Everything."

Being hurried along like an errant child on her way to the principal's office didn't make Deme happy, but nothing could erase the level of pure lust she'd experienced in her room only a few minutes ago. Knowing she was in control of her own emotions once again felt almost like freedom.

As they passed the administration building, the offices closed and dark, a scream ripped through the air.

Cal let go of Deme's arm and ran toward the sound.

Deme followed. In good shape, she still had trouble keeping up with Cal, his stride leaving her far behind.

Deme neared the garden fence at the center of the campus, her chest heaving, the air growing as thick as it had been in her dorm room. She struggled to fill her lungs, the darkness more menacing with each step closer to the wrought-iron gate.

Cal stood with his feet apart, his fists up in the fighting position. Behind him on the ground was Rachel, her face in the shadows, her shoulders shuddering with muffled sobs.

"What's going on?" Deme stepped up beside Cal.

Standing in front of him was Mike Hubbs, Rachel's date, his shirt torn, hanging out of his waistband, his hair mussed, his eyes wide, glazed and wild. "She's mine," he said, his shy voice low and guttural, unrecognizable from the young man Deme had met in the hallway of the dorm.

"Don't let him touch me. Please." Rachel huddled on the ground, her knees drawn up to her chin, her arms wrapped around her legs. "Please." Another sob shook her body and she whimpered.

Deme dropped to her haunches beside Rachel. "What happened?"

"I don't know..." She took a shuddering breath and wiped her arm across her eyes. "One minute we were walking, the next he...he...tried to...rape me." She sobbed, burying her face in her hands.

Mike lunged for Rachel.

Cal stepped in front of him, landing a punch to the young man's jaw that sent him flying backward. He landed with a thud on the ground and lay still for several seconds.

Rachel cried out, attempting to rise.

Deme's hand on her shoulder kept her in place.

Mike pushed himself to a sitting position and gazed at the people staring at him, his eyes wide, the glaze gone, confusion taking its place. "What are you doing here? Where's Rachel?" He struggled to stand.

Cal stepped in front of him, blocking his access to the troubled girl on the ground. "I suggest you leave Rachel alone."

"But we have a date."

"Date's over." Cal held his fists at the ready for round two.

"I don't understand."

"I bet you don't." Deme snorted and stood, adding her body as a barrier between Mike and Rachel. "For your information, most girls don't like to be raped."

"Rape?" He shook his head. "What are you talking about?" He leaned to the right, peering around Deme. "Rachel? Are you all right?"

"No thanks to you." Cal grabbed Mike's arm when he tried to step around Deme. "You aren't getting near her. I'm calling the police."

"No." Rachel lurched to her feet, streaks of mascara making dark tracks on her face. "Don't call the police. It may have been my fault. I never should have done it."

"Done what?" Deme asked.

"I never should have changed."

"No man has the right to rape a woman."

"But he didn't mean to, did you, Mike?" Rachel tried to push Deme aside, but she refused to let her by.

"I would never rape Rachel. Hell, I'm still a virgin." He clapped a big hand over his mouth, his face turning so red that even in the shadows Deme could see the glow. He removed his hand and said softly, "I wouldn't know how." He shoved his hands through his hair. "I swear I didn't rape her. I wouldn't try. I respect her too much."

As much as Deme tried not to, she couldn't help but believe that Mike meant what he said as the truth. "Then explain why you attacked her."

He shook his head. "I don't remember attacking her. I must have blacked out. I swear, Rachel, I would never hurt you."

"But you did." Her voice hiccupped on a sob.

Mike backed away a step, tears glistening in his eyes. "I'm sorry. I don't remember." He took another step. "I wouldn't…" Mike turned and ran.

Cal started to follow, but Rachel's voice stopped him. "Please, don't." She laid her hand on his arm. "Let him go. He wasn't himself."

"He can't get away with this," Cal said. "What if he tries it again?"

"He won't." Rachel stared into the darkness where Mike had disappeared.

"How can you be sure? You have to turn him over to the police." Deme took Rachel by the arms. "What if he tries to rape someone else?"

Rachel shook her head side to side and jerked out of Deme's hold. "It's not him. It's me."

"What do you mean, it's you?"

"It happened that night."

"What night?" Deme grabbed the girl's arms again. "The night Aurai disappeared?"

"Yes." Rachel's head hung down, her eyes shadowed, unreadable. "Everything happened, everything changed."

"Tell me." Deme shook her gently.

"I can't." Rachel broke free, backing away much as Mike had done. "They'll kill me."

"Who will kill you?" Cal asked.

"Leave me alone," Rachel pleaded. "Please."

"What happened that night, Rachel?" Deme demanded. This girl knew something, and she'd shake it out of her if she had to. "Where is Aurai?"

She shook her head, tears streaming down her face. Rachel turned toward the Gamma Omega dormitory.

Deme captured her arm and spun her around. "At least tell me where it happened."

The younger girl looked into Deme's eyes and whispered, "In the garden." She glanced over Deme's shoulder and gasped, her eyes round. Before Deme could stop her, she'd knocked aside the hand holding her and ran away from the dorm and into the darkness.

Deme glanced behind her.

A group of five girls emerged from the shadows near the gate to the wrought-iron fence surrounding the central garden. A garden Deme had been told was strictly off-limits to all students and faculty.

At the point was Zoe Adams, her blond hair shining in the light from the windows of the Gamma Omega dormitory.

She didn't advance on Deme and Cal. She stood with the others fanning out to each side of her. Five girls in all, each as beautiful as the next.

"There's something not right about them," Cal muttered.

"You're telling me." Not in the mood for another confrontation with the Stepford sisters, Deme hooked Cal's arm and led him toward the parking lot. "Come on. Let's get away from campus. I'm supposed to meet my sisters at Burger Barn at nine o'clock. You might as well meet the rest of the Chattoxes."

Cal took the lead, guiding Deme to where he'd parked his motorcycle. He slung his foot over the seat and jerked his head. "Get on."

Without hesitation, Deme climbed on the back, wrapped her arms around his waist and held on. The danger of falling in love with Cal all over again seemed minor compared with the sinister darkness of a face-off with the leader of the Gamma Omega sorority.

Chapter 7

"Who is this Zoe Adams, anyway?" Brigid tapped her fingernails on the table to the same rhythm as her petite foot encased in black leather boots. "She doesn't scare me. I'll rip every hair out of her head and make her beg for mercy."

Cal suppressed a grin. He'd already gotten a taste of Brigid's brand of finesse at the police station earlier that day.

Sitting among the four sisters, it struck him how different they all were. As though they came from completely diverse families. Not one looked like the other, and each had unique characteristics and personalities. But they all wore the silver pentagram and they all cared about their missing youngest sister. That they turned to Deme's strength and maturity to bring order to the group seemed natural since Deme was the oldest.

"No matter how much the girls disturb us, we can't

go in like a bunch of ninjas kicking ass." Deme's gaze moved from one sister to the next. "We have to find out what's going on by blending in, getting to know them or at least some of them. Not everyone is Zoe Adams. Rachel might come clean given enough time."

Gina nodded. "Or that Shelby chick."

Brigid slammed a palm on the table. "We don't have time. While you're out playing college coed, our sister is missing. She could be in danger."

"She is," Selene said, her voice quiet, intense.

Deme sighed. "I know and we'll get to her. In the meantime, the girls of Gamma Omega are afraid of something. I want to know what it is. I think it has to do with Aurai's disappearance."

"Not Zoe Adams." Cal's words were spoken in a low, calm tone, but every feminine eye turned toward him. "Zoe isn't afraid of anything."

"It's as though she has power over them," Deme agreed.

"You think she'd kill them if they leak information?" Gina asked.

Deme's gaze met Cal's. "You know…I wouldn't put it past her. She's trouble."

That she'd looked to him warmed his insides more than Cal cared to admit. On the outside of this band of sisters looking in, he could use an ally, even if Deme didn't have the best reputation for sticking around.

Deme tore her gaze from Cal's and aimed it at her sister Gina. "You start cleaning the aquariums in the library tomorrow, right?"

Gina nodded. "They're a mess."

"Good. You can use that opportunity to dig through any information you can find on the history of Colyer-Fenton, the Gamma Omegas and especially the central garden. I want to know why it's off-limits. Did something happen there that could have an impact on the aura?"

"You felt it, too, didn't you?" Selene asked, her brown eyes glazing over. "The garden has a dark aura, a sense of anger and frustration...and ultimate doom." She stared across the table at Cal, but he could tell she wasn't looking at him so much as through him.

A tingling sensation rippled down the back of his neck as though Selene's fingers trailed across his spine. Which was ridiculous. Cal looked around the room for an air vent, something that would cause him to shiver.

"What else can you sense? Earlier you said there were voices calling to you. Back when you were in my room. Who did they belong to?" Deme asked.

Voices? Cal frowned.

Selene continued to stare, her brow knitting into a pained frown. "I can't...quite...see them."

"Them? More than one. Male or female?" Deme shot out.

Cal stared at Deme. The line of questions she shot at her sister made less and less sense.

"Female," Selene responded with conviction.

"Alive or dead?"

Okay, that bordered on downright weird. Cal started to rise and thought better of it, remaining seated to see this conversation through, no matter how bizarre.

Selene closed her eyes. "Screaming. Pain. Horror. Must leave." She opened her eyes and stared around at her sisters. "What?"

Cal could swear she'd been in some sort of trance, like the one Deme had been in when the vine went berserk in her room. What was with the Chattox women? Were they all a little...off?

"Go on." Brigid leaned forward. "What else can you tell us about these females?"

Selene cocked her brow. "What females?"

"The ones you said were warning us off in Deme's room. Don't you remember?"

Selene squinted. "Vaguely. In your room?" She shifted her gaze to her oldest sister.

"My room. The one that overlooks the central garden," Deme affirmed. She turned to Cal, her eyes narrowing.

He could almost see the gears in her mind turning. Off balance by all the talk of hearing voices and sensing dead people, Cal worked hard to maintain his outward appearance of stoic understanding, when all he wanted was to shout, "What the hell?"

"Rachel was walking with Mike just outside the gates of the garden when he attacked her. I'd like to know where the other girls were when they were attacked. Is something about the garden causing people to act out of character?" Deme's gaze shifted from Cal's, her cheeks stained in a subtle flush.

His eyes widened as he made the connection she was referring to. Had something influenced his and her behavior when they'd been in her room? Cal wanted Deme to look at him, to acknowledge him and the violent desire that had transpired between them. "Are you suggesting the garden is influencing behavior?"

As much as he would like to think he wasn't responsible for his actions earlier, he didn't buy in to the forces of nature or the spirit world making people perform unthinkable acts.

Still…he had never been more out of control than he had been for those passion-filled minutes with Deme. What scared him was the intensity, the violence of the sex. His back still stung from where her fingernails scraped his skin.

The shame and horror on Mike's face echoed in Cal's mind. A guy like Mike didn't force himself on a girl. In his gut, Cal knew that. But then Jeffrey Dahmer had appeared to be such a normal kind of guy to most of his acquaintances.

Deme turned to Selene. "Do you have any of the Gamma Omega girls in your drama workshop?"

"I checked my list of students and addresses. Seems like one Shelby Cramer had an address of the Gamma Omega dorm."

Deme nodded. "That's the one who tried to pull me aside earlier. Zoe scared her silent. See if you can gain her confidence. Maybe she'll tell you something when she's not surrounded by sorority sisters or Zoe."

"I'll do that." Selene sighed. "I wish we had something to go on. I'm really worried about Aurai."

"As we all are." Deme reached out to the sisters on each side of her. They joined hands with each other, forming a circle Cal didn't try to be a part of. Each closed her eyes and they chanted softly in unison.

"Feel the power
Free our hearts
Find our way
Be the one
With the strength of the earth
With the rising of the wind
With the calm of the water
With the intensity of fire
With the freedom of spirit
The goddess is within us
She is power
We are her

We are one
Blessed Be."

As the last word was uttered, a breeze shifted through the café.

Cal glanced toward the door. No one had gone out or stepped in.

"Did you feel her?" Selene opened her eyes.

The other three nodded, their eyes glassy with unshed tears.

Deme whispered, "She's still alive."

Brigid followed with another heartfelt, "Blessed Be." Then she stood. "We have our work cut out for us. Let's get to it."

The sisters stood and filed out of the café, leaving Deme alone with Cal.

Brigid was the last one out, glancing behind her at Cal. She tipped an imaginary hat and grinned.

"What was that about?" Deme frowned at Brigid's back.

"I could ask the same." Cal captured Deme's hand as she rose to leave. "Uh-uh. We've only just begun."

She sank into her seat and sighed. "Where to begin?" Her fingers curled around the medallion with the pentagram hanging around her neck. The one just like those each of her sisters wore.

"Start there." Cal reached out, his fingers touching hers and the medallion. A brief shock of electricity reminded him of how she'd felt in his arms earlier.

Deme glanced down at the necklace. "Oh, this." She smiled. "Our mother gave each of us one. It's a pentagram." She pointed to the top point of the pentagram. "This point represents Spirit. That's Selene. She senses the feelings and emotions of others, both live, dead and otherworld." She held up her hand. "Let the otherworld comment go for now and let me finish."

Cal nodded.

She touched the point to the left of Spirit. "This point represents Water—that's Gina. She can see, smell, taste and influence all things water, from the smallest drop of perspiration to the grandest ocean."

Despite his disbelief, Cal couldn't help but be mesmerized by Deme's voice. Clear, calm and completely convinced. The love for her sisters shone through above it all, making his own convictions of what was true and logical waver.

"The bottom left point is Earth." She smiled up at him. A brief smile, one that told him she didn't expect him to understand or believe what she was saying, though she did so absolutely. "That's me. I can feel the vibrations of the planet, tell you when someone is coming and influence the flora. If I really get cranked up, I've been known to shake a few rocks." She chuckled, the sound more self-deprecating than humorous.

She touched the point to the right of Earth. "This point represents Fire."

Cal frowned. "Brigid?"

Deme tipped her head to the side and stared across at him. "Yes. How did you know?"

"Gut feel." His palm still tingled where Brigid touched him earlier. That and the heat in the war room made him think of her.

Cal stopped there. If he didn't watch out, he'd start believing all this garbage.

"The final point is Air." Deme smiled softly, the look on her face one of such sadness, it made Cal want to reach out and pull her into his arms.

"Aurai?"

She nodded. "The youngest of the five of us." Deme looked up, her eyes glistening. "She just wanted to live a normal life. That's all any of us ever wanted."

Cal pressed his lips together. "You *are* normal."

"No." Deme shook her head, her smile fading, her jaw tightening. "We're not."

"What exactly are you telling me?"

She inhaled and let out a long, steadying breath. "We're witches."

"Brigid said the same thing." Cal leaned back, his arms crossing over his chest. "Is this the secret you couldn't tell me? The reason you left without saying goodbye, good luck or get lost?"

Deme nodded. "You're a cop. You live by a book of rules. Everything is either black or white. There's nothing in between to you. How could you understand?"

"You're right on one count. I don't understand. But you could have had the decency to give me a chance." He heaved a huge sigh. "Look, I can't say that I believe in witches. I can't say that I believe in magic, but I'll tell you this—something strange happened back in your room tonight."

"Strange things like that happen a lot around us."

"Maybe so, but they don't happen to me. I like to think there's still a logical explanation for the vine." His fingers curled around his coffee mug, the sting of the puncture wound he'd received bringing back the struggle.

"What about what happened between us in my room?" She raised her eyebrows. "You felt it, didn't you? The anger, the rage, the overwhelming desire, didn't you? Everything dark intensified."

He hesitated, a residual heat pooling in his loins. "I think that can be explained. I was mad."

Deme shook her head. "You never lose control."

"Really mad." His argument sounded lame even to his own ears.

Deme reached out and touched his arm. "Do you really think you could have stopped?"

He wanted to say yes. Being in control was who he was. He hated to admit it, but she was right. "No."

"It wasn't you. I felt it, too. I think it has something to do with the garden."

"Why? We had passion in our relationship before."

"Not that much. Not that violent."

Cal's jaw tightened. "I still don't believe in magic."

"Think about it...Mike attacked Rachel. Did he look like someone who could hurt a girl?"

"What do we know about the things a man is capable of? We don't know Mike well enough to make that call."

"Maybe not." Deme's gaze circled the restaurant before landing on him. "What about the two attempted rapes by model students? Think they were acting on their own?"

He shrugged. "It happens."

"Is everything a coincidence? I thought you didn't believe in coincidence?"

Cal didn't have an argument for that. "Let's agree to disagree on the magic thing. I'll investigate the students involved in the hazing, get some information from the staff and leave the woo-woo to you."

"Fair enough." Deme stood. "I need to get back to the dorm. Duty calls and I'm still the R.A." She hooked her handbag over her shoulder. "Besides, I need to check on Rachel."

Cal lifted his jacket and slipped it over his shoulders. "I'll check with the lieutenant and get him to run a background check on Zoe and Mike."

Deme rode on the back of Cal's motorcycle, her arms wrapped around his waist, glad he couldn't see her expression. He'd recognize the hunger in her eyes, the need for physical contact with him. Her body ached for this man, but she couldn't commit to him or any other.

What had happened to Aurai could happen again to any one of her sisters and herself. One minute there, another being dragged into some unknown hell. Being witches, having certain powers, made them targets. What kind of normal life could she live with a mortal?

She almost laughed out loud. Even to her own ears, using the words *witches* and *mortals* sounded so farfetched. She and her sisters had played down their abilities, refusing to live up to their full potential. Their mother had told them they could live whatever lives they wished, if they wanted it badly enough. Unfortunately, normal wasn't one of the choices.

As the motorcycle came to a stop in front of the dorm, Deme peered up. She wished this would all go away. But it wouldn't until she found her sister.

She swung her leg over and straightened.

Cal dismounted, pulled off his helmet and grabbed her arm as she turned to leave. "Deme—"

"Look, Cal." She faced him, her face set, her lips firm. She hadn't wanted to confront him, not when her emotions were still raw from their earlier encounter, but she had to set him straight. "What happened earlier shouldn't have. I don't intend to start where we left off a year ago. Once this case is solved, once Aurai is home and safe, we go our separate ways."

His lips twisted. "Who said I wanted it any other way? I was just going to say, be careful."

"Oh." She frowned. "Well, then, good night."

Before she could turn, his hand lifted to cup her cheek.

"Sweet dreams, little witch." He bent and pressed his lips to hers.

Fire shot through every nerve in her body. Deme knew she should pull away, should put a stop to something that couldn't be, but she didn't.

She leaned into him, her lips parting.

His tongue delved deep, wrapping around hers as his arms circled her waist, dragging her closer.

The hard ridge behind his fly pressed into her belly, making her exceedingly aware of her effect on him. The power of bringing a man to this surged through her, blasting her blood through her veins. She squeezed the apex of her thighs, the ache so prominent she wanted to crawl all over him, make love in the moonlight, discard all reservations and inhibitions to be naked with this man. All this without the added push she'd gotten in her room.

"Get a room, will ya."

Deme broke away from Cal, her breathing heavy, her heart racing.

Zoe Adams stood in the entrance to the dormitory, her hand on her hip, a sneer marring her perfection. She didn't repeat her comment, only stared.

Fighting the urge to squirm, Deme straightened her shirt and touched Cal's face. "That's one for the cover story," she said quietly enough only he could hear.

As she turned toward the dorm, squaring her shoulders, she caught a flash of pain winging across Cal's features. But when she looked back, his jaw was tight, his brown eyes expressionless.

Deme couldn't sense the vibration of his movement, so he must be waiting for her to get safely inside. She could feel his gaze following her as she neared the entrance to the Gamma Omega dormitory and Zoe Adams as the younger woman stood guard over her domain.

Zoe's smile was anything but welcoming. She didn't say anything as Deme stepped around her, the college coed's concentration fixed on Cal.

Deme's fists clenched as a flash of unexpected jealousy painted her vision green. Not that Cal would go for a college coed. He was more mature, had more class.

Still, Zoe was gorgeous, perfect in every way. Why wouldn't a man like Cal be attracted to her? He wasn't committed to any other female. Deme had seen to it that he wasn't tied to her. She had her reasons. But those reasons were beginning to wear on her.

As Deme opened the glass entry door, Zoe tossed over her shoulder, "Don't think you're going to change anything, R.A. We like things the way they are."

Deme froze, her fingers poised on the metal handle. "What makes you think I'll change things?"

Zoe didn't respond, her shoulder rising in a hint of a shrug.

"Are you afraid I'll get in your way of the games you play with the sorority?"

"I'm not afraid." She shot a glance at Deme before she fixed her gaze on Cal again. "I just wouldn't want to see anyone get hurt."

Deme let go of the handle and marched back down the steps to face Zoe. "Is that a threat?"

Zoe's mouth curled in a smile that didn't reach her eyes. "Do you feel threatened?"

Deme fought her desire to throttle this prima donna. "Not in the least. You don't scare me, Zoe. As the R.A., I determine who lives in this dormitory and who should be booted. Give me just one reason, and your ass is out of here."

Zoe's pale blue eyes narrowed. "I wouldn't do that if I were you."

"But then, you aren't me." Deme stared at her a little longer. She could almost see the steam rise from Zoe's reddening face. She could feel the heat in the air. The steps beneath her feet hummed with something she couldn't quite place. When the other girl didn't respond, Deme left her standing there and entered the dormitory.

Out of Zoe's sight, Deme's body shook. Something about Zoe Adams wasn't right. Her aura was dark, the air around her hung heavy, oppressive. Even the earth beneath her feet seemed thick with antagonism.

As she climbed the steps, her vision wavered. Or was it the steps shifting? Either way, she clung to the railing until she reached the second floor. For once the corridor was empty. Not a single girl ventured out to the sound of the stairwell door closing behind Deme.

The silence was eerie, unnerving. The closer Deme moved toward the R.A.'s room, the less she looked forward to sleeping there. What had happened between her and Cal still hung in the air. Her body thrummed with desire. She wanted to run back down to him and spend the night in his arms, preferably in his apartment.

She held true to her course, entering her room with the key. Her first glance shot to the window. The vine that only a few hours ago had attacked Cal was safely outside the window, the thorns appearing less intimidating, the leaves a lighter shade of green.

Was it her imagination? She checked the lock on the window and leaned over the angelica root plant. It looked normal, if a little more green since she'd brought it into the room. She moved it to the counter by the sink, away from the window.

Moonlight shone through the glass, drawing Deme back to overlook the garden. Tall pine trees framed the garden, and dark blobs of shadows indicated the locations of rosebushes. Nothing appeared sinister, yet Deme couldn't help how her chest tightened as though a hand squeezed her ribs, making it more difficult to breathe.

"Where are you, little sister?"

A whisper of air stirred the hair around her neck, as if a gentle hand settled on her shoulder, a silent voice calling out, *I am here.*

Restless, Deme couldn't imagine laying her head down to sleep. So much had happened in one day and they still hadn't found Aurai.

A glance at her bed, neatly made and untouched even after the violent sex she'd had with Cal, made her think of Rachel and Mike's attack. Was the girl okay? Would she feel more like talking if Zoe wasn't around to scare her silent?

Deme left her room and hurried down the hall to Rachel's room. Again, the hallways were deserted. At eleven o'clock at night on a weekend in a dorm, it wasn't right. She recalled staying up all hours. If not her, then others ran the hallways, giggling and making noise until the wee hours.

When she reached the room Rachel had shared with

Aurai, she knocked softly, hesitant to make any noise, the silence in the dorm so complete it gave her chills. There were girls behind the doors. Deme could feel them shuffling quietly.

No response.

Deme knocked again. "Rachel, let me in?"

The floor vibrated, feet moving toward her. "Go away." Her muffled voice barely carried through the solid door. Deme had her ear pressed to it and could feel the girl's sobs. Her lingering fear, regret and thoughts of self-inflicted harm flowed through the barrier, filling Deme with Rachel's frame of mind.

Deme had to get in. If Rachel was having thoughts of suicide, she had to talk to her. Get her some help. "Please, Rachel."

"Go away." The feet moved away, the door remaining locked, Rachel's aura drifting away from where Deme stood pressed to the door.

Deme straightened, pulling the keys from her jeans pocket. It took only a moment to find the master key and insert it into the lock. She turned the handle and, with a quick glance at the empty corridor, ducked inside, closing the door behind her.

"Rachel?"

The girl lay wrapped in a fuzzy pink robe, curled in the fetal position on her bed, her back to Deme. "What do you want? I told you to go away."

"I can't. I'm worried about you. About what happened."

"Don't. I'm fine. Mike didn't do anything wrong. It was my fault."

"It wasn't your fault. No man has the right to attack you like that." Deme crossed the small room and sat on the edge of the bed. When she reached out to touch the back of Rachel's neck, the girl flinched and groaned.

"Rachel?" Deme brushed the girl's dark hair aside, exposing the column of her neck and the angry bruise marring her smooth white skin. The bruise resembled the shape of teeth marks. Human teeth.

"Did Mike do this to you?" The edge of another bruise was barely covered by the robe.

Deme pulled the lapel farther down. She had two more bite marks, equally purplish-red.

"He didn't mean to." Rachel tugged the edges of the robe up to her neck. "He wasn't himself."

"That's not an excuse for what he did." Deme pulled the girl up and into her arms. "No one should do this to another human."

"You can't turn him in, unless you turn me in, too."

"Why?"

"I bit him, too."

She pushed Rachel to arm's length. "You bit him?"

"Yes. I don't know why. I've never done anything like that ever. He made me do it."

"Mike made you do it?"

"No, not Mike."

"Then who?"

"I don't know. It sounds crazy, but he got in my head and made me act like an animal. I didn't want to, but I couldn't stop."

She stared at Deme, her eyes widening. "He got to you, too, didn't he?" She pointed at Deme's neck.

"What do you mean?"

"There." She pointed again.

Deme left the girl on the bed and walked to the mirror on the wall between the closets. She pushed her hair aside and there on her neck just below her ear was a bite mark, just like the one Rachel had.

Cold washed over her, her stomach clenching, her skin clammy. Deme's world grayed around the edges as she realized just how out of control Cal's actions had been.

Chapter 8

Cal lay in his bed in the apartment he'd had for the past five years, wishing he'd stayed with Deme. Instinct told him she wasn't safe on that campus, in that dorm, with the craziness infecting people right and left. Someone was playing with them. With all the students and faculty at Colyer-Fenton College. The sooner he found out who, the sooner he could put a stop to it.

In the meantime he lay awake waiting for dawn and the start of another day of investigation.

He must have drifted off because the next thing he knew his alarm clock buzzed. He rolled over and hit snooze, but the alarm kept ringing. Then he realized it wasn't his alarm but his cell phone.

After fumbling on the nightstand, he found it, flipped it open and answered, "Black."

"Cal, I need you at the hospital."

Cal sat up straight, all vestiges of sleep wiped from his mind. "Who?"

"A young man, a college student from Colyer-Fenton, was just brought in comatose."

"What happened?"

"Attempted suicide." The lieutenant hesitated. "He might just have succeeded."

"Has he been ID'd?" Cal balanced the cell phone between his shoulder and his ear while he pulled on his jeans.

"Mike Hubbs."

"Damn." The phone slipped from Cal's ear. He barely caught it before it hit the floor. He jammed it against his ear to hear the lieutenant as he continued.

"I take it you know him," Marty said.

"Ran into him earlier. He'd attempted to rape his date, Rachel Taylor, on campus."

"No one turned him in?"

"The girl didn't want to press charges."

"I'm not liking this, Cal." The lieutenant sighed. "Get here, will ya?"

"On my way." Cal clicked the off button and zipped his jeans, slipping the cell phone into his pocket.

He tugged a black T-shirt over his head and was pulling it down when his phone vibrated in his pocket.

Without looking at the caller ID, he answered, "Black."

"Cal?"

Deme's voice brought him to a standstill.

"What's wrong?"

"I just left Rachel in her room."

"Funny you should mention her."

"She's in bad shape." Deme didn't sound in such good shape herself. Her voice was tired.

"Tell me."

"She's covered in bite marks."

"From Mike?"

"Yeah." She paused. "And Cal?"

"You mean it gets worse?"

"Yeah." Deme sighed.

Cal's gut clenched, his hand tightening around the phone.

"I have a few myself."

Cal's stomach took a freefall and he sat hard on the bed. "I did that?"

"Yeah."

"I don't remember doing it." He shoved a hand through his hair, bile rising in his throat.

"It's like I said earlier, it wasn't you."

"The hell it wasn't." He stood, rage flowing through him.

"There's something else."

"As if this isn't bad enough," he muttered.

"She said *it* made Mike do it. *It* made *her* bite Mike, too. Do me a favor will you?"

"Anything," he said, feeling like the lowest form of life on the planet.

"Go to the mirror and check yourself."

He stood and crossed to the mirror over the dresser. "Hold on." Cal set the phone on the dresser and tore off the shirt he'd just put on. There on his collarbone and again on his right shoulder were teeth marks. He touched them, pain an affirmation of the bruising.

He lifted the phone, his gaze pinned to the marks. "I'll be damned."

"You, too, huh?" she asked softly. "I'm sorry, Cal. I don't know what came over me."

"Same here."

Is this what had happened to Mike? Was there another being making them act this way?

If so, everything Cal believed to be true and logical teetered on the edge of crashing in around him.

He shoved his feet into his boots and ran out the door. Answers. He needed answers and fast, before someone else got hurt.

After a thorough look around the dormitory to verify all was quiet and no one wandered the halls, Deme returned to her room.

As soon as she walked through the door, she felt watched, which was ridiculous. No one else was in the room, and being on the second story of the building, no one could be hovering outside her window. Still the feeling persisted, even as she dressed for bed in conservative pajamas.

The skimpy baby-doll nightgown she normally slept in would have to wait for a night she didn't think she might have to risk running out of the building.

Deme didn't think she'd fall to sleep as keyed up as she'd been after her talk with Rachel. But as soon as her head hit the pillow, exhaustion claimed her.

Suddenly she was being lifted and spun in the air, her cries being sucked into a vortex along with her body and soul. Dragged down, down, down, she entered a dark world where light barely penetrated and slithery things skittered through the shadows.

"Deme?" a voice called.

"Aurai?" she answered, moving toward the sound, her eyes open but seeing nothing but black. With her hands out in front of her to keep her from bumping into things, she continued moving in the direction she'd first heard her sister's voice. "Aurai? Where are you?"

"Here," she said. "I'm right here."

"But I can't see you. Come into the light."

"I can't. I'm trapped."

"Where, Aurai? Where are you trapped?"

"I don't knooooowwwww." Her voice faded into an abyss, swallowed like everything good and bright.

The darkness ebbed around her, undulating like a seductive lover, pressing closer until she backed against a wall. Feathery black tendrils stroked her skin, swirled around her face and into her mouth.

She couldn't breathe, couldn't cry out. Her fingers clawed at her throat trying to dislodge the evil. She had to get out before it consumed her, too.

"Go, Deme! Leave before he takes you, too!" Aurai cried out.

No. Deme didn't want to leave her sister. She had to get her out with her.

"You can't. He's too powerful. Let me go…"

Deme jerked awake, gasping for air, her heart thundering against her chest. She sat up, her gaze darting around the interior of the dorm room, pushing back the panic that threatened to take over.

Light from the hallway edged underneath the doorway.

As the panic receded, tapping increased on the window.

Almost afraid to look, Deme glanced across at the glass and almost screamed.

An image of her sister's face wavered against the inky blackness of night. Ghostly pale hair whipped in the wind and her eyes rounded in terror.

"Aurai!" Deme leaped from the bed and raced for the window. As she reached for the latch, her sister's face disappeared and in its place the vines formed a gaping maw, thorns pressing against the window like teeth, slashing at the glass.

Deme jumped back, her hand releasing the clasp, the lock remaining tight. For a long time she stood with her hand pressed to her chest. Then she heard it.

Chanting. Soft at first, rising in waves with the wind. It was coming from outside...in the garden.

Afraid to trust her own senses, and still shaking from her last encounter, Deme leaned toward the window, peering through the choking vines distorting her view.

Below in the open area between the towering pines, a circle of people stood in black robes, candle flames flickering in front of each one.

What the hell? The garden was forbidden. After Aurai had disappeared, Deme would think no one would venture into the deadly paradise.

The floor beneath her feet trembled as if warning of danger.

Dressed in her pajamas, her feet bare, Deme shot out of the room.

Cal arrived at the hospital in time to catch an ambulance preparing to leave.

"Crazy shift." A blond EMT shook his head as he closed and latched the outside door at the rear of the ambulance.

Cal paused beside one of the techs and flipped out his badge. "Did you guys deliver a Mike Hubbs here a little while ago?"

"The guy who attempted suicide?" The EMT, perched on the running board, about to climb into the driver's seat, nodded. "Yeah. That's what I'm talking about. Crazy."

"Who reported it?"

"His roommate found him. The guy slit his wrists and would have bled out if his roommate had gotten in a few minutes later. I think the kid was high on something."

"Hubbs?"

"Yeah, he was delirious, talking about a beast trying to come out of his chest."

The EMT at the rear of the vehicle joined them. "Yeah, he kept ripping at his shirt and disturbing the pressure bandages on his wrist. He slipped into a coma before we got to the hospital."

"Probably just as well. He was losing blood fast and all that jerking around only made it worse."

"The doc thinks they might save him, though." The radio inside the truck chirped static, a call going out to a unit.

"That's us. You need anything else, catch us at the end of our shift. We've been hopping tonight. Must be a full moon."

The EMTs climbed into the ambulance and drove out of the emergency entrance.

Cal looked up at the sky. Clouds obliterated the moon. He entered the hospital, immediately hit by the scent of disinfectant. His first instinct was to turn and leave, hating the sterile environment, the injuries and traumas that passed through the doors, but he had to see Mike for himself.

His hand went to the bite mark on his collarbone. Had Deme really bitten him? He couldn't remember any of that, only the hot sex and the need to do it again and again.

Even now his jeans tightened, his groin filling, pulsing to life.

As he entered the elevator, he adjusted, chastising himself for his continued lack of control. How could this be happening to him? He respected Deme more than that. Another wave of guilt plagued him, pressing down on him like a heavy weight. If he was a weak man, he'd be tempted to punish himself.

Cal's breath lodged in his throat, refusing to move any farther. The urge to punish himself grew, and he realized what Mike had felt and why he'd attempted suicide.

The logical side of his brain tried to reason with the side that piled more and more guilt on top of him. By the time the door slid open on the floor where Mike was being kept in ICU, Cal was sagging against the handrail.

"Black?" Marty hurried over from the nurses' station and helped Cal out of the elevator. "What's wrong?"

"I don't know." Cal staggered to the counter and leaned on it, breathing hard. "I can't seem to pull myself out of it."

"Of what?"

"That's just it, I don't know. It's as though I'm on drugs or something. Everything seems too much to handle. I can't fight it." Cal crumpled to the floor, the world going dark.

"Mr. Black? Cal?" A woman in blue scrubs waved something under his nose.

The pungent smell stung his senses and pulled him back to consciousness. Cal sat up, running a hand through his hair. "What happened?"

"You passed out." Marty squatted on his other side.

"Passed out?" Cal never passed out. But then he'd

done a lot of strange things he never thought he would in the past twenty-four hours. He pushed to his feet.

"Whoa, steady there." Marty rose beside him, a hand on his elbow.

The nurse had his other arm.

"I'm fine." He straightened, shaking off their hands. "Really."

"Still, you should see a doctor."

"Not necessary. I came to see Mike."

"Look, we don't need another patient in ICU. Let us help you." The nurse grabbed his arm again.

"I said I'm fine." Cal glared at her until she let go.

"Have it your way, but I'm not picking you up off the floor."

Cal turned to Marty. "Where's Hubbs?"

"Second door on the right."

Cal crossed the corridor and entered the room to find the big undergraduate covered in white, tubes running into his arm and down his throat, his arms wrapped in bandages.

"He's still in a coma. They'll try to bring him out in the morning when the doctor makes his rounds. He's not much help as he is."

Cal only half listened. He strode to the young man's bedside, pulled the sheet back and tugged the collar of the hospital gown down.

Just like Deme predicted, the man had bite marks on his chest.

"Human, aren't they?"

"Yes," Cal responded.

"Know who did it?"

"His girlfriend."

"Jeez. What's with kids nowadays?"

"I'm beginning to wonder that myself, but I'm thinking it's not the kids."

"Drugs?"

"No." He pulled the gown up, covering Mike's chest, and tucked the sheet around him. "Make sure they take good care of him."

The lieutenant's brow furrowed. "After what he did to that girl, you care?"

"I don't think he knew what was happening."

"Care to explain?"

"Not now." Cal turned and left the room.

Marty jogged to keep up. "What's going on?"

"I don't know, but I get the feeling Deme Chattox is in over her head."

"Well, hell." Marty stopped in the middle of the hallway. "Keep me informed, Black."

Cal passed the elevator, opting for the staircase. He took the stairs two at a time, leaping past the last four to land on the street level. He burst into the open, breathing for what felt like the first time in days.

Worry had a way of making your vision sharper, your hearing more penetrating and your focus dead-on. Without a doubt, he knew he needed to get back to the campus. The sooner the better.

Deme entered through the garden gate. The lock and chain lay on the ground nearby. Who had the key? Who would be stupid enough to let these people in when they could be banned from campus if caught?

Keeping to the shadows of the buildings surrounding the garden, Deme eased closer to the circle. For the first time since she came to Colyer-Fenton, Deme realized the garden was in the shape of a pentagon, a building at each side, one of which was the Gamma Omega dor-

Her voice got stronger. "But know this. It wasn't us. Something else is at work here."

"You know I don't believe in all that magic stuff." He blew out a frustrated breath. "I'd love to blame something or someone else, but I can't. I did that to you."

"And I did it to you. Think, Cal," Deme said, her voice tense. "In our past relationship, we never got that violent. Never."

"But how could something or someone else cause this?"

"What Rachel said made sense."

"What is this *it* she's talking about?"

"I don't know. But it's having an impact on more and more people. We have to find its source."

"Let's assume I believe there's some supernatural force at work here. How do we find it?"

"Again, I don't know. But I bet it has everything to do with Zoe's attitude, the attempts at rape…and Aurai's disappearance."

"I'm headed to the hospital now."

"Why?"

"Mike Hubbs was admitted. He attempted suicide last night."

Deme gasped. "Is he all right?"

"I'll know more once I swing by. Want to meet me there?"

"No, I get the feeling I'm needed around here. In case something happens. Let me know how it goes."

"Will do." He started to hang up and thought again. "Be careful, Deme. Even if you don't want me in your life, I care."

"Thanks." She clicked off.

Silence surrounded him and with it guilt so overwhelming he wanted to throw himself out the window.

mitory. She recognized the student commons building as another and the administration building as a third. The other two she couldn't identify but made a mental note to check into it when she got back to her room and could locate them on the campus map.

As she neared the circle, the chanting grew louder. All the voices were pitched high and soft. Girls. Probably the Gamma Omegas doing some hazing ritual.

The robes they wore looked much like the one she'd found in Rachel's closet—black with a full hood to hide their faces.

When she got close enough, Deme could make out the words, and she gasped. They were calling on the spirit of the dark lord of the underworld.

Deme couldn't feel power emanating from any one girl, but she knew you didn't mess with dark spirits, witch or not. Dark magic was unstable, hard to control and even harder to cleanse from your aura once it invaded.

Was that what had happened? Had dark magic invaded this campus, disturbing those who got too close to its center?

One girl stepped forward and pulled back her hood, exposing her face to the candlelight.

Zoe Adams.

She set a blue vial in the center of the ring of candles. With a flick of a match, she lit a sandalwood incense wand and jabbed it into the earth beside the bottle. Then she stood and, instead of lifting her face to the moon as a good witch would, she stared at the ground.

"God of love and beauteous might
Come unto us this moonless night
We cast this circle to ask thy boon
Bless beauty on us, bless us soon

We cast this circle one more time
Upon us let your splendor shine
Lord of Darkness great and wise
Let others see us through your eyes
We cast this circle one two three
We pray you bless us for all who see
So mote it be."

From a velvet bag tied to her waist, she tossed rose petals around the ring of candles and stepped back to the outer circle of robe-clad girls.

The members who'd obviously done this before bowed their heads and chanted.

"Night cloaks all with beauty
Shadows grow with power
Darkness, we embrace thee."

They continued chanting, repeating the words over and over until all the girls joined in.

Deme stood transfixed, dread pressing into her chest like an iron fist. These girls played at black magic. Didn't they understand? Dark spells like this one were dangerous.

Zoe knelt to retrieve the blue vial from the center of the circle and poured a single drop onto her lips. She passed it to the next girl in the circle, who repeated the performance and handed it to the next.

As the vial made its way around the circle, a cry rose up from one of the robe-clad girls. "No! I can't do this!"

Rachel Taylor collapsed to the ground, her hood flung back, exposing thick brown hair and pale, translucent, smooth skin. Her body shook with the force of her sobs, the earth vibrating beneath Deme's feet, sharing her sadness and something else.

Deme had to stop this ritual before it went too far.

She was afraid she was already too late, but she couldn't stand by and do nothing.

Calling on all the power of the earth she could muster, Deme pressed her bare toes into the grass, feeling the cool earth beneath. She closed her eyes and drew in a deep breath, her concentration nearly shattered by the amount of effort even a breath of air required in this cloistered garden.

"Mother of earth
Goddess of beauty
strength of spirit
I call upon thee
Ancient the stone
stalwart the tree
Your gifts of safe harbor
impart upon thee
Embrace these children
let peace once more reign
Bring moonlight to shadows
and ease to their pain
Mother of earth
Oh, radiant one
With prayers I beseech thee
Let darkness be gone."

Deme opened her eyes, her prayers echoing in her mind, hope rising inside her as she hid among the shadows. The earth beneath her bare feet quivered. Moonlight peeked out from a cloud, casting light upon the circle of girls.

A tentative smile curled the corners of Deme's lips. The goddess would shine down on the garden and protect the girls from the dark forces at work here.

The cloud slipped back over the moon, choking out all light but for the candle flames. A dark wisp of air whipped through the clearing, snuffing out every flame, leaving the garden in shadows except for the few lights shining from windows of the buildings surrounding them.

The hooded girls gasped.

"I can't see," a voice called out, quavering in the gloom.

"Anyone have a flashlight?"

"I do." A light flickered on, spreading a narrow ray through the ranks of the girls. The circle collapsed inward, the girls moving closer to one another, gathering around the beam of the flashlight.

"What's that?" a girl cried out. Then a scream ripped through the air.

The beam of light swerved toward the scream.

The ground parted, roots pushing up from beneath.

Girls screamed and ran in all directions, but the roots tripped them, wrapping around their ankles, bringing them crashing to the earth.

What was happening?

Deme watched in horror as more roots exploded from the ground, grasping at those girls racing for the open gate.

The gate swung shut, trapping all within the garden.

One by one, the girls were dragged to the earth, the roots weaving back and forth over their bodies.

Deme threw herself toward the nearest girl, clawing at the relentless root that twined and circled the girl's neck. The hood fell back, revealing the pale blond hair and gray eyes of Shelby Cramer. She reached for Deme, her eyes wide, fearful.

"Help me," she cried, then the root tightened.

Shelby clutched at the root strangling her.

Deme grabbed the root, pulling to free the girl.

Beside her the ground parted and darkness in the form of a bare black vine snaked up, twisting around her legs, dragging her to the ground and away from Shelby.

Deme dug her fingernails into the earth, reaching for the girl, her hand grazing the robe, but not for long.

The earth shook, the ground trembling as more and more roots sprang from below, slithering along the surface, attaching themselves to all those who occupied the garden.

"Deme!" From the second floor of the dormitory, Cal pushed aside the thorn vine blocking Deme's window and cursed. "Deme!"

Hope filled her chest and made her fight harder at the roots that bound her, dragging her deeper into the earth. "Cal! Help us!"

He disappeared, and with him all hope faded.

The roots around her arms swept up to her neck, cutting off her air. Deme couldn't draw a breath, the darkness more and more pronounced as her head grew light and fuzzy. Images of Cal flitted across her memories. Why had she run from him? From the potential for happiness. If she lived, she'd tell him how she felt. *Please, I have to live.* She closed her eyes and prayed, *Goddess of the earth, please let me live.* The more she prayed, the tighter the roots became, pressing her body into the earth, the dirt parting to let her slip beneath.

"Deme, hold on!" Suddenly Cal appeared wielding a big knife, slashing at the roots clinging to his feet. He cut and hacked his way across the garden until he reached Deme.

In two great swings, he severed the roots pulling Deme deeper into the earth. Air filled her lungs and she sprang to her feet, refusing to give in to the peace of death.

With Cal hacking and Deme pulling, they freed one girl after the next, shoving them through the gate and out of the forbidden garden. Bushes and vines reached for them as they exited the garden, the last to escape.

Cal slammed the gate behind himself and wrapped the chain around, bolting the lock in place.

Deme fell to the ground, breathing hard, her arms and legs laced with scratches and bruises.

"We can't stay here." Cal lifted her in his arms and carried her to the edge of the building farthest away from the seething garden.

There he stopped and crushed her to his chest. "Deme." He buried his face in her neck, his body shaking. "I thought I'd lost you."

"You and me both." Her arms wrapped around him and she held him close, tears wetting her cheek and his. "I tried to help them."

"Shh…it's okay now."

"But everything I did made it worse. My spell turned against the girls." The tears came faster and sobs rose in her throat. "They almost died."

"Deme." Cal set her on her feet and gathered her face between his palms. "*You* almost died."

"I'm okay, thanks to you." She pulled away, her gaze panning the yard surrounding the dorm. Not a single girl remained. Only Deme and Cal occupied the area. "Where are the girls?"

"They must have gone in."

"Let's check on them. I hate to think they went back into the garden."

"Surely not."

"Come on." She led the way into the dorm and

knocked on the first door with a Gamma Omega symbol on it.

A pretty girl with dark brown hair opened it, blinking at the light in the hallway. She yawned. "You're the new R.A., right? What's going on?"

"Random check," Deme said. "Were you outside earlier?"

"I got in from my waitress job around nine. Why?"

Deme shook her head. "No reason. Go back to bed."

As the brunette closed the door, Deme shot a narrowed glance at Cal. "I swear I saw her out there in one of the robes."

He nodded. "Did you see the dirt on her bare feet?"

"No, but I'll be looking next time." She walked to the next door with the Gamma Omega Greek letters and knocked.

It took longer this time for the girl to answer. When she did, the scratches on her ankles and calves and the dirt on her feet were all too obvious. "What's happening?"

"Maybe you can tell us." Deme crossed her arms over her chest. "Were you just in the forbidden garden?"

The girl shook her head, her eyes glassy. "I don't know what you're talking about. I've been in bed since ten o'clock. Got an exam tomorrow."

"How do you explain the dirt on your feet and the scratches?" Cal pointed to her feet and ankles.

The girl looked down and blinked, her eyes widening. "What the hell? How did those get there? Oh, my God." She looked up, tears welling. "I should call the campus nurse."

Deme frowned. "You don't remember getting them?"

"No. I swear I've been in my room all night. Ask my roommate."

Another girl lay in bed, completely out, her arm hanging over the edge, displaying cuts and bruises.

"Oh, God, she's been hurt, as well." The girl ran to her roommate and shook her. "Wake up, Abby."

Deme held her breath until the girl stirred and her eyes opened. "Lissa? Whadya want?" she asked, her words slurred.

"What happened to us? Why do we have cuts and bruises?" Tears poured down Lissa's face and she collapsed on the floor beside her roommate. "I don't know what happened."

Deme stepped into the room, pulling Cal in behind her to keep from waking the entire dorm with Lissa's sobs. "Mind if we look around?"

"No." Lissa scrubbed the tears from her face and held on to her roommate's hand. "Please do." She pulled her knees up under her chin and watched as Deme and Cal checked beneath beds. As Deme opened one closet, Cal opened the other. There hanging inside each were the black robes used in the ceremony.

Deme pulled one out on the hanger. "Do you remember wearing this in the garden earlier?"

Both girls shook their heads. "We only wear those when the Gamma Omegas have a sorority meeting."

"And you don't remember having one of those tonight?"

Both girls looked up at Deme, shaking their heads. "No," they stated in unison.

Lissa climbed up on the bed beside Abby and hugged the girl close. "We'd remember something like that."

Deme stared hard at both, but her gut told her that these girls thought they were telling the absolute truth. Obviously they didn't remember being attacked by roots in the garden and almost killed.

"What's happening?" Abby asked.

"I don't know." Deme replaced the robe in the closet even though she wanted to take it out and burn it. "But I'm going to find out. Use a clean washrag and soap to clean your scratches. I'll bring ointment and bandages by in a few minutes."

Deme and Cal left the girls, closing the door behind them.

"What do you make of that?"

"You were there. You saw what happened." Deme faced Cal. "It happened."

He nodded, stroking his hand down the side of her cheek. "It happened."

"Right before I cast my spell, they were passing around a blue vial of liquid. Do you think it was a drug?"

"Could be."

"Then there is one more person I need to talk to." Deme pushed her dirty pajama sleeves up and marched to the stairwell door.

She climbed the steps two at a time, Cal keeping up with little effort.

Once on the second floor, she aimed for Rachel's room.

She got only halfway down the hall when Zoe Adams stepped out of her room in front of her. "What's going on?"

Deme came to a complete stop, her jaw tightening. "Why don't you tell me."

"Tell you what? That you're breaking the rules of the dormitory by bringing a man in after midnight?" Zoe cocked her eyebrows up into the sweep of her blond bangs. "I could have you fired for that."

Deme didn't back down. Instead she took another

step forward, putting herself toe to toe with the sorority leader. "What did you give the girls that made them forget what happened in the garden, Zoe?"

"I'm sure I don't know what you're talking about."

"I can have you kicked out of the dormitory and the school for drugging students, so don't mess with me."

"I'd like to see you try." One lip curled upward in a smirk. "My father is a major contributor to this school. You can't kick me out of anything."

"No matter how much money your daddy contributes, drugging others without their consent is illegal." Cal stepped up beside Deme, his hand resting at her waist.

Despite her self-righteous anger, Deme had to admit she was intimidated by Zoe's sordid, cocky self-assurance, and Cal's show of support made her feel better.

"Like I said...I don't know what you're talking about."

"Where's the blue vial you were using in the garden ceremony just a few minutes ago?"

Zoe frowned. "I wasn't in the garden a few minutes ago."

"What about the dirt on your feet and scratches on your legs? How do you explain that?"

She glanced down at her legs. "Well, you're right. There are scratches and dirt on my legs." She tipped her head to the side. "Now, how did they get there?" Zoe glanced up, her eyes narrowing. "You wouldn't have had anything to do with that, would you?"

Deme stared at the girl. She wanted to believe that Zoe was lying, but her confusion at the dirt and scratches was too convincing. "Good grief, Zoe. Go clean yourself up. Oh, and Zoe, something isn't right around here, and I intend to get to the bottom of it."

Zoe's gaze narrowed into a squint. "I can't tell you how this happened tonight, but I can tell you the Gamma Omegas stick together. Not one of them wants out of the sorority. They like what it's done for them and they won't go back." She turned on her bare heel and stomped back to her room, closing the door with a thump.

"What do you think she meant by they won't go back?" Cal asked.

"I don't know. But I'm getting really tired of Zoe's attitude." Deme sucked in a deep breath and let it out. "I want to check one more room then I need to distribute ointment and bandages." Exhaustion was dragging her down fast. No sleep and being attacked by a possessed garden had taken its toll.

"Where to?" Cal looked at the remaining doors.

"Rachel Taylor's room." Deme moved down the hallway and tapped on the door. "Just so you know, my sister used to occupy this room." Deme didn't wait for a response from Cal. She raised her hand and knocked on the door. The door swung open to darkness.

Cal reached inside and flipped the switch. Light filled all four corners...of an empty room.

Chapter 9

Cal didn't sleep the rest of the night. Though Deme insisted that she would be okay without him there, he hadn't gone far. He'd camped out beneath a tree where he could see the Gamma Omega dormitory.

Twice, the campus cop had circled. Twice, Cal had ducked into the shadows to avoid questions. As the campus maintenance man, it wouldn't do for him to be caught more or less stalking a dorm full of girls. Especially given the fact they'd had several attempted rapes. Despite the danger of getting caught and blamed for what he was trying to stop, Cal stayed put, managing to nod off near dawn.

Not until the sun shone down on his face did he awaken. Students passed by on the nearby sidewalks, carrying books to the commons for breakfast and a cram session before class.

Cal stood and stretched, checking his cell phone for

any text messages or missed calls. None. He dialed Deme's number and hit Send, only to punch the end call button before the first ring. She needed her rest, and he felt certain nothing else had happened since the garden incident.

With the grunge of a restless night making him feel sticky, he straddled his bike and headed for his apartment and a warm shower. He had to report for his first day of work as maintenance man in less than an hour, and he was certain that he would have a lot to do besides investigating the case.

After a shower, he headed back to campus, swinging through the local gourmet coffee shop for a strong dose of caffeine. Gritty eyes and an empty stomach didn't seem to be the best way to start the day. He had toilets to fix, drains to unstop and lightbulbs to change out, based on the repairs list his supervisor had given him the day before. He also wanted to ask a few questions while he had the opportunity.

Cal stepped into the maintenance shop fifteen minutes before his shift was due to begin.

Fred Knowlton sat at his desk, staring at the computer. "Damned thing is slower than molasses," he muttered.

"Morning, Mr. Knowlton."

"Fred. Call me Fred or I'll fire you on the spot," he groused, without looking up. "Know anything about computers?"

"A little." Cal stepped behind Fred and looked over his shoulder.

"Can't get this application to come up."

"Mind if I drive?"

"Not at all." Fred stood and let Cal take his seat. "I have a kind of love-hate relationship with these things.

I love to hate 'em. I had the work schedule up and was adding your name to the list of employees when it locked up on me."

Cal checked the task manager and canceled the program that was locked up and restarted it. "That should do it." He stood and let Fred resume his seat.

Fred spent a few seconds keying in information using the one-fingered typing method and pressed Enter. "There." He grinned up at Cal. "You saved me a lot of heartburn. What can I do for you this morning?"

"I was just curious about the guy I'm replacing. What happened to him? I heard rumors he disappeared."

Fred frowned. "Damnedest thing. I gave Kyle his list of repairs and sent him off about three weeks ago. Guess he didn't like the kinds of repairs and decided it was time to quit. He didn't come back that afternoon to clock out, didn't call and tell me he was quitting, and I haven't seen him since."

"Did you report it to the police?"

Fred shrugged. "I told the campus cop and HR. Figured if they were worried, they'd follow up. In the meantime, I've had some of the other guys working to pick up his slack. Glad you've come on board." His eyes narrowed. "You will let me know if you decide to quit, won't you?"

Cal grinned. "Don't worry. I will."

"Here's an updated list of repairs for the day." Fred handed him a printout. "If there's anything on the list you need help with, give me a call."

"What was on the list you gave Kyle when he disappeared?" Cal looked down at his list and back up. "Not anything on this list I hope."

"No. I seem to recall the only major repair was to a steam pipe in the basement of the student commons.

At least he fixed it before he disappeared." Fred stood, clipped a tool belt around his waist and stepped away from the desk. "Still have a lot to do today. Been short-handed so long, I've been helping out, as well." He slapped a campus maintenance hat on his head and handed another to Cal. "Here." He pulled a set of keys from his pocket and handed them to him, as well. "The master key should get you in most places on campus. Oh, and you should be able to find a coverall in the locker room that will fit you. See you at quittin' time."

Cal followed Fred to the locker room and the older man left him there with a map of the campus and a stack of coveralls in various sizes.

Dressed in a coverall and the maintenance cap, Cal hoped to blend into the woodwork. He quickly tackled the replacement bulbs in a couple of the lecture halls, keeping his ears open for anything out of the ordinary. Working through the list took up most of his morning, more than he would have preferred. But his next stop was a leaky faucet in the student commons kitchen. He wanted to check out the basement while there and see if he could find a clue to the missing maintenance man, Kyle.

It didn't take him long to replace the washer in the faucet, successfully stopping the drip. Then he located the stairs leading down into the basement. The doors were locked, but the master key Fred had given him worked to open them.

The first thing he noticed was the rumble of ma-chines, completely obliterating any other noise he could hope to hear. If he worked down here long, he'd require earplugs or suffer hearing loss.

The basement was a maze of pipes, air-conditioning ductwork and stuff Cal didn't recognize. The lighting was less than adequate, forcing him to pull out the flashlight he'd grabbed out of the toolbox he'd been assigned. He searched the length of the basement, checking in, around, behind and over everything. He located several steam pipes Kyle could have worked on, none of which were leaking steam.

When he thought he had exhausted every inch of the space, Cal turned toward the stairs, in the process of hitting the off switch on his flashlight. When the beam swung across the concrete floor, it flashed on something beneath the metal stairwell. His hand froze on the switch. He'd missed it before because it wasn't all that obvious. Beneath the metal stairwell, he noticed metal rivets standing out on the floor. An iron ring the size of a softball stood vertical, as if it had been used not long ago and the rust caking the hinge kept it from dropping back down.

This was the basement. What could be below it?

Cal reached for the iron ring and tugged.

The door didn't budge. He searched for a lock, hoping he had a key to match. No lock. Which meant the door should open. He pulled again, putting his back into it.

This time the door creaked upward, but the weight of the door pulled it back down, dragging Cal with it.

Determined to get the door up this time, he used both hands, bent his knees and pulled with all his might. It took a lot of effort to get it open, but once he did, it was as if whatever suction had hold of it from below let go.

The door swung upward and clanked against the concrete wall beneath the steps. With the door's opening the stench of rot, sewer and damp wafted up into his face, making him gag. He pulled the collar of his coverall over his nose and shone the beam of his flash-light into the hole.

Metal ladder rungs led down into a dark abyss, the sublevel of the building. He knew that Chicago had an entire labyrinth of tunnels beneath the city. Could this be part of it?

His heartbeat kicked up the pace as he placed his foot on the first rung while holding on to the staircase above. He wondered if he'd find Kyle down here, and if so, would he be dead and decomposing?

Cal braced himself for the worst as he stepped another rung lower. In the back of his mind he thought maybe it wasn't such a good idea to go below without backup. He'd about decided to come back up when the cell phone vibrated in his jeans pocket.

His jeans were buried beneath his coverall. In order to access it, he had to climb back out of the hole and unzip his coverall.

The caller ID indicated Deme. He punched the talk button and pressed the receiver to his ear. "Deme? Are you all right?"

"Cal? Where are you?"

"In the basement of the student commons. What's up?"

"Gina's been working in the library all morning and found something interesting. I'm headed that way. Can you join us there on the second floor in the east-side stacks?"

"I'll be there." He flipped the phone shut and stood for a moment shining his light down into the darkness and obscurity of the subterranean level below. It would have to wait. He'd check with Marty and see if he knew anything about the tunnels before he ventured farther.

As he lowered the heavy iron door to the ground,

he could swear he heard something like a groan from down below. An unwanted chill spread through his skin right down to the bone. All the talk about magic had his imagination working overtime.

He jerked the door open again. "Hello!"

No response. Not even an echo, as if the ground below swallowed his call.

Maybe he'd imagined it.

He lowered the door again. The hinge gave with an eerie creaking sound almost like the cry of a child. That must have been it. Nothing a little oil wouldn't cure. He left the trap door and walked up the staircase into the student commons, feeling as if a weight had lifted from him.

But the creepy feeling he'd gotten followed him all the way across campus to the library.

Deme knew the exact moment when Cal entered the building. The vibration of his movements were his alone, and she recognized it from the many weeks they'd dated. Each time he'd entered her apartment complex, she'd known, her body anticipating their greeting and the tumbled mess they'd make of the sheets on her bed. Every minute of every day had been spent thinking of him and what he'd do to her when they finally got together. She'd been so completely obsessed with him, it had ultimately scared her into running.

Even now, every one of her nerve endings alerted her to his presence. She'd arrived a minute before him and hadn't met up with her sisters yet. But her feet wouldn't take her farther, forcing her to wait near the central staircase. Her pulse quickened, her breathing becoming more ragged in anticipation of seeing him again.

No amount of self-chastisement slowed her beating

heart. She really had to get a grip on her reaction to the man's presence. When they found Aurai, Deme would be on her way back to St. Croix and the thriving private investigation business she'd established there. Cal had said in no uncertain terms he didn't believe in magic. Therefore he'd never understand her.

Not that she'd been dabbling much in magic. She preferred to live a normal life much as Aurai had aspired to, touching on magic only to help solve investigations no weightier than finding a missing pooch or a cheating husband.

The distance from Cal hadn't lessened her longing for him and the physical ache of not having him to lie next to her in bed. Even now, she wanted him.

This is ridiculous. She couldn't go on mooning over a man she'd left behind a year ago.

Deme turned away, determined to move on and join her sisters in the stacks.

A sound behind her made her look over her shoulder.

Cal stood at the top of the stairs. Dressed in a Colyer-Fenton College maintenance uniform, he looked no less handsome. The tool belt hanging from his hips actually increased his appeal.

Her heart flip-flopped in her chest, her cheeks burning, the heat flooding her body, dipping low into her belly. The apex of her thighs flamed, and ached with longing.

Cal reached out and cupped her face. "Are you okay? You look a little feverish."

Deme almost laughed out loud, her face smoldering with heat. "It's a bit warm in here." She told herself to turn, to walk away from where this man stood touching her cheek. But she couldn't. She wanted to lean into his palm and press a kiss there. Again, she couldn't.

"Come—" Deme squeaked, cleared her throat and started again. "Come on. Selene and Gina should already be here."

As his fingers left her cheek, the cool library air barely helped to bring her temperature back under control. Her feet finally cooperated and she moved one step at a time toward the east-side stacks.

"Aren't you afraid of blowing your cover?" Cal asked. Deme shook her head. "Gina chose this location because no one uses this corner of the library. We should have no problem as long as we keep it quiet."

Gina and Selene leaned over a microfiche reader, pointing at the screen. Brigid stood beside them, her arms crossed, her brows pushed low.

"They still use those things?" Deme leaned over Gina's other shoulder.

"The librarian said they're in the process of converting everything to digital format. They just hadn't gotten this far back." Gina spoke without glancing up. "Look at this." She maneuvered the film backward to the beginning of a copy of an article from an old *Chicago Tribune* newspaper.

The headline read Five Sisters Die in Colyer-Fenton Fire.

"What the hell?" A cold hand squeezed Deme's heart, making her chest hurt almost as if the old article was a portent of her and her sisters' deaths. Which was crazy. "What's the date on that paper?"

Brigid stared at Deme. "It'll be exactly thirty years ago tomorrow."

All four sisters were silent.

"It doesn't mean anything to us," Gina finally said. "What's interesting is the location. Apparently the fire occurred in Lion Hall and it was burned completely to the ground." She looked around at the people assembled. "Anyone have a copy of the campus map?"

Cal pulled a wrinkled paper out of his pocket and handed it to Gina.

She spent half a minute scanning the page and the legend detailing the names of the buildings. "Just like I thought. There isn't a Lion Hall."

Brigid shrugged. "Which means they didn't rebuild the hall after it burned. So?"

Deme leaned over Gina's shoulder, reading down through the entire article, skimming over the details of the emergency response. The more she read the colder the room became until a shiver shook her from head to toe. "Says here in the article that it was the central building in a spokelike design. The five adjacent buildings suffered minimal damage."

"You think the forbidden garden is where Lion Hall used to be?" Gina asked.

Selene stood straight, her eyes closed, her body swaying. "Yes. That's exactly it. And the five sisters have to be the voices calling to me in my night and day dreams." She pressed her fingers to her temples. "Thank the goddess. I thought I was going crazy. I hear them now."

Deme shot a glance at her sister. "Really? Can you hear what they're saying?"

Selene's brow scrunched. "No. But the closer I get to the garden, the more I hear them and the more chaotic their voices are."

"Has to be where Lion Hall stood. That's why you can hear the sisters. They burned with the hall thirty years ago."

Brigid touched Gina's shoulder. "See what else you can find during that time frame. Any strange happenings, unexplained events, attacks, problems with students?"

Gina nudged the microfiche tray, skimming across several days' worth of newspapers, searching for anything related to Colyer-Fenton College.

A headline on the front page of the *Tribune* captured Deme's attention. "Go back."

Gina eased backward slowly, coming to a halt on an article.

Local College Coed Attacked on Campus

Deme read over Gina's shoulder. "'A young woman was attacked on the Colyer-Fenton College campus late last night. Miss Baker is being treated for injuries at an area hospital. The police questioned the victim, who was so traumatized she spoke of a huge beast, ravishing her.'" Deme looked up at Cal. "Sound familiar?"

Gina continued reading aloud, "Doctors and psychiatrists are working to help her in the aftermath of the ordeal. The president of the campus has hired additional security personnel to keep students safe, but some parents have pulled their students out of school until the perpetrator is caught."

"See if you can find the full name of the girl."

Gina swept across film, but no other news mentioned the campus or the student.

Deme straightened and paced the length of a shelf of books. "We need to get into student records."

"I'll see what I can do." Cal pulled a lightbulb from his coverall pocket, a smile tugging at his lips. "Surely there has to be a lightbulb burned out in there."

Deme almost laughed, glad he was there and helping them find her sister. "My gut tells me that the building that burned and the sisters who died in it are related to what's happening now. It's too much of a coincidence, especially considering there are five sisters involved now."

"I'll keep looking through the newspaper articles and historical records of the college," Gina offered.

"Good." Deme looked to Brigid.

Brigid rolled her eyes. "I'll check out City Hall and see what records they have on file for the buildings on campus back then. Although I'd rather be kicking ass than digging through moldy old papers."

Deme touched her sister's arm. "Thanks, Brigid."

Brigid's expression hardened. "Anything for Aurai."

"I have a class to teach right now in the theater. I can ask around and see if anyone knows where Rachel disappeared to," Selene said.

A student carrying a huge stack of research books passed by where they stood, casting a questioning look in their direction.

When he'd passed, Deme sighed. "We should meet off campus later this evening. I don't want too many people seeing us together. If someone on campus is causing all these problems, we don't need them to find out they are being investigated."

"Right." Brigid tapped a finger to her temple. "I'm outta here."

"Me, too." Selene slung the long handle of her bag over her head and across her chest, looking every bit the artistic drama teacher. "Wish me luck. I've never taught drama."

Deme smiled at her. "You'll do great. It's all about empathy and expressing emotions. Exactly what you're good at."

"Thanks. I just wish I could get rid of this headache. It's dragging me down."

Deme stared at her sister, for the first time noticing

the dark shadows beneath her eyes. "Are you sleeping at all?"

She shook her head. "Not much. I'm having nightmares about being sucked into the earth by a wind tunnel."

Deme's breath caught. "You, too?"

Brigid, three steps away, turned back, her hand raised. "Me, three."

The three of them turned to Gina.

She nodded, her mouth set in grim lines. "Is the dream about Aurai?"

All the girls nodded as one.

Deme was the first to break the long silence. "Well, let's get to work and find our sister."

Brigid and Selene left.

Gina bent over the microfiche reader.

Cal touched Deme's shoulder and motioned her aside.

"Are you going to be all right?" Cal asked.

Deme frowned. "I can handle myself. If you can find out about the students who were here thirty years ago that could be a big help."

"I'll come up with an excuse to get inside the records."

"And Cal, find out anything you can about Zoe Adams, Mike Hubbs and Rachel Taylor. If we can get an address, we might want to check with Rachel's family and see if she made it home."

"Will do." He closed the distance between them, cupping her face. "Be careful, will ya?" His thumb brushed across her cheekbone, his gaze capturing hers.

Deme stared into his eyes, trying to read into his mind and soul. "Tell me, Cal. After last night, do you still think magic is a bunch of talk?"

"Let's say I'm teetering on the fence."

"You can't deny what you saw in the garden."

"No. And I have no explanation for it. But like you said, I'm a black-and-white kind of guy. It's going to take time for me to accept the gray." He touched her lips with his, briefly, bringing his head up so fast, Deme thought she might have imagined his kiss.

"Did you just kiss me?" she asked.

"Looks like it."

"No. This is a kiss." She wrapped her hand around the back of his head and drew him down to her, kissing him hard and long. Her tongue pushed past his teeth to claim his, twisting and tasting. Her chest pressed into his, and she wished with all her heart she were naked in bed with this strong cop who'd saved her ass the night before.

A discreet cough reminded her where she was.

Deme pulled back, brushing her hand across her lips. "Sorry, I didn't mean to put on a show."

Cal grinned, then sobered. "Don't be sorry. Just be safe." He kissed her again, his lips pressing hard against hers. Then he left.

Deme watched him until he rounded the corner and disappeared. She sighed and turned toward Gina.

Her sister sat facing her, arms crossed over her chest and a smirk on her face. "Wanna tell me what's going on with you two?"

Deme straightened her shoulders. "No."

"Oh, come on. What are sisters for if they can't share the sordid details of their love lives?"

"Shh." Deme glanced around at the empty section of the library. "We've been here long enough. If we stay any longer someone's bound to see us together."

Having been the oldest sister forever, she had never

shared her life with her younger sisters, feeling the need to hold herself to a higher standard while her siblings struggled through hookups and breakups during their teens. Not that Deme hadn't struggled. Being a witch with "talents" had its own kind of strain on every relationship she'd ever been in. When she'd finally found Cal, she'd been gun-shy and afraid to let herself care too much.

Her voice little more than a whisper, Gina continued, "Really, Deme. We're all adults now. You don't have to be the model sister anymore."

Gina's comment hit too close to home, knocking a chink in the wall Deme had built to hold herself up. "It's just…"

"He's a mortal and you're a witch?" Gina's brows cocked upward.

Deme sucked in a deep breath, finding it difficult to let go and share after carrying the burden alone all those years. "Yes."

"So?" Gina shook her head. "And here we all thought you were the smart one." Her sister tsked. "So disappointing."

"See?" Deme flung her hands in the air. "That's why I never shared. I couldn't let you see how messed up I was. You all counted on me to be the perfect sister, to lead by example."

"And you're not so perfect." Gina stood and wrapped her arms around Deme. "Which makes you all the more lovable and perfect in my eyes." She held Deme at arm's length. "Do you realize how hard it is to live up to your example?" Gina grimaced. "It's exhausting."

Deme stared at her sister. "Really?"

"You're a tough act to follow, and some of us would rather give up than try."

Deme's eyes widened. "Brigid?"

Gina nodded. "I've hit a few roadblocks myself in the path to being Deme."

"I'm sorry." Deme hugged her sister close. "I didn't know I was being a pain."

"Well, you are." Gina brushed a tear from her cheek and pulled away. "Speaking of pain, I need to check the archives in the basement. The librarian said there are boxes of old documents and manuscripts down there that haven't been converted to microfiche."

"I'll go with you. The Gamma Omegas are probably all in class about now."

"Good. I didn't want to go there by myself. It's dark and creepy."

"My kind of fun." Deme nodded at the microfiche reader. "Let's print off copies of what we've found so far. As we collect more data, maybe it'll all fit together like a puzzle."

"And we'll find Aurai."

Deme's body chilled, her heart squeezing hard in her chest. "Do you think she resents me?"

"Aurai?" Gina snorted. "Never. She worships the ground you walk on. Why do you think she wanted to live a *normal* life?"

"Because of me?" Deme shook her head. "She does not want my life. I've screwed it up so much, she'd be crazy to be like me."

"Looks like you have an opportunity to make it right," Gina said, avoiding Deme's glare. "I sure would make it right if your maintenance dude was the Right in the Mr. Right."

"Sharing is over." Deme gave Gina a pointed look. "Aren't you supposed to be cleaning aquariums?"

"Did the big one on the main level. I'll work the one

on this floor and the third floor tomorrow. Poor fish were swimming in algae."

"Well, make yourself at least look like an aquarium cleaner while I print those articles." Deme parked in the chair behind the microfiche reader and located the articles they'd scanned earlier, printing out copies. When she was done, she paid the librarian and left ahead of Gina, headed for the basement.

As she descended the steps to the main floor, her head reeled with the realization that she'd been holding herself up to a standard too high for any normal person to live up to. She was allowed to have faults, foibles and to screw up every once in a while.

And her biggest mistake was leaving Cal. Was it too late to tell him she'd been wrong?

Chapter 10

Cal entered the administration building. The first office he came to was filled with middle-aged women answering telephones and giving out information concerning admissions and costs for the college. When one of the women hung up, Cal asked where he could find the student records archive room. "Someone mentioned a light out in there." He held up a bulb for good measure.

The other ladies in the room all turned their attention toward him, their gazes sweeping over him.

"I'll show you." The first woman he'd asked jumped from her chair and hurried toward him.

Cal resisted groaning. "No need. I don't want to disturb your work." He'd have a tough time going through student records with someone looking over his shoulder.

"No problem. I needed a break." She waved over her shoulder at the other women and trotted down the hall ahead of Cal, the color in her cheeks high. "My name is Monica."

"Nice to meet you, Monica."

"You're new around here, aren't you?" She smiled back at him.

"First day."

"Well, I hope you'll stay. We can't seem to keep the cute ones around here."

"What do you mean?"

She paused at a closed door marked Records and faced him, her blush deepening. "Like you don't know you're cute." Monica giggled. "Look at me flirting with a younger man."

"No, what did you mean by not keeping the cute ones?"

"I assume you took Kyle's place in maintenance."

"You knew him?"

"Yeah, he changed the outlet in the wall by my desk." She sighed. "Nice guy and closer to my age. Not that I wouldn't go for a younger man if the opportunity presented itself." Monica winked. "This is the place. I'd better get back to my desk. Let me know if you need anything else."

"Thank you, Monica. I'll keep what you said in mind." Cal smiled at her, just a little, not wanting to encourage her flirtation, but liking the frankness of the woman.

He made a show of fiddling with his keys until Monica disappeared around a corner. Once the hallway was clear, he pushed the master key into the lock and entered the room.

Rows of files stood in long rows. The edges of paper stuck out in many places, aging, turning yellow.

Starting at the first one he came to, he noted they

were in alphabetic order, many of the files dating back over twenty years. No new students were in this menagerie, those records and signed documents scanned and saved online. He spied a computer terminal in the corner, making a mental note to attempt to research Rachel, Mike and Zoe through the database.

After scouring the first three rows, he finally made it to the records dating to the year Lion Hall burned.

With only one name to go on, he quickly searched the records for a Miss Baker, locating several. On a small notepad, he jotted down the first names of the girls in the files and the last known addresses. All together there were five girls with the last name of Baker—Diane, Brenda, Katherine, Lisa and Paula. He spent a moment in each record, looking for anything out of the norm, then he moved on to the task of finding the five sisters.

How in the heck was he supposed to know which ones belonged to the girls who'd died in the fire? He didn't even have a name to start with.

In most circumstances, he'd consider the effort futile. What could students from thirty years ago tell him about what was going on today?

Given what had happened in the garden, he didn't want to leave any stone unturned, even the really weird and bizarre. Last night's fight with killer roots had left him questioning all his beliefs.

He started with the *A*s and worked his way through to the *C*s when he came across two files where the pages were packaged in large envelopes and written across the top was the word *Deceased*.

The last name on top of the first one read *Chattox*.

Cal's skin went cold as he read the first name following the comma.

Deborah.

He breathed again and moved to the next file. Again the last name was Chattox. The first name Ellen.

Only two files.

He opened Deborah's and scanned the admissions data. Under family, he noted other siblings were Ellen, Francis, Georgia and Hannah, ages ranging from twenty to twenty-six years old.

These had to be the sisters who died in the fire.

That they had the same last name as Deme gave Cal the willies. What were the chances? And as Deme had reminded him, there was no such thing as coincidence.

Had fate sent Aurai Chattox to this school? And if so, what did fate have planned for the rest of the sisters who'd followed? Would they end up like the other Chattox sisters?

A dark lump of dread settled in Cal's gut and his hand shook as he shoved the documents back in the envelope.

He tucked the two files into his coverall and zipped it. After rifling through the rest of that year and the years on each side, he didn't find any more Chattoxes. He moved on to the computer in the corner, sat down and brought up the menu.

The computer required a log-on and password. Without the ability to hack into the system, Cal had done all he could do here. He left the room, locking the door behind him.

Once out of the administration building he headed for the quiet of the library, hoping to catch Deme and Gina to share what he'd found.

As Deme descended the staircase into the basement, the walls, air and atmosphere changed, growing darker and more oppressive.

"You'd think they'd improve the lighting in here." Gina stepped past a table laden with several boxes of old books. "Basements always seem so dark." A shiver shook her frame.

"You feel it, too?"

She nodded. "It's more than just the dark, isn't it?"

Deme found a light switch against the wall and flipped it, eliminating even the little bit of light they had to begin with. "Oops, sorry." She switched it back on and moved toward the dusty stacks arranged in rows. "Let's get this done and get back topside. I don't like it down here."

"I'm with you." Gina rubbed her arms, hugging herself as though the cold was seeping through to her bones. "What exactly are we looking for?"

"Anything that can shed a little light on what's going on around here." Deme's mouth twisted into a rueful grin. "No pun intended."

"Right. That should be easy." Gina wandered past the first stack. "You can have this row. I'll start at the other end. We can work our way to the middle."

Deme skimmed over the titles of ancient books whose bindings were well-worn, some crumbling due to the damp. "Why would they store books down here? With all the pipes and dampness, you'd think they'd relegate the old stuff to the attic instead."

"Who knows." The sound of books being placed back on shelves came from the back row where Gina worked. "All I know is it's been more than three days since Aurai disappeared and we still don't have any leads on what happened."

Nothing on the first row jumped out at her as important. As Deme passed to the second row, Gina moved another row closer, as well. A look passed between them, their light banter forgotten as the dank air pressed in around them.

"Not liking this, sis," Gina called out.

"Me, either."

"Hey, I think I've found something here," Gina's voice was more muffled, barely making it through the stacks of books and documents. "There's an entire room filled with binders and schematics of the Colyer-Fenton campus—"

A loud thunk cut her off before she could finish.

"Did you drop a book?" Deme walked to the end of her row and looked to the rear of the room, where Gina had gone.

Gina appeared around the corner of a row. "No, I thought you did."

Deme moved toward Gina, placing her feet gently to avoid additional noise. "It came from your direction."

"No, it came from yours." Gina moved toward Deme, peering down each row as she passed. "We are alone, right?"

"I thought so." Deme glanced down a row. Nothing moved, nothing looked out of place.

As they converged, Deme looked down the only row they hadn't checked. A book lay on the floor, its pages open and yellowed with age.

Deme shot a glance at Gina. "Coincidence?"

Gina shook her head. "I wasn't anywhere near it to knock it off and neither were you."

They both looked over their shoulders before advancing down the row toward the book.

A draft of frigid air wafted over them, lifting the pages of the book, one after the other. The draft stopped as suddenly as it began, the pages settling.

"As if we didn't get that this was weird," Gina muttered.

Deme stared down at the book. "Someone's trying to tell us something."

"Wish Selene was here. Maybe she'd know who." Her sister glanced up at Deme. "Do you want to, or should I?"

With a deep breath, Deme squatted and lifted the book, careful to keep it open at exactly the page it had landed on. "I need more light."

"Over here." Gina led the way to the end of the stack to a table that stood against the wall. A bare lightbulb hung down from a cord, shedding a convenient glow over the tabletop.

Deme flipped the book over to read the binding. *Tales of Myths and Monsters.* A draft didn't precede the chill snaking down Deme's spine this time. "I don't know about you, but I'm not liking this any better."

"Something tells me little sis is in bigger trouble than we thought."

Deme didn't need the reminder to spur her into action. She flipped the book back over and glanced at the ink drawing of a creature, reading the title of the page out loud. "'The Chimera, Myth or Reality?'"

"Do we have a choice?" Gina quipped.

At a sharp glance from Deme, Gina raised both hands in surrender. "Okay, okay, I'll keep my comments to myself. Read on."

"'The Chimera is fabled to be a fire-breathing creature with the body of a lion. It has two heads—one of the lion, one of a goat—and it has a serpent for a tail.'"

"I haven't seen anything like that, have you?"

Deme closed her eyes, recalling the image in the window of her dorm room after her sister's face disappeared. She'd thought the vines on the window were teeth. Could they have been a lion's gaping jaw?

She squeezed the bridge of her nose, closing her eyes briefly before going back to the text, eyes wide open.

"'The Chimera has many weapons at its disposal that it can use in multiple dimensions. Some say it has tele-kinetic abilities as well as the ability to force thoughts into the heads of the weak or impassioned.'"

"Holy crap," Gina whispered. "The attempted rapes."

And her violent sex with Cal. Deme's hands shook.

"Is this what we're up against?" Gina asked.

Deme forced herself to continue. "'The Chimera draws on the magical powers surrounding it, twisting it to suit its own evil purposes.'"

"That's why when I tried to call on the goddess to help the girls in the garden, my magic turned against us." Deme breathed in and out, trying to calm her racing heart. "Wow, we might be in over our heads here." She looked across at Gina. "If Aurai tried to use her powers, the Chimera could have turned them against her, as well."

Gina clasped Deme's hand. "Aurai is all right. You heard Selene, and you feel it. She's still alive. We will find her and free her from whatever has her."

"Damn right we will." Deme glanced down at the book. Though it mentioned what the creature was capable of, it gave no advice on how to deal with such a being.

"We need to show this to the others," Deme said.

"What I want to know is where it's coming from." Gina's eyes opened wider. "And I might have that answer." She headed to the back of the basement. "I'd found a room filled with schematics of the buildings on campus, dating back to when it was originally built," she called over her shoulder. "I'll bring them out here where we can see them under the better light."

"I'll keep looking through the rest of the stacks for anything else that might be important, then I'll join you. Maybe there's a historical account of the college somewhere in here." Deme scanned the rows of books, brushing aside dust to read the titles, the book of myths and monsters tucked under her arm.

When she'd reached the end of the stack, a sharp scream pierced the rows of books, followed by a loud slam.

Deme's heart stopped in her chest then shot into overdrive. She ran to the end of the stack and raced toward the back of the basement where Gina had gone.

As she neared the last row of books, water pooled around her feet. "Gina!"

"Help!" Her cry came from the other side of a closed door. "I'm in here."

Deme tried the handle. It wouldn't budge. "The door is locked. Unlock it."

"I can't. It's dark in here. The light blew out."

"Hang tight. I'll see what I can find to break down the door."

"Hurry. Look out, Deme, a man tried to attack me. I called on the goddess of water..." Gina sobbed. "You were right. The Chimera is turning it against me. The room is filling with water."

Deme glanced behind her. When she saw no sign of a man waiting to jump her, she looked at the base of the door. Liquid leaked from beneath it. "How big is the room?"

"Not very. It's already up to my knees."

Deme's gaze shot right then left. Nothing struck her as useful in prying a door open.

She spun, heading back to the table. If she could break a leg off it, she might be able to pry the door open before the water got too deep.

As Deme ran past the stacks, something long, dark and thick slithered out on the floor in front of her feet.

Too late to stop herself, her foot caught on it and she flew forward, landing on her belly, knocking the wind from her lungs. She lay in the seeping water until she could catch her breath. Then she lunged to her feet.

An arm reached out to grab her from behind, hooking around her neck. Dank, moldy rot filled her nostrils as a filthy coverall sleeve pressed into her throat, cinching off her air. Her fingers pried at the arm to no avail, the pressure increasing until the air around her grew fuzzy, her vision blurring.

She had to get loose. Having lost one sister, she'd be damned if she'd lose another. Deme grabbed on to the arm, lifted her feet and pushed hard against the closest shelf of books.

Cal entered the library and took the steps to the second floor two at a time. He swallowed his disappointment when he couldn't find Gina and Deme. Retracing his steps to the first floor, he stopped in front of the information desk.

The librarian manning the computer didn't look up.

"Did you see a redhead and a sandy-blonde woman go by here?"

"A lot of people go by here." The librarian glanced up, her gaze raking over Cal and his coverall, a blush replacing the placid, bored look of a moment before. "Oh, do you mean the two who went to the basement to research the college?"

"How long ago?"

She glanced at her monitor. "Fifteen minutes."

Before the last syllable left her lips, Cal had reached the door to the stairs leading down to the basement. God, he hated basements. Like hospitals, basements had unique smells...not all good.

The concrete-and-metal stairs clanked with every footstep as he ran down. A sense of foreboding filled his chest the lower he went. The same damp, decaying scent that he'd experienced from the trapdoor in the basement of the student commons filled his nostrils, gagging him.

When he reached the bottom, he landed in a puddle of water.

What the hell? His gaze swept across a floor, the lights above reflecting across the inch of water spreading to all corners. Where was Deme?

A loud crashing sound, followed by another, followed by another roared through the cavernous area. He ran toward the sound, splashing through the water, and rounded a corner to see stacks of books toppling one after the other in a domino effect. Each shelf and tons of books slammed into the next, headed directly for where he stood.

Cal dodged to the side, hugging the wall beside him as the shelf in front of him hit the one beside him, slamming it to the floor. Books spewed out to the side and bounced upward with the force of impact, the ground quaking beneath his feet.

"Deme!"

She didn't answer. The swirl of dust was so thick it fogged the limited lighting, making the view impenetrable. "Deme!"

Sounds of a scuffle alerted him that he wasn't alone.

He picked his way across the fallen books and shelves, his feet slipping and sliding on the shifting books.

As dust and shelves settled around him, he finally saw Deme.

Someone had her by the throat.

Deme hung on to the arm with her fingers, her feet flailing, trying to gain purchase.

Adrenaline pumped through Cal's veins, pushing him forward, faster and faster as he leaped and slid toward her, slamming into her attacker.

Not until he was right on him did Cal realize the man holding her wasn't right. His face was black with decaying skin and the rot of polluted earth. Blank, soulless eyes stared at nothing. As if powered by some unseen force, he continued to choke Deme.

Cal hit him in the side, taking the man and Deme down in a flying tackle.

The arm holding on to Deme loosened and she managed to scramble free.

As she crawled across a pile of books, the creep snagged her ankle with a clawlike grip.

Cal rolled to his feet and stomped the man's wrist, again and again until the hand released Deme. "Run!" he yelled.

She crab-crawled over fractured bookshelves and the mess of tumbled books to a clear area where shelves still stood, the books still neatly aligned. Deme reached for a wooden splinter the size of a sword sticking up from a jumble of broken shelves and damaged books. She headed for the back of the room.

The vacant-eyed man pushed to his feet and lumbered toward her.

"Look out!" Cal yelled, his feet moving, but the

books slipping from beneath him hampered his progress. He wouldn't get to her before her attacker did.

"I don't have time for this." Deme raced around one of the shelves still standing and rammed into it with her shoulder. "Get back, Cal!"

The shelf teetered toward the creepy dude and back at Deme. She hit the shelf again. This time it leaned far enough to fall, crashing down on the guy in the dirt-caked coverall.

Cal jumped back, avoiding the worst of the wreck.

Deme didn't wait for the dust to clear. She dove behind the next stack, disappearing out of Cal's sight.

His heart hammering in his chest, and with Deme out of sight, Cal could imagine all kinds of horrible things happening to her. He leaped over the downed shelf and the piles of ruined books, splashing through two inches of water.

When he rounded the corner of the last stand of shelves, he found Deme.

She had the large splintered board in hand, shoving it against a door frame. "Help me!"

"Where's Gina?"

"In here. We have to get her out."

Cal ran the last few steps, his hands closing around her shoulders. "Move."

"But it's locked. We can't get in and she's going to drown." Deme hit the door with the board, tears running down her cheeks.

Cal took a deep breath and threw all of his weight into the door. The door frame split, but the lock held. Water leaked from beneath the door at an alarming rate. "What the hell's happening in there?"

"She tried to use her ability to influence water to slow down the man who attacked me. Only she got locked in and water is filling the room now. We have to get her out before—"

Cal stepped as far back as he could get and slammed into the door. Pain shot through his shoulder, but the door gave enough for the lock to break loose, water rushing through the gap at chin level.

"Help me!" Gina called through the crack as the pressure of the water forced the door shut again.

"Get back," Cal yelled.

Deme joined him this time, and together they hurled themselves at the door.

Once they had the door open a foot wide, Deme shoved a book in the opening sideways as high up as she could reach, creating a six-inch gap.

Water rushed through.

Gina squeezed into the space, creating a damming effect, the water pushing against her back, running over her head. "I can't do it," she gasped.

Cal grabbed her hand and leaned as hard as he could on the door panel. He pulled her through, water gushing out, carrying Gina past Cal and Deme. The pressure on the book made it pop out of position, forcing the door closed again.

Gina washed to a stop, sprawled across the soggy books, coughing and sputtering, soaked to the skin and pale. She sat up, pushing hanks of blond hair out of her eyes. "What the hell happened?"

"That's what I'd like to know." Deme rushed to her sister's side and helped her to her feet. "Are you okay?"

"I'll live, but I don't understand what happened with my precious water. It's as if it turned on me."

Deme hugged her sister. "Things just aren't right around here."

Gina laughed and coughed. "You're telling me."

"The man who attacked you didn't look right, either. I want to get a look at him." Cal walked over to the shelf unit beneath which their attacker lay. He shoved and tugged, lifting the heavy case off the man.

Together he and Deme dug through the books until they reached him.

Deme reeled back first, and Cal followed, the stench from the man more than either could stand.

"He smells dead." Gina held her hand over her nose and mouth.

Cal reached out and felt for a pulse, finding none and the skin cold and sticky. "If he wasn't dead before, he is now."

With her hand over her nose and mouth, Deme shook her head. "He looks and smells like he's been dead for days."

"That's impossible." Cal flipped the man over. Beneath the dirt and stains, he recognized the coverall of the Colyer-Fenton maintenance staff. "He attacked Deme."

"And a room filling with water isn't any less impossible?" Gina asked.

"One thing is for sure." Cal stood and wiped the grime against his trouser leg, his mouth set in a grim line. "I think we've accounted for one of the missing persons."

Beneath a smudge of grease, the name tag read Kyle Scruggs.

Chapter 11

"You found who?" Brigid straddled the chair in the diner, her black, leather-clad leg bouncing with the tapping of her booted foot.

"Kyle Scruggs," Deme repeated. "The maintenance man who'd gone missing three weeks ago."

"Well before Aurai disappeared." Selene shook her head. "What's happening now didn't start with our dear sister's disappearance."

"It started with the beginning of the semester when Aurai arrived on campus." Deme stood and paced next to the table. "From the looks of it, the girls of the Gamma Omega sorority are playing with fire."

"Do you think they've really conjured some kind of evil?"

Deme tipped her head toward Gina, whose hair was almost dry from her battle for life in the basement of the library. "Before the basement flooded, we found a book on monsters."

"Monsters?" Brigid's brows twisted. "Seriously?"

Deme nodded, her gaze steady on Brigid. "Seriously."

"The book actually found us," Gina added.

"How so?" Selene asked, her face open, curious.

"It fell out of a shelf on an aisle neither of us were anywhere near."

Brigid stood. "Could the Scruggs guy have pushed it out?"

"I don't think so." Deme paced again, coming to a stop in front of the table. "I think the sisters who died when Lion Hall burned down died fighting whatever it is we're up against now. And I think they were trying to tell us just what it is by showing us the book."

"And what is it?" Brigid asked.

Deme's gaze caught and held Gina's. "A Chimera."

Selene stared straight ahead, her eyes bright, far away. "Body of a lion, tail of a serpent and two heads, one of the lion and the other of a goat." She closed her eyes. "It has great power. It was what pulled at me back in Deme's dorm room."

"Are you sure?" Deme asked.

She nodded. "Yes. The voices...my dreams...were the sisters warning us away."

Cal, who up to this point had sat in a chair and held his silence, suddenly sat up straight and reached inside his coverall. "I forgot all about this." He pulled out two folders and handed them to Deme. "I think I can help you with names of at least two of the sisters who died in the fire. Seems there have been Chattox sisters on this campus in the past."

"Chattoxes?" Deme accepted the files and laid them out on the table. "Where did you get these?"

"In the student records room."

She ran her hand over the files, a strong current flowing through her fingertips. "Feel this." She guided Selene's hand to the folders.

Her other sisters reached out and the package glowed, levitating off the tabletop.

Deme slapped it down, glancing around nervously. "That wasn't supposed to happen."

"But it did." Selene looked up at Deme. "Which proves it's them."

"What are the chances of running into a group of sisters with the last name Chattox?" Deme demanded.

"One in a bizzilion." Gina's voice was unsteady, her hand shaking as she pulled it away from the files.

Deme sat down hard. "I'm not liking this at all. It's way out of our league."

"Speak for yourself." Brigid crossed her arms over her chest. "I've been following strange occurrences for the past year in my efforts with the Chicago Police Department."

"You've had something like this happen before?"

"No, but some of the people I've come across in our investigations have been pretty darned scary."

"But as powerful as a Chimera? A creature that has been legended to manipulate others for its own gain?"

Brigid shrugged. "So it can manipulate others. We're smart, and now that we know, we can be ready."

Gina stared down at her hands, her face pale. "But we can't use our own powers. They work against us."

"Then we use our heads." Brigid's mouth thinned into a tight line.

"Whoa, wait a minute." Cal held up his hand. "And

you think *you're* out of your league. I have no clue what you're talking about."

"I told you, cop, we're witches," Brigid said. "We have a certain amount of powers when we choose to use them." She smacked the back of her hand against his chest. "Keep up with us."

Deme smiled across at Cal. "It's true. When something isn't sabotaging our power, we can do some pretty amazing things." Her smile faded. "Up until now, we chose not to, preferring to keep a low profile so as not to draw attention."

"Why?"

"I personally have no desire to be dissected by some wacko scientist," Brigid said.

"It tends to make people look at you differently." Deme's gaze refused to meet Cal's. "Some of us just want to live normal lives."

"But you can't." Cal shook his head. "I have to admit, I didn't believe in all that crap about magic, but I can't begin to explain what's been happening on this campus. Unless someone is a truly gifted illusionist, which I doubt."

"So you believe us when we say we think there is a monster on this campus?" Gina asked him.

"I don't know what to believe anymore." Cal pushed a hand through his hair, standing the dark strands on end.

Deme noted how her sisters' gazes followed his movements. And why shouldn't they? He was a single, very attractive man. But that didn't help how her heart squeezed in her chest and her fists tightened.

Cal's hand dropped to the pocket on his coverall. "I have five names that could be the student who was attacked thirty years ago."

Brigid held out her hand. "I'll look into those since it doesn't have to be done on campus."

"Good. I want to check in with the lieutenant back at the office." Cal stood and stretched. "I'm almost afraid to get too far from campus now, given all that's happened. None of you are safe."

"And neither are Aurai or the students." Deme gathered her rental-car keys and handbag. "I should be getting back."

"Stay vigilant." Cal looked directly into her eyes. "Especially going near the garden."

His look and words warmed Deme all over. She wanted to walk into his arms and let him hold her until all the ugliness went away.

"You don't have to tell me twice," Selene said. "I have to go. Play practice is at five." Selene left the café.

"Me, too. Think I'll follow Cal back to the station and see what I can find online." Brigid slipped her helmet over her head and snapped the strap in place, her black hair flowing down her back.

"I'm going to search through the copies of articles we made and do more research on the Chimera." Gina gathered her purse, slinging it over her shoulder. "There has to be a way to stop it before it does irreparable harm."

"Seems it already has." Deme tapped the article at the top of Gina's pile of pages, the one about the burning of Lion Hall and the demise of five sisters just like them.

A shiver shook Deme from head to toe.

"I'll be at the hotel I'm sharing with Selene," Gina said. "You might check on her while she's at practice. That theater is on the garden axis."

Deme nodded as Gina slid by and exited with Brigid,

tossing a wink over her shoulder as she let the door close behind her.

That left Deme and Cal alone. Well, as alone as they could be in a diner with a waitress, a cook and a cashier waiting for the evening rush of patrons.

Deme smiled. Her sisters were setting her up. She moved toward the door, pushing through to stand outside in the cool evening air.

Cal closed the door behind him and captured her hand, pulling Deme up against him. "I meant it. Be careful." He touched her cheek. "What happened earlier..."

"Won't happen again. We all know now not to use our powers." Deme closed her eyes and leaned into his palm. "Thanks, Cal."

"For what?"

She opened her eyes and stared into his. "For being there when I needed you." They stood so close, Deme could almost feel his heat. If she leaned nearer, she'd feel the beat of his heart against hers.

Cal closed the distance, leaning down until his lips hovered over hers. "Wouldn't have it any other way." He kissed her, drawing her into his arms and holding her tight. When their lips parted, he didn't release her, pressing his cheek against the side of her temple. "I don't think I've ever been more afraid in my life than when I saw Scruggs choking you to death." He chuckled. "Unless you count the time in the garden when the roots were pulling you into the earth." He sighed, his chest rubbing against hers deliciously.

Deme flattened her palms against him, loving the feel of his muscles beneath her fingertips—all that power tensed for action. "That's two times you've saved me in the past twenty-four hours. This could become a habit."

"Don't let it." He squeezed her again and set her at arm's length. "Go. I have work to do. If I stand here much longer, I'll forget what it was." His hands slid down her arms to clasp hers. "I'll come by and check on you later tonight."

Deme wanted to tell him not to, that she could handle being in the dormitory on her own, but her lips wouldn't let the words through. She wanted him to come. Wanted the reassurance of his presence in that creepy room she was obligated to occupy until they found Aurai and resolved the problems on campus. "Later."

She pulled her hands from his grip and turned to her car.

Behind her, the rumble of a motorcycle engine drew her attention.

Cal, straddling his Harley, roared out of the parking lot and into the traffic headed toward the station.

Deme wanted to be on the back of the bike with him, urging him to get far away from Colyer-Fenton and the craziness they'd found there.

Sisters, come to me! Aurai's call echoed in her head, reminding her of what had to be done. Standing around mooning over an ex-boyfriend wasn't getting her any closer to finding her sister.

Before the courthouse closed, Cal stopped in the records department and asked for help locating schematics of underground tunnels in the area of Colyer-Fenton College.

The lady behind the counter frowned and glanced at the clock. "We close in fifteen minutes."

Loading all his charm into one big, sweet smile, Cal leaned over the counter. "Please?"

The woman, probably in her late fifties, plump, graying and overworked, blushed. "Well…okay." She wheeled her mouse across the mouse pad, clicked her fingers on the keyboard and hit Enter with a flourish. "That should do it." She looked over the top of her reader glasses. "Mind you, it's old and probably not accurate anymore, what with the newer tunnels and subways built, but it's the only schematics I have on file." She stood, walked toward a printer and returned with a single sheet of paper. She handed it across the counter. "You might also try the Metropolitan Water Reclamation District of Greater Chicago for the Deep Tunnel schematics, as well. I haven't compared them to these so I don't know how they relate." She glanced at the clock again and gathered her purse from under her desk. "I have to catch my train, or I'd stay and chat."

Cal smiled. "Thank you." He left, tucking the schematic into his jacket before climbing on his motorcycle and heading for the station.

Traffic being hell, he didn't arrive until well after five, narrowly missing being hit at least three times by motorists too busy talking on their cell phones to pay attention to those around them.

Lieutenant Warner sat behind his desk, an empty coffee mug beside him, staring at the computer screen.

Cal knocked on the door frame and leaned into the office. "You look busy."

"Please, deliver me from reports." Marty pushed back from the keyboard and rolled his shoulders. "I miss the days of being a beat cop."

"Know what you mean."

"Whatcha got?"

"Been a busy day on campus." He filled in the boss on the activities of the night before and the incident in the basement of the library to include the names of the victims of similar events thirty years ago.

Cal looked at his boss, expecting him to question the roots grabbing people and the water issue in the basement, but he didn't even blink.

When Cal finished his report, Marty nodded, his brows drawing together. "You mean to tell me these two sequences of events might be related?"

With a nod, Cal pulled the schematic of the rail tunnels from his jacket and laid it across the desk. "Another thing. While I was in the basement of the student commons, I found a trapdoor leading to a level even lower than the basement."

"Lower than a basement? How can that be?" The lieutenant slipped a pair of reader glasses onto his nose and leaned over the schematic.

Cal pointed to the map, his finger on the street running through the Colyer-Fenton College campus. "As you know, beneath the older streets of Chicago is a labyrinth of railroad tunnels built for the movement of freight during the early nineteen hundreds."

"Yeah. I remember stories the old cops used to tell about troubles with vagrants finding their way down in there. They did a big push to seal off the entrances to keep them out."

"Well, I think they missed one." His finger traced the line beneath the campus that ran through the five-building circle surrounding the closed-off garden at the center of campus. "I'll check the basements of the other four buildings in this area to see if they have similar access to the train tunnels."

"Good idea." Lieutenant Warner looked up. "Are we

to the point where we should evacuate students from campus?"

Cal drew in a deep breath and let it out before answering. "No. I'm not sure who all is involved in this. If there really is a creature traversing the tunnels, that's one thing we'll have to deal with. If someone human is making it appear to be a creature, we need to catch him in the act. Right now, I haven't even got a suspect. I need more time to investigate."

"That missing girl doesn't have time."

"Tell me about it." Cal's chest tightened. Deme took personal responsibility for every one of her sisters. To lose one would be devastating.

"Are you ready for reinforcements?" the lieutenant asked.

"Not just yet."

"Even to check out the basements?" Marty shook his head. "After the near-drowning incident, you don't think you need help? Sounds to me like you do."

Cal's fists clenched. He'd almost been too late, and he didn't even want to think about that. Deme and Gina would have been lost. "We managed."

"Barely, by the sounds of it." Lieutenant Warner nodded. "Fine. I'll wait another day before sending more help. In the meantime, what can I do for you?"

"Help Brigid find more information on the names I gave her. She's not as familiar with some of the systems available here."

"I'll get one of the detectives to assist." He looked over the top of his glasses. "Anything else?"

"Yeah." Cal crossed his arms over his chest. "You didn't even bat an eyelash when I mentioned the abnormal attacks. Why?"

Lieutenant Warner's lips turned up briefly. "I've

been working this city a lot longer than you have, Cal. Some crazy stuff has passed over my desk and before my eyes. I don't take anything for granted, and neither should you."

"You believe all this magic stuff?"

"All I got to say is keep an open mind and watch your back."

Cal went straight for the war room, where he found Brigid hard at work on the computer. "Any luck?"

"You're not going to believe what I've found." She turned the laptop toward him and maneuvered the cursor to a tab on the browser, then clicked. The website was the courthouse records page. On it were the names of Diane Baker and Richard Masterson.

"That would make her married name, assuming she took her husband's surname, Diane Masterson."

"Bingo."

"I need to let Deme know."

"Right. Nothing is coincidence. And look at this." She clicked on another tab and a genealogy site appeared with a family tree dating all the way back to the early sixteen hundreds of Pendle Hill, Lancashire, England. At the top of the tree were five women, all by the surname of Chattox. To the far right was one Anne Chattox. "It gets weirder." Brigid clicked on Anne Chattox's name, bringing up a new screen with a full-length story of the Pendle Witch Trials of 1612. With it was a drawing depicting a figure of an old woman dangling by the hangman's noose.

Brigid's body shook. "I get a chill every time I look at that picture." She rubbed her arms.

"Can't say that I blame you. Bring up the previous screen."

She clicked the back icon and the tree reappeared.

"If you follow it through the centuries…" She scrolled down through the names of each generation until she came to bottom. "Voila! There we are. The five Chattox sisters of the present. Gives me the creeps." She rolled the screen up a little. "And there are our counterparts from thirty years ago. Apparently not every sister has five girls, but at least one in every generation does and they keep their maiden name to pass on to their daughters."

"Did your mother know about this?"

Brigid snorted. "I always thought she was a throwback to the women's liberation movement, that that was why she kept her maiden name and had it inscribed as our maiden name on the birth certificate. Wish she was still alive. I have a lot of questions for her."

"Are any of your aunts still alive?"

"As a matter of fact, yes. Aunt Rose lives in Portland. I think we're about due a familial visit."

"A phone call will do for now. We need you too much here."

"Gotcha. I'll check with Deme and see if she'd like to do the honors."

"Do you always check with your oldest sister before making decisions?"

Brigid cocked a brow at him. "Seriously?" She shook her head. "No. But when it comes to our search for Aurai, I defer to her. I want my sister back as much as the rest of us."

"Good work. I'll check out Dr. Masterson's office and see what I can find."

"How you gonna get in without her knowing?"

Cal held up the set of master keys his supervisor had given him that morning and smiled. "It pays to be working on the inside."

"No fair. Next time I get the undercover job."

"Next time?"

"Yeah. You don't think this is the only case you'll be working for the Special Investigations Team, do you?"

Cal hadn't thought of that. "You've been working with them for a year?"

"That's right. Mostly on arson investigation cases."

"Your forte is fire, right?"

"You got it. I have an uncanny sense of smell where fire is concerned. I can tell exactly where a fire started and even visualize an arsonist as he's lighting it."

Cal nodded. "Impressive. What else can you do?"

"I've been known to throw a few fireballs when needed." Her eyes opened wide and she smiled. "Oh, and I have some pretty cool friends. Check this out." She snapped her fingers and two bright spots of flame appeared out of thin air, hovering over her hand like spirits. Then they took off and flew around the room, buzzing past Cal, singing the hair around his ear.

"Hey!"

"I call them dragonflies."

Cal ducked and batted at the little creatures as they dived toward his head. "Yeah? Why?"

"They have nasty little tempers and they breathe fire."

As Cal swatted at the pests, one of them turned on him and shot a stream of flame at him. Cal grabbed a pad of paper and held it up in front of his face. "Call them off."

Brigid snapped her fingers again and the two dragonflies disappeared in a puff of smoke. She waved her hand to clear the air. "Sometimes they set off the fire alarms." She smiled across at him. "Still a disbeliever in magic?"

"You put on a very convincing show."

"It would have gotten me hanged in the witch trials, hands-down." She stood, crossing her arms over her chest. "So what's up between you and my big sis?"

Unprepared for her sudden change in conversation, Cal didn't have a canned answer. "I don't know."

She pinned him with a dark-eyed stare. "Are you the one she ran away from a year ago?"

He shrugged, reluctant to discuss Deme with her sister. "If you mean were we seeing each other a year ago and she left for another job, then yes."

"She not only left Chicago, she left the country." Brigid took a step closer, her hands dropping to her hips. "What did you do to her to make her run?"

Cal shook his head and smiled. "I asked her to marry me."

Chapter 12

Deme paced her room, afraid to get comfortable, ultra-sensitive to anything that might even remotely be construed as using her powers. When she'd arrived in her room, she expected things to be out of place, the vine at the window to be tapping, something weird.

Instead, the room appeared like any other college dorm room. Normal and generic. Except for the missing comforter on her bed.

She strode to the window and glanced down at the darkened garden. The vine had retreated from her window, hopefully for good. Exhausted by the lack of sleep the night before and the trying events of the day, Deme still couldn't imagine closing her eyes to sleep.

The elusive moon hid behind a thin layer of cumulus, turning the edges of the clouds a silvery blue. The ground below was nothing more than a black abyss, trees and shrubs hidden from view.

A light blinked on in a building across the garden. A lone figure stood silhouetted in a window.

Crossing the room to the folder she'd been given upon acceptance of the resident assistant position, Deme pulled out the campus map. With the map in hand, she returned to the window, orienting the map to the lay of the structures surrounding the garden.

The administration building stood across the garden and to the right of the Gamma Omega dorm. When Lion Hall had been standing, none of the surrounding buildings faced each other. Not so now. Although she couldn't make out the features of the other person, instinct told Deme who it was. The president of the college, Dr. Diane Masterson. What was she doing in her office this late?

With half a mind to go over and confront the woman, Deme hesitated. What could she ask without alerting the woman to her investigation of the staff and students? No. She couldn't barge in and demand to know why the woman stayed so late into the night. Likely she was as concerned as the police about the recent attacks and disappearance of one of the students.

For a long moment, Deme stared across at the other woman, wanting to extend a little magical nudge to read the woman's mind.

Deme tugged at the collar of her shirt, the air in the room feeling stuffy, muggy and dense. She looked away and beneath her breath muttered, "No magic. No magic. No magic." She hoped that by reminding herself constantly she'd remember not to cast even a simple spell. Not that she performed magic on a daily basis, but sometimes she sent a quiet prayer to the goddess for help or protection, or she used a little of her influence to tap into thoughts. After what happened in the garden and the library basement, she was afraid to speak to the goddess at all.

When Deme looked across the garden again, the woman had disappeared. At that exact moment, the light blinked out.

With nothing to stare out at but darkness, Deme resumed her pacing.

The more she paced, the more her legs dragged until finally she pulled a clean tank top and a pair of shorts from her suitcase and prepared for bed and another sleepless night.

Before she lay on the sheet-covered mattress, she checked the room thermostat. Why was it so hot and humid in the room? Eighty degrees? Good Lord. She maneuvered the dial to a cool sixty-eight. No wonder it was so hot.

Cal had promised to come by before he called it a night. Where was he? The digital alarm clock on her nightstand glowed a bright green eleven forty-five.

The air in the room didn't seem a bit cooler with the change in the thermostat. Deme checked it again. It was back at eighty. She tapped the box, cursing her inability to fix anything mechanical. Maybe when Cal got there he'd take a look at it. In the meantime, she reset the dial to sixty-eight, for what it was worth, grabbed a washcloth from her suitcase and dampened it with cool water. She pressed it to her warm skin, dragging it across her face and down her neck to her breasts.

So damned hot.

As she lay on the thin mattress, Deme pushed aside the sheets, fanning the cool, damp cloth over her and then draping it over her face.

With the cloth blocking the overhead light, Deme

closed her eyes and breathed deeply, letting her body relax. Sleep would come if she'd just let it.

The air in the room thickened, and the effort to draw a breath grew more labored. Deme couldn't seem to bring a full deep breath into her lungs, so she took shorter, faster breaths until she panted like a dog in the full summer sun. The faster she breathed the more light-headed she felt.

So tired from her day, she didn't care, couldn't move more than to raise her hand to her chest. She lay still, the only thing stirring her fingers, trailing across her breasts. The air around her seemed to swirl and lift her hand, guiding it lower.

Half-asleep, not fully awake, she let her hand travel down her belly, to the juncture of her thighs. That throbbing area low in her body, aching for a touch, a stroke, a gentle hand to soothe away the tension. Or better yet, to create more.

Deme's fingers slipped beneath the elastic band of her shorts, lacing through the mound of curly hair. When she found that spot, she caressed it with the tip of her finger, stroking, coaxing, teasing.

Her back arched from the bed, her hips lifting to greet the steady ministrations of that magical finger. Her body tensed, climbing up the ragged peak to the climax. Intense vibrations rocketed through her body, sending her spiraling to the top of who knew where, lifting her higher with each minuscule brush of her finger.

A groan filled the air. She was surprised it was her own. In her body, but not, Deme couldn't control her responses, couldn't back down from the most intense orgasm she'd ever experienced. So intense she sensed it was wrong, but she couldn't stop herself from riding the wave on and on like a surfer on a never-ending crest.

The exquisite ache built into a painful desire, growing and changing with each passing moment. Deme's groans transformed into low guttural growls, her fingers curling into claws, scratching at her belly, tearing at her shirt.

Naked, she had to be naked. She ripped the cloth from her heated face, clawed at her shirt, ripping it away in shreds. Her shorts fell to the floor in nothing but tatters. Her eyes remained closed, the darkness a balm to the strengthening desire racking her body.

This is wrong.

The small voice whispering in the very back of her mind fought to push aside the animal expanding within, only to be beaten back, slammed against the wall of doubt.

Help. The essence of Deme struggled to surface from the quicksand of darkness drawing her down.

Piercing the darkness, a voice called out in a clear, sweet tone, *Deme, fight it!*

Aurai? Deme tried to open her eyes to see her beloved sister, but no matter how hard she tried, she couldn't.

Don't let it win!

I can't fight it. It's so strong.

You have to fight or it will consume you.

Deme shoved and pushed against the inky darkness, her body weakening, her will dissolving. *It's too strong. Need help.*

He'll come.

Cal raced along the Eisenhower Expressway and took the exit leading to Colyer-Fenton College, a sense of urgency he couldn't justify pushing him faster and faster.

Since he'd left Brigid at the station, he'd had an increasing sense of doom the closer he got to the campus. If he believed in intuition, he'd say someone was in trouble there.

Deme.

When he arrived at the Gamma Omega dormitory, he drove up on the lawn and parked his motorcycle in front of the door, hopping off before the engine stopped roaring.

He hit the door at a full run, slamming into the locked glass so hard he banged his nose.

Damn. He squeezed the bridge of his nose to stop the stinging, his eyes tearing. He'd forgotten the doors were locked at eleven o'clock. Only those with a pass key could enter.

He whipped out his master key and inserted it into the lock, twisting hard.

Down the hallway to the staircase and up two at a time, he ran. When he arrived on the second floor, girls lined the hallway in varying states of dress, from baby-doll nightgowns to sweats and T-shirts. One girl stood wrapped in nothing but a towel. All of them had one thing in common. They stared ahead, their eyes blank, their footsteps stilted like so many zombies in a horror film.

When Cal tried to dodge past one, she stepped to the side, directly in his path.

"Excuse me." He grabbed her by the shoulders and set her to the side, eager to clear the path to Deme's room.

Sounds of muffled screams and animal roaring

drifted from the end of the hall where Deme stayed. Cal had to get to her. Something wasn't right.

"It's with her." The girl Cal remembered as the president of the sorority, Zoe, stood in front of him, dressed in a sheer nightgown that left nothing to the imagination, her blond hair hanging down over her shoulders,. "Wouldn't you rather have me?"

"No." He reached out to grab her arms, but she moved fast, closing in on him, wrapping her arms around his neck, her legs lifting to clamp around his waist.

He staggered with the surprise attack and the impact. As he struggled to pry her off his body, the other girls closed in around him.

The closer they came, the louder the roars from the room down the hallway.

He had to get past these girls and get to Deme.

Cal pried the legs from around his waist. As he worked at the arms clinging to his neck, Zoe wrapped her legs around him again. For a thin young woman, she had surprising grip and strength in her thighs. She squeezed her legs together, making the contact more painful.

This time Cal pulled her arms free and jerked one up behind her, then with his free hand, he got one leg free and slung her around, knocking several of the girls aside in the process.

With little gentleness, he pushed and shoved the young ladies out of the way and raced for the end of the hall.

"Deme. Let me in," he called through the door.

Guttural growls were the only response.

He pulled his master key from his pocket and inserted it in the lock. When he pushed the door to open, it pushed back.

Cal leaned his shoulder into it and the door flung open.

Darkness greeted him, the overhead light covered in a thick layer of what looked like moss. The walls had the same coating. The air was as thick, humid and dank as though he was deep in the rain forest, not a Midwest college dormitory.

The light from the hallway shone across the green algae-covered floor to the single bed in the corner.

Levitating above the thin mattress was a naked woman, long red hair splayed out as though charged with static electricity.

"Deme!"

Her body jerked, her back arching. She turned to face him, but her eyes were closed.

"Deme!" Cal rushed forward, stopping a foot away, unsure what to do, how to bring her back from wherever she was. "It's me, Cal," he said, his voice cracking. "Deme, what is it doing to you?"

One slender hand reached toward him.

He took it. "Deme, please."

Her eyes opened, the pupils golden, like those of a lion.

Cal staggered backward. This wasn't Deme, but it was.

"You can't have her," he said, his tone intense, almost as much of a growl as he'd heard from Deme.

Deme's body twisted and dropped to the mattress, then like a cat, she flung herself at him, her arms and legs wrapping around his body, clinging to him in a choking hold.

Cal struggled to breathe, no clue how to handle the

possessed Deme without hurting her, but if he didn't get her to loosen up, he'd be the next victim taken by the Chimera.

"Deme." He clasped her cheeks between his hands. "Look at me." He gazed into her eyes, determined to make her see him. "You have to fight whatever has you."

The tension in her body eased a fraction. "That's what...Aurai...said." Deme's gaze softened, the irises more green than gold. For a moment, Cal thought she was back. Then a growl rose up from her throat and she dug her nails into his skin, her legs wrapping even tighter around his middle. "Take me." One hand raked over his shoulders and down below her bottom, where she worked the rivet on his jeans.

Cal covered her feverish fingers just as she loosened the button. "No, not like this." He raised her hand to his face and pressed a kiss to her palm.

She stared at the place where his lips had touched, as if mesmerized by the gesture, the gold irises fading into emerald-green. Until she blinked, her eyes narrowing, her lips curling back into a feral snarl.

Her tongue snaked out to lick a coarse path along his neck to his earlobe, where she bit down hard.

"Ouch!" Cal jerked away from her teeth. "I won't let you have her, damn it. She's mine." He dragged her face close to his, almost nose to nose. "I love you, Deme, damn it, and you love me, too." His voice was low, determined, insistent, begging Deme to come back from the hell the Chimera had her in.

Her legs loosened and her feet dropped to the floor. A broken sigh escaped from her throat and she was leaning into him. "Help me," she whispered. Her arms circled his waist where her legs had been and she pressed her face into his shirt.

"I'll help you, Deme. Just don't give up on me." He stroked her hair.

"It's stronger than me."

"No one is stronger than you."

Her body jerked, her head flung back, her eyes widening, the lion eyes back. Rumbling growls rose in her chest, her fingers curling into his skin.

"Fight it, Deme."

Her teeth clenched, her lips pulling back. "I am," she said through clamped jaws.

Thumbs slipped into the waistband at the back of his jeans, shoving them downward. He swatted at her hand, knowing it wasn't Deme doing this, but at the same time he couldn't ignore desire straining against his zipper. "Not like this. I won't make love to you when you're like this."

"You will," she said, her voice low and raspy, nothing like normal. Before he could stop her, her hands snaked to the front of his jeans, whipped the zipper down and shoved the denim downward.

His engorged cock sprang forward into her hands.

Despite all his attempts not to react, he sucked in a gasp and held it, teetering on the verge of knowing he should do the right thing, and wanting to slam into her, burying himself to the hilt.

Her hand wrapped around him, a slow smile rising on her lips, her golden eyes narrowing. She pressed her face into his neck, her breasts crushed against his chest, sliding across the fabric of his shirt.

Naked wouldn't be close enough. Cal groaned, resisting the overpowering wave of desire washing over him. He couldn't make her stop when she shoved his jeans down around his ankles, couldn't find the strength to halt the progress of her hand, sliding up his leg between his thighs.

She had him by the balls before he could voice even a mew of protest.

Breathing like a man topping a steep climb, he grabbed her hand, drawing it up to his chest.

The growl in her throat was only the beginning of her protest. She whipped her hand free and ripped his shirt in half from hem to chin. Clawlike fingers traced a line down his torso to the jutting member pressing into her belly.

"Not like this," he repeated like a mantra to her and himself. With every ounce of control he could muster, he smoothed a hand over her hair and along her neck. "When I make love to you, I want to make love to the Deme I know and care for." He pressed a kiss to her temple. "You, Deme. Not some creature from the Black Lagoon." He trailed his mouth along her jawline until he brushed across her lips. "Kiss me, Deme. Only Deme."

For a long moment, the woman in front of him remained poised, gaze on his lips, her irises crossing from gold to green and back to gold. Finally the green solidified, the pupils returning to normal.

Deme reached up to cup his chin. "Cal? When did you get here?"

He laughed low in his belly, his breath catching in his throat. "A few minutes ago."

She blinked, her gaze capturing his. "How did you get in?"

Cal cupped her chin with both hands and brushed his thumbs across her lips. "Master key." He bent to take her lips. "I'm glad you're awake."

"Was I sleepwalking?" She turned her cheek into

his palm and pressed her lips against his skin. "I don't seem to remember."

"You were having a bad dream."

Her eyes turned toward the ceiling and the green moss coating it. "Am I still dreaming?" She moved, her breasts rubbing against his naked chest. "I must be. We're both naked." She smiled, a hand trailing over his shoulder and down his arm. "I like the way your skin feels against mine."

Cal wanted to laugh, cry and yell all at once. Deme was back, but she didn't remember any of what had happened only a moment ago.

Deme's hand continued downward to his hips, circling behind to press him closer. "Were you about to make love to me?"

"To you, yes." He did laugh and kissed her. "Only you, babe." He kicked off his boots, shed his jeans and came to her, hard and fast. The tension of fighting his desire fueled his passion. He lifted her. Unwilling to wrap her legs around his waist, he settled her on the solitary mattress, her legs falling over the edge.

She parted her knees, opening to him.

Invitation accepted, he drove inside her, burying himself deep. Her tight channel engulfed him, coating him with the juices of her own desire, only a moment ago fueled by a demon.

As he thrust in and out, the tension building, rising, bursting over the edge of sanity, he remembered what he'd told her to get her back. He loved her.

He still loved this woman. No matter what happened after they found Aurai and returned Colyer-Fenton to a safe place of learning again, he would always love her. Even if she didn't return his feelings.

Having bared his soul to her once, Cal had no intentions of doing it again. Deme had some kind of misguided perception about who she was and what he'd be willing to accept. Until she got over it, he'd do his best to keep his dreams of a white picket fence and children running around the house as just that. Dreams.

The more he stroked her inside, the more ragged his breathing ran. If he wasn't mistaken, the room temperature had risen at least ten degrees since he entered her. Perspiration slickened his body and hers until the smack of skin on skin sounded more like slaps.

Deme planted her feet in the mattress and rose to meet every thrust with one of her own, her hands clenching around his waist, guiding him in and out, faster and faster. Her eyes closed, her breasts bounced as she dug her nails into his buttocks and slammed him into her.

With his body strung so tight, Cal catapulted over the edge, so intent on milking every last sensation from his body and hers. As he drifted back to earth and to Deme, he sucked in a deep breath. "I've missed you."

Deme didn't respond at first, her eyes still closed. Then they opened and a smile slid across her lips, her bright gold, feverish eyes staring up at him. "I missed you, too."

Chapter 13

Deme woke to sun streaming in through the window, the sheet draped over the lower half of her body and her head aching. With the brightness of the light shining into her eyes, she couldn't see the rest of the room.

Movement at the far corner captured her attention, but the angle of the sun blurred her vision. "Cal?"

"Afraid not." The figure moved out of the corner and closer until Deme could see who it was.

"Dr. Masterson?" Heat rose in Deme's cheeks as she pulled the sheet up to her neck, hiding her naked breasts she was sure the president of the college had already gotten an eyeful of. "What are you doing here?"

"I regret to inform you that your services are no longer required as the resident assistant of the Gamma Omega dormitory."

"What?" Deme sat up straight, dragging the sheet with her. "Why?"

"Several of the girls have informed me that you've broken the most important rule of the dormitory. A rule you, as the resident assistant, are supposed to be enforcing."

Guilt raised the temperature even higher on Deme's body thermostat and she gulped. "Which rule?" she asked, knowing full well that fornicating with a man in your dorm room was top on the list of no-no's of the Gamma Omegas, although she was positive a majority of the girls had violated that rule more than once.

"If you'd bothered to read the manual, you'd know." The college president lifted the folder with the manual inside and tapped it against her palm. "No men in the dormitory after the door is locked at eleven o'clock." Her brows rose on her forehead as her gaze skimmed over Deme and her rumpled sheets. "I'm sure you've broken other rules as well, based on your state of undress."

"My apologies, Dr. Masterson." Deme forced what she hoped was an apologetic smile. All the while her head ached as if she'd been on an all-night bender. "Would it help to tell you that I won't let it happen again?"

"No." Dr. Masterson crossed her arms over her chest. "It wouldn't surprise me to get calls from some of the parents with their concerns over their daughters' well-being."

"You're telling me," Deme muttered.

"What was that?" The older woman's eyes narrowed.

"Understood. I'll need time to arrange for alternate accommodations. I'll let you know the moment I find some."

Even before Deme finished her sentence, the older

woman was shaking her head. "I want you out by this evening."

Deme gasped. "I can't. We won't be finished." Hope plummeted to her belly.

Ms. Masterson's jaw tightened, her arms still firmly crossed over her chest. "Finished?"

Back-paddling like a kayaker facing a waterfall, Deme grasped for the first thing she could think of. "I'm working on a project with some of the students. I need to finish it before I can go apartment hunting."

"That would be your problem."

"Please, Dr. Masterson. The other girls are depending on me to make sure we get it right." She sat up straighter, hating to beg to a woman she'd had doubts about last evening. "Let me stay another day. That's all I ask."

The president of the college drew in a long, deep breath and let it out slowly before saying, "One day." She followed quickly with, "Too many strange things are happening around here. I don't want your involvement to make things worse." She pointed at Deme. "If you do, you'll discover that I can be your worst nightmare. Do you understand?"

A cold chill raced down Deme's spine and didn't dissipate even after the other woman left the room, closing the door firmly behind her.

Just what did she mean by she could be her worst nightmare? Did Dr. Masterson have any idea what Deme's nightmares had been about lately?

Deme tossed the sheets aside and got out of bed, her legs sore, the place between her thighs tender. She must have been really tired when Cal had visited her last night. Her memory was pretty sketchy on a few things. Based on her nakedness and soreness, she could assume they'd done more than just sleep. Why she couldn't say no to the man was beyond her level of comprehension.

Her brows drew together as she stared around her room. Nothing looked out of the ordinary. The plain white walls needed some form of decoration to make them less sterile, but other than that, the room was no more threatening than any other dorm room on campus.

Deme scratched her head. Had she dreamed of being in a jungle last night? Something about moss-covered walls, heat and humidity tugged at her subconscious, but not enough to wrap her mind around. Next time she saw Cal, she'd ask him if she'd talked in her sleep.

Deme slipped into a bathrobe and tossed a clean towel over her shoulder before emerging from her room. A shower sounded damned good about now. Then she'd get on with the investigation. She had only one more day to eke out any information she could from the Gamma Omegas before her cover was blown. Just as well. Enough time had passed since her sister's disappearance.

Halfway to the bathroom, the muffled sound of sobbing reached Deme through Rachel Taylor's closed door. Really wanting the shower, she almost ignored it and moved on, but the sobbing grew louder.

Deme raised her hand and knocked on the door. "Rachel?"

"Go away."

"It's me, Deme, the R.A." Okay, so she technically wasn't the R.A. anymore, but Rachel probably hadn't spoken with Dr. Masterson yet. "Let me in."

The sobbing subsided. After a full minute and a half, just when Deme thought the girl was going to ignore her, the door opened a crack and Rachel looked out, her hair hanging like so much black straw around a face deeply marked with acne scars.

Deme gasped. "Rachel?" She could have kicked herself as soon as she made the sound.

Rachel's eyes welled with yet more tears and she slammed the door.

Thankfully, Deme got her foot in the crack before she could shut it all the way. But the impact on her toes made her cry out in pain. "Holy cow! Open the damned door before you cripple me."

Rachel clapped a hand to her mouth and flung the door wide. "I'm so sorry. I didn't mean to hurt you."

Playing on the girl's guilt, Deme winced. "I'll be okay, I hope." She moved into the room and closed the door behind her. "Now tell me what all the crying is about."

Rachel turned away. "I can't do it anymore. I can't be someone I'm not."

"What do you mean?"

"The sorority. I've asked to be moved to another dorm. I can't take it anymore."

Deme gripped the girl's arms and forced her to look her in the eye. "Take what?"

"The lies, the secrecy, the rituals. I don't care if I'm ugly on the outside."

Deme studied the girl, who a day ago had been another Zoe clone, perfect complexion, perfect hair and face. Today, she met the exact description Aurai had given Deme about her roommate—hopelessly homely, but sweet. "You aren't ugly, Rachel."

"I wasn't when you met me, but I am now." She stared into Deme's face with red-rimmed eyes. "Look at me!"

Deme choked back a lump in her throat. This girl

wanted so badly to fit in she'd practically sold her soul to the devil to be beautiful. "You're more beautiful to me now than any of the Zoe clones in this dorm." She hugged Rachel to her and stroked the back of her head as the younger woman's shoulders shook with the force of a new wave of weeping.

"I wanted to be pretty, just once." Rachel's tears soaked through Deme's robe.

"We all want to be accepted."

"But not the way they're doing it." Rachel pushed away, scrubbing her sleeve beneath her nose. "It's wrong."

"Tell me, Rachel." Now was her chance to get to the bottom of the Gamma Omega shenanigans. "What rituals are they performing?"

Rachel strode across the room, wringing her hands. "Apparently Zoe found a book in the library. A book of spells. She decided to use it as part of the sorority initiation, only it didn't work out exactly as planned."

"How so?"

Rachel looked across at the empty bed that used to be Aurai's.

A lump the size of Texas rose in Deme's throat, and she fought back the ready tears thoughts of her youngest sister inspired.

"That night was horrible." Rachel buried her face in her hands, her body shaking. "They swore me to silence, but I can't be quiet anymore." She looked up through her tears straight into Deme's eyes. "My roommate disappeared that night." She shook her head side to side, her eyes glassy as if seeing the drama replayed over and over. "She was lifted into the air, her robe wrapping around her like she was in a funnel cloud."

Deme took a step toward Rachel. This was the most

she'd heard about her sister's disappearance from any-one. "Then what?"

"The candles had blown out and there weren't any lights coming from any of the nearby buildings. A cloud must have passed over the moon because it got really dark. I could hear her scream as though she was being drawn into a vacuum, dragging her away in a final blast of wind." Rachel blinked, her brows drawing down low over her eyes. "You see why I couldn't tell anyone? Who would believe me?" She clutched at Deme's arm. "You believe me, don't you?"

Deme pulled Rachel into her arms and hugged her again. "Yes, sweetie, I do."

After a long minute, Rachel pulled away enough to brush the tears from her cheeks. "Now Mike is in the hospital because of me."

"Why do you think it's your fault?"

She snorted. "My vanity. I wanted so much to be like the other girls. The spell Zoe used made it happen."

"What exactly was this spell?"

"It makes ugly girls like me…" She ducked her head, her cheeks reddening. "It makes them pretty."

"You are pretty without spells and rituals."

"That's what Mike said, but when I drank from the vial, I became beautiful and Mike couldn't control him-self around me. It made him an animal." She wrapped her arms around her middle. "It made him attack me… and made me attack him."

"What's in the vial?" Deme took Rachel's hands. "Are you sure Zoe didn't drug you?"

The younger girl's mouth drew into a tight line. "No. It was the spell."

"But she could have put some kind of date rape drug in the bottle."

Rachel shook her head. "The spell and the potion in the vial are what made me beautiful and then aggressive. I've never hurt another human being in my life. Neither has Mike. When he found out what he'd done, he couldn't live with himself." Rachel's voice caught on another sob. She swallowed hard and continued. "He tried to commit suicide. Thank God he failed. I told him it wasn't his fault, but he wouldn't listen. That's when I decided enough was enough. I stopped drinking the potion. I haven't been out of my room since. They'll know as soon as they see me."

She held up a blue vial and pressed it into Deme's hand. "Here, take it. I won't be needing it. I'm done with Gamma Omega. I was just fooling myself to think I'd ever fit in."

Deme took the vial and Rachel's hand. "You're doing the right thing. You don't belong with Zoe's group."

Rachel nodded, her shoulders sagging.

"Not because you're not beautiful, but because you're beautiful where it counts." Deme touched her hand to her chest. "Don't let anyone tell you that you're ugly. Do you hear me?"

Rachel nodded. "Yeah. That's what Mike said. If only I'd listened, he'd be okay, not in a coma." The younger girl slipped her arms into a hooded sweat jacket, pulling the hood up over her head. "I'm going to the hospital now to visit him. Maybe he'll be out of the coma today. Wish him luck, will you?"

"You bet." Deme stepped out of the room with Rachel and ran right into Zoe.

This girl had caused enough trouble with Rachel and Aurai to remain on Deme's blacklist for life. Even if something else was manipulating her actions, Deme couldn't seem to forgive her at this moment. "What do you want?" Deme asked, none too gently.

"Nothing. Should I want something?" Her gaze went over Deme's shoulder to connect with Rachel's, her eyes narrowing at the girl's appearance. "Just checking on my Gamma Omegas. This sorority sticks together, don't they?"

An implied "or else" hung in the air between Zoe and Rachel, making Deme's blood boil.

"Look, Zoe." Deme stepped in between the two coeds and stood nose to nose with the striking sorority president. "If anything happens to my new friend, Rachel, you'll answer to me. Got that?"

Her beautifully arched brows rose into her low-slung bangs. "I don't have a clue as to what you're talking about."

"Then I suggest you get a clue and leave us alone." Deme pushed past her and marched to the exit, shoving Rachel in front of her.

Deme had had her fill of Zoe Adams.

Cal had a job to do, or he would have stayed until Deme woke up. As it was, he'd eased her eyelids open to get a glimpse at her emerald-green eyes before he'd climbed out of the bed and dressed for work in campus maintenance. No more cat eyes. Whew!

Most of the night he'd lain awake, watching out for a return of the Chimera. He must have dozed off because when he woke, the room had returned to normal, no sign of algae, moss or the jungle humidity that had greeted him earlier.

Convinced the threat had abated for now, Cal rose from the bed, put on his jeans and slipped out of the dorm shirtless. The one he'd worn in had been ripped to shreds by the Chimera-possessed Deme. One thing was certain, she could not sleep in that room another night. He'd talk to her about it later.

First major stop on his list of assigned maintenance duties had to be the office of one Dr. Diane Masterson. What he hoped to find, he had no idea. Maybe he'd run into her and discuss her past and the attack that happened on this very same campus thirty years ago.

He couldn't imagine any woman in her right mind returning to a place where she'd been brutally raped. And to overlook the area where it had occurred day after day...

Cal couldn't begin to fathom the woman's reasoning. He hurried through the morning tightening faucets, unclogging toilets, replacing hinges and door handles, unjamming locks and performing the myriad other duties required by his supervisor. By noon, he was just heading for the administration building when his cell phone rang.

"Black speaking."

"Cal?" The voice sounded like Deme.

Cal's heartbeat quickened. "Deme?"

"No, it's Selene. Something weird's going on here at the theater. Think you can come give us a hand?"

"I'll be right there." His heart pounding, he dashed past the student commons, weaving his way through the maze of students lounging on the grass or sitting at the outdoor tables.

It never ceased to amaze him how the sun could go on shining when crazy, soul-defining and dangerous events happened. People could be dying and the sun would continue to rise and set.

He arrived outside the theater in time to see a stream

of students gathering in front of the door, waving at their friends to come.

Cal ran past them and pushed through to the door. Gina stood in front of the glass double doors, refusing to let the students pass. When she saw Cal, she motioned him forward. "Thank goodness you're here." She opened the door and let him slide through. "I was here cleaning the theater aquarium when it started. Selene and Deme are on the stage."

The auditorium was half-full of gawking students, some pointing toward the stage, others pressing hands to their mouths, their eyes wide.

Selene stood on the stage looking up into the rafters. Deme stood beside her.

Cal's groin tightened just at the sight of Deme. He squelched his reaction and climbed the steps up the side of the stage.

"Have you tried to talk her down?" Deme had her back to Cal and didn't see him approach.

"I've tried everything short of calling the fire department. I thought since you are her R.A., you might have more luck." Selene glanced around. When she spotted Cal she blew out a long breath. "Blessed Be, you're here. Maybe you can help."

"What's going on?" he asked, his gaze sweeping over Deme's face, noting the dark smudges beneath her eyes.

"Not what—who." Deme pointed up at the catwalk twenty-five feet above the stage. "Shelby Cramer is up on the catwalk and won't come down."

"And she's acting really funny," Selene added.

"Funny how?" Cal stared up into the shadows of the catwalk.

"She's growling and hissing at anyone who tries to climb the ladders."

At first he couldn't see the girl. Then a movement caught his attention and he spotted her. Crouched on the metal mesh, the pretty blonde stared down at the people gathered below.

A student hurried forward, handing Selene a flashlight.

"Oh, thank the goddess." Selene shined the light up at Shelby, the beam reflecting an intense red off the girl's eyes.

Shelby shrank back and hissed.

"That's not normal," Selene stated.

"Goes along with the way she's acting." Deme stared into her sister's eyes. "When did she start acting this way?"

"I don't know. She was quiet when she showed up for rehearsal, but she wasn't acting strange until halfway through the first act." Selene's gaze shifted to the young woman in the rafters. "Do you think the Chimera has her?"

Deme nodded. "That's where I'd put my money." She turned to Cal. "I'd have gone after her, but I'm not much bigger than she is. Can you help me take her?"

Cal's jaw clenched. "I'll get her." Before he could take two steps toward the ladder in the far corner of the backstage area, Deme's hand shot out and grabbed his arm.

"I'm going with you."

"No."

"She's acting like an animal. If you chase her one way, she'll run the other. We need to come at her from opposite directions. Corner her."

"I don't want you up there." He didn't want to tell Deme what he was really afraid of. If Shelby was possessed by the Chimera, what was to keep the beast from possessing Deme as it had last night?

"I'm going." Deme took off toward the ladder leading up into the rafters.

Cal grabbed her shoulders and forced her to stop. "I don't want you up there."

"Why?" she demanded, her green eyes blazing, the air practically crackling between them. "Don't you trust me?"

"You, yes. The Chimera, no." His grip relaxed. "Do you remember any of what happened last night?" He asked the question softly enough only Deme and Selene could hear.

Deme frowned, rubbing her temple. "Not much. You came over late and we must have done something because I woke up naked."

Selene's lips twitched and she opened her mouth to comment. At a glare from Cal, she closed it.

Cal's face softened and his fingers rubbed her shoulders. "Let's just say you weren't quite yourself last night."

"Really?" She looked up at him, her frown deepening. At last she shook her head and planted her hands on her hips. "Well, I am myself this morning, and you can't do this without help."

Cal stared at her long and hard. Metal rattled overhead as Shelby ran along the catwalk, ducking low to stare at them beneath the thin handrails. "Okay, but you take direction from me."

"Fine."

Cal ran to the far backstage corner while Deme headed for the other. They arrived at the same time. Cal pulled himself up the ladder, keeping his eye on Shelby and Deme alternately.

He reached the top first and he waited for Deme. When she stood on the catwalk, he motioned her forward.

Shelby crouched in the middle of the walkway, her head swinging back and forth as she watched the movements of Deme and Cal. A low rumble rose from her chest, ending in a teeth-baring hiss.

Cal edged closer from his end. "Shelby," he called out, appealing to the girl buried beneath the Chimera's trance. After what had happened to Deme last night, he knew how easily the Chimera could manipulate others. He also knew that the person was still there and could be reached if you were persuasive enough. "Shelby. Come with me and you'll be all right."

Deme moved faster, closing the gap between herself and Shelby more quickly than Cal.

He picked up the pace, afraid that Shelby would attack Deme before he could reach her.

Shelby crouched lower, her catlike gaze shifting from Deme back to Cal. Her hands curled into claws, her body tensed. She was going to pounce.

"Watch out!" Cal yelled.

The girl let out an ear-piercing animal scream and leaped at Deme.

Deme, standing her ground, refusing to let the girl by, was hit full force in the midsection. She staggered, fell backward and landed on her back, Shelby on top of her. The structure shuddered, metal creaking, followed by a loud pop.

The old strut beside Deme that attached the catwalk to the ceiling beams broke.

The footbridge tilted sharply toward the front of the stage.

A collective scream rose from the students in the

audience as Deme and Shelby slid toward the edge and the twenty-five-foot fall to the hardwood flooring of the stage.

Deme hooked an elbow around the strut on the opposite side and wrapped her legs around Shelby's middle as she slipped over the side.

His heart hammering against his ribs, Cal's first instinct was to dive for Deme and grab her before she fell. But he was too far away. Instead, he held tightly to the handrails until the shaking stopped. Then he was running down the listing walkway toward the two women. If they fell the way they were, both could die or be terribly injured.

After a full year without her, Cal couldn't lose Deme again.

The muscles in Deme's shoulder burned, the weight of her own body enough to make her cry. The additional weight Shelby represented was making it nearly impossible for her to hold on.

Footsteps pounding toward her on the grate alerted Deme to Cal's approach. Hope surged inside. But shifting metal beneath her killed that hope. "No!" she gasped. "Stay back! If you come any closer, the other strut will break."

As if to emphasize her point, the structure creaked loudly and the catwalk shuddered again.

Shelby clawed at Deme, trying to climb up her onto the catwalk. Her eyes were wide and feral.

"Shelby Cramer, I know you can hear me. Listen up, girl!" Deme yelled, her back and legs straining. She had to get through to the young woman. If she didn't, the Chimera would take them both to the ground in a very uncomfortable landing. One they might not survive.

The woman stopped clawing and stared up at Deme, her eyes narrowing, her lips pulling back over her teeth.

"You don't own her." Deme's arm was going numb. She reached up with her other hand and clutched at the strut to relieve the pressure on her elbow. She wouldn't last much longer. "Shelby, take your body back. It's yours!"

"I can get closer," Cal called out.

"No!" Deme said between clenched teeth. "It's too dangerous." With every muscle in her body screaming for release, Deme forced her voice to calm. "If you let her die, you die with her. What's it going to be?"

Shelby stared up at Deme, her chest rumbling with a low, wicked growl. Her eyes flashed red and then back to gray. The girl's head lolled backward.

Then as though coming up for her first breath of air, Shelby gasped, her eyes wide, her body rigid. "What the hell?" She looked down and twisted violently, almost jerking Deme loose from her hold on the strut. "What's going on? Help!" She wrapped her arms around Deme, clinging tightly, pressing her face into Deme's belly.

"Shelby…keep calm." Deme's arms and legs shook. "Can you reach up and grab on to the catwalk?"

"No! Oh, God. Help. Oh, God." She hung on to Deme with a death grip, refusing to let go.

"I can't hold on much longer, Shelby. You have to help yourself."

"Deme, we have to risk it." Cal inched forward. "I'm coming to you."

"It'll break." By this time, Deme's refusal was weakening. If she didn't get some relief soon, it wouldn't matter, they'd fall anyway.

Shelby turned her face toward Cal.

Cal lay flat on the catwalk and crawled toward them,

distributing his weight across a broader surface to ease the strain on the lone strut standing between the two women and a tragic fall. The metal creaked but held.

When he got within two feet of Shelby, he reached out a hand. "Take my hand, Shelby."

"I can't." Her voice shook and she buried her face in Deme's belly again.

"Yes. You. Can." He scooted forward a little more.

Deme's arm was slipping, and her legs couldn't hold up under the strain. Shelby was sliding farther down her body.

"Give me your hand now," Cal shouted.

Shelby cried out and slapped her hand into his.

Deme's legs lost their grip on the girl and she slid free. "No!"

Shelby screamed. The metal of the catwalk groaned and jerked as the girl's weight shifted from Deme to Cal.

Deme, her arms shaking, struggled to pull herself up to the section of catwalk still firmly attached to the roof. She lay facedown, breathing hard. As the blood rushed back into her arms, the pain of a thousand pins and needles stabbed into her.

Dangling from Cal's grip, Shelby hung twenty feet above the hard wooden floor of the stage. "Help! Oh, God, please," she sobbed.

"I've got you," Cal said, his voice low, steady, calm. He reached with his other hand and pulled her up a little more.

"Why is this happening to me?" Shelby whimpered.

"Everything is going to be okay," Cal said.

Across the broken catwalk from Cal, Deme let Cal's words wash over her, warming her where she'd felt so cold. If he hadn't been there today...

When Cal finally had Shelby close enough, he grabbed the back of her jeans and hauled her the rest of the way onto the walkway, scooting her back to the undamaged portion.

As Deme lay gasping for breath, arms aching and her face pressed against the catwalk's grate, Cal's words washed over her. *Everything is going to be okay.*

She pushed to a sitting position, then stood, her resolve hardening. Tired of reacting to every curveball the Chimera threw at her. Deme realized the only way everything was going to get better was to make it happen.

Chapter 14

Cal worked with Fred to stabilize the catwalk, repairing the damage and reinforcing the struts so that they wouldn't fail again. Not until nearly quitting time did he get a chance to check out Dr. Masterson's office. He told Fred he had one more thing to check on his way back to the locker room and not to wait on him.

"What you did for that girl…" Fred patted him on the back. "You do good work, Cal. Get some rest."

Cal used his key to enter the administrative building through a side utility door accessed only by maintenance personnel. Most of the staff had already left for the day, leaving the desks empty and many of the lights off. He quickly located the college president's office and knocked on the door. When no one answered, he let himself in.

The walls were lined with framed diplomas from the University of Illinois. He scanned all of them, taking pictures with his cell phone. Not even the under-graduate degree read Colyer-Fenton College, as if the attack had driven her from the college to complete her education elsewhere.

"With this arsenal of education, why did you come here?" Cal wondered out loud to the empty room.

"I had to come back," a voice said behind him. "To face my fears."

Cal froze, his hand in the air in the middle of snapping another picture of her doctorate diploma. Lowering his arm slowly, he turned to face the woman. "Of what?"

"I spent years hiding in my room, only venturing out to go to and from class. I was so afraid of every shadow. Not until I decided to come back here did I find purpose."

"What were you afraid of?"

She rolled her eyes. "Don't play stupid with me. I saw what you did for that girl in the theater. You're not some Cal Smith, the maintenance man. You're here because of the happenings on campus."

Cal didn't respond. By not replying, he agreed. "So what are you going to do?"

"I don't think you're responsible, if that's what you mean. And if you can help find what's causing all this chaos, all the better." She walked across the room to sit behind her desk. "I'm of the opinion that whatever it is, it has been here before."

"Thirty years ago?"

She steepled her fingers, looked directly at him and nodded. "Just do me a favor."

"And what's that?"

"Keep me in the loop, will you?"

"I can't make that promise."

"I can have you thrown off campus."

He tipped his head. "Yes, you can."

Her lips twisted into a wry smile. "But I won't. I owe you for Shelby."

"Thanks. Do you mind my asking what happened thirty years ago?"

She laughed, the sound harsh in the fading light from the window. "The news article didn't give you enough?"

"Only that a young woman was raped."

Dr. Masterson stood and faced the window, the one looking out onto the garden. "That's all there was to the story." Her tone didn't invite further questions nor any hope of additional answers.

"Then I'll be going. If you can think of anything else that might help solve this case, I'll be around."

Silhouetted against the window, Dr. Masterson looked dark and alone. "Next time, wait to be invited into my office. I'm kind of particular about people invading my privacy." She looked back over her shoulder, her eyes narrowed. "And do be careful whom you associate with. There are those on campus who aren't what they appear to be."

His lips curled up on the corners. "Like me?"

"You'd be surprised. And so might they."

Somehow, he didn't doubt that. Cal left, closing the door behind him. His last view of Dr. Masterson was of her looking out her window, down into the garden.

Deme spent the day talking to sorority sisters and searching every inch of the Gamma Omega dormitory for any evidence leading her to find Aurai. Having come up empty, she'd turned her search to the student commons and finally returned to the library, where she'd called a meeting of Brigid, Gina and Selene in the relative privacy of the second floor east stacks.

"Relatives!" Gina gasped.

"Coincidence be damned," Selene said in an unusual display of frustration. "You know what this means, don't you?"

Deme nodded. "We're on this campus for a reason. Apparently the same reason the five sisters had been here."

Brigid held up a finger. "With one difference…" She planted her hands on her hips. "I don't plan to die taking down the big, bad Chimera."

"Right," Deme agreed. "And I'll be damned to eternal hell if one of my sisters pays the ultimate price. We're a family and we will all emerge intact, if I have anything to do with it."

"Here! Here!" Gina clapped.

"Sounds all well and good, but you listen to me." Deme's eyes narrowed as she looked into the steady gazes of her sisters. "Don't try to fight it alone. The Chimera is strong. You saw what it could do to a regular girl when it took over Shelby. It seems to turn our powers against us, so beware."

Gina put her hand into the center of the circle of sisters. "Be safe, sisters."

Deme's palm covered hers, and Brigid and Selene piled a hand on top. "Blessed Be."

A whirl of wind lifted their hair, and the women smiled at each other.

Deme's eyes misted. "Same goes for Aurai," she said softly.

"We will find her." Selene's arm circled Deme's shoulder. "We have to believe that."

"I do." The responsibility of being the oldest sibling

weighed more heavily than ever before. "Look, you guys get off campus and get some rest. We have more work to do tomorrow."

After her sisters left, Deme couldn't give up. She spent the rest of the evening searching through more news clippings for anything else she could find on the five sisters. There had to be something useful to lead her to Aurai.

Fatigue pulled at her eyelids long before she closed the books and packed it in. She hated to admit that fear of last night's black hole of memories made her reluctant to return to her room, thus she had pushed on longer than she should have.

When she finally left the library, Deme trudged toward the dorm, not at all looking forward to staying another night alone in the room against the garden. Having seen what the Chimera could do to a young college coed, she shuddered to think what it could do with her as semiconscious as she was.

A man pushed away from a light pole and ambled her way.

Deme's pulse sped. She could tell that walk anywhere. Cal Black moved like a panther, his steps smooth, measured, lean and sexy.

After the day she'd had, she couldn't think of anyone she'd rather see. She needed a few answers to questions she had concerning what had happened in her room the night before. Questions aside, she was glad to see him. No amount of self-denial would change that, and frankly she was tired of fighting her attraction. Hell, she was flat-out tired, period.

"Tough day at the office?" he asked.

She fell in step beside him, heading for the parking lot. "Yeah. I'm glad you came by."

He chuckled. "That's a change for the better."

His laughter filled the emptiness threatening to drag her spirits ever downward. "Mind if I ask you a few questions about last night?"

"Can it wait for a few minutes?"

"Sure."

He hooked her arm with his big, rough hand and took off across the campus lawns toward the parking lot.

The tallest of her sisters, even Deme's long legs had a tough time keeping up with Cal. She arrived at his motorcycle slightly out of breath. "Needing a little exercise, big guy?"

"Huh?" He looked up as if he hadn't realized Deme was beside him all the way.

"You're hitting the old ego hard these days." Deme laughed. "If you want to be by yourself, why didn't you say so? I'd understand."

"No, I don't." He shook his head, his frown showing his confusion. "I want to be with you."

Cal's words had an instant warming effect, leaving Deme feeling more alive than she had since she'd almost plummeted to the stage that morning. She didn't respond to his comment. Didn't feel as if she had to.

He shoved a hand through his hair and breathed deeply. Then he handed her a spare helmet. "Get on."

She looked down at the helmet and shrugged. "Okay. Where are we headed?"

"Somewhere...anywhere...away from here. I need to get my head on straight." He climbed onto the bike and kicked the engine to life, the roar echoing across the quiet campus.

Deme climbed on behind him and wrapped her arms around his waist.

The motorcycle shot out onto the road and soon entered traffic on the Eisenhower Expressway, headed east toward Lake Michigan.

As Cal dodged vehicles, Deme leaned into him, letting herself go for the few short minutes she could, the wind blowing the cobwebs from her mind and clearing her head. Away from campus her mind wasn't clouded with the oppressive presence of the Chimera. She needed this break in order to think straight and plan her next move.

Cal dropped off the expressway, heading south. He came to a stop on Lake Shore Drive near the John G. Shedd Aquarium.

After the short, swift ride, Deme was more alert and awake than she'd been in days.

Cal parked the bike, removed his helmet and took hers from her, securing it to the motorcycle. Then he grabbed her hand and led her along a broad, concrete walkway. The flotilla of sailboats lining the bay on Lake Michigan, the night skyline of Chicago and the Navy Pier spread out before them.

"Where are we going?"

"Shh…" He left the sidewalk and crossed over grass, pulling her along behind him. "It's almost time."

"Time?"

Over the steady hum of traffic, a loud *pop* sounded across the water toward the Navy Pier and a trail of color shot into the air high above the lake, where it exploded in a burst of brilliant pink light.

"Oh, yeah. I'd forgotten all about the fireworks." She stood beside Cal, staring up at the display as, one after another, rockets shot into the air. "Our mother used to bring us here in the summertime. We'd spend the afternoon on the beach and stay until the fireworks ended. Aurai would fall asleep before they started."

Cal slipped an arm around Deme and pulled her against him. Nothing sexual, but it had a tremendous pull on her in the area of her heart.

She'd expected him to make love to her on the beach, or try to kiss her in the moonlight, but to just stand there and hold her while they watched the fireworks...

Tears welled in her eyes. How had she gone so wrong where this man was concerned? He'd once asked her to marry him. She'd answered by running away.

How could she make it right again? All because she was strange, different...a witch. "I don't lead a normal life."

"Neither do I."

"I can make things happen with earth, plants and vegetation that would scare most people."

Cal shrugged. "I chase bad guys and get shot at."

"Everything about me and my sisters is bizarre and unusual."

"Is that a bad thing? Some people would kill to have what you and your sisters have."

"Something has." She stood in silence a moment, reflecting on the people who'd been hurt or killed by the Chimera's manipulations. "All we wanted was to lead normal lives, have careers, maybe fall in love..." Her voice faded off. She hadn't meant to mention that *L*-word, but there it was.

Cal let the word pass, instead asking, "What do you remember about last night?"

"Not much. I was hoping you could fill in the blanks." Deme stared up at him, his face illuminated by the night sky, brightened occasionally by the flash of the pyrotechnic display.

He stared up at the fireworks exploding high above Lake Michigan. "You weren't quite yourself."

"The Chimera had me, didn't it?" A shiver raked over her body, shaking her all the way down to her toes. "Was I as bad as Shelby?"

He chuckled. "You had your moments."

"Did I hurt you?"

Cal hesitated, his gaze remaining on the lights of Navy Pier. "No."

Deme didn't believe him. "Show me your shoulders."

"You didn't bite me this time. Except on the ear." He reached up to touch his earlobe. "But it's fine."

"Then how else did I hurt you?" Deme couldn't help but feel he wasn't telling the whole truth. Her lapse in memory frustrated her.

"You didn't." His arm tightened around her. "Look, I just came to see the fireworks."

Deme faced the display, a thousand questions racing through her mind. Had she said something hurtful to him while possessed by the Chimera? He'd once asked her to marry him. After she'd disappeared for a year, he probably harbored some pretty ill feelings toward her. Had she jabbed at that pain? Did he even care anymore?

Her heart squeezed inside her chest. Though she'd run away from him, hoping he'd forget her and move on to a normal life with a normal woman, she couldn't help wishing he still loved her.

She glanced up at him, wanting more than anything to ask if he still loved her, but she couldn't. Her gaze returned to the pier and she forced herself to say, "The fireworks display is pretty, isn't it?"

"Yeah. My father only brought us once while my mother was alive. She loved it. When she died, he couldn't bring himself to return."

"I'm sorry."

"Why? It was a long time ago."

"You must have been close to your father."

His hand dropped to his side. "It was a long time ago."

The fireworks died away and a stream of vehicles made a slow, lighted procession out of the Navy Pier parking area. Families on their way home after a fun-filled day. Life couldn't be more beautiful and simple for some.

Only Deme's could never be that uncomplicated. Hadn't her mother said from the moment she could understand that because she was blessed, she had a responsibility to use her gifts to help others? She'd told herself that was what she was doing with her private investigative service in St. Croix. But she'd really only been lying to herself.

Trying to live a normal life ignoring her talent except to further her own financial pursuits had given her what? A great, big empty feeling.

What Cal had hoped to accomplish by bringing Deme out to watch the fireworks was a mystery to himself. He'd spent the past couple of days working nonstop to discover anything there was to know about a missing girl. The discoveries had been more than weird, shaking his knowledge of the world he lived in. It was a lot to comprehend and believe, all being shoved at him one frightening incident after another.

Standing on the shores of Lake Michigan, on the edge of the city he'd called home for his entire life, he had to admit, he knew less now than he thought he'd known last week.

He needed this. A chance to stand back and evaluate.

"I spoke with Dr. Masterson." Cal broke the silence.

Deme shot a glance his way. "And?"

"She more or less admitted she was the woman raped thirty years ago."

"Why did she come back?"

"She couldn't move on until she laid her ghosts to rest."

Deme snorted. "Like that's going to happen now?" She breathed in and let it out. "Sorry. I don't mean to be sarcastic, but I have a feeling it's going to get a whole lot worse before it gets better."

He nodded, his hand tightening around her waist. "I'm afraid you're right."

"Did you learn anything else?" Deme asked.

Cal had yet to tell Deme of what he'd found in the basement of the student commons, but he couldn't keep it from her long. Sooner or later, Lieutenant Warner would spill the beans to Brigid, and she'd be all over him for not letting her in on the secret tunnels sooner. "I found out there is a labyrinth of tunnels beneath the city."

"The old freight tunnels they used back in the early nineteen hundreds? Yeah, so?"

"I did a little research and got with an engineer friend of mine." He faced Deme. "Did you know that one of the tunnels runs directly beneath the Colyer-Fenton campus?"

Deme's eyes widened. "Do you think that might be where the Chimera is hiding?" Her hand clutched his sleeve. "It could have Aurai there." She turned toward the parking lot. "We have to go."

Cal grabbed her arm and pulled her to a stop. "Whoa, wait a minute."

"Why? You could have found her."

"We don't know what's in the tunnels or even if the

air is breathable. You can't go chasing down there until we get the right equipment."

"But Aurai could be down there. If the air isn't breathable, she'd be…"

"Dead."

Deme gulped down the lump in her throat. "But she's not. We felt her. She's still alive."

"The place where she is might be okay, but getting to her could be deadly, not only because of the Chimera, but poisonous air."

"Cal, we have to go. If there's any chance at all that she's down there, we have to find her."

"And we will." He pulled her into his arms and held her. "Tomorrow. I have a tunnel expert meeting us at the diner in the morning. He'll bring breathing apparatus and the equipment we need to test the air."

Deme stared up into his eyes a long time before her shoulders slumped. "You're right. We need to do this correctly. I don't want anyone else hurt."

He held her arms, his hands squeezing tighter. "Deme, only me and the tunnel expert are going down."

She jerked out of his hands and backed up a step. "No way."

"I can't risk losing you or another one of your sisters."

"I'm going with you. You tell your expert to bring enough equipment for me to go, too."

"No."

"Come on, Cal. You knew how I'd respond to this. If you didn't want me to go with you, you might as well have kept it to yourself. The cat's out of the bag now." She fisted her hands on her hips, her legs planted wide, daring him to refute her claim.

And he wanted to. The thought of Deme getting hurt

in the nasty, smelly, dank tunnel below the campus made him crazy. But with her standing there in front of him, her green eyes blazing, the wind off the lake lifting her wild red hair around her, she looked like a Valkyrie ready to do battle with the devil himself.

A smile crooked the corners of his mouth, spreading into a grin. "Okay. But only you. The rest of your sisters will have to remain ignorant until we know more."

She stuck out a hand. "Deal."

Cal grabbed the proffered hand. Instead of shaking it, he pulled her into his arms. "Now, we need to get some sleep. I haven't had a good night's rest in three days."

"You can drop me off at the campus."

"Not sure that's a good idea. Not after what happened last night."

"You never did give me all the details." She fit perfectly against him, her breasts rubbing against his chest with every breath. "There are a few memories missing from that particular event. Are you ever going to tell me what happened?"

"Maybe someday." He leaned down and kissed her. "As for now, I think we should make some new ones." His lips pressed against hers, his tongue slipping into her mouth to taste hers. Yeah, this is what he'd wanted. Far away from the influence of the Chimera, he could be certain that the woman he kissed was indeed Deme, not some jacked-up creature from the underworld.

Her hands slid beneath his shirt and up across his back, her fingernails lightly scraping his skin.

Cal tensed.

When she didn't dig deep, he relaxed and tugged her shirt from the waistband of her jeans, letting his own hands roam across her warm, naked skin.

Not until a cool breeze off the water caressed the side of his face did he come up for air and remember where he was. He set her at arm's length, removing his hands from beneath her shirt. "We better go before we're arrested for indecent exposure."

Deme leaned into him, her fingers finding his nipples beneath his shirt. "But we still have our clothes on."

His hand slid up her arms, gripping her shoulders. "We won't for long at this rate." He pushed her away and took her hand, leading her up the grassy slope to the concrete walkway.

In silence, he climbed on the motorcycle. Deme slipped on behind him, the inside of her thighs sliding around his. Cal almost pulled her into his lap and made love to her there in the park. Instead, he kicked the engine into life and revved it, shooting out onto Lake Shore Drive, headed for his apartment.

When he passed the exit off Eisenhower Expressway to the Colyer-Fenton College campus, Deme shouted, "You missed my exit."

He shook his head and kept going. No way in hell he'd let her sleep in that room one more night.

When he pulled into the parking lot of his apartment and parked the bike, Deme hopped off the back, her face set in grim lines. "I need to go back to campus."

"No." He took off his helmet and headed for the stairwell.

She stood beside his bike, refusing to follow. "Then I'll just call a taxi."

He stopped and turned around. "You can't."

"Can't call a taxi?"

"No, you can't sleep in that room tonight."

"Why?"

"I don't want what happened to Shelby today to happen to you...again."

Deme's eyes rounded. "It had me last night?" She walked toward him, slowly, as though in a trance, her gaze seeking his in the dimly lit parking lot. "How bad was it?"

He took her into his arms. "It made Shelby look like a kitten stuck up in a tree."

Deme leaned her forehead into his chest. "Damn."

"Yeah."

"But I can't impose on you."

"Who said you were imposing?" He swung her up into his arms. "I would have taken you to your sisters if that had been the case." He gazed down at her. "I still can, if that's what you want." His breath held in his throat as he awaited her answer.

Chapter 15

Deme wrapped her arms around Cal's neck. "No. This is what I want." She leaned forward and pressed her lips to his. Every nerve in her body burst into flame, blood rushing low in her belly to that aching, throbbing place at the juncture of her thighs.

She wanted Cal. Tall, sexy…naked…Cal.

He carried her up the stairs, as if she weighed nothing. When he reached the upper landing, he wasn't even breathing hard.

"You know, I could have walked." She kissed his lips and laughed. "But it was more fun watching you play the he-man."

"And here I thought I was impressing you with my chivalry." He dropped her feet to the ground and jammed the key into the lock.

As soon as the door opened, Deme pushed through,

ripping her shirt up over her head and tossing it to the corner. "What's taking you so long, Detective?"

Deme couldn't explain the feeling of coming home. Was it the amount of time that had passed, the distance she'd traveled, the events of the past couple of days or the emotions evoked by returning to Cal's apartment after a year? She couldn't put a finger on the one thing that made her want to grab for what little happiness she could find and hold on. Tomorrow was another day of trouble, but tonight was hers and Cal's.

She shimmied out of her jeans and kicked them off, standing there in her bra and panties, her chest rising and falling with the rapid breaths of a sprinter.

Cal closed the door behind him and leaned against it, his arms crossed, his brows raised. "Is this the reason you think I brought you here?"

A moment of doubt struck Deme as her skin cooled, her stomach fluttering with a sudden attack of the nerves. Her arms wrapped around her middle. "Didn't you?"

He shook his head.

Deme's eyes narrowed and her arms dropped to her sides. Was he testing her, or did he really not want to make love to her? "Not interested?" She walked toward him, her hand slipping up her back to unclasp her bra.

He tipped his head to the side. "Thinking."

Deme held the cups of her bra in place, letting the straps slide down her shoulders.

Cal didn't move, but the flare of his nostrils gave him away.

Oh, he wanted her all right.

Deme let the bra fall to the end of the fingers on one hand and she lifted it in the air before tossing it across a lamp shade. "Still thinking about it?"

He pushed away from the door but didn't close the distance. "Yup."

After a day full of stress, this little game of cat and mouse should have pushed Deme over the edge. Instead, it was reviving her, making her want more.

Standing in nothing but her black bikini panties that left very little to the imagination, she straightened her shoulders, pushing out her chest, proud of what genetics had blessed her with.

Still he stood there waiting for her to make the next move.

Deme remained rooted to the floor three feet away from Cal, her body on fire, ready and waiting for him to take her. Apparently he wasn't ready and it was up to her to make him want her as badly as she wanted him.

Deme let her fingers trail slowly across her belly, sliding into the indention of her belly button, tracing a path upward. When her hands reached her breasts, she cupped them, squeezing gently, lifting them and massaging their firm roundness.

The nipples peaked, hardening into tight little nubs. With the tips of her fingers, she tugged at them, pinching and teasing.

Her breathing became more erratic, what she was doing to entice Cal making her hotter and more needy with each stroke.

With one hand on her breast, continuing the sensual massage, she slid her other hand downward to the apex of her thighs, beneath the elastic of her panties.

She threaded her fingers into the mound of hair, parting her folds to caress the sensitive little nubbin hidden between.

Deme's breath caught in her throat. Her hips thrust forward as her finger stroked the sweet spot.

Her head fell back, her hair brushing over her back and lower to the top of her buttocks, the swish of the fine silken tendrils as erotic as a man trailing feathers over her nakedness.

Lost in her own sensual arousal, Deme didn't realize Cal had moved until he grasped her face between his palms. "Look at me."

She blinked her eyes open, unaware she'd even closed them. When she looked into his deep brown eyes, she could see a fire burning bright.

He stared for a long moment before he let out a steady breath. "Good, it is you." His hands skimmed down her neck and over her shoulders to cup her breasts in his palms. His lips pressed into the pulse thrumming along the side of her throat, his tongue flicking and tasting a path down to her collarbone.

Deme's head fell back, exposing the mounds of her breasts to his lips. "What is that supposed to mean?"

"Just what I said." He pushed her breast up with his hand and took the nipple into his mouth, teasing it with the tip of his tongue. One hand glided down her waist, edging beneath her panty line to join her hand there in a sensual stroking motion.

Deme gasped, pressing her breast more fully into his mouth. "Were you expecting someone else?"

His lips left her breast to kiss her full on the mouth. "I was hoping we were alone so I could do this." He backed her up until her bottom hit the edge of his dining table. With a rough thumb, he hooked the elastic of her waistband and dragged her panties halfway down her thighs. Then he lifted her until her bottom slid across the table, her knees draping over the side. With her perched above him, he dropped to his knees and finished the job of taking off her panties, one agonizing inch at a time, pressing his lips to every inch of exposed skin all the way down to her ankles.

When he finally pulled the panties free, Cal parted her legs, pulling them over his shoulders, bringing her aching entrance within inches of his lips.

Deme cupped the back of his head, urging him closer. All the worries of the day were washed to the back of her mind. The only focus she had was on what Cal's mouth could do to her.

Cal pressed his lips to the inside of her thigh, mere inches from heaven, sliding his tongue closer.

Her body throbbed, nerves jumping as his fingers parted her folds, thumbing the center with gentle precision. When his tongue replaced his thumb, Cal teased and flicked, dropping lower to thrust into her, laving her channel with warm, wet strokes.

Deme's hips pushed forward, meeting his thrusts and wanting more. When he transferred his attention back to her own point of desire, the little nubbin of tantalized nerves, Deme's hands braced behind her, her bottom rising off the table.

A brilliant explosion of sensations, every bit as spectacular as the Navy Pier fireworks display, burst through her, rocking her world into a bliss so intense, she didn't know she'd screamed out until the sound of her voice echoed in her ears. She rode the wave of pleasure, hips rocking, breathing erratic, her heart beating a thousand times a minute.

As the intensity diminished enough so she could breathe, a new burgeoning need swept over her. She grabbed Cal's ears and pulled him up.

"Hey. Do you mind?" He climbed to his feet, eager to get ahead of her pull on his ears, and stood between her thighs.

With her breath still coming in erratic heaves, Deme yanked at the rivet on Cal's jeans. "You have..." She breathed out and sucked in another breath. "Too many clothes on," she said, her words coming out in a rush. With a quick flick, she had the button undone and the zipper down.

Cal's erection sprang forward into her palm and she guided it swiftly into place.

With one hard thrust, he filled her.

Deme let out the breath she'd been holding and sucked in another, her legs wrapping around his middle, drawing him closer.

Cal started slow, sliding in and out.

Deme had no patience for it. She wanted him hard and fast. The more punishing, the more alive she felt. With both hands on his buttocks, she set a pummeling pace.

As she climbed that tension-filled peak yet again, she let go of her hold and lay down across the table, her fingers digging into her folds, coaxing more from her climax as she catapulted over the top.

With one final thrust, Cal clutched Deme's hips, holding her hard against him for one last second, sliding free before he spilled inside her.

Replete, fulfilled and completely satisfied, Deme lay across the table, her legs falling over the edge, her body limp. After several cleansing breaths to refill her starving lungs, she sighed. "I can't move another muscle."

"Yes, you can." Cal pulled his jeans up around his hips without buttoning or snapping. Then he scooped his hands beneath her legs and back and lifted her. "You can hold on so I don't trip carrying you to our bed."

Surprisingly, her arms did work as she draped them

around Cal's shoulders. "Hey, why is it I'm naked and you're not?"

"My error. I haven't mastered pulling my jeans off while still wearing boots. When you come up with the magic that will do it for me, let me know."

"I'll work on that." Deme liked the feel of his cotton shirt rubbing against the skin of her hip and the way his fingers curled around her thigh and beneath her breast. That he could make a joke about spells was icing on the cake.

In his bedroom he laid her across the comforter and straightened, staring down at her. "You're so beautiful, I'm beginning to think you've cast a spell on me."

She leaned up on her elbow, letting her legs fall open. "So, Mortal, when did you decide you believed in witchcraft?"

"Since I met you." He started to work on the buttons of his shirt.

Cal sat beside Deme at the diner the next morning. With her thigh pressed against his, heat singed a path to Cal's groin, making him wish they were back in his apartment twisting in the sheets. Or better yet, making it on the table.

Cal was eying the table in front of him with more than casual interest when Lieutenant Warner and Dustin Zoeller, the Chicago tunnel expert, slid onto the bench across from him.

Heat rose up in his cheeks as he worked to squash images of a naked Deme lying on the smooth tabletop in front of him.

"Good morning." He cleared his throat and extended a hand across the table to Dustin. "Glad you could make it."

The lieutenant nodded toward Deme. "You must be one of Brigid's sisters."

"Deme Chattox." Deme held out her hand to the lieutenant and to Dustin. "I'll be going on this little spelunking expedition with you this morning."

Cal cringed. Nothing like Deme taking the lead on the happenings of the day.

Dustin's brows rose along with the lieutenant's. "What's this?"

Cal jumped in. "I didn't have time to tell you that there's been an addition to our little group." He hadn't had time because he'd been buried inside their little addition, making love to her into the wee hours of the morning. A bit of information he had no intention of sharing with his boss.

Dustin shook his head. "No can do. I can't authorize a civilian to enter the tunnels. It leaves the city open for lawsuits."

Deme smiled. "Sorry. I didn't mean to put you on the defensive, but my sister is the victim here. I know things you can't possibly understand. You need me."

"We could get Brigid to go. She's at least on the payroll," Lieutenant Warner offered.

"No. I'm the oldest. My sisters are my responsibility." Deme's eyes narrowed. "I take it you haven't told Brigid about the tunnels yet, am I right?"

"No." The lieutenant frowned. "But—"

"Good. Let's keep it that way until we know what we're dealing with."

Cal chuckled. "You see what *I'm* dealing with?"

"Remind me to recruit her, will you? And while you're at it, I want to meet the rest of the Chattox women." Marty grinned. "I have a feeling they are Chicago's best-kept secret."

The tension in Cal's shoulders lessened. He thought he'd have to fight his boss to get Deme on this mission. She'd been right that she understood more about the world of magic than any of the men did. She could feel things they didn't, maybe even sense trouble before it happened. They needed her or someone like her when they descended into the bowels of the city.

"Sir, I don't think it's a good idea," Dustin protested again. "She's not an expert in the tunnels. How can she know more?"

"She has other special talents."

"What? Like a psychic?" Dustin snorted and blushed. "No offense."

"None taken. But I'm going." Deme smiled sweetly. Cal recognized the spark in her emerald eyes as one of challenge. She wasn't going to be easily dissuaded. He almost felt sorry for Dustin. The man obviously didn't know who he was up against in Deme Chattox.

The tunnel expert appealed to the lieutenant with raised brows.

Lieutenant Warner's jaw firmed and he glared at the younger man. "She goes. If anyone takes the heat, it'll be my ass."

The expert's lips pressed into a thin line. He wasn't happy, but the lieutenant was in charge. The man finally shrugged. "It's your life, lady."

Deme laid a hand on the expert's arm. "It's my sister's life we're talking about."

A surge of pure jealousy so strong it surprised him ran through Cal's veins like a shot of adrenaline. Not until Deme removed her hand from Dustin's arm did Cal's pulse slow back to normal. He couldn't even attribute his jealousy to a mind-manipulating Chimera this time. They weren't anywhere near the campus.

Cal drew in a deep breath and concentrated on what Dustin had to say.

"I have breathing equipment, ropes and a device that can test air quality as we proceed down into the tunnels. I prefer to have a full team of rescue personnel on hand to pull us out if things go south." The man held his hand up when Cal started to protest. "I understand we're on a college campus. We need to protect the entrance location to keep others from finding it and misusing it."

"I've got it covered." Lieutenant Warner grinned. "I've arranged for the fire department to conduct a recruiting demonstration on campus today. The chief will be on call in case of emergency. He's loaning two of his finest to our efforts in the basement of the student commons. They'll be there under the pretext of performing an annual fire inspection."

Cal nodded then asked, "What about weapons?"

Dustin shook his head. "We don't know if any of the gases down below are flammable. If you discharge a weapon in a flammable environment, you could blow half of Chicago to hell in a heartbeat."

"Whoa." Cal held up a hand. "No weapons? Do you have any idea what we're up against?"

Dustin looked from Cal to Lieutenant Warner and back. "I thought we were looking for a kidnapping victim. I assumed we'd be looking for her and her kidnapper. Is there more than one?"

Cal glanced across at Lieutenant Warner.

The lieutenant shook his head, just enough for Cal to get the message not to share any more than necessary. Why would the lieutenant keep information about a monster running loose beneath the city to himself?

Cal almost laughed out loud. As if he'd have believed it a few days ago? Not likely. He'd originally thought it was a big hoax and that anyone who'd believe such bull needed his head examined. Yeah, maybe the lieutenant was right.

"Look, if you'll get us down there and show us how to use the equipment, we'll take care of finding our girl."

Deme tapped her foot as the group converged in the student commons basement thirty minutes later. The sooner they got moving, the better. After four days being held captive by the Chimera, Aurai would be getting weak. Given the beast's methods of attack, Deme guessed it didn't have access to its own physical form, moving through the actions of others, or as in Aurai's case, by manipulating their talents to capture them.

Dustin Zoeller gave them a brief training session on the dangers of being in the tunnels, the gases that could be poisonous and how to use the air-testing device.

He then showed them how to wear the oxygen tanks and masks and checked all the equipment for proper functionality.

"I feel like I'm going scuba diving." Deme fitted the breathing mask over her face and adjusted the elastic straps.

"The subterranean environment can be just as deadly." The tunnel expert pulled the straps holding the mask to Deme's face tighter.

The heavy metal door beneath the stairwell stood open, the dark cavity already sending chills across her skin. How she wished her sisters were there for moral support.

She had chosen not to inform them, sure they'd insist on accompanying her into the tunnels. Deme couldn't let them. Not until she knew more.

Cal hooked his D-ring to the rope the firemen would use to haul them out if need be and climbed onto the top rung of the metal ladder. He paused, giving Deme a thumbs-up. "Ready?"

"As ready as I'll ever be." Her heart hammering in her chest, she edged toward the tunnel, every instinct in her screaming for her to keep out.

"Deme!" The clatter of footsteps on the metal staircase rang out as several people clambered down from the main level of the student commons. "Deme, wait!"

Deme turned to face an angry phalanx of sisters as Selene, Brigid and Gina reached the basement floor, breathing hard, eyes blazing.

Brigid led the charge. "What the hell are you doing?"

Deme pushed the mask to the top of her head. "I'm going after Aurai."

"Without us?" Gina stepped up beside Brigid.

"I didn't want to worry you."

"Bull." Selene, the usually calm, collected sister, glared at her. "You didn't want us here."

They'd caught her and nailed her. She yanked the mask off her head. "That's right. I didn't want you here."

"I thought we were in this together." Gina tipped her head to the side, her blue-gray eyes reflecting her disappointment.

"Only when it's convenient for her." Brigid planted her hands on her black-leather-clad hips. "You aren't our mother."

Deme flinched. "I never said I was."

"Yeah, but whether we wanted you to or not, you've been calling the shots since Mother died."

"I had to." Who else would have kept them together?

"No, you didn't. And for the record, this past year

while you were in St. Croix, we were on our own." Gina crossed her arms over her chest, a frown drawing her brows together. "We managed fine."

The implied "without you" hung in the air.

"We proved to ourselves that we could live without Big Sis guiding our every movement." Selene stood with her hands on her hips just like Brigid. "We don't need you."

The blow hit her square in the gut, and she stepped back as if it had been a physical punch. Her eyes stung, but Deme refused to let the tears fall.

Selene reached out for Deme's hand. "We don't need you as our *mother.*"

Gina joined Selene, placing her hand over their joined hands. "No, we don't." She glanced back at Brigid.

The black-haired sister hesitated and then closed the distance, adding her hand to the rest. "We don't need you as our mother. We need you as our sister."

Deme stood, surrounded by her sisters, the love she felt for them swelling in her chest. "Sisters who need to find a missing member of the family."

"Right." Brigid was the first to break the circle. "So what's happening here?"

Deme gave them an abbreviated version of the plan. "I was going to tell you about it once we got an idea of what's down there."

"Well, the cat's out of the bag." Brigid's chin lifted in challenge. "We're coming with you."

Deme shook her head. "There's not enough breathing equipment."

"Then I should go since I have a better psychic connection," Selene insisted.

Brigid planted herself in front of Deme, hands on

hips. "No, I should go because I'm working with the city on this case."

Gina pushed Brigid aside. "I should go because… well…just because."

Lieutenant Warner pulled Deme out of the middle of the women. "Deme's going. She's been briefed on the equipment and we're running out of time. The fire department won't be on campus all day. You three can help the rest of us monitor their progress."

Brigid glared at the lieutenant. "I'll pick a bone with you later."

"No, you won't." Lieutenant Warner nodded to Cal. "Go."

Deme's pulse quickened as his head disappeared below the top of the ladder. She pulled the mask in place, tightened the elastic straps and checked the oxygen meter.

The lieutenant clapped her hard hat fitted with a headlight on top of her head. "Be careful down there."

She pulled on thick work gloves, gave the lieutenant a thumbs-up and got in line behind Dustin Zoeller as he waited for the firemen to snap the rope through his D-ring. Then he stepped over the edge and descended the rungs of the metal ladder into the tunnel below.

When it was her turn, Deme stood steady while the fireman tugged on her web seat and snapped the rope through the D-ring. It was scary to think that thin rope was their lifeline to escape if the shit hit the fan down below.

With a deep breath, Deme grabbed the ladder rungs and lowered herself into the darkness. The only light chasing back the shadows was the thin beam from her helmet. She leaned over, pointing her head at the ladder below her, catching a glimpse of the top of Dustin's head and the tiny glow from his headlight. She couldn't see past him to Cal, making her want to hurry her progress to the bottom.

With the mask fitted tightly to her face, Deme couldn't smell the air, but she could feel its coolness through the long-sleeved coverall the tunnel expert had provided. The dampness of the air made her exposed skin sticky.

The descent took longer than she expected. Just how deep were the tunnels? After five minutes, claustrophobia became a real concern. The not knowing how much farther had her breathing harder. Several times she had to stop and remind herself to breathe slowly so as not to use up all her oxygen before she had a chance to look around.

When she thought the ladder would never end, she emerged from the vertical tunnel into a horizontal tunnel large enough for a man to stand up straight without hitting his head on the pipes and conduit hanging above.

Before she could make the last four rungs, Cal grabbed her from behind and set her on her feet. She turned in his arms and clung to him for a few seconds, more relieved than she cared to admit in front of the tunnel expert.

Dustin stood in the middle of a train track, holding the bright yellow toxic-gas monitor. After five minutes, he slid his mask off. "Hydrogen sulfide's a little high, as is the carbon monoxide, but not enough to be alarmed. At this point, the air's breathable. You might want to conserve your oxygen."

Cal and Deme switched their oxygen off and removed the masks.

The dank, metallic scent of wet rocks filled her nostrils.

Cal unclipped the chem light from his web harness and clicked it on, flooding the tunnel with light.

Dustin unfolded the tunnel map he'd brought along and shined his headlight down at the lines. "We're headed toward the foundation of Lion Hall—the one that burned down—right?"

Now that she was down here, Deme just wanted to get this whole adventure over with. The same oppressive feeling she had in her dorm room of being watched by a malevolent being hung in the air, making it difficult to breathe. She was tempted to put her mask back on, but knew it wasn't the lack of oxygen that was doing it to her.

If her sister was down here, she had to find her or some evidence that this was where the creature had her trapped. She couldn't draw on her ability to "feel" for her sister on the off chance the Chimera would tap into her powers and trap her, as well.

Frustration made her impatient. "Which way?"

The tunnel expert nodded to his left. "That way. Should be a junction in fifty feet that will take us there." He hesitated. "Are you sure we don't need additional backup?"

"If you want to go back up, do. Just leave the air monitor with us."

"No, no. I'll go." Dustin tucked the map in his pocket and unbuckled his chem light from his web belt, holding it out in front of him like a weapon. "Lead on."

Cal took point, moving ahead carefully, stepping over old pipes, discarded equipment and crumbled bricks.

Picking her way across the uneven ground was slow but gave Deme a chance to study her surroundings, to feel without pushing too much into the consciousness of the Chimera. Hypersensitive to being manipulated now, Deme kept firm control of her mind and senses, determined to keep the beast at bay.

She kept a close eye on the tunnel expert, as well. Cal knew what was ahead. Dustin hadn't a clue. She and Cal had discussed it with the lieutenant and decided to stop short of their destination to keep the other man safe.

The closer they moved toward the center of campus, the heavier her steps, as though something pushed her down, making it harder and harder to move.

"You all right?" Dustin asked from behind.

"Yeah," Deme said, feeling anything but right.

"Should be an open area one hundred yards ahead right below the old foundation of Lion Hall."

Deme pushed forward, determined to get close enough to see what they were up against, without placing Cal or Dustin in the line of fire. Problem was, she didn't have any idea how close was too close.

A waft of air lifted the loose tendrils of her hair that had escaped the rubber band securing a ponytail at the back of her head. Dust particles stirred and floated in front of the chem lights. The closer they came to the foundation of Lion Hall, the stronger the wind current until the three were bent double, straining to take another step. They stayed close to enable them to see each other as the dust particles thickened.

"This isn't right!" Dustin yelled. "There shouldn't be this much air moving through the tunnel."

His words whipped away, but Deme heard them and agreed. She knew what was causing it, and it made her blood boil.

The Chimera was manipulating her sister's power.

At this point, they'd reached the end of the rope. Unless they unclipped, they couldn't go any farther.

Cal dropped back and grabbed Deme's shoulders. "This is as far as you two go."

"No way." She shook off his hands and tried to step around him, the wind slamming her backward into Dustin.

"This is getting too dangerous," Cal shouted above the gale ripping through the tunnel.

"It's my sister! She's in there!" Deme unclipped the D-ring from the rope, ducked around him and dashed forward, head tucked low, shoulder to the force pushing against her.

Chapter 16

Cal pointed to Dustin. "Stay here."

When he ripped the rope out of his D-ring and turned, he could barely see Deme disappearing into the swirling dust. He bent under the force of the wind pushing past him and hurried after her.

As he caught up, the blasting air pushed harder against him and the tunnel seemed to close in, his light nothing but a thin beam in the darkness.

Deme came to an abrupt stop at the end of the leg of tunnel. Roots climbed the arching walls, twisting and interlacing with each other to form a tight web, blocking their path.

Still pushing hard to catch up to Deme, Cal wasn't prepared for the sudden cessation of wind. He plowed into her, slamming her body into the web of roots blocking the passageway into the cavernous chamber below the expired Lion Hall.

He grabbed Deme and tugged at her, attempting to pull her away from the vines that had quickly wrapped around her wrists and ankles. Even as he yanked and jerked at the snagging vegetation, the roots inserted themselves between him and Deme, pushing him away as they pulled Deme forward.

Cal reached for the knife attached to his belt and hacked at the roots winding around Deme's wrists and ankles. As he sliced each one away, more appeared and replaced the damaged ones.

When a vine wrapped around his wrist, Cal caught the knife in his free hand and sliced it clean away from him. Before the plants could draw Deme through the web, Cal cut and hacked, finally yanking Deme free. Like a fireman running from a burning building, he hitched her up over his shoulder and hauled her several yards away, where he set her on her feet. When she lunged toward the web again, Cal wrapped his arms around her waist. "Deme, I won't let the Chimera have you."

Deme strained against Cal's arms, leaning toward the seething, slithering mass of living plant life. The roots and vines waved in the air, crawled ten feet into the tunnel and stopped, as though an invisible barrier barred their ability to spread.

"Please," she cried. "Let me go."

"It seems the Chimera is unable to manipulate your powers outside the perimeter ring of buildings surrounding the rose garden."

Deme swayed toward the cavern, her eyes glazed, her face pale. "Can you feel it?"

"Feel what?"

"The energy sucking me in. It's draining me, pulling me toward it."

"I've got you, babe, and I'm not letting go." He hugged her against his body, his wrists locked around her waist.

"You have to let me go. Aurai is in there. I know it. The Chimera used her power of wind to push us away."

"If it wants you to come now, why did it try to push you away? And why the web of roots blocking our approach to the Lion Hall foundation?"

"It wants me, not you." Deme's eyes closed. "Aurai is calling me. She's there." Her eyes opened and she clawed at Cal's arms. "Let me go. She's in there. Aurai is in there, and she's alive."

Cal clenched his teeth and held on tightly even as Deme's fingernails dug into his skin. "I can't let you go, Deme. You'll end up trapped just like Aurai."

"I have to get to her."

"We will. But we need to work it out with your sisters. The Chimera has too strong a pull on you. It defeated your younger sister. You're strong, but it has manipulated you, as well."

Deme ceased her struggles and looked up into Cal's eyes, tears shimmering in the meager light from the top of his helmet. "I can't abandon her."

"You're not. *We* are going to regroup and come back with a plan to free her. Right now I have to get you out of here."

"No!" she shouted, renewing her efforts to claw her way free of his arms. "I can't leave my sister."

"Deme!" Female voices sounded behind him. Cal and Deme ceased their struggles and turned as one to face the three sisters they'd left topside in the basement.

"I thought we told you to stay put." Deme planted her fists on her hips.

"We couldn't." Gina snorted. "We passed the tunnel expert a few minutes ago. He was shaking and scared."

Deme glared at her sisters. "What if the air down here wasn't breathable?"

"Obviously it is." Brigid started forward, her gaze moving past Deme to the wall of interlaced roots and vines blocking their entry into the area beneath where Lion Hall had once stood. "The Chimera wants us, doesn't it? I can feel its lure."

"Don't get too close," Deme warned. "It tried to drag me through but pushed Cal away." Deme tugged at Cal's hand holding her back from charging into the Chimera's lair.

He refused to release her hand in case the Chimera managed to make another grab for her.

Brigid pushed past Deme and Cal and stood as close as she could get to the blocked entrance without being snagged by the waiting vines. "Why you and not him?"

Gina joined them. "We have the power."

Selene stood behind Cal, her eyes wide, her face pale. "It wants our power."

"The Chimera already has Aurai's power. We can't risk it taking the rest of us."

"It would be catastrophic." Selene's voice shook.

Deme turned toward her brown-haired sister. "Do you know what would happen?"

Selene stared straight ahead, looking at neither her sisters nor Cal, her focus on something none of them could see. "If the Chimera has all our powers, it will be undefeatable."

"Then we won't let it have the rest." Brigid flicked her wrist, cupping her hand. "And we're taking Aurai back." A ball of flame erupted in her palm.

The flame startled Cal and he stepped backward, loosening his grip on Deme.

"No, Brigid. Don't use your powers." Deme made a dive for the entrance to the underground chamber beneath the rose garden.

As if sensing her approach, the vines and roots parted, lashing out to snag her wrists. "Damn!" Deme fought with all her might to free her arms and legs, twisting and kicking to push back the onslaught of vegetation dragging her into the Chimera's lair.

Cal reached for his knife as he ran for Deme.

Before he got more than three feet, Brigid put out a hand, stopping him. "Let me."

"No!" Deme yelled. "Remember what happened to Gina."

His hand on the hilt of his sheathed knife, all Cal could do was watch.

With the ball of fire swirling in her palm, Brigid reared back like an all-star pitcher and launched the fireball into the web in front of Deme.

The roots shrank back, absorbing the fireball, and then with a whoosh of air, they shot it back at the people standing in the tunnel.

Gina ducked, and Selene cried out and fell against the side wall.

Cal dove for the uneven floor, his knee crashing against a fallen brick, sending a sharp pain lancing up his leg.

The fireball ricocheted off the ceiling and bounced back and forth from side to side on the walls, growing in size and intensity, filling the gap behind them, creating an impenetrable wall of fire. Heat built in the confines of the tunnel.

Cal glanced up at the piping carrying natural gas

throughout the city. If the pipes grew too hot, they'd explode, possibly leaving a gaping hole in the Chicago cityscape. "We have to get out of here before the gas lines blow."

Deme screamed as vines slithered around her neck and sucked her toward the interior of the chamber. Her cry ended as the air was cut off to her windpipes, the creeper cinching tighter around her throat.

Cal pushed to his feet, yanking his knife from the scabbard. He attacked the vines, slicing them in two and pulling them away from Deme's throat.

Brigid's hand curled again.

"Don't!" Selene and Gina yelled.

Another vine snaked out and snagged Brigid's wrist before she could wind up another fireball.

The vines and roots dragged her toward the chamber. She fought them off, but for every one she freed herself from, two more appeared and wrapped around her limbs.

His hand wielding the knife as fast as he could, Cal cut away at the deadly plant life threatening Deme and Brigid.

Gina and Selene crowded against his back, the heat intensifying, edging closer.

"We'll be burned alive if we stay here." Selene buried her face in her arms, the glow of the fire making her skin red.

Gina raised her hands, closed her eyes and whispered something Cal couldn't hear.

Too busy hacking away at the vegetation intertwining around the other two women, Cal couldn't tell what was happening with the sisters at his side until a sudden swoosh sounded beside him.

His arms tiring, Cal sliced into the last vine holding Deme hostage and he shoved her behind him. He turned to Brigid and cut a root holding her wrist. When he had her free, he pushed her back, as well. The vines turned on him and lashed out.

Cal backed away, his feet splashing through ankle-deep water.

"Gina, what did you do?" Deme shouted.

"I don't know. I only wanted to put out the fire so we wouldn't burn to death."

"Hang on to something," Selene warned.

Cal turned in time to see a wall of water bearing down on them. "Grab the pipes or cables. Don't let it suck you into the chamber."

All four women wrapped their arms and legs around the pipes on the sides of the walls or ceilings.

Cal had barely enough time to latch on to the pipe above him before the wave slammed into him, nearly yanking his hand free. The tunnel around them filled with water, covering the tops of their heads.

Miraculously, the light on his helmet continued to glow an eerie yellow in the swirling fluid. Cal kicked his feet, pushing himself upward to the roof of the tunnel, where he gulped in air. Then he submerged and checked for the women. Gina was closest. Selene's dark hair swirled like black ink in the murky water. Deme kicked and fought to reach the pocket of air above her head and Brigid swam toward him, working her way back through the tunnel.

Cal moved aside and gave Brigid a push to send her on her way. He grabbed Gina and shoved her after Brigid. Selene floated toward him, her face pale, her eyes wide. He squeezed her hand as he pushed her after her sisters. Deme clung to the pipe above, her head tipped back, her mouth and nose pressed against the roof. A ghostly white root slipped through the water toward her.

Cal yelled, the sound muffled by the liquid. He bunched his legs and thrust himself toward her, cleaving through the water, his lungs burning with the need to breathe. He reached Deme at the same time as the root did.

He grabbed Deme and shoved her after her sisters, the movement sending him backward toward the chamber entrance, right into the clutches of the root.

With the ease of a snake, it slipped around his ankle.

Desperate to breathe, Cal kicked and fought to reach the roof and the pocket of air. But the root yanked him down, refusing to let him surface even for a moment.

He'd lost his knife in the blast of water. Cal had nothing to defend himself from the Chimera's hold on him. If he didn't get air soon, he'd die.

Several yards down the tunnel, Deme emerged from the water and slid across the floor into her sisters' legs. "What the hell just happened?"

Brigid, Gina and Selene reached for her and hauled her to her feet. "The Chimera used Gina's water against us."

"Cal?" Deme spun to face a wall of water, held in place by the force of a being far beyond her limited powers and comprehension.

Selene shook her head. "He hasn't come out yet."

"Damn!" Deme's heart raced, her breathing coming in gasps. She couldn't lose Cal. Not now. She cared too much about him. Hell, she loved him.

Deme shook off her sisters' hands.

"Don't, Deme," Brigid yelled. "He can get out on his own."

"And I should stand here and wait?" Deme sucked in a deep breath and dove back into the water. The light from her helmet provided a narrow beam in the cloudy water.

She swam as fast as she could, using the sides of the walls and the floor to kick off, propelling her forward.

Where was he? Her chest hurt, her lungs desperate for air. Light reflected off something shiny on the tunnel floor. Deme recognized Cal's knife, scooping it up as she swam forward. If the vines had him in their clutches, he didn't have a way to fight them off.

When she finally caught a glimpse of Cal, he was thrashing around in the water, kicking against a thick root that had him by the ankle.

Careful to stay far enough away to keep from being caught up in the same trap, Deme reached for Cal, pressing the knife into his flailing hand.

As quickly as she handed it to him, he sliced through the root and kicked free, bumping into her as he pushed farther away from the web of vines and roots.

Not until he'd gotten several yards away from the wicked vegetation did he swim to the top of the tunnel. Deme joined him, gasping in huge gulps of air. "I thought you were right behind me," she said between breaths.

"I would have been." He grabbed her hand and squeezed, letting go almost immediately. "Ready? Let's get back."

Deme dragged in another deep breath and pushed off the wall, headed back to where her sisters waited.

The farther they moved from Lion Hall, the more shallow the water became until they emerged on their feet, slogging through the tunnel toward Selene, Brigid and Gina. They stood in the dark, their irises contracting as the lights from Cal's and Deme's helmets illuminated their surroundings.

The sisters fell on Deme, hugging her close. "We thought you weren't going to make it out." Gina hugged her so tightly, Deme couldn't breathe.

"But I did." Deme looked back toward the chamber. The water had drained away. The passage appeared as it had when she and Cal had first walked down it what seemed like a lifetime ago.

"We have to go back." Deme took a step back that way. "I can still feel Aurai in there."

"Me, too," Selene whispered.

Cal blocked the tunnel, his feet braced wide, his arms crossed over his chest. "You're not going back. Not now."

"But we have to," Deme insisted. Aurai's voice called to her, desperate, afraid.

"No." Cal twisted her around and slung her over his shoulder. Ducking as low as he could, he ran back down the tunnel.

The wind picked up, this time clutching at him like a giant hand trying to suck them back toward the garden and the subterranean levels below the foundation of Lion Hall.

Deme bounced along, the air whooshing out of her lungs with each jarring step Cal took. Her sisters ran behind them, keeping pace.

When Cal reached Dustin Zoeller, he shouted, "Get out of here!"

Dustin, eyes wide, his face pale, spun on his heels and ran back in the direction of the student commons basement where they'd entered this maze.

When they reached the vertical tunnel, Dustin didn't

slow, but grabbed the steel bars of the ladder and pulled himself up, his monitor bumping against the rails.

Cal dropped Deme to her feet and turned her toward the ladder rungs. "Go, Deme. Get out of here. Now."

She hesitated.

Cal lifted her hand and curled it around the ladder sides. "Please." He kissed her neck, his hands cupping her butt, then he shoved her up the ladder.

Pushing her every step of the way, Cal arrived at the top, breathing hard and exhausted.

Deme's sisters emerged behind them, all of them talking at once.

Beyond her endurance and fresh out of steam, Deme swayed, her eyes rolling backward in her head. Before she could respond to any of her sister's questions or concerns, she fell, darkness consuming her.

Cal was there, scooping her up into his arms.

"Is she going to be all right?" Lieutenant Warner asked.

"I don't know." Cal stared down at Deme, lying limp in his arms.

"I tried to keep the other women out, but they wouldn't be deterred." Marty glared at the sisters. "What happened down there?"

Cal snorted, hitching Deme higher in his arms. "The Chattox women are a force unto themselves."

"Holy crap!" Dustin Zoeller joined them, ripping his mask off the top of his head and throwing it to the ground. "I've never seen that kind of wind in the tunnels before." He shook his head. "It shouldn't be that strong. I don't get it." Then for the first time he noticed the others were soaking wet. "How did you get all wet?"

"Slipped in a puddle." Cal locked gazes with the lieutenant, unwilling to enlighten the tunnel expert. The fewer people who knew what was going on beneath the city streets, the better off the residents of Chicago. They couldn't afford a mass panic and the resulting exodus that could cause more deaths than the Chimera could achieve on the campus of Colyer-Fenton College. "We need to get Deme and her sisters away from here."

"I know where we can take her." Brigid nodded toward the steps leading out of the basement. "Let's get her to my apartment. It's only a couple miles from campus. Far enough away that nothing here can affect us." She closed her eyes and drew in a deep breath before opening them again. "I feel it even as we stand here."

Cal would rather have taken her to his apartment, but he didn't want to fight the three sisters, whose worried expressions indicated they wouldn't let him waltz away with Deme.

"We can go in my SUV." Gina hurried up the stairs, followed by Cal and Deme. The other two sisters brought up the rear.

When they arrived in the parking lot next to Gina's midsize four-door SUV, Deme's eyes blinked open. "What… Where am I?"

Cal gave her a wry grin. "We're getting you the hell off campus."

"Put me down." She struggled ineffectually against Cal's arms around her.

He shook his head. "No way."

"Why are you carrying me, anyway?" She glared at him and then noticed her sisters standing in a circle around her. "Why are you all staring at me?"

"You passed out, sis." Brigid grabbed the keys from Gina's hand and clicked the button to unlock the door. "We're getting you away from campus so we can discuss what happened and what we plan to do next."

"I felt her." Deme fought against Cal's hold, but he held tighter. "Aurai's down there. We can't leave her there."

"And we can't afford for the Chimera to take another one of us." Selene laid a hand against the side of Deme's face. "Remember, you don't always have to take care of us. We're in this together. Let's make this a group decision and effort."

"We can stand around arguing, or we can get moving." Brigid jerked open the car door. "Either way, you're coming with us. We can talk when we get to my place."

Cal squeezed Deme and set her inside the car in the front passenger seat. "I'll be right behind you."

She looked up at him and nodded, her forehead wrinkled in a stubborn frown. "I'm counting on it."

Selene climbed in the backseat and Gina in the driver's seat. Brigid mounted her Harley.

As the SUV drove away, followed by the motorcycle, Lieutenant Warner joined Cal. "I expect a full report." He held up a hand to stem the flow of words Cal had poised on the tip of his tongue. "I know…after you've had a chance to calm Deme down."

"Thank you, sir."

"I think it's time to evacuate campus. To hell with what the college president might say."

"Good idea." Cal looked back at Colyer-Fenton. With the sun hidden behind a bank of gray clouds, the campus looked hunkered down, ready to weather a tempest. As if sensing an impending storm, students hurried across the manicured lawns, clutching their books to their chests to keep papers from flying out in the rising wind.

Even as Cal observed, the wind increased, neither

from the west nor the east, but seeming to come from all around, swirling toward the center of campus and the rose garden where Lion Hall once stood.

Cal nodded again. "Yeah, get the students out."

"I'm on it." Lieutenant Warner wrapped his coat around him and charged back toward the administration building and the office of Dr. Diane Masterson.

Cal slung his leg over his motorcycle seat and reached down to insert his key in the ignition.

A slender hand reached out and grabbed his.

His heart slammed against his chest and his gaze shot up to capture the brown-eyed stare of a student he should know, but couldn't quite place.

"You're Deme Jones's boyfriend, aren't you?"

On the verge of correcting Deme's last name, Cal bit hard on his tongue and nodded, maintaining his cover story.

The girl threaded her fingers together. "Is she going to be all right?"

"Yeah."

"Tell her Rachel said hello and that I hope she feels better soon." Rachel stared down at her clasped hands. "And not to worry. I'll make it right."

Before Cal could ask her what she meant by that, she turned and ran back toward the Gamma Omega dormitory.

Cal glanced to where Gina's car had already disappeared around the street corner headed for the campus exit. He kick-started his motorcycle and drove after Gina's car. As he neared the edge of the parking lot, his gaze shifted back behind him to the girl who'd identified herself as Rachel. If he had it right, she was the young woman whose boyfriend almost raped her near the garden over Lion Hall.

Torn between following the student and following Deme, Cal turned his bike around and parked it. If the girl had any intention of going up against the Chimera, he had to stop her.

Deme had her sisters to look out for her. This college coed had no one and, from what Deme had told him in the early hours of the morning, even her sorority sisters had turned against her when she'd quit taking the potion they'd concocted to make them beautiful.

His mind with Deme and her sisters, Cal dismounted from his Harley and hurried after Rachel.

Cal had stepped into the Gamma Omega dorm and stopped the first girl who passed him. The girl had light blond hair pulled back with a headband, every hair in place. She wore a short jean skirt and a cotton-candy pink tube top that exposed more of her midriff than it covered.

Cal cringed. Another Zoe clone. "Where can I find Rachel Taylor?"

"Men aren't allowed in a girl's dorm without an escort." The blonde's perfect brows arched. "Besides, you're too old for her." She flounced away without having answered his question.

When he turned to find another girl to ask, Zoe Adams stood before him, her head tipped slightly to the side. "That seems to be the sixty-five-thousand-dollar question. When you find Miss Rachel, tell her I'm looking for her." Zoe's eyes narrowed into thin slits. "She has something that belongs to me."

"Me, too." Another girl joined Zoe, then another, and another until the hallway filled with angry Zoe clones.

Cal knew when he should cut his losses. If he really thought Rachel was in the dorm, he might push past the phalanx of beautiful women to find the ugly duckling.

But since they were looking for her, too, he decided to look elsewhere.

"Thank you, ladies." Cal tipped an imaginary hat and backed out of the building, pushing through a throng of girls who'd crowded in behind him.

Dr. Masterson hurried toward the dorm, her serviceable low heels clicking on the concrete sidewalk. "Mr. Black, perhaps you could help me clear the boys' dormitory. Lieutenant Warner insisted the students were in danger and should be evacuated at once."

"Yes, ma'am, I'll get right on it."

She paused, her brows pulling together. "You're working with him, aren't you?"

Cal was past needing a cover for his work. "Yes, ma'am."

"Well, I'm certain you'll see to the boys' safety then, won't you?"

Without waiting for his response, she hurried into the Gamma Omega dorm, shouting to the girls as she went.

Cal jogged away from the circle of buildings at the center of campus to the boys' dormitory. Inside, some of the guys had already received word of the evacuation via text message from other students across campus.

Young men streamed out of the dormitory toward the parking lot, carrying suitcases and laundry bags. He tasked one guy per floor to knock on the doors and make sure the dorm was empty before leaving. Once he'd set the evacuation of the boys' dorm in motion, he resumed his search for Rachel, the clock ticking away the minutes since the time he'd told Deme he'd be right behind her.

He returned to the Gamma Omega dormitory one more time to see if Rachel had returned to gather her belongings.

When he stepped through the doors, the dorm was a flurry of activity. All the doors were open and girls shouted across the hallway as they shoved clothing into suitcases.

With no sign of Zoe or a blockade of girls to obstruct his passage, Cal raced up the stairs to the second floor where Deme's room had been. Hadn't she said Rachel had been her sister's roommate and hadn't their room been on the same floor as Deme's?

A scream ripped through the hallway.

Cal raced toward the sound.

A door blasted open and a girl with dirty-blond hair and a pockmarked face stumbled through, her hands covering her cheeks, tears streaming from her eyes. "Where is it? I need more."

Cal grabbed her arms and made her focus on him. "Where is what? What do you need?"

"The vial, the blue vial with the potion. I need it, can't you see?" She clawed at her face, her jagged fingernails leaving deep scrapes across her already scarred skin, blood oozing from the wounds. "I can't go back. I won't go back to being pathetic."

"You're not pathetic. You're human and beautiful in your own right."

"Shut up." She shook his hands free and ran toward the stairs. "Zoe, help me. Make me beautiful again."

Cal stood in the middle of the hallway for a moment longer, then turned to face a door with the words *Rachel Must Die* written across it in black Magic Marker.

What the hell?

He grabbed the knob and tried to open the door. It was locked from the inside. With heavy, metal door frames, no amount of banging against it would open it.

Then he remembered the master key on his assigned key ring. He quickly opened the door and pushed it open.

The room was a wreck. Black fabric lay in shreds across the room, drawers had been emptied onto the floor and everything in the closet was scattered across the room.

Cal's stomach took a steep dive.

The window stood wide open, wind flapping the thin curtains hanging on each side.

He ran across the floor and stuck his head through, expecting the worst. When he looked directly below the window, he let out the breath he'd been holding in a whoosh. "Thank God."

He'd expected to see Rachel's broken body lying in the bushes. But the bushes remained as they had been before all the commotion began. And he still hadn't found her. Based on the cries of the other occupants of the dormitory, she might have found the vials of potion Deme had told him about that made the girls beautiful. If he didn't find Rachel before the sorority sisters did, the Chimera would be the least of her worries.

Cal left the room and raced to Deme's room, peering out her window into the garden below. No Rachel. The garden was empty, appearing calm, serene, no sign of the beast beneath the manicured grass.

If he didn't find the coed soon, he was sure Deme and her sisters would launch some half-cocked plan before he could get to them and inject a voice of reason. Cal left Deme's room and took the stairs to the lower floor, leaping the last four steps entirely. Rachel was nowhere to be found. Where would she have gone? He headed for the student commons. Maybe she'd gone for a bite to eat.

He frowned. Rachel didn't know about the trapdoor

in the basement, did she? His footsteps quickened until he was jogging across the campus.

An employee stood outside the glass doors of the student commons, twisting a key in the metal lock. "Sorry, got orders from the big boss, we're shutting down and evacuating campus."

"I'm maintenance staff. Are you sure everyone's out?" Cal looked over the worker's shoulder into the open bay lined with tables, the chairs scattered haphazardly as though they'd been vacated in a hurry.

"Positive."

"Did you check the basement?" Cal pulled the ring of building keys from his pocket.

"Why would I check the basement? Only staff goes down there." The employee nodded toward Cal's key ring. "You have keys, check it out yourself. I'm out of here." The young man turned toward the parking lot. "Just lock up when you leave. I don't want to get blamed if someone loots the place."

Cal didn't bother to respond, wasting precious moments finding the right key to unlock the door. Once inside, he dodged in and out of the tables and dashed through the kitchen to the rear of the building where the door led down to the basement. He ran down the stairs, arriving at the bottom, his heart racing. Where the hell was Rachel?

Chapter 17

Deme sat at the diminutive dining table in Brigid's apartment. Despite Brigid's tough-as-nails exterior, her apartment made up for it in feminine decorations, ranging from impressionistic landscapes to fluffy floral throw pillows on the white leather couch. Brigid was a contradiction, the one sister Deme could never quite connect with. The leather and motorcycle riding screamed nonconformity and a harsh demeanor.

Yet her apartment was her realm of peace and tranquility.

"You realize this is the first time I've been to your apartment?" Deme commented.

Brigid shrugged. "Kind of hard to visit when you're in St. Croix."

Deme's lips pressed together and she stared across at her second-oldest sister. "I know. I'm sorry. I deserted you. I deserted all of you."

"Why?" Brigid stepped forward, her fists balanced on her hips. "Were you ashamed of us?"

"No, never."

"Then were you ashamed of what we were? What we are?"

"In a way, yes. As much as Aurai wanted to live a normal life and attend college like any other nineteen-year-old, I wanted to live a normal life, too. But I knew I couldn't."

"So you ran away?" Brigid snorted. "Apparently being the oldest doesn't make you the wisest."

"I didn't say what I did was right. I'm just saying I had to do it at the time."

Selene stood behind Deme and laid a hand on her shoulder. "Because of Detective Black?"

Deme turned in her seat to face the sister who seemed to see right through her. Selene's image swam before her in a pool of tears welling in Deme's eyes. "I couldn't be with him, knowing he wouldn't understand who and what we are."

"And now?"

Deme huffed, a single tear slipping down her cheek. "He's handling it just fine."

"Did you ever think of giving yourself a chance? Giving him a chance?" Brigid rolled her eyes. "For the oldest and smartest, you're pretty dumb sometimes."

Deme smiled at Brigid, pushing her damp hair out of her face. "You got that right. I wasted an entire year thinking I was doing the right thing when I could have been…" She gulped back a sob.

"With him," Gina finished. "And we almost lost him today to the Chimera."

"Which brings up another issue. I don't want him involved in this anymore."

"Sorry, chica," Brigid quipped. "He's in up to his neck. You're not going to keep him out of it. Hell, wild elephants couldn't keep him away. In case you haven't noticed, he's in love with you."

Deme's face heated, an image of them lying naked in his apartment flaring in her memory. Yeah, they were highly compatible in bed, but could they build a relationship on lust alone? "I'll be glad when we get Aurai back and things get back to normal."

Gina snorted. "What is normal?"

Deme sucked in a breath and let it out. "You're right. I don't think we were destined to lead normal lives. Any of us who think we can are sadly mistaken."

Though he seemed to be handling the witch thing well, would it all catch up to Cal and overwhelm him when they finally got Aurai back, took care of the Chimera and life returned to a semblance of normalcy?

"Time's wasting." Selene slapped a heavy volume in the middle of the table, her normally sweet expression one of intensity. Her ice-blue eyes glowed with a light of challenge and determination. "We have to defeat the Chimera in order to get our little sister back."

"Right." Deme stood, pushing her chair back from the table, giving all four sisters space to gather around the *Book of Spells* their mother had given into their keeping. Deme had left it with Brigid when she'd gone to live in St. Croix. As much as she'd tried to divorce herself of her heritage, she couldn't.

Deme laid her hand on the leather binder. Brigid laid hers down on top of Deme's then Gina and Selene added theirs until all four sisters' hands rested on the book their mother had bequeathed to them. Together they closed their eyes and chanted.

"Feel the power

Free our hearts
Find our way
Be the one
With the strength of the earth
With the rising of the wind
With the calm of the water
With the intensity of fire
With the freedom of spirit
The goddess is within us
She is power
We are her
We are one
Blessed Be."

A surge of energy built beneath Deme's hand until it blasted through her, slinging their arms up and away from the book.

The tome flipped open, one page at a time, slowly at first, building in speed until the pages fluttered, creating a breeze.

Deme stood back with her sisters, watching and waiting. No one dared speak until the pages drifted to a stop, halfway through the book.

As one, each sister leaned over the book to read.

"*To free the Spellbound,*'" Deme read aloud.

"*Give shape to the victim*
with the bones of a rat
Give voice to the trapped
with the scream of bat
Give substance and life
with the seed of a thistle
Then cast out your troubles
Repeat on a whisper
The call to the caged
of all shapes and size

Repeat it five times
and watch your quarry rise
With the strength of the earth
With the rising of the wind
With the calm of the water
With the intensity of fire
With the freedom of spirit
Rise from the darkness
take shape in the light
come to our sisters
bring substance to might
When the ground thunders
it will rise through the rift
Capture it quickly
Before the grounds shift.'"

Deme glanced up at her sisters.

Brigid gave voice to the question in all their faces. "We save her without facing the Chimera?"

"No!" Selene shook her head. "We shouldn't play with magic."

"How else will we get to Aurai? We can't fight the Chimera. It's too strong." Selene pressed her fingers to her temples. "We can't." Her face scrunched in pain.

Deme lifted her sister's chin. "Why?"

"The other sisters…the ones that died…they say it's too dangerous."

"I say we go for it. Aurai's been down there long enough." Gina entered Brigid's kitchenette and opened her pantry door. "What have you got in here? Any rat bones or bat screams?"

"I'm with Gina. Aurai's been gone long enough." Brigid stared across at Deme. "I have everything you left in my care. Unlike you, I didn't plan on ignoring that part of my life."

Deme hugged her sister. "Once again, you prove to be the smarter sister. Thank you."

As she pulled away, Brigid's cheeks flushed.

Deme stood back and looked at each of her sisters. "Are we in this together?"

Gina and Brigid gave a resounding "Yes!"

Which left Selene.

"I want to believe this is the right thing to do." Tears trickled down her sister's face. "But the voices in my head are screaming for us not to. They want us to go away and never come back."

"Not an option." Deme shook her head. "We can't leave Aurai."

Selene wiped the moisture from her face and straightened. "No. We can't."

Deme went to work. "Mom didn't want us to use this stuff until we were good and ready. She didn't even want us to look through it. I have no idea if we have the ingredients we need to perform the spell."

"We have everything but the bat. And I know where we can get one of those on the way." Brigid's voice sounded confident. When the other sisters all looked at her, she shrugged. "I catalogued everything. I'm anal, so sue me."

Gina grinned and hugged Brigid. "Let's get our sister out of there."

"Damn right." Brigid switched the light on in the small pantry and reached to the top of the shelf to grab a bag labeled Rat Bones. She grabbed another labeled Thistle Seeds.

Brigid disappeared for five minutes to the top of the apartment building, returning with a bagged bat. "Don't ask how I knew it was there."

Ingredients in hand, including the live bat, the sisters returned to the Colyer-Fenton campus as the sun set.

For the first time since their mother's death, Deme felt closer to her sisters than ever. Between the five of them, they'd survive and overcome the power of the Chimera.

As Deme stepped out of Gina's SUV, the sun had set and a fat new moon slipped up the horizon, glowing a deep orange. "Ladies, do you realize the fall equinox is upon us?"

Gina reached into the SUV and pulled out the sack with the bags of ingredients and one live bat. "We will give thanks to the goddess for our bounty and for our family."

"Once we have Aurai back in our arms," Selene amended.

"Right." Brigid looked around. "Where to? The tunnels?"

Deme shook her head. "No. We return to where it all started."

"Can we go to the garden without being captured by the Chimera?"

Deme handed each sister a thumb-size leather pouch attached to a leather strap. "Put these around your necks."

Gina draped the charm over her head. "When did you have time to make a protection charm?"

"I didn't. I found these in a jar in Brigid's pantry. Mom must have made one for each of us. Seeing as our pentagrams aren't protecting us like they had in the past, I thought a little added boost might help." She slipped hers over her head and held one more in her hand. "This one was for Aurai."

"She might not be where she is now if she had been

wearing it." Selene's voice quietly echoed the thoughts Deme had had when she'd found the charms.

"We can't change the past, but we can shape our future if we choose." Deme set off for the garden, wondering where Cal had gone. He'd said he'd catch up to them and yet he hadn't even left campus. His motorcycle stood where they'd left him over an hour earlier.

With her sisters ready to take on the Chimera for possession of Aurai, she didn't dare take time out to look for him. She prayed to the goddess he was all right.

With the comforting softness of the leather pouch resting between her breasts, Deme lifted the latch of the garden gate between the Gamma Omega dorm and the student commons. The campus appeared deserted. No kids standing around chatting, exchanging notes or flirting with each other. No one hurried to a night class.

A chill shivered along the surface of her skin. She could have sworn there had been a chain and lock securing the garden the last time she was there.

Brigid nodded toward a bush where a chain, a heavy set of bolt cutters and a severed lock lay almost out of sight. "Someone beat us here."

Deme held her hands out to each side. The sisters joined hands in a circle. "We may only have one shot at this before the Chimera tries to take us down."

Gina nodded. "Hit hard and fast. Got it."

"And don't use your regular powers," Selene added.

Brigid nodded. "Yup. That's suicide."

Deme gave a short, sharp bark of laughter. "Like what we're about to do isn't?" She looked around at the familiar faces, her heart swelling inside her chest. "I love you guys."

"Ditto." Brigid's normal tough voice broke. She

squared her leather-clad shoulders and said, "Let's go get our sister."

Deme led the charge, carrying the ingredients, her gaze panning the grounds for live roots and vines ready to claim her and reel her into the Chimera's lair. Strangely, no obstacles blocked their path or tried to grab them.

"I smell a trap," Gina commented from Deme's left.

"I smell gasoline." Selene pointed ahead. "We have company."

In the center of the garden, Rachel Taylor shook a plastic gas jug over a pile of robes and little blue vials. "Die, you son of a bitch! Whatever you are. I hope you burn in hell!" Tears streamed down her face and gasoline splashed across her jeans and shirt.

Rachel flung the jug to the ground and pulled a matchbook from her pocket.

Deme's breath caught in her throat. If the Chimera didn't get her, her attempt to incinerate the trappings of the Gamma Omega's foray into witchcraft could include herself. "Rachel, don't!" Deme ran forward.

"I have to do this. I have to stop it from hurting anyone ever again." Rachel struck a match. "We need to be proud of who we are, not ashamed. This is for all the ugly girls dying to become beautiful." The match dropped to the pile of robes and flames leaped into the air, spreading everywhere the gasoline soaked.

A finger of fire raced across the garden lawn and up Rachel's leg.

The girl screamed and backed away from the bonfire growing in size and intensity.

Deme hit Rachel in a flying tackle, pushing her away from the trail of fire. In a desperate attempt to douse the flames, Deme rolled Rachel in the dirt, the flames on her pants and shirt refusing to extinguish until they had thoroughly burned through the fuel feeding them.

Gina joined her, yanking at the girl's shirt, pulling it up over her head.

Rachel screamed and fought to be free, her eyes rolling back in her head, fear and pain making her movements frantic, her young body strong in her effort to be free of the sisters.

Brigid removed her leather jacket and dropped it over Rachel's flaming pant legs, using it as a hot pad to remove the girl's jeans.

When they had her out of the burning clothes, Deme jumped to her feet and hauled Rachel up with the help of her sisters. "Get out of here! Get out while you can."

Brigid draped her jacket over Rachel's shoulders and the sisters pushed her toward the gate, shoving her through and pulling it closed behind her. Then leaning her back against the gate to keep Rachel from pushing through again, Deme shouted to her sisters, "Give me your hands." She grabbed Gina's hand and Brigid's. Gina and Brigid clasped hands, completing a circle of three, and Deme closed her eyes.

She said a silent prayer to the goddess of earth to protect the gate and keep it closed. When Deme opened her eyes, vines were pushing up through the earth, intertwining around the bars of the wrought-iron fence, wrapping around the gate to keep anyone from opening it to come in or out.

With Rachel safely outside the Chimera's range, Deme, Gina and Brigid turned back to the center of the garden.

Selene had gathered the fallen bags of ingredients and the cloth sack with the live bat, then walked toward the fire, her footsteps slow, measured, trancelike.

"What the hell is she doing?" Deme asked. "She needs to wait for the rest of us."

"Wait, Selene!" Brigid ran ahead and laid her hand on her sister's shoulder.

Selene didn't look at her, just shrugged loose and continued toward the fire.

"The Chimera must be manipulating her." Gina broke into a sprint, racing across the lawn, Deme in close pursuit.

Brigid tried to wrest the bags from her hands, but Selene wouldn't let go. Then she was running toward the fire, her pace quickening with each step.

Brigid reached her first and grabbed her around the waist to hold her back from throwing herself into the fire. She stopped her just in time. But she couldn't stop her from tossing the bags into the flames.

"No!" Brigid lunged for the bags, but she couldn't let go of Selene to save them from being burned. An agonizing, high-pitched scream filled the air as the live bat was consumed by flames.

Gina grabbed Selene and pulled her farther away from the fire. "Selene. Snap out of it. Don't succumb to the Chimera. He's using you."

Selene blinked and stared at her sister as if seeing her for the first time. "What do you mean? What's happening?"

Brigid stared into the fire where the bags had disintegrated beneath red-hot flames. "That's it? Did we just lose our last shot at getting Aurai out of this alive?"

"No." Deme grabbed her sister's hands. "The Chimera won't win. It won't keep our sister. The ingredients are there. We just need to say the spell. Do it now, before the Chimera can stop us!"

"But we don't have Aurai to complete our circle," Gina cried.

Deme turned to Selene. "Can you reach her? Can you call to Aurai and let her know we need her?"

Selene squinted, a frown drawing her brows together. "The other sisters are warning me. They say we are making a mistake."

"We have to get our sister out of there," Deme reminded her. "We have to do whatever it takes."

Selene shook her head. "They want us to leave, to get out now while we can."

The fire behind them flared higher, the heat bearing down on them.

"Bullshit," Brigid said. "We're not leaving without Aurai."

Using her best calm voice when all she wanted to do was scream, Deme entreated her sister, "Selene, ask them to help."

Selene closed her eyes, the frown on her forehead smoothing. "I feel Aurai's presence, and the sisters are here, too."

"About damned time," Brigid muttered. "Let's do it."

With one last look around the garden, Deme searched for the angry vines, sudden tidal waves or flash fires they'd been up against before. Nothing stirred and the fire behind them slowly died.

A stillness settled over the garden, so still not even a cricket dared to chirp.

Slowly at first Deme chanted the spell, her sisters joining in until their voices sounded in unison, growing in strength and determination.

"With the strength of the earth
With the rising of the wind
With the calm of the water

With the intensity of fire
With the freedom of spirit
Rise from the darkness
take shape in the light
come to our sisters
bring substance to might."

The four sisters repeated the chant five times. With each repetition, the air around them thickened.

When they finished, Deme said a silent prayer to the goddess and opened her eyes, hoping beyond hope she'd find her youngest sister standing in front of her.

For a long moment, the garden remained still, an energy she couldn't see building, rising in intensity.

Wind blew in from the east and twisted in a circle around the sisters, forming a funnel and rising higher into the night toward the full moon. In the middle of the funnel a ghostly image appeared, a girl in a black robe, with long, flowing blond hair.

"Aurai!" Deme wanted to reach up to grab for her sister, but she couldn't break the ring of truth she and her sisters formed with their hands. All they could do was watch as she rose higher, her image solidifying.

Then the wind died down, lowering the sister until her feet touched the ground.

Aurai's legs crumpled beneath her and she fell in a heap of black robes and blond hair at the sisters' feet.

Deme, Brigid, Gina and Selene broke the circle and rushed forward.

When they gently rolled her over on her back, her eyes blinked open and she whispered, "I knew you would come."

"Thank the goddess, you're okay." Deme hugged her sister, tears running down her cheeks. She couldn't believe it had been as easy as that. All they'd had to do was work a spell and their sister was back among them. She hugged her sister again and sat back to give Brigid and Gina a chance to be with her.

Selene stood back from the group, hovering around Aurai, her eyes wide, her face pale. "Deme."

Deme frowned. "What is it, Selene?"

"We have a problem." She swayed, her eyes blinking closed and open again. "We've made a terrible mistake."

"What do you mean?" Deme rose to join her sister, looping an arm around her shoulders.

Selene shook, her teeth chattering in her head. "We have to stop it."

"Stop what?"

The wind that had delivered Aurai lifted the hair around Deme's face in a gentle fluff. Then it swirled again, twisting around the five sisters on the garden lawn.

"It's coming." Selene stepped back, her face tilting to the heavens. The trees in the garden swayed and lashed out in a frenzy, bending nearly double in the gale-force winds.

Clouds blocked the full moon, darkening the sky. Then they opened up and rain pounded down on the women, hard, heavy drops that slapped against Deme's face, stingingly painful. The rain came in sideways, joining the whirling funnel. The fire Rachel had started flared.

The twisting wind shifted over the flames and added their power to the building tempest. In the midst of the fire, rain and wind, an image grew and grew until it was twice the size of a tour bus.

Deme sucked in a deep breath and let it out. "By the goddess, what have we done?"

Chapter 18

The trapdoor to the tunnels stood open, the vertical tunnel a gaping, dark maw. Someone had gone down recently, might even still be down there.

Cal leaned over the black hole. "Rachel?"

No one responded and he couldn't see anything in the abyss. Without a flashlight, he'd be of no use.

Too much time had passed since he'd last seen Deme. The fool woman wouldn't wait for him to join her before she made her next move against the Chimera. Cal could only hope her sisters would hold her back, talk sense into her—make her wait until he could get to her.

Cal ran up the stairs to the kitchen and searched cabinets, drawers and a broom closet before he located a flashlight that worked. Back down in the basement, he tied the flashlight to his belt loop with a thin strap and climbed onto the ladder.

Although it had been only a couple hours since he'd

been down in the tunnels, it felt like a lifetime. And he didn't want to go down now any more than he had wanted to go then. But he had to suck it up to save Rachel from doing something completely stupid. Having seen what the Chimera was capable of, Cal knew one girl didn't stand a chance against it. Much as he'd rather be with Deme, she would want him to take care of Rachel first.

He lowered himself down the ladder, moving as quickly as possible. When he reached the horizontal shaft, he ran in the direction of the Chimera's lair. He slipped once on crumbled bricks and nearly twisted his ankle tripping over the abandoned railroad tracks. On the final turn toward the foundation to Lion Hall, he saw a light ahead—a woman's body silhouetted by its glow.

"Rachel!"

The figure paused for a moment, and the light bounced away from him. She was running toward the Chimera's lair.

Cal leaped over a rail switch and ran down the tracks, fearing he wouldn't be able to stop her in time.

Halfway to her, a roaring rumble filled the tunnel and the walls trembled. A blast of wind sucked Cal forward, lifting him off his feet. He'd been running full sprint, and with the added force shoving him along, he couldn't slow down fast enough to stop his headlong rush. The ground beneath his feet shifted so sharply, the force threw Cal forward. He tumbled, falling to his knees, rolling head over heels in a painful somersault. The flashlight flew from his hands, light bouncing then blinking out three feet from where Cal came to a jolting landing.

His head throbbed, probably from hitting the train

railing. It hurt to breathe, indicating a bruised or broken rib, and his ankle ached, but he could move. Cal patted the ground in the direction he'd seen the flashlight fall, dust filling his lungs, choking him so badly he had to pull his shirt up over his nose in order to breathe.

So far his fingers found only the ice-cold steel of the train rails and crumbled brick. No flashlight. Without a light to guide him back to the exit, Cal doubted he'd make it. He could be trapped in the dark maze for a long time. No one knew where he was, and he still hadn't reached Rachel. His chest tightened, his breathing labored as he fought a full-scale panic attack. Now wasn't the time to be thinking negative thoughts. He would find the flashlight and he would get himself and Rachel out of this mess so that he could return to Deme.

His fingers closed around a smooth, round cylinder. The flashlight. He picked it up and flicked the switch on and off. Nothing. Frustration raged through him, kicking adrenaline through his veins. "Damn it," he growled. "You're going to work." He slapped the metal tube against his palm and a beam of light flashed across the tunnel.

Dust particles filled the air, reflecting light back into his eyes but not into the distance. One slow, painful step at a time, Cal limped toward the chamber that had once been the foundation of Lion Hall. Blinded by the light reflecting off the dust, Cal could only inch along, checking his footing as he went in case he happened to trip on the woman who'd run from him.

"Rachel?"

When he thought he'd gone far enough to be at the tunnel's end, his foot connected with something soft.

A feminine groan rose up from the ground.

"Rachel?" Cal squatted, cringing as pain shot through his knees and ankles.

"Not Rachel," a lower, familiar voice said.

The woman pushed up into a sitting position and scrubbed the layer of dust from her face. "It's me, Diane Masterson."

Cal reached out to the woman. "What are you doing here?"

She laughed, the attempt bringing on a coughing fit. "I came to kill it."

"Kill what?"

"The beast. I came to kill the beast."

"What do you know about it?" Cal asked. Had Lieutenant Warner filled her in on all the details of what lay beneath campus?

"I know it can't be stopped by just anyone. I know it's evil. I know that it's what raped me thirty years ago." Her words grew louder and faster as tears welled in her eyes and made dirty tracks running down her face. "It ruined my life by impregnating me with a baby. A baby I had to abandon, to throw away because it was so hideous." She buried her face in her scuffed hands, sobs shaking her shoulders. After several seconds, she sucked in a sharp breath, raised her head, her lips pulling back in a sneer. "That beast has to die so that I can live."

Cal placed a hand on her shoulder, not sure what to do to ease the woman's pain. She had seemed so strong, so well put together. For her to fall apart... It shook him to the core. But that didn't get them out of the mess they were in.

"Can you stand?" Cal gripped her arm at the elbow.

"I think so." She reached out for her flashlight and

then leaned on his arm, letting him leverage her to her feet.

"Come on, let's get out of here before the ceilings cave."

"No!" She jerked out of his grip and stepped backward, toward the chamber where the Chimera resided. Her light panned the vast cavern.

The dust had begun to settle and as it did, their flashlight beams revealed...nothing.

Cal moved into the chamber. Only hours ago, it had been a seething mass of impenetrable vegetation. Now it was concrete pillars, pipes, old rail tracks and open space. Complete silence surrounded them, the scuffs of their feet the only sound echoing off the concrete walls.

"It's gone."

"No." Dr. Masterson stumbled forward. "It has to be here. It was here earlier. I could tell by your faces as you emerged from the tunnel. It has to be here."

"It isn't now." In Cal's gut, he knew this. Just as he knew that although it was gone from here, they weren't out of danger. That same gut feeling told him that Deme and her sisters were in more danger than ever before. If he wanted to be there to help defeat the Chimera, he had to get out of the tunnels and back up on campus. "Let's get out of here. The tunnels aren't safe."

"It isn't fair. I've spent the last thirty years living in fear, afraid of my own shadow, sleeping with lights on. Afraid of its return. It can't end like this."

Cal didn't have time to be nice. "Get a grip, Dr. Masterson. If we don't get out of here soon, it won't matter. And there are people I love up there who just might need my help." He gripped her arm and manhandled her toward the tunnel and their exit out of the maze beneath the city.

After they'd traveled several hundred feet, Dr. Masterson pulled out of Cal's grasp. "I can manage on my own." She cinched the belt on her trench coat, the jacket hanging heavy on one side.

Cal didn't have time to contemplate why. He pushed forward. If Dr. Masterson decided to stay behind, he couldn't take the time to drag her along. Deme needed him. He knew this as he knew the sun wouldn't rise in the morning for him if she wasn't in his life anymore. His long strides ate the distance and soon he was back at the ladder, staring up at the small circle of light shining down from the basement.

He turned back to see that Dr. Masterson had managed to keep up with his pace. Her light bobbed along as she hurried toward him.

Without delaying any longer, he tied his flashlight on his belt and grabbed the rungs of the ladder, beginning the long climb upward. The bang of the light hitting the metal rungs and the sound of his breathing getting heavier were the only noises he could make out. He made it to the top in less than five minutes.

"You gonna be all right?" He called down to Dr. Masterson.

"Yeah. Go on. Don't wait for me." She was only halfway up when he turned away from the trapdoor and left the basement.

Deme needs me. The mantra reverberated in his head, setting the pace, pushing him faster. When he burst through the exit doors of the student commons, he was running all out toward the garden.

When the garden came into view, Cal saw Rachel crowded against the gate, screaming through the wrought-iron bars.

He caught her by the shoulders and spun her around. "What's wrong? What's happened?"

"They're in there." Rachel pointed toward the garden.

"Who's in there?"

She shook her head, her gaze darting past him to the sky over the top of the gate. "It'll kill them."

Cal peered through the gate covered completely and held securely by twisted vines.

Wind whipped past him, the moon cloaked by sinister clouds, the light of the city reflecting off their blanketing thickness.

Thunder rumbled and lighting slashed the sky, fingering offshoots that spread out in a thousand different directions. As the thunder died down, an eerie roar started low and built until it made Cal's eardrums burn. He'd heard a similar sound like that in a zoo. The roar of a lion.

Cal ripped his knife from the casing on his belt and cut at the vines. "I...really...hate...vines!" His last word coincided with his final hack, freeing the gate enough that he could push through.

Once inside he passed a stand of bushes and trees to where the lawn opened out in a wide swath between rosebushes. What had been empty minutes before was filled with a monster that consumed the majority of the space between the buildings.

On the other side of the beast, Deme and her sisters crouched low. Only there were five women, one with pale blond hair, pushing up from the ground, her hands and face dirty, her skin white.

The beast reared back on its hind legs, its two massive heads rising as high as the clouds, one a goat with wicked horns, the other a ferocious lion with long, razor-sharp teeth. Its tail whipped around and struck at Cal, the shape of a serpent with the fangs of a pit viper.

Cal leaped backward, the snake's teeth ripping through the thick layers of coverall, missing his skin by a fraction of an inch.

Gina raised her arms to the beast and a wave of water swelled in front of her. Like a tsunami, it bore down on the raging titan. Before it could smash into the creature, the wave twisted and elongated into the shape of a giant paw, and it altered course, swatting Gina, knocking her five feet into the air. She screamed as she sailed across the garden, her cry cut off when she crashed to the earth.

Deme and Brigid advanced on the beast with nothing but their hands and their questionable powers of the pentagram to defend themselves. Deme took no more than five steps before her feet were mired in briars, enveloping her legs like concertina wire, bringing her to a complete standstill.

Brigid moved forward, eyes narrow, palms cupped, fireballs swirling and ready to launch.

She reared back and flung the first one straight at the closest head. The goat opened its mouth and swallowed the fireball.

Without pausing, Brigid launched the second at the lion's head.

It, too, swallowed the fireball. Then at the same time, the two heads shot the fireballs at Brigid.

"Look out, Brigid!" Cal yelled, but the speed was too great. Brigid didn't have time to duck or dodge the attack.

The fiery orbs hit her dead-on, knocking her on her butt and catching her shirt on fire. Brigid crab-walked backward, slapping at the spreading flame. Finally, she rolled over, smothering it out in the grass.

With Gina, Deme and Brigid incapacitated, that left Selene and a weak Aurai standing against the beast that moved toward them.

"Run, Selene," Aurai cried. "Our powers are of no use against it."

Selene stood still, her gaze pinned to the advancing monster, her arms rising out from her sides.

The Chimera roared and reared again, its paws rising above Selene. If it dropped to all fours, it would land directly on top of her.

Cal ran forward, knife drawn, yelling like a banshee.

The snake struck out.

Fast and true, Cal swung his knife, severing the serpent's head.

The lion roared and dropped down, barely missing Selene.

Before the giant could turn, Cal grabbed its mane and hauled himself up onto the demon's back.

The Chimera flung its head back and forth, roaring, angry.

Cal plunged his knife into the beast's neck again and again. The injury didn't seem to have any effect on the beast but to make it more annoyed. Its body twisted and bucked.

Cal felt himself losing grip. He flung his knife down to Deme. "Get out, Deme," he yelled, then he was flying through the air. He hit tree branches, crashing from one to another as gravity brought him down to earth, flat on his back, the wind knocked from his lungs.

For several seconds, he couldn't move, couldn't lift a finger. He just lay there stunned and immobile.

Like a one-woman vigilante, Diane Masterson charged

into the fray, her hair standing on end, tunnel dust covering every inch of her body from hair to feet. She waved a forty-five magnum and screamed like a demented Valkyrie, "Die, you son of a bitch!"

Cal sucked in a breath and yelled. "Get down!"

Aurai tackled Selene, throwing her to the ground.

Deme, having cleared the briars, dove for cover, and Brigid rolled over where she lay as a loud bang ripped the air.

Masterson was flung back, landing hard on her butt.

The Chimera flinched, the bullet having pierced its front shoulder. It reared again, spinning on its hind legs, and landed in front of the college president.

Holding the pistol in both hands this time, Dr. Masterson fired again.

The bullet slammed into the beast's chest, bringing it to a complete halt.

"That's for what you did to me. The creature you impregnated me with. For ruining my damned life!" Tears streamed down Dr. Masterson's face as she raised her weapon again. She pulled the trigger but the gun jammed.

The Chimera growled, a low gurgling sound that made the trees shake.

Diane Masterson tried to pull the bolt back to dislodge the bullet, but it wouldn't budge.

The beast stumbled forward, its lips stretching over fangs the size of butcher knives.

The college president flung the pistol to the side and crab-walked backward, scrambling to get to her feet.

Cal sucked in a deep breath, pulling air into his lungs, finally able to move again. He leaped from the ground and ran for the Chimera.

Deme beat him there. Dodging the beast's massive

paws, she dove beneath it and rolled to her feet directly below its throat. With both hands, she rammed the knife into its jugular, ripping a long gash downward. Blood gushed like a geyser.

The Chimera roared, the sound less menacing, gurgling with the fluid filling its lungs.

With its last breath, the Chimera lurched forward.

Cal dove beneath it, knocked Deme out from under and rolled to the side as the giant crashed to the earth.

Dr. Masterson screamed.

The beast landed on Cal's leg, trapping him beneath a mound of fur and bones.

Deme lay in the grass a few feet away from him. So very still.

Unable to reach her, Cal cried out to her, "Deme!"

For the longest moment of his life, Cal struggled to free his leg, his gaze on Deme.

Then her hand twitched and she moaned.

Cal's eyes misted. Thank God, she was alive. He shoved and pushed, but the weight of the creature pinned him to the ground.

"Let me help." The pale-haired Aurai stood beside him, her hands rising palms upward, her eyelids drifting closed. A gentle breeze lifted the fine strands of her hair, spreading it out to the sides like a cape of gold.

The lifeless body of the Chimera rose from the ground, just enough that Cal could slide his leg free.

His first stop was to check on Deme.

She pushed up to a sitting position. "I'm all right. What about my sisters?"

"I'm good," Brigid called from the other side of the creature's corpse.

"Me, too," Gina said, coming up behind Cal.

"And me." Selene appeared around the side of the Chimera.

"What about Dr. Masterson?" Deme asked.

"Not so good for her." Brigid rounded the front of the beast, carrying a forty-five Magnum pistol. "One of the beast's fangs pierced her heart. Likely she died instantly."

Selene shook her head. "Poor woman. What a terrible truth to live with."

"What did she mean about being impregnated?" Brigid asked.

"I don't know." Deme heaved a weighty sigh. "Now we can't even ask. At least we're all here and alive." She climbed to her feet and gathered her baby sister in a hug. "And you're back."

Aurai laughed. "I was beginning to wonder how long it would take you to find me."

Brigid, Gina and Selene crowded in for a group hug.

Cal took the pistol from Brigid and cleared the misfired round, waiting for the women to finish their reunion hug.

"We wouldn't have found you without Cal's help." Deme opened the circle of sisters and grabbed Cal's arm.

Suddenly he was drawn in and included in the family hug.

Awkward at first, he couldn't help the way his chest swelled. He hadn't felt this loved…well, since his parents passed on. He could easily get used to being a part of this family of sisters.

But for how long would Deme include him? Now that Aurai was safe amongst them, would Deme return to St. Croix?

Cal pulled free of the sisters.

Deme's brow wrinkled and she stared across the top of Aurai's head into his eyes.

"We need to talk," Cal said.

Deme nodded. "Yes, we do. Let's do it now."

With all five sisters staring at him, Cal fidgeted. "Can we go somewhere more private?"

"I share everything with my sisters. Anything we have to say can be said in front of them."

Cal gazed into five pairs of eyes so different from each other, but bearing the same stubborn streak he so admired in Deme. "Okay, then, for starters, you can't go back to St. Croix."

Deme nodded. "Agreed."

"You're staying here close to family. Your sisters need you. You need them and you need me."

"Right." Deme smiled, detangling herself from her sisters' arms and walking toward Cal.

"I don't care how much you like living on a sun-baked island in the Caribbean, you have to come back to Chicago, where I can see you every day."

She walked right into his arms and wrapped her hands around his neck, dragging his mouth close to hers. "I'm with you so far."

"And you can't leave again." He pressed a brief kiss to her lips. "Did I mention that part?" His lips found hers again, taking her mouth more completely.

"I love you, Detective Cal Black. I'm not leaving you ever again. So get used to it."

"I was just thinking how easy it would be to get used to you being around all the time. And I wouldn't mind it if your sisters came to visit us."

"Oh, really?" Brigid stood with her legs parted. "Does that mean you're not going to freak out every time one of us uses our powers?"

Cal's gazed didn't leave Deme's. "I think your powers are what make you special."

Deme smiled up into his eyes. "And here I thought
you'd run screaming."

"I don't scream." He kissed the tip of her nose. "I
yell on occasion, but I don't scream."

"I'll have a few loose ends to tie up in St. Croix."

"I feel a honeymoon coming on." He kissed her full
on the lips, hard and fast, then dropped to one knee.

Selene sighed. "How romantic."

Aurai hugged her brown-haired sister. "I hope we
find a man like Cal."

"Not me." Brigid huffed. "Men are overrated."

"Only because you haven't found one who makes
your knees weak." Gina backhanded her leather-clad
sister in the belly. "Shut up and let him finish."

Deme shot a quelling glare at her sisters and they
fell silent.

Cal laughed and took her hand in his. "Deme Chattox, can you find it in your heart to love me as much
as I love you? To live with me through thick and thin,
through Chimeras and whatever else this crazy world
has to throw at us? I live a dangerous life. It can be
hard on a woman."

"I'm not just any woman, Cal Black. As you said, I'm
special." Deme dropped to her knees and took both of
Cal's hands in hers. "But let's be perfectly clear. What
exactly are you asking?"

"I'm asking you to marry me and be my partner
for life."

Deme sucked in a deep breath and let it out slowly.

Her pause had to be the longest seconds of Cal's life.

Then her eyes shone with moisture that spilled down
her face.

For a moment, Cal's stomach clenched.

"By the goddess, if you won't say it, we will." Brigid joined hands with the other four sisters.

"Yes!" The four sisters said in unison.

"Do you mind?" Deme glared at them, then her frown cleared and a smile shone across her face. "In case you didn't get the message, the answer is yes." She closed the distance between them, cupping his face with her hands, and kissed him long and deep.

Cal threaded his fingers through her tangled auburn hair and sealed the deal, his tongue thrusting past her teeth to stroke hers.

"Ahem." Brigid rolled her eyes. "If you two could finish, we might get this place cleaned up and the kids back in time to finish out the semester."

Cal gathered her in his arms and rose to his feet, hugging her tight.

"I'll need to get a job or open another investigation agency," Deme said. "I won't be a kept woman."

Brigid walked by her, tossing over her shoulder, "Or, you can come to work for the Chicago Police Department with me and Cal."

Deme stared up into Cal's eyes. "And investigate things like what happened here?"

"It seems Brigid and I have been recruited for special projects. Lieutenant Warner thinks we have the necessary skills to tackle the weird and unusual."

"Probably because we are weird and unusual." Brigid laughed. "What do you say, sis? Want to work for the city?"

Deme's gaze never left Cal's. "You okay with that?"

"More than okay. It means I get to see a lot more of you."

Deme's smile turned sexy. "Oh, you'll get that as soon as we get back to your apartment."

"Mind keeping it G-rated?" Gina jerked her head toward Aurai. "Child here."

"I'm not a child." Aurai stomped her foot. "I'll be twenty in a couple weeks."

"Sure you can put up with my family?" Deme asked. "I don't plan on running out on them again."

"I'm positive." Cal tipped her head back and kissed her again. "Especially if it means I get to be with you."

When Deme broke the kiss, she looked around at her sisters. Aurai stood nearby, a rumbling sound emanating from her belly. "We need to get Aurai some food."

Aurai laughed, her hand covering her stomach. "I could use a bite."

Selene stood beside the Chimera, her face tipped back, her eyes closed.

"Feel anything?" Deme and Cal walked across the grass to join her.

"They're leaving," Selene said.

"Who?" Gina joined her.

"Our sisters." Selene smiled. "They said thanks for doing what they'd tried to and failed." Selene opened her eyes and stared around at her living sisters. "They need one last favor."

"What's that?"

"To help them dispose of the body."

"Civic-minded of them." Brigid walked across to Selene.

Selene held out her hands.

The sisters came together in a circle beside the Chimera, all closing their eyes and raising their faces to the full moon breaking through the clouds. Their voices rose together into the night.

"With the strength of the earth
With the rising of the wind
With the calm of the water
With the intensity of fire
With the freedom of spirit
The goddess is within us
She is power
We are her
We are one
Blessed Be."

Cal didn't pretend to understand, still mystified by the magic these sisters wielded. He stood by and witnessed the unexplainable union of their spirits.

As they repeated the chant over and over, the Chimera rose from the ground, its massive body appearing weightless in the light from the moon.

The sisters' voices grew softer and softer until they stopped as one.

On the final "Blessed Be," the Chimera's body trembled then shimmered and exploded in a cloud of vapor.

"They're gone." Selene's eyes filled with tears. "I feel empty."

"You have us." Gina slipped an arm around her waist and drew her close.

"And we have Aurai back." Brigid pulled her younger sister into the group hug.

Deme wrapped her arms around them. "We have each other."

Cal stood by, waiting patiently, feeling as if he was spying on a family gathering he wasn't a part of. He hoped to change that soon.

When Deme held out a hand, he smiled. Maybe sooner than he expected. He joined the sisters in the hug. Part of a very unique family, and damned proud of it.

Epilogue

The next day, Cal and Deme met with Lieutenant Warner and Dustin Zoeller at the trapdoor in the basement of the Colyer-Fenton College student commons.

A welder stood by to seal the metal door for good. No student or campus employee would ever descend into the maze of tunnels below the city from this entrance again.

The door stood open for the last time as the welder inspected the hinges and prepared his equipment.

"Deme tell you that she accepted the job?" Lieutenant Warner rocked back on his heels, a grin spreading across his wrinkled face.

"I told him," Deme responded.

Marty patted her on the back. "I think you'll make a great asset to the team."

Cal grinned. "Yeah, she has great assets."

Deme swatted him playfully.

Cal had spent the entire night making love to her. She definitely had assets, every one of which he intended to explore more thoroughly tonight.

"What about the Gamma Omegas?"

"They've had their sorority charter revoked and Zoe Adams was expelled from campus." Deme smiled grimly. "I confiscated the Book of Spells from Zoe's room and, since Rachel stole all of their vials of potion, almost all of the girls have reverted back to normal coeds."

"What about Rachel and her boyfriend?" Cal asked.

"Brigid visited Mike in the hospital. He's out of the coma and Rachel was with him." Deme stared at the welder's back, her mind miles ahead. "Both of them are transferring to a community college to complete their core courses and will probably go on to the University of Illinois to complete their bachelor's degrees."

The lieutenant nodded toward the vertical tunnel leading down into the bowels of the city. "Think we've seen the last of the trouble from the tunnels?"

Deme shook her head. "No."

"What makes you say that? The Chimera is dead."

"Gut feel."

Cal nodded. "I get that feeling, too. I think Chicago has its share of trouble brewing. Will sealing the tunnel stop it?" He shook his head. "Probably not. But then we wouldn't have a job, now would we?"

The lieutenant sighed. "I was looking forward to coasting into a peaceful retirement in a few years."

Cal laughed. "Not a chance. This city has a life of its own."

"You think Dr. Masterson meant anything by what she said about her baby?"

"If it's a monster, I hope she killed the thing. Otherwise, what happened to it?" Cal stared into the darkness of the tunnel.

"I had Brigid do a search on public records of births and had her check hospital records in and around Chicago. No one by the name of Diane Masterson delivered during the year following the rape. If she had a baby, she delivered it somewhere else or at home."

"Think it survived?" Deme asked.

Lieutenant Warner grimaced. "I don't even want to speculate."

The welder closed the trapdoor and set his tools out to begin the welding.

"I think that's our cue to leave." Lieutenant Warner turned. "By the way, good work on getting this case closed and cleaned up."

Despite their vow to act professional in front of the boss, Deme slipped her hand into Cal's. "We had a little help from some sisters."

"See if you can get some more help from them on your next case. I have a file waiting on Cal's desk. Don't wait too long to get started. We've had a number of attacks reported in the past forty-eight hours in downtown Chicago. One in particular stood out."

"What's special about this one?" Deme asked.

"One woman survived long enough to tell the paramedics it was a beast with a man's body and lion's head that attacked her. Maybe this lion creature is Diane Baker's missing son."

Cal looked at Deme. "Let's get to work."

* * * * *

POSSESSING
THE WITCH

For friends and lovers who accept you for who you are, no matter your physical or social flaws.

To Cleve for inspiring my drive and ambition to succeed in this crazy world of publishing and for being there when I need a swift kick in the pants to get back to work. You're more than just a husband. You're my cheerleader, coach and team. You love me for all my successes and my flaws and encourage me to push on. I could not have accomplished so much without your love and support.

Chapter 1

She glanced behind her, certain she'd heard something that sounded like a growl. When the sound did not repeat, she shrugged and pulled up the collar of her jacket to block the bite of the chilled autumn air. Now, she wished that she'd accepted an offer of a ride to the garage from her friends. At least then she wouldn't be alone, on a dark street, jumping at every noise.

She knew better than to go anywhere alone in downtown Chicago, especially after dark.

As she entered the parking garage, she let out the breath she'd been holding and laughed. All that worry for nothing. She climbed the stairs to the second level and there, in the middle of the empty bay, stood her car, a shiny, creamy, pearl-white Audi, the heated leather seats beckoning to her.

As she dug in her purse for her keys, she heard it again. This time louder. The deep rumble of an animal's growl sent shivers coursing down her spine.

It sounded as though it was coming from her car.

The growl burst into a roar, echoing off the concrete walls of the garage, so real and frightening she screamed and dropped her purse, keys and all, and ran back toward the stairs.

"No," she cried, her heart in her throat, her breath catching on a sob. "No."

Although hampered by high heels, she made it all the

way to the bottom. As she turned toward the street, fifty feet away and still busy with traffic, something big and heavy slammed into her back, knocking her facedown on the concrete.

Too far from the traffic to be seen, she lay pinned beneath the weight of an animal, its heated breath sniffing at the back of her neck.

She whimpered, struggling to crawl from beneath it, her heart racing, her hands scuffed and bleeding. "Please..."

The creature's nose nuzzled the line of her throat, then a long, hot, wet tongue snaked out and licked her skin.

She screamed, renewing her frantic fight to free herself from the faceless beast.

The animal roared again and sank its teeth into the back of her neck, shaking her viciously.

Her arms and legs went numb and she couldn't move any part of her body, but her thoughts were clear and frightened beyond comprehension.

The creature dragged her from the garage into the shadows of an alley, pavement scraping her face. He stopped behind a stack of bound cardboard, dropped her to the ground and roared, the sound reverberating off the walls.

"Please...don't kill me."

Selene Chattox jerked awake, drenched in sweat, her heart racing.

Please...don't kill me.

She snatched her cell phone from the nightstand and speed-dialed her sister, Deme.

"Yeah...what...who is this?" A loud banging noise was followed by a muttered curse. "Sorry, I dropped my phone. Selene? What's wrong?" Her voice was hoarse, filled with the gravel of sleep.

"She's dying."

"Who's dying?" All raspiness cleared, Deme's words were clear and clipped.

"I don't know."

"Can you tell where?"

"In an alley."

"Can you be more specific? Do you see anything else, a street sign, a building name, something?"

Selene inhaled, closed her eyes and let her mind drift back into the dream. Her cheek stung where the pavement had scraped against her skin in the nightmare—blessedly, the rest of her body felt no pain. Hot breath snorted down on her neck and Selene jerked out of the vision, her hand shaking so hard she could barely hold the cell phone to her ear. "I smelled water. She was in a parking garage, leaving the theater, when she was attacked. It dragged her into a nearby alley."

"A theater near water…" Deme spoke to someone on the other end. "River or lake?"

"River."

"The Civic Opera House on Wacker Drive?"

"Maybe."

"I'm coming over. Cal's calling Lieutenant Warner. We'll have someone there in minutes."

"Hurry," Selene whispered. "It's going to kill her."

Wind blasted down the back alley as Gryphon Leone emerged from the Civic Opera House, wrapping his long cloak around him. The chill of fall had settled in far sooner than he'd expected. He sniffed the air, his keen sense of smell picking up on the delicate nuances of coming rain and the dampness of the river.

He'd waited until the other theatergoers had departed before leaving the shadows of his box. He arrived early and left late, valuing his anonymity and privacy. The fewer people he encountered, the better. Despite years of exercising his control, he didn't trust himself with the people of the light and didn't put himself in too many situations that required him to remain in the public eye for long.

With the rise of his business and philanthropic ventures, he feared his anonymity would soon be a blessing of the past.

He hurried toward the street, determined to return to his apartment at the base of his office building, a haven beneath the surface of the oldest part of downtown Chicago, before the rain came.

The scent captured him, bringing him to a sudden halt. He lifted his nose to the air, a low rumble rising in his throat.

Blood. Fresh blood and animal musk.

His apartment, and the need to return before the rain, slipped through his thoughts, forgotten as his inner animal pushed to the surface.

Gryph fought back, breathing deeply in and out until the growling abated and all that was left was the scent—blood, tantalizingly fresh, tainted by the musk of another animal and the accompanying stench of fear.

He wanted to turn and walk away, but he couldn't, his feet moving of their own accord, closer to the source. Rounding a corner, he spied a parking garage and something dark staining the sidewalk near the stairs leading up.

The stain spread like someone had taken a large paintbrush and dragged it along the walkway, until the paint ran out at the entrance to an alley.

Go home. Return to your apartment. Don't get involved.

Balthazar's words echoed in his head, the old man's warnings etched firmly in Gryph's brain since as far back as he could remember.

Still, the trail begged to be followed. He'd go as far as the entrance to the alley, no farther.

Gryph crossed the street, keeping out of the inky liquid staining the concrete, and worked his way quietly to the entrance to the alley.

As he stepped into the opening, a bellow blasted against the brick walls, followed by a woman's scream.

A huge shadow rose up from behind a stack of wooden pallets, the shape that of a giant wolf, rearing back on his hind legs.

Gryph's beast exploded from inside, answering with a deeper, more ferocious roar, thundering into the alley, echoing against the brick walls. His skin and bones moved, spread and stretched as his physical form altered, expanding, his clothing ripping at the seams. He shrugged out of his cloak, the long folds falling to the ground at his feet.

The creature in the alley rumbled again, launching itself toward him.

Caught in midtransformation, Gryph was helpless to defend himself.

The wolf, equal in size to Gryph's inner lion, hit him full in the chest, knocking him back into the side street. The air slammed from his lungs.

His attacker flew past him and hit the opposite building, his feet glancing off the bricks, then landed on all fours, launching a new attack within seconds.

His transformation complete, Gryph dodged to his side and sprang to all fours, reaching out to pound the animal with a powerful swipe from his forepaw.

The wolf tumbled across pavement, sprang back on his feet and tore into Gryph, his fangs slashing for Gryph's jugular.

Gryph twisted to avoid the worst of the bite, but not all of it. The wolf's teeth sank into his skin, ripping through his shoulder near his collarbone. Pain rocketed through his senses, blinding him briefly.

The wolf pounced on him, pinning him to the ground.

Had the creature wanted to finish him off, it could have with one more fatal bite.

Instead it stared down at him, its chest heaving, and it growled low and menacingly, like a warning. Then it leaped over Gryph and disappeared out of the alley and around a corner.

His shoulder bleeding, Gryph pushed to his paws, his racing heartbeat slowing.

A moan alerted him to another being's presence in the alley. With his focus on survival, Gryph hadn't moved on to the source of the long, thick bloodstain.

He staggered toward the banded stack of compressed cardboard boxes, his nostrils filled with the scents of blood, woman and fear.

Before he reached her, his body began its transformation back to man, the change made more difficult given his wounds.

His arms and legs completed before his face and head, allowing him to reach out to the woman and feel for a pulse.

Her eyes blinked open, widening, a scream bubbling up in her throat.

Gryph tried to reassure her with words, but all that he could emit was a rumbling growl.

The woman's eyes rolled back in her head and she passed out.

The pavement was soaked with her blood from a wound in the back of her neck. If she had any chance at survival, she had to get to a hospital as soon as possible.

He left her on the ground for only a moment to retrieve his cloak, his cell phone tucked in the inside pocket.

Quickly he dialed 911 and gave a description of the victim, her injuries and her location. When the dispatcher asked his name, he clicked the off button and pocketed the phone.

He returned to the woman and applied pressure to her wound to stem the flow of blood from her body, but her face was deathly pale.

As he leaned over her body, blood dripped down on her.

Until now, he hadn't realized how much blood he'd lost. He could tell he was weakening, but he couldn't leave the woman until the police or ambulance were close.

A siren sounded in the distance, growing closer by the second.

Gryph had to leave before the emergency personnel arrived—how else would he explain his tattered clothing? And given his injuries and the pain they caused, he couldn't risk being around surface dwellers should the pain increase, summoning his inner beast.

He stayed until the last possible moment. When the flashing lights of an emergency vehicle pulled into the side street, Gryph leaped over the chain-link fence behind him, raced for the opposite end of the alley and rounded the corner to the next street.

Keeping to the shadows, he ran until his feet slowed, the blood running in a stream down his arm, dripping onto the sidewalk, draining his strength. The police would follow his trail. He couldn't let that happen, he couldn't let them find him. Then he remembered how close he was to the river, its scent drawing him to the corner of Washington Street and Wacker Drive. Making a sharp left, he stumbled toward the bridge. An ambulance passed him, its lights blinding. A police car followed, slowing as it passed by.

Exhaustion pulled at Gryph—he wanted to sleep, but he knew he couldn't. He leaned against the bridge railing and stared down into the water.

The police car stopped and backed up.

Gryph leaned out and let himself tip over the edge. Then he was falling, racing to meet the black shiny surface of the river.

When he hit the water, the force of the fall sent him deep into the murky black depths.

His shoulder burned, the effort to move it too much. But he kicked his feet, propelling himself upward, hoping the current would carry him far enough away they wouldn't find him.

He surfaced a hundred yards from the Washington Street Bridge. A cop stood at the rails shining a flashlight below, sending a sweeping arc back and forth across the water.

Gryph sucked in a breath and sank below the surface, letting the current carry him farther away. As he flowed downstream with the river, he wondered what it would feel like to drown, to let his lungs fill with water and the river claim him. His chest burned for oxygen and he kicked his feet to send him closer to the river's edge. Dying in a river wasn't in the cards for him tonight.

When he came up again, he had drifted far enough that the cop's light couldn't find him. Tired beyond endurance, he kicked and pulled with one arm to the side of the river, searching for a place he could crawl out. Several minutes later, he found a metal ladder pinned to the concrete walls of the river and dragged himself up the east embankment onto a walkway, where he collapsed, the night sky of the city fading to black.

Chapter 2

Pain...tired...can't breathe.

Selene staggered to the door of her basement apartment below the vintage dress shop she owned that was situated among the quaint little buildings of old-town Chicago.

She could barely breathe and her shoulder ached unbearably, the pain draining her strength, sucking the life from her body.

Holding on to the handrail, she pulled herself up the steps to ground level. Headlights flashed on the street in front of the building.

Once outside the door of her shop, Selene met Deme, as her sister climbed out of her Lexus SUV. "Thank the goddess, you're here."

"Were you going somewhere without me?" Deme asked.

Selene lurched toward the car and leaned against the door. "We need to get there."

"Are you all right, sweetie?" Deme started to round the car.

"I'm okay, but we need to move fast." She opened the car door and slid into the passenger seat. "Hurry."

"Where exactly do we need to get?" Deme climbed back into the driver's seat and inserted the key in the ignition.

"Head toward the Washington Street Bridge."

Deme shifted into gear and spun the SUV around in a tight U-turn, bumping over the curb on the other side of the street. When they'd gone several blocks, she looked across at Selene.

"Is it the girl? The one you called about earlier?"

Selene shook her head. "No. Someone else. He's injured and alone." She closed her eyes, shivering. "And cold. He'll die if we don't get to him soon."

"What about the girl?"

"The EMTs are with her now. But *he's* alone."

Deme's foot sank to the floor, shooting them along the streets, dodging the occasional driver unfortunate enough to be out on the city streets so late into the night.

As they crossed the Washington Street Bridge, Selene leaned forward, her gaze panning the landscape, the steel, glass and concrete buildings rising high into the night sky, blocking the moon. "Turn left on Wacker."

On such short notice, Deme slammed on her brakes and skidded into the turn. The rear end continued around and she goosed the accelerator to keep her SUV from making a complete three-sixty.

As they shot down Wacker, Selene dug her fingers into the dash, leaning so far forward her nose almost touched the windshield. He was near, very near. Selene leaned back in her seat, braced herself and yelled, "Stop!"

Deme hit the brakes, bringing the vehicle to a standstill, tires burning into the asphalt.

Selene burst from the door, rounded the car and raced across the street. So intent on reaching the wounded man, she didn't see the car until almost too late.

A horn blared, tires squealed and an older model Lincoln Town Car swerved, barely missing her.

Without slowing, she ducked between buildings and headed for the river.

"Selene, wait for me," Deme called out behind her.

But she couldn't wait, his need drove her forward, sending

her on a headlong rush toward the river. She found a stair-case leading down to the walkway along the water's edge.

"Selene!" Deme called out behind her. "Damn it, this area is dangerous at this time of night."

She knew. He'd been injured by a dangerous animal, his blood running into the river. Selene ran along the wa-ter's edge, heading north. Something moved in the shadow beneath the next bridge.

Fear had a place in Selene's race to save him. But it wasn't for herself. It was for him. She didn't slow until she reached the bridge.

A moan echoed off the steel supports.

A man lay across the concrete, a soaked cape pulling at the string around his neck, but otherwise he was shirt-less in the late autumn chill. His soaked trousers were torn and ragged, as though they'd been through a shredder. No shoes, no jacket, his hair, longish and tousled, was hang-ing in his face.

Selene ripped the coat from her back and covered him, pulling it up to the wounded shoulder. Blood oozed from a deep gash. Not a gunshot wound, but the vicious bite of a raging animal. She tore the hem of her blouse, wadded the material into a pad and pressed it into the gash, stem-ming the flow of blood.

His eyes opened and he gasped. A low growl rumbled in his throat and his hand reached out to grab her wrist in a fearsome grip, pulling her hand away from the injury. The strength of his grasp hurt, cutting off her circulation.

Selene bit her lower lip, pushing back the pain. He didn't know what he was doing. "Shh…I'm here to help. We have to stop the bleeding. Let me help." Tears stung her eyes as his grip tightened. She stared into his face, trying to read his expression, the shadows blurring her view.

If he squeezed much harder, he'd snap her bones. Such strength in an injured man was extraordinary.

She sent soothing thoughts into his consciousness.

Deme skidded to a halt behind her. "Let her go," her sister said to the man.

"It's okay, Deme. He's delirious, he doesn't know he's hurting me." Selene sucked in a breath and let it out slowly. "Please, let go. I need to stop the blood. Do you understand? Otherwise you'll die." *Please, I only want to help.*

His eyelids drooped. "Tired. Can't hold on."

"That's right, let go." Selene peeled one finger loose, then another. "We need to get you help."

"No hospital," he whispered. Then his hand slackened and dropped to the ground.

"About damned time he passed out. I was going to have to knock him out so that you could help his stubborn ass." Deme dropped to her haunches and pulled her cell phone from her pocket. "I'll get an ambulance here."

"No!" Selene's response came swift and sure. From where, she didn't know. All she knew was that this man wouldn't want to go to a hospital, no matter how injured he was. "Help me get him back to your vehicle."

"Are you kidding? He must weigh close to two hundred pounds. There are stairs and…"

"Please. We have to get him out of the cold and bandage his wound before shock sets in or it won't matter." She pressed the wad of material to his shoulder. "Give me your scarf."

"But it's my favorite."

Selene held out her hand.

Deme unwound the scarf from around her neck and reluctantly handed it to her, a frown creasing her brow. "You don't even know this guy. What's so special about him?"

Selene didn't answer, instead wrapping the scarf around his shoulder and knotting it over the wound to apply more pressure. Then she stood and grabbed him beneath the injured arm.

Deme took the uninjured side.

The man growled again, guttural and animal-like.

"Get up," Selene said in a strong voice any drill sergeant would envy. "Get up!" With her sister's help and the efforts of the half conscious, half naked man, they got him to his feet and led him to the stairs.

After nearly losing him twice, they got him up the steps and onto the street above. Selene leaned him against a light pole to help hold him up as Deme ran for the vehicle. She pulled up beside them and they guided him into the backseat, bumping his head and shoulder in the process.

A low roar ripped through the car, startling the women.

Deme stared across at Selene. "No man should make that kind of noise, I don't care how delirious."

"Just get him in." Selene lifted one of his legs, shoved it in and closed the door quickly. She climbed into the passenger seat and twisted around to watch him.

Deme eased into the driver's seat and stared into the rearview mirror at the man. "Sure you don't want me to drop him off at a hospital emergency room?"

"No." Selene's jaw set in a hard line. "Take me home."

Deme shook her head, her lips pressing into a thin line. "I'm not leaving him at your place."

"You have to." Selene shot a pleading glance at her sister. "I'm his only hope."

"Look, Selene, you don't know this guy. He could be a mass murderer or a rapist. He could be the person who jumped the woman from your vision."

"He's not."

"How do you know?"

"I just know."

"He was in the same area, Selene."

"He didn't hurt that woman." Selene's words were low, intense.

Deme stared into her sister's eyes for a long, hard minute. "Okay, then."

Selene breathed a sigh as the SUV pulled away from the curb and headed back across the river toward her apartment. Why she'd insisted on taking him to her home, she didn't know. He'd insisted no hospital. Why?

Selene stretched out her mind to read into his thoughts, but the more she pushed the more frustrated she became. So many questions spun through her own thoughts, she couldn't see into his.

The man in the backseat moaned. He'd lost a lot of blood and from the looks of him, had gone into the river, a very unsanitary place. If he didn't die of exposure, the bacteria from the river water might kill him.

"Could you hurry?" Selene urged.

Deme shook her head, but the SUV's speed picked up. A red light ahead made her slow the vehicle enough to look both ways before blowing through.

In what seemed like an interminable amount of time, but had been less than ten minutes, Deme pulled up in front of Selene's shop.

"We're here, now what?" Deme cast a glance into the backseat, where the man lay semicomatose. "How are we going to get him in the basement? Assuming I agree to this plan of yours."

Selene bit her lip. "I don't know. But we have to."

Deme reached into her purse and pulled out her cell phone. "Cal can be here in fifteen."

"No." Selene put her hand over Deme's phone. "I'd rather we kept this to just you and me."

"What? You and me carrying a large unconscious man into your basement apartment?"

Selene nodded. "Yes. And I don't want Cal to know that he's even here. I don't want anyone else to know. Not even Gina and Aurai. Especially not Brigid."

"We're your sisters. Why keep it from us? Look, just let

me take him to the hospital. Let them handle him. They have big strong burly orderlies that—"

"No." A deep voice cut into Deme's words. The back door to the vehicle opened and the man got out.

Selene ripped her door open, but not in time.

One second he was holding on to the door, the next he'd crumpled to the ground.

Her heart beating hard against her ribs, Selene dropped to her knees. "Are you all right?"

"I don't need your help," he said.

Deme stood over them both, her fists planted on her hips. "Like hell you don't."

"I won't go to a…" He lay still with his eyes closed, his breathing shallow, almost nonexistent.

Selene slid one of his arms around her neck. "Help me get him up."

Deme sighed. "Stubborn witch."

Selene's lips twitched. "Shut up and get his other side."

Deme lifted his arm to drape over her shoulder, but as soon as she moved it, he jerked, growling like a rabid animal, his teeth peeled back over sharp incisors. With her head down to get the arm over her shoulder, Deme didn't see the pointed fangs.

But Selene did. Her stomach flip-flopped and she ducked her head to avoid Deme's gaze. "Just get an arm around his waist and help me haul him to the stairs." To him she said, "Could you manage to stay with us long enough to help yourself down a flight of stairs?"

"Must get below," he said through gritted teeth.

"That's where we're going, just help us get you there." Selene glanced across at her sister. "Ready?"

"Whenever you are." Deme's arm tightened around his waist.

Selene stepped forward at the same time as Deme.

The man between them lurched and stiffened, then a low rumble rose in his chest.

"Either stop growling, or I'll drop you here and leave you on the pavement," Selene threatened, her voice sharp, her back straining under his weight.

"You go, sister." Deme grunted, easing toward the building and the next hurdle. The steps.

The rumbling abated, but his grip tightened around Selene. He snorted. "And I thought you were an angel come to rescue me."

Deme laughed out loud.

Selene shot an angry glare at her before she responded. "Hardly. I'll be your worst nightmare before this night is over." She shuddered thinking of how she needed to clean his wound and how painful it would be for him. She guessed he wouldn't like it in the least.

When they reached the narrow stairs leading down into the basement apartment of the shop, Deme laid the man's hand on the rail and moved down the steps in front of him. "The stairs aren't wide enough for three. You'll have to help yourself down the stairs, big guy."

The man groaned, his eyes rolling to the back of his head, the hand on the rail turning white with the strength of his grip.

Selene turned his face toward her and tried to probe his mind.

His chaotic thoughts were a jumble of pain, darkness and overwhelming sadness.

Unable to bear the ache and sorrow, Selene jerked out of his head and swayed.

"What is it?" Deme asked.

"Nothing. I just can't read his mind." She could sense emotions and pain, but not thoughts or words. She'd have to use other means to get through to him. "Listen, mister,

"Not yet. You're soaked to the skin." Selene pushed him toward Deme. "Hold him up while I get his clothes off."

"You're going to strip a stranger?" Deme asked.

"You want the honors?" Selene quipped. "He's not lying in my bed in those wet, smelly clothes."

"Why is he going to lie in your bed? I'm not liking this arrangement, Selene. You don't know this guy. He could be a serial killer."

"I can't leave him on the streets, Deme." Though her back hurt, she held on to the man. "Look, if it makes you feel better. I can sense that he won't hurt me."

Deme's lips pressed together and her eyes narrowed. "You said you couldn't read his mind."

"I can't read his individual thoughts, but I can tell he's harmless to me."

Deme stared hard at her sister. "I'm not convinced, but I'll hold on while you do the stripping. I don't think Cal would be thrilled to know I'd stripped a strange man." She took over by sliding beneath the arm Selene had been holding him up by. "Just hurry. He weighs a ton."

The man groaned, his knees buckling.

Selene helped Deme straighten him, then she went back to work, reaching for the waistband of his trousers. She wasn't a virgin, but removing a strange man's tattered pants was…well…disturbing. She quickly flicked the buttons loose and stripped the damp trousers down thick muscular legs coated with a fine layer of tawny hairs.

Her heartbeat quickened when she realized he wore nothing beneath his trousers.

Breath caught in her throat and she hurriedly removed his pants, setting them in a pile on the floor.

"Holy smokes, the man is hung like a frickin' horse!" Deme grunted and almost fell over. "Damn, I think he's out again. It's all I can do to hold him up." She shifted his weight, leaning hard to keep him up.

With her heart already beating a rapid tattoo inside her body, Selene hoped Deme wouldn't mention the man's nakedness again. Her older sister couldn't be happy about this stranger being totally nude in her sister's bed. She'd never leave him alone with Selene at this rate.

Selene knew, by way of her "gift," that she had to get Deme out of the apartment before she tried to clean this man's wounds. Something about him screamed danger. But not necessarily a danger to her. Those eyes, that growling and the roar, were only the beginning, she feared.

Deme wouldn't understand. She didn't have the gift of spirit like Selene.

Trousers off, completely naked, the man swayed. Selene helped Deme maneuver him to the bed, where they sat him on the edge and laid him back gently, lifting his feet up onto the mattress. Once settled, Selene pulled the sheet up over his legs and hips.

Selene went to work on the padding she'd tied over the wound, pulling it carefully over his shoulders, easing the fabric caked in sticky blood loose from his injury.

He sat straight up, his hand reaching up to grasp hers in a surprisingly strong grasp.

"Easy now. We have to clean it so that it doesn't get infected," she said in a stern but gentle tone.

His grip loosened, his hand falling to his side. Golden eyes, glassy with pain, stared at her before they rolled back in his head again, and he slumped against her.

Selene braced herself to keep from falling over with his weight.

Deme moved forward to steady Selene. "You got him?"

"Yeah. Thanks."

Selene and Deme held on, lowering him back to the mattress. Once there, they stood back and flexed their arms and shoulders.

Selene took a deep breath and let it out. "I'm sure you have to get back to Cal. I can take it from here."

Deme crossed her arms over her chest. "I'm not leaving you alone with him."

"Yes, you are. If I need your help, I'll call you. I have you on speed dial."

"Selene, be serious. You don't know him and what he's capable of."

"I told you. I can sense he won't hurt me. Trust me, Deme. I need you to leave me and go check on the woman who was attacked earlier."

"He could be her attacker." Deme's brows rose and her gaze captured Selene's. "Your sense of spirit has been wrong before, hasn't it?"

Selene shook her head. "Never. And no, he didn't attack the woman." She knew beyond a doubt this man wasn't the girl's attacker.

"Still, I don't feel comfortable leaving you with him." Deme's cell phone buzzed and she pulled it from her back pocket. "Hey, Cal. What's happening?" She listened for a minute, her gaze going from Selene to the man on the bed and back to Selene. "Okay, I'll be there in ten minutes." She clicked the off button.

Selene's brows rose. "Cal wants you at the hospital to question the woman, doesn't he?"

Her sister nodded. "He'd like you to be there, too."

Before Deme could finish the last word, Selene was shaking her head. "I'm not leaving him. His wounds must be treated."

"He's unconscious. We could take him to the hospital with us and let the professionals fix him up."

Selene stared down at the man's pale face. "Even if I wanted to, we couldn't get him back up the stairs."

"The woman regained consciousness. I need to get there before they knock her out completely."

"Go. I'll be fine." Selene didn't wait for her sister to

leave—she started gathering supplies to clean and bandage the man's shoulder.

"Well, then, I'll check back here when I'm done at the hospital."

"No need. I tell you, I'll be fine."

Deme snorted. "I'll be here." She touched her sister's arm. "Be careful, and whatever you do, don't trust him. You're my sister and I care about you. I don't want you to be the next woman in the hospital, or dead."

Selene took Deme's hand and squeezed it. "Then trust me. I know what I'm doing."

"Fair enough." With one last pointed stare, Deme left.

As the door closed behind her sister, Selene filled a bowl with hot water and set to work cleaning the wound.

She dabbed at the dried, caked blood all around the jagged, ripped skin, careful not to cause him more pain. But the effort was hopeless. She'd have to scrub to get the dirt and grime off. She applied more pressure, anxious to get the river water off and treat him for infection with one of her mother's poultices made of the dried herbs she kept in her pantry.

After she'd cleaned the skin surrounding the injury, she took a breath and, with a fresh, clean cloth, attacked the wound itself.

Her first dab was hesitant and as gentle as she could be and still get it clean.

The man, whose hair was drying to a tawny gold, jerked with each touch. As she worked toward the center of the jagged, torn skin, his chest rumbled, his body tensed, the muscles in his arms seemed to grow.

Selene tried to hurry but she didn't want to be careless and hurt him further. Her next touch set him off.

He flinched away and a bellow erupted from his throat. His back arched off the bed and his arms and legs writhed against the sheets.

Selene jumped back, tripped over his pile of clothing and fell hard on her butt.

The man rolled to his side, away from her, twisting and jerking, his skin stretching taut over bulging muscles. Thick golden hair sprouted from the skin covering his back, arms and neck. His hair grew longer, thicker and coarser around his head.

The man's back arched again and he roared, falling to the floor on the opposite side of the bed from where Selene sat on the floor in stunned silence.

As soon as he hit the ground, another roar echoed off the walls of the small bedroom and knocked sense back into Selene. She pushed to her feet and threw herself across the bed.

If he continued to thrash around, his wound would start to bleed again.

"Stop it," she yelled. "Whatever's happening to you, stop it now." Selene's heart raced as she stared down at the back of an animal that appeared to be half human, half lion. "What are you?"

He roared again, his back bowing upward.

Selene fell back on the bed, knowing that deep inside, this man was in pain, and the pain wouldn't get better until the injury was tended to. Pushing back her fear, she forced her voice to be calm while she shook inside. "If you don't get back in the bed and lie still, you could die. And I'll be damned if you die on my watch."

The beast's body stilled, the only movement the heaving of his chest as he breathed in and out, his thick, hairy skin twitching.

Taking a deep breath, Selene slid off the bed and crouched on the floor beside the huge creature, touching his uninjured shoulder. "Please. Let me help you."

He flinched away from her.

"You might as well let me help you. I know your secret now. We're past the awkward part. I know why you don't want to go to a hospital. But that doesn't mean your wound can't be treated here." She touched him again.

This time he didn't withdraw.

Taking that as acquiescence, Selene urged him to roll over onto his back.

He laid still, his eyes those of a lion, staring up into hers, unblinking. The hairs on his naked body receded back into his skin, the huge bulk of his lionish muscles reduced to those of a bodybuilding hulk of a human.

Selene reached for his hand, her own shaking. "Come. Get back in the bed where I can clean that wound."

His eyelids fluttered.

She tugged on his uninjured arm. "I can't do it for you and you're not staying on the floor."

He let her help him back into the bed, where he lay completely naked, his skin returning to normal.

Selene's breath caught in her throat as her gaze ran from his toned calves up to thick thighs to the juncture of his legs, where a thick, hard erection, bigger than any Selene had ever witnessed in her limited sexual experiences, jutted upward. As she ran the sheet over his body, she forced her gaze up to his head. The angles in his face eased from the animal he'd become back to the handsome, clean-skinned complexion of the man she'd rescued from beneath the bridge.

Once settled, he lay as still as death, his face pale, his breathing shallow and uneven.

Selene collapsed on the chair beside him, her heart racing, her confidence in the world she'd known shaken even more. What had she gotten herself into? This man obviously wasn't human. Selene laughed shakily. Deme would be livid if she knew what she had in her apartment.

Selene shook her head, staring at the man lying so innocently against her clean white sheets.

What the hell was he?

Chapter 3

Gryph floated in and out of consciousness, pain forcing his beast to the surface more than once. Each time he was coherent enough to realize his body's metamorphosis, he fought the change. A gentle but firm voice led him through the darkness, each time bringing him back from that place so primal and dangerous that he feared he'd go there and never return.

In a burst of pain his body stretched, flexed and altered, his lion surfacing, ready for battle. But an angel's voice cut through his confusion, through the instinct driving him to lash out against the source of his suffering.

Once his eyes opened and he thought he saw a brown-haired beauty hovering over him. A halo of light surrounded her head. A dark angel there to drag his sorry ass back from the grave. She dabbed something cool and moist across his brow, whispering assurances to him. Then she pressed a glob of thick, oozing paste into the angry wound on his shoulder, bringing him fully awake and off the bed. The pain stabbed through his muscles and his jaw tightened. He could feel the lion fighting to break through. He opened his mouth to yell, but the lion's roar erupted from his throat, echoing off the walls.

The angel became the devil, glaring at him, her dark eyes flashing. "Shut up and lie down. That's the second poultice I've applied that you've shaken off." She laid her cool hand on his heated, good shoulder and pushed him down onto the pillow.

A wave of nausea washed over him and he let her guide him back to the mattress. As soon as his head hit the pillow, the lion backed off and his human thoughts became clearer. "Why?"

"Why what?" Her hands dug into a stainless steel bowl on the table beside the bed and came up with a glob of greenish-brown mud. "Let's try this again, and this time don't sit up, or roar. And most of all try not to kill me, will ya?"

Her words cut through his pain, causing him to clench his teeth and focus on maintaining his humanity. "Why did you help me?"

She laid the poultice over his wound.

He gasped, his fingers clenching the sheets at his sides to avoid lashing out at his angel.

The woman shrugged. "I didn't see anyone else coming to your rescue." She adjusted the sheet around his waist and tucked a blanket over him.

For the first time, Gryph realized he was naked. His brows shot up. "My clothes?"

"What's left of them are in the dryer." Her lashes swept down over her deep dark eyes, her cheeks reddening. She pushed a long wavy strand of rich brown hair behind her ear. "They smelled like stinky river water. I washed your trousers, but I'm not sure they'll be fit to be worn." She looked up, her gaze capturing his.

"Did you…?" He nodded toward the sheets covering his body.

"Undress you?" Her chin tipped upward. "You weren't lying on my bed in the soaked clothing. And you weren't cooperating much in a semiconscious state."

Gryph chuckled, and regretted it immediately as the

if you want to get off the street and lie down, you have to help me get you down these stairs. Do you hear me?"

He moaned and leaned heavily on her.

"Wake up." She shook his good shoulder. "I need your help."

"No angel," he muttered, his eyes opening.

"I'll be the devil himself if that's what it takes to get you down those steps. Now, move!"

Deme chuckled. "Didn't know you had it in you, sis. Sure you don't want me to get him down here? I'm bigger than you are."

"I got him." Selene fished in her pocket for her keys and tossed them to Deme.

Her sister hurried down in front of Selene and the stranger to open the door to the little apartment.

Straining against his weight, Selene stepped down first. In a combination of deliberate steps and clumsy falling, she got him down the short flight so quickly he slammed into the door frame.

The big man roared, his eyes flashing open, exposing deep, tawny gold irises, like a lion.

Selene gasped.

"What?" Deme leaned past the man to stare out at her sister. "Did he hurt you?"

"No, no." Selene couldn't meet her sister's gaze. "Let's get him to the bedroom." No need to worry her sister. Especially when she wanted her to leave as soon as she got the injured man settled. If Deme had seen what Selene had, she'd have this man out of her apartment so fast his head would be spinning more than it was already.

By the time they reached her antique cast-iron bed, the man teetered on the verge of passing out. He was more a dead weight than a help. Or that's how he felt to Selene, bearing the brunt of his weight. He leaned toward the bed, but she held on.

movement shook his shoulder. Pain sliced through him and he growled.

Her eyes narrowed and he stopped.

"Perhaps you can tell me your name." She ripped a white sheet in half, then in half again. Her movements were smooth, capable and graceful. Slim flingers made quick work of reducing the sheet into bandages.

Despite his pain, Gryph found himself fascinated by the firm, capable movements of her slender fingers, wondering what they'd feel like running over his naked skin. The animal in him purred.

Her brows rose. "Is it so hard to tell me your name?"

He hesitated. Having spent his young life avoiding answering questions posed by surface dwellers, he still didn't feel comfortable sharing anything about himself with those above the world he'd grown up in. But something about this woman inspired his confidence. "Gryph."

She nodded. "Gryph." On her lips, his name sounded like the music he listened to with Balthazar in the Lair. "I am Selene."

Her fingers folded the sheet into a neat pad, which she laid gently over his wound. Using white medical adhesive tape, she taped it down firmly, holding the poultice in place.

"What is that foul-smelling stuff you put on me?"

"A poultice my mother used to make when we fell and scraped our knees. Guaranteed to help you heal quickly."

"Was your mother an angel like you?"

The woman's lips tipped upward. "*She* was the angel. I'm not. In case you don't remember, I cleaned your wound earlier. You were somewhat out of it. But not enough that you didn't raise a ruckus several times throughout the procedure."

Gryph cringed, his fists tightening into knots. "Did I say or do anything?"

"You didn't *say* anything. You *growled* and *roared*."

She'd only answered half of his question. Gryph's eyes narrowed.

The woman wouldn't meet his gaze and she busied herself gathering the bowl and washcloths on the nightstand.

Gryph grabbed her wrist.

The bowl upended and fell to the ground. The woman's eyes widened.

"What did I *do*?" His voice came out gravelly and as more of a growl than he'd intended. The flash of fear in her eyes told him everything he needed to know. He dropped her hand.

She stepped back, rubbing at the red marks where his fingers had been.

Gryph sighed. "You didn't turn me over to the authorities." He shook his head, staring hard into her eyes. "Why?"

"Should I have?"

"Any surface dweller would have."

Her brows dipped together. "Surface dweller?" She bent to retrieve the bowl, scooting back out of his reach as soon as she straightened, clutching the bowl to her chest. "What do you mean by surface dweller?"

His lips clamped shut. *Damn.* He'd said too much. The less this woman knew the better off he was, and the safer the community of souls was who lived far below the hustle and bustle of Chicago in the dark tunnels under the oldest part of the city. The scarred, the unusual, the mutants and the physically and mentally disfigured freaks who slid beneath the surface to live out their lives unnoticed by the beautiful, so-called normal people of the light.

"I should leave." He pushed to a sitting position and the room spun so fast, he tilted toward the edge of the bed.

The woman was there to catch him, steadying him against her breast. Her tantalizing scent cut through the gray fog consuming him, bringing him back from the edge of unconsciousness.

"You're not going anywhere in your condition," she said, her voice firm.

As much as he wanted to remain with his cheek leaning into the softness of her breast, he straightened. "I'll be fine. I heal fast." His voice sounded weak, even to his own ears.

"If you let yourself." She held on to his arm, her gentle fingers urging him toward the pillow.

Too exhausted to fight her, Gryph lay back, the slightest movement shooting pain through his shoulder. The gray fog swirled around his peripheral vision, shadows sneaking up to claim him. He closed his eyes, giving in to the darkness. "Why didn't you turn me in?"

As if from the bottom of a deep well he heard her answer, "Because I know what it's like to be different."

Selene stayed by his side through what remained of the night. When it came time to open her dress shop above her apartment, she would leave it closed for the day. The man in her bed needed her more than women needed the vintage and whimsical dresses, beautiful, colorful blouses and artistic jewelry her business was known for in the city.

Gryph's wounds had taken more out of him than he would have admitted. He burned with fever for hours and every time he moved, the pain shot through him, triggering the beast within.

Exhausted from little sleep and the stress of caring for her strange patient, Selene was drifting off in the chair beside the bed when her cell phone rang.

Selene hurried to the kitchen to answer and keep from disturbing her patient.

As soon as she clicked the talk button, Deme's urgent voice asked, "Selene, honey, are you okay?"

"Yes, I'm fine." She laughed softly. "Did you expect anything else?"

"With a strange man in your apartment, I didn't know what to expect. Is he still there?"

Selene turned toward the bedroom.

Gryph lay as still as death, his face flushed with fever. "Yes, he's still here."

"Do you want me to come over? He hasn't attacked you or anything?"

"No, he's too far out of it to be a danger."

"What about when he comes to? I can be there in five minutes. Just say the word."

"No." Selene was firm. If Gryph changed in front of her, Deme might not understand. She sure as hell wouldn't agree to let him stay in Selene's apartment after that. "What's the status of the woman who was attacked?"

"She regained consciousness for a few minutes, but she was so distraught, we couldn't get her to answer questions or identify what attacked her. We're at the hospital now, hoping she'll come to long enough to describe her attacker." As a member of Chicago PD's Special Investigations Division, Selene's sisters, Deme and Brigid, had an inside track on any case that defied the norm. Last night's attack was right up their ally.

"Let me know what you learn."

"We had the ME examine her wounds."

"Isn't that a bit premature?"

"Her physician wanted a forensic look at what he saw."

"And?"

"They both confirmed it was some kind of animal attack."

Selene's hand tightened on the cell phone. "Did they say what kind of animal?"

"No, only that it was large enough to snap her neck and

paralyze her. If she lives, most likely she'll never walk again."

Selene drew in a long breath, empathy for the girl weighing deeply in her mind. What if she was wrong? What if the man in her bed was the beast who'd attacked the woman?

She focused on the man lying against her sheets for a long moment. She could sense no latent savagery in him. No hunger to kill. Even when he'd half shifted in pain, she hadn't sensed that he was capable of killing without cause. He wasn't the one.

"Selene, are you there?"

Selene shook her head and returned her attention to her sister. "I'm sorry, what did you say?"

"Brigid is with me. I can send her over to assess the guy in your apartment, if you'd like me to."

"No, Deme." She gripped the phone. "You didn't tell her about him, did you?"

"No. I respected your wishes. Although if you're comfortable with him in your home, why be secretive? We're sisters. Since when do you keep secrets from any of us?"

Since the man in her bed had a beast inside him. "Please, just let me get him well. I'll tell the others once he's able to get around on his own."

"By that time, he might be well enough to attack you. I tell you, Selene, I'm not happy with the situation. It's bad enough watching over a stranger who's been attacked. I don't want to know what it feels like to stand over one of my sister's hospital bed."

"I'll be okay. I promise."

"Well, I'm coming by later today. Whether you like it or not."

"He's unconscious now. Let him wake before you do."

She snorted. "I'm not liking this."

"Duly noted." Selene sighed. "Don't worry, Deme. I'll be careful."

"Yeah, yeah. I'm sure that's what this woman said as she stepped into that parking garage." Deme hung up.

Selene sagged against the counter.

She could hear the man in her bed moan, the moan changing to a low rumbling growl as he thrashed, the sheets slipping low over his waist.

Tired, but determined, Selene prepared another of her mother's poultices, wet a clean washcloth and filled a basin with fresh water. She laid them on a tray and carried them into the room.

With great care, she removed the bandages and plucked away the old poultice a little at a time. The wound was an angry red around the edges. When she applied the damp washcloth, the man jerked to a sitting position, his gaze wild as he slapped her wrist away as if slapping a paw at her. His eyes were glazed, his cheeks flushed with fever.

"It's okay." She pressed a hand to the uninjured shoulder. Speaking softly, she urged him to lie down.

As if he understood, he eased to his back, grimacing, his lips drawing back over long catlike fangs.

As she removed the poultice from the wound, she talked softly. "I've never met a man quite like you."

He winced and growled, small hairs rising on his neck and arms. Fascinated, she stopped cleaning and reached out to touch the hairs. "What are you? Half man, half beast? I have a million questions for you when you are up to answering." She sang her words, soothing him as she applied the new remedy and bandages.

By the time she finished, his face had paled alarmingly and his body shook so hard his teeth rattled.

She pulled the sheet up over his chest.

"Shh, you'll be okay," she said, worried when he shivered so hard he shook the bed. Even after she'd covered him with a blanket, he trembled and his jaw clenched.

Afraid he would go into shock, Selene did the only thing she knew to do. She stripped down to her panties and slipped beneath the blanket and sheet, pressing her warm body against his cold skin. Careful, so as not to touch his wound, she draped an arm over his belly and a leg over his thigh. Curling her body around his, she held on, praying to the goddess the fever and shock wouldn't be the end of him.

Slowly, the tremors lessened, dropping from constant to intermittent and finally, they stopped altogether.

Warm alongside him, and tired beyond exhaustion, Selene lay her face against his chest and closed her eyes. His deep, even breathing reassured her that he would be okay while she took a short nap. Sleep claimed her instantly and with it began the dreams...

Wandering through the dark, she recognized the tunnels. They were just like the ones she and her sisters had traversed beneath Chicago to save the youngest of her sisters from an evil Chimera a couple of years ago.

So dark...

Selene carried a flashlight, the beam barely lighting the way, pushing against the inky blackness like a hand shoving back heavy drapery.

The longer she walked, the longer the tunnel seemed. She stepped over old railroad tracks, discarded pallets, pipes and debris, searching for...whatever, she wasn't quite certain.

Something clattered behind her. Selene stopped to listen. Nothing but the eerie silence. When she started walking again, she sensed something moving with her, getting closer.

At a T-junction, she ducked to the left, clicked off her

flashlight and waited, barely breathing so that she could hear the sound of footsteps treading softly in the passage.

There it was.

The soft steps, moving slowly toward her. Not those of a human but the close succession of patters on the ground like those of a four-legged creature.

The closer it moved the faster her heart beat and the more shallow her breathing. She was afraid if she made even the slightest sound, she'd give away her position.

Just as the creature eased to the junction, Selene flicked her thumb over the on switch, shining her light into the eyes of the predator, hoping to blind it while she made her escape.

The red eyes of a wolf shone back at her like twin blood orbs in a face so dark it blended into the black of the tunnel.

Selene screamed and backed away, the hand holding the flashlight shaking so badly she almost dropped it.

It was huge, as big as any man, only twice as menacing. Its lips curled back, exposing long, sharp teeth, and it emitted a growl so frightening, Selene spun and ran through the tunnel.

"Help me!" she cried, her voice echoing off the empty walls. No one was there—most sane people didn't venture into the subterranean underworld beneath the city. She was alone, being chased by a wolf. She ran, knowing she couldn't outrun the creature.

Her foot caught on a broken rail and she crashed to her knees.

The wolf caught up, braced its paws on either side of her and breathed its hot breath onto the back of her neck, as if waiting for her to turn over. To face her death.

Selene rolled to her back, clutching her pentagram between her fingers, unable to close her eyes to the wicked gleam in her attacker's face, knowing she would witness her own death.

The wolf's body tensed, his mouth opened and he bunched his muscles.

Then a tawny golden flash of sinew and fur hit him head-on, knocking the wolf onto his back.

Selene scrambled backward, grabbing for her flashlight as a mighty battle for supremacy raged in the beam of her light between the wolf and a glorious male lion.

The wolf lunged at the lion, his teeth sinking into the lion's shoulder.

Selene gasped. "No!" She pushed to her feet and would have thrown herself at the wolf, but hands held her back.

"Let me go. I have to help," she whimpered.

"Shh," a low male voice crooned. "It's okay."

"No, it's not." She wept, struggling to free herself. "He'll die."

"It's only a dream," the voice said. A hand smoothed the hair back from her forehead. "It's only a dream. Come little angel, wake up."

"A dream?" Selene whispered. Rising from the darkness, she blinked her eyes open...

Selene stared at the glow-in-the-dark stars she'd tacked to the ceiling shortly after she'd moved into her small apartment. The stars reminded her of the night sky filled with twinkling stars that dispelled the darkness and gave promise of the vastness of the universe.

A solid warmth pressed against her side. She turned her face, her cheek resting against skin—a lot of skin. Selene tipped up her chin and stared into golden eyes and lips quirked at the corners.

"The angel awakens." His words rumbled in his chest, echoing into her ear. His arm shifted beneath her head, his hand cupping her shoulder.

"I must have fallen asleep," she said.

"I think you and I must have been having the same dream. I woke only moments before you."

"I was being attacked by a—"

"Wolf?" His brows descended. "I saw you."

"But then a lion saved me." Selene's eyes widened. "Was that you?"

His gaze grew guarded. "I should be going." He tried to sit up, growled in pain and fell back against the pillow, wincing at the effort.

"You're in no shape to go anywhere."

"I can't stay here."

"Why not?" Selene leaned up on her elbow before she realized she was only wearing her bra and panties. She lay back down, her face burning.

His eyes flared, the pupils dilating. He opened his mouth to say something.

Selene placed a finger over his lips. "Don't get any ideas. I only lay here to warm you when you were going into shock." She cupped his cheek. "It seems the fever is gone." Sitting up, she pressed a pillow to her breasts. "You won't need me to keep you warm."

His good hand closed gently around her wrist. "Stay."

"But I'm not dressed."

"I know. And neither am I." His voice had lowered to a warm rumbling purr. "I feel a chill coming on."

Selene frowned. "Yeah, right."

His body shook and his face tightened in pain. "Please. It's your bed, and you need sleep as much as I do."

"I don't know you."

"I'll keep the monsters away from your dreams."

"What if *you're* the monster?"

"You've already proven you can tame my beast."

She wavered, the warmth of his skin tempting her. "I'll need to change your bandages soon."

"They can wait." He tugged on her hand, drawing her back to the bed.

"I *am* tired." She settled against him, trying to read into his mind. She couldn't hear his thoughts, could only feel his emotions or see flashes of images. They weren't malevolent so much as hot and lusty, sparking an answering heat deep in her core. "I shouldn't." Her hand rested on his chest.

His muscles hardened, his skin stretching tight. "You should sleep," he whispered.

Ha! Sleep was the furthest from her mind as she lay almost naked against this ruggedly powerful and mysterious man. The longer she lay there, the more she wondered what it would feel like to press her lips to his skin.

An image of lips brushing the top of her head was followed by a featherlight stirring at her temple. Selene's breath caught in her chest.

Her heart tripped over itself then thundered against her ribs. She shifted until she faced him, staring up into his eyes. "Did you kiss me?" she asked, her voice little more than air.

His mouth quirked upward. "Had I really kissed you, you would know."

Every logical thought in her head screamed for her to get up, get dressed and throw this man out of her apartment. But logic didn't rule when it came to Gryph. Her heart had firm control and was moving forward, the momentum sweeping her with it.

Bolder than she'd ever been in her life, she leaned up until her mouth hovered over his. "Then kiss me so that I'll know."

He chuckled, the mirth dying as his gaze claimed hers and his head rose to close the distance between them. His hand wrapped around her hair and pressed her into him and he claimed her lips, his mouth slanting against hers, his tongue snaking out to dart between her teeth, sliding the length of hers, the surface coarse, sensual, enticing.

Selene slipped her hand behind his head, her fingers threading through the longish, thick, golden mane, tangling and tugging, to get closer still. Half lying on his good side, she inhaled the musky scent of male and something more primal. Her body ignited, her skin on fire from breast to thigh where it met his. Her center tightened, her channel growing slick.

A low purr rumbled in his chest and his hand flexed and skimmed across the small of her back to cup the curve of her buttocks. His fingers massaged the flesh, sliding into her panties and between the seam of her thighs, finding her entrance.

Her insides clenched, a wash of liquid dampening the path as he pressed his finger inside her.

Her mouth consumed his, she sucked his bottom lip between her teeth and moaned as he swirled the digit inside her.

Selene let go of his lip and arched her back, her head tipping back as she basked in the rush of sensations shooting fire through her veins.

Gryph raised his injured shoulder and cried out. "Damn!"

Yanked back to reality, Selene slid off him and stood in her bra, then adjusted her panties, her eyes wide. "That shouldn't have happened."

The man in her bed nodded, his hand pressing gently against the bandage over his shoulder. "You're right. I'd be taking advantage of the situation."

"You? You're the injured party." Selene grabbed a short champagne-colored silk robe and jammed her arms into the sleeves, pulling the edges closed around her. "I'm sorry. I don't know what came over me." She grabbed the washbasin and rag and rushed from the bedroom into her little kitchen, where she stood with her back to the open door, her body trembling. Not from fear, but from coming so close to making love with a stranger, and then pulling back. She still wanted him and—damn it—he was injured, practically a prisoner in her bed until he could get around on his own.

Selene sucked in a deep breath and let it out slowly. She had to get a grip, go back in there and dress his wound. The sooner he was well, the sooner he'd be out of her bed, her apartment and her life.

As she filled the basin with fresh, clean water, mixed more of the magical poultice and grabbed another clean cloth, she squared her shoulders and called herself a fool for falling into bed with a stranger.

With her mental pep talk fresh on her mind, she entered her bedroom.

Gryph lay on the bed, the sheet covering all the right places but it was tented.

By the goddess.

Selene nearly dropped the basin. Her hands shook so badly and her body burned, craving to be beneath the sheet sporting the evidence of his desire.

"You don't have to do this," he said.

"If I don't, your wound will get infected and you could die."

"So?" he said. "You don't owe me anything."

"I owe you human kindness. I'd take care of anyone injured as badly as you."

"Anyone," he said softly. "Selene, what happened a moment ago—"

"Don't." She set the basin on the nightstand. "Let's forget it ever did."

"Problem is…I can't." He nodded toward the tented sheet.

"You can and will." She refused to glance at his groin,

focusing on the injured shoulder. "It should never have happened."

"Because I'm different?"

"No, because *I* am."

He frowned and opened his mouth to say something else, but the cell phone in the kitchen rang, saving Selene from further argument. She didn't want to explain why she was different. How would any man like to know she could read his thoughts? What if she could project her thoughts? What if all of Gryph's desire could be a manifestation of what Selene was feeling? Her gift was being able to connect to other's minds. A telepathy of emotions and images.

She ran from the room and grabbed her cell phone.

"We need you at the hospital," Deme said without preamble.

"Why?"

"The victim is awake and we don't know for how long. Hurry."

"I can't leave right now."

"Brigid is already on her way. She should be there to pick you up in less than two minutes." Her sister sighed. "I don't like you being alone in that apartment with that man."

"I'm fine." Selene's gaze shifted to Gryph. "He's not going to hurt me."

"We'll know more as soon as the woman can tell us. We need you here for that, in case she can't speak."

"But—"

"Come, or I'll tell Brigid about your guest."

Her hand clenched around the phone. Her sister wouldn't understand Selene's trust in a stranger. And for that matter, Brigid was more likely to throw a fireball first, ask questions later. With the threat of letting Brigid in on her rescue, Selene had no choice. "Fine. I'll come."

Selene clicked the phone off and scooted back to her bedroom, grabbing her jeans from the floor. "I have to go."

"When will you be back?"

"I don't know." She jammed her legs into her jeans and pulled them up over her hips. Her hands hesitated on the robe. "You won't go anywhere, will you? You're not healed enough."

His gaze met hers, the heat of those golden eyes warming her body all over again. He gave a brief nod. "I'll stay until I'm better."

Selene dropped the robe, without breaking visual contact.

His golden eyes flared, his lips tightened and a low, rumbling purr rose from his chest.

Then she pulled a T-shirt over her head. "I'll be back as soon as I can."

Chapter 4

"I don't know why I had to come." Selene couldn't help worrying about the stranger she was forced to leave behind in the bed, back in her apartment. Alone, injured and sexy as hell.

"I'm sure Deme had good reason. Probably because you can read minds better than any of us." Brigid parked her Harley in the visitors parking area outside the emergency room and kicked the stand down to hold up the big machine.

Selene climbed off, pulling the helmet over her head.

In her biker leathers and with her badass attitude, Brigid was hard enough to stand up against. To keep Brigid from asking questions or entering her apartment, Selene left without inviting her sister in, claiming they'd better hurry. Her Chicago police special detective sister didn't need to know about the man. She'd go ballistic, possibly even fling a fireball or two, if she even knew Selene had him in her apartment.

In the dark hours just before dawn, Selene and Brigid slipped in through the emergency entrance to the hospital. They headed straight for the elevators and the ICU floor where the injured woman was being cared for.

As they rode up in the elevator, Selene let her guard down and stretched her thoughts out, gathering in emotions, thoughts and fears of the people in the hospital. Most were asleep, some dreaming, some having nightmares. Those who lay awake in their beds worried about their loved ones or whether they would live to see another day.

The overall feeling was one of worry and sadness, with one exception. A dark malevolence slithered through Selene's thoughts, skimming at the edges, slipping in and out like a thief. One moment the darkness took shape, the next it pushed her away, making her head hurt with the pressure.

A hand on her elbow made her open her eyes.

Brigid stared at her, her brows furrowed. "Are you all right?"

Selene hadn't realized she'd closed her eyes. Nor had she realized the elevator door had opened onto the ICU floor. She blinked and forced a smile. "Yeah." Then she stepped out onto the highly polished tiles, rolling the strain from her shoulders. Surely she'd imagined the darkness. "Let's get this over with." That way she could get out of this hospital and back to the man called Gryph, lying semiconscious in her bed.

As she rounded the corner of the elevator bank, Selene saw Deme and Cal, Deme's fiancé, standing at the nurses' station, consulting with a doctor.

Deme looked up, the strain in her face easing slightly when she recognized Selene and Brigid. "I'm glad you came." She introduced them to the doctor, who immediately excused himself, leaving the four of them standing beside the nurses' station. Deme tipped her head to the right. "Let's go somewhere we can talk. I could use some coffee." She led them back to the elevator and down to the cafeteria that remained open 24/7.

"Was the woman able to identify her attacker?" Brigid asked.

"The victim's name is Amanda Grant," Cal said.

Selene leaned forward, her breath lodged in her chest. "What did she say?"

Deme's gaze connected with hers and she continued without looking away. "We had a sketch artist draw from her description. Show her what we got, Cal."

Cal Black, the tall, handsome Chicago police officer, pulled a white page from the folder he held and handed it to Brigid. "I've never seen anything like it."

"Me, either," Deme said, her gaze fixed firmly on Selene.

Brigid whistled. "What is it?"

Selene leaned over, her heart beating so fast, it pounded against her eardrums. When the page came into view, she gasped.

Lion eyes stared out at her, and a full mane of hair encircled a half human, half lion face. The same face she'd seen when Gryph had suffered severe pain and changed into something she'd never encountered before. Selene swallowed the lump in her throat. "Miss Grant said this was her attacker?"

Deme nodded. "About that time she passed out. She's been unconscious since. The police chief has a copy of this and will be circulating it to the press."

That dark spirit flitted through Selene's thoughts again and she winced, pressing her fingers to her temples.

"Are you okay?" Deme leaned forward and grabbed Selene's wrist. "What the hell?" She stared down at where her fingers touched Selene's skin. "Where did you get these bruises?"

Selene pulled her hand free. "Must have hit my arm against my stair rail."

"Like hell you did." Deme reached out and pulled her close to study the marks. "*He* did it, didn't he?"

"He who?" Brigid closed the gap between them and took Selene's hand from Deme. "Who did this?"

"No one." Selene glared at Deme, wishing she'd shut up and left Brigid out of it.

"Selene and I found a man down by the river and took him to her apartment," Deme announced. "Against my better judgment."

"He was injured." Selene tried to pull her hand free form Brigid's grip. "I only wanted to help."

"And a hospital wasn't good enough for him?" Brigid snorted and let Selene have her hand back. She stood with her arms crossed over her chest. "What am I missing here?"

"Yeah. What are we missing?" Gina, followed by Aurai, stepped into the cafeteria. Now all of her sisters were here. "The nurses' station said we could find you here."

Selene stared across at Deme. "You called everyone?"

"I got the feeling this was something that could potentially involve all of us."

"It doesn't. It only involves me." She spun around and paced away from her sisters, turned and marched back. "I only needed assistance getting him into my apartment, or I wouldn't have asked for your help."

"Thanks." Deme's lips twisted. "I thought we were sisters. Aren't you the one always preaching that we shouldn't keep secrets from each other?" she demanded. "What is it about this man that has you ready to lie by omission to your family?"

With her four sisters staring at her accusingly, Selene had no other choice but to tell the truth. "He's different."

Brigid shook the paper with the sketch at Selene. "Just how different?"

"He…" She shook her head, the dark, painful consciousness stabbed through her mind, closer this time. Selene gasped, clutched her head in her hands and doubled over.

"Selene?" Deme grabbed her arms and helped her straighten. "What's wrong?"

"Something dark…" She pressed fingers to her temple to stop the pain. "Evil."

"Where? At your apartment?"

"No." She looked up, her gaze turning toward the hallway outside the cafeteria. "Here."

"Here? Something evil in the hospital?"

Selene staggered toward the door. "Amanda...must get to her." Without waiting for an answer, she ran to the elevator, stabbed at the button and then waited, her hands twisting together as the elevator made its slow descent to the cafeteria, every second stretching excruciatingly. When the doors finally opened, Selene fell in and jabbed the button for the floor where the ICU was located. Cal jumped in with Deme, Brigid, Aurai and Gina close behind before the doors closed.

"Hurry," Selene whispered as the elevator whisked upward.

"What is it? What do you sense?" Deme asked.

"Amanda's in trouble." The elevator door opened and Selene darted out.

"Selene!" Cal called out. "Wait. Let me go first. It might be dangerous."

Selene couldn't hear him for the roaring in her ears, the pounding of her heart nearly beat out of her chest. The pain throbbed with so much intensity that her breathing grew shallow and she couldn't get enough air into her lungs. She dropped to her knees, clutching at her throat.

"Selene." Cal reached her first.

She pushed him away, pointing to a hallway, unable to push any air past her vocal cords because she couldn't get air into her lungs. When he wouldn't go, she pushed him again.

Brigid squatted in front of her. "What is it, Selene?"

She pushed her away, too, her vision dimming, her head getting light. "Amanda—"

Brigid's eyes widened and she sprang to her feet. "Something's happening to Amanda."

"I'll stay with Selene, you guys go!" Aurai dropped to the tiled floor with Selene and slipped an arm around her sister. "Breathe, Selene. You can do it. Please. Pull yourself out of Amanda and come back to me." Aurai turned Selene's face to her. "Look at me."

Selene stared into her sister's pale blue eyes. The overhead lights glowed off her bright gold hair, almost blinding her with the intensity. A light, a bright light to follow, to drift toward.

"Selene!" Aurai shook her head. "Snap out of it." She raised her hand and slapped Selene across the face.

The contact brought Selene back from the light, back to the cool hard tiles of the hospital floor. She stared into her sister's eyes, seeing her for the first time, kneeling on the ground beside her.

Selene gasped in a huge breath and let it out, her breathing returning to normal, her vision clearing. Then the malevolent presence wavered in her mind, making her jaw tighten and her temple ache. "He's getting away." She lurched to her feet, holding on to Aurai.

"Who's getting away?"

"The one who attacked Amanda." Selene stumbled down a hallway toward a stairwell.

"You can't go after him, Selene." Aurai grabbed her arm and held her back.

Cal ran out of an ICU room shouting, "Get a crash cart in here!" Gina, Deme and Brigid joined him.

Critical-care nurses raced for the woman's room and for the equipment necessary to save her life.

Selene and Aurai ran to join the others in the hallway, staying well out of the way. "What happened?"

Deme shook her head. "Someone smothered Amanda."

Selene pointed to the stairwell. "He went down the stairwell."

Cal ran for the stairwell and shouted over his shoulder, "Deme, call Security, get them to block the exits."

"I'm coming with you," she said.

"I'll make that call." Aurai ran for the nurses' station.

"I'll take the elevator down." Brigid ran in the opposite direction.

Selene started to follow Cal and Deme, but Aurai yelled at her. "No, Selene. Go with Brigid. You're not strong enough yet." She pointed toward the elevator where Brigid waited. The bell rang, announcing the car's arrival, and Brigid stepped in.

Selene dove for the elevator, catching it as the doors closed.

When she turned, she saw Aurai talking on the telephone, a frown denting her smooth young forehead.

The sense of evil was fading, the tightness easing in Selene's head. "He's getting away."

"Not if I have anything to say about it," Brigid said through clenched teeth.

Thankfully, the elevator went all the way down without stopping on even one floor. Whether it was because Selene was willing away anyone who dared to touch the buttons or just luck, she didn't know or care. The main thing was to get to ground level before the killer.

The bell rang, the door opened and Brigid leaped out. Selene followed more slowly. She closed her eyes and felt for the presence. Her senses only picked up on the worry and sadness surrounding the hospital. The evil had gone away…vanished.

"Brigid!" Selene called out as her sister hit the exit door.

Brigid came to a sudden halt and looked back over her shoulder.

Selene shook her head. "He's gone."

Deme and Cal emerged from the stairwell, breathing

hard. They stopped in the emergency room lobby, staring across at Selene.

She shook her head. "We're too late."

Brigid cursed. "Well, I'm going out to look anyway."

"I don't even feel him anywhere close. It's as though he dropped off the face of the earth, his presence disappeared so quickly."

Aurai emerged from the bank of elevators and ran across the lobby to join her sisters. "We missed him?"

Deme nodded.

"Damn." Brigid punched a fist into her palm. Then she turned toward Selene, her eyes blazing. "The man you took to your apartment, did you lead him here?"

Selene shook her head, her stomach knotting. "He didn't do this."

"Are you sure?" Brigid crossed to stand in front of Selene, anger flowing from every pore of her body, her very presence heating the air around them all.

The anger surrounded Selene, filling her senses. She staggered backward. "I'm sure. He didn't do this."

"What about the picture? The one Amanda had drawn before she was murdered." Brigid's lip curled up in a snarl. "Was your guy the one in the picture?"

Selene stared out at the faces of her sisters, all waiting for her answer, all wearing accusing expressions. She couldn't lie to them, but if she answered, she'd damn the man in her apartment. She inhaled and let the breath out before she said, "Yes."

"What do you want to bet when we get back to your apartment, your guest is gone?" Brigid punched out of the hospital, running toward her Harley.

Selene had to sprint to catch up to Brigid or be left behind. She prayed the man was still lying in her bed. Then at least it would prove he wasn't the man who'd attacked Amanda Grant and returned to finish the job.

* * *

Gryph's eyes fluttered open. It took him a few moments to comprehend that the puffs of clouds and blue skies were nothing more than a mural painted on the ceiling of the room he found himself in. Stars were tacked amongst the clouds in an odd day-night combination. The soft bed and sweet-scented air contrasted sharply to the musty dampness of the underground he'd grown up in. He sat up, wincing at the soreness in his shoulder.

He must have dozed off or passed out after Selene left. Over an hour had passed, his shoulder already felt better, and his vision had cleared. One of the benefits of being a shifter was that once the injuries had been addressed his body regenerated quickly. He rose, wrapping one of the sheets around his middle, and paced the interior of the tiny two-room apartment, his strength returning with every step, even as the walls closed in around him.

Light, colorful fabrics draped the windows. The furniture, a scattered array of mix-and-match items, most likely found at yard sales, appeared lovingly restored with new fabric and accessorized with bright throw pillows and blankets. Every color in the rainbow was represented, none appearing out of place, as if they all worked to get along in the close confines of the interior.

In the living area, a rich red overstuffed sofa took up most of the space. On a coffee table in front of the sofa stood a candleholder in the shape of a pentagram, each point holding a small tea candle whose wicks had been burned at some point in time. Facing the sofa was an old-fashioned gas fireplace set against one wall and surrounded by a bright mosaic of tiles, adding even more color to the room. Over the fireplace hung a large filigreed pentagram, encased in a circle. Fine images inscribed in the design of each point of the pentagram represented spirit, air, fire, earth and water.

On the wooden mantel stood a photograph of five women, one of whom was Selene with her rich brown hair. Another was the red-haired woman he vaguely remembered, who'd helped get him into the basement apartment. The women held hands as they faced the camera and smiled. Clearly they cared about each other. Sisters, if not biologically, then by their strong connection to each other.

Despite being at the bottom of the stairs and in the basement of an older building with only a couple of windows filtering sunlight into the room, the space breathed of warmth and comfort—what Gryph had always thought a home should be. The atmosphere filled Gryph with a sense of longing he hadn't experienced since he'd been a small child, and was led to the surface at nightfall to experience a sunset so grand and beautiful he'd cried.

Gryph shook off the feeling of home and spied a small television settled on a corner of the breakfast bar between the kitchen and the living area. He switched it to the local news station and rolled his sore shoulder, gritting his teeth at the pain.

A newswoman stood in front of the Chicago trauma-and-critical-care hospital, the wind whipping her hair into her face as she gave her late-breaking report of an attack on the streets of Chicago.

"A young woman was brought to the hospital late last night after being brutally attacked and left to die when leaving the theater in downtown Chicago. Admitted to the trauma center, she only had minutes to speak to the police before she was taken into surgery. A forensic artist was able to compile a rough sketch of her attacker before the surgeon arrived. Just to let you know, the woman made it through surgery and is now in recovery, expected to live. Whether she'll walk again remains in question.

"Folks, as crazy as it appears, were posting the image of her attacker. The police department isn't quite sure what to make of it, and neither am I, but if you see anything like it, call 911 and report the location and time of the sighting. If such an animal is loose in the city, the sooner we capture or kill it, the safer we *all* will be."

A drawing replaced the images of the reporter and the hospital.

Gryph's heart thudded against his ribs as he stared at a crude drawing of a lion's head with a man's face. It was him.

Chapter 5

Gryph continued to watch the television newscast. The sketched image of him was replaced by the reporter. "This just in—the victim was in ICU after surgery when she was attacked again and smothered to death before anyone could get to her." Police units, lights flashing, rolled in beside the newswoman. Officers leaped out of their squad cars and raced into the building.

His blood freezing in his veins, Gryph realized what saving the woman had cost him and the rest of the outcasts who lived their lives beneath the city streets. With an animal like him identified as the beast who'd ravaged a woman on the streets, every police officer would be searching all the nooks and crannies in the city. If they dug too deeply, they would locate the Lair.

He'd put them all at risk of discovery. And whomever had attacked the woman outside the theater in the first place was still running free and had gone back to finish the job.

He had to get out of Selene's apartment. She'd seen him in his half-changed form. She'd know the drawing was of him, and she might return with the police to haul him in for murder. Or if she didn't turn him in, and the police found him there, he'd bring her down with him. The evidence was stacked against him by an eyewitness, who was dead. If Selene chose not to hand him over to the authorities, she could be arrested for aiding and abetting a suspected murderer.

With purposeful strides, he entered the kitchen and pulled open the compact clothes dryer, removing his cloak and the tattered remains of his trousers. He stepped into the ripped pants. The shirt was beyond repair. Rather than leave it there as evidence against Selene, he shoved it into a pocket, slung his cape over his shoulder and hurried toward the door.

Gryph paused by the small window beside the door, pushed aside the frothy mauve curtain and lifted the edge of the blinds to peer out at street level. It wouldn't be long before people ventured out onto the early morning city streets. The sidewalks would fill with workers headed to their jobs.

He unlocked the door and eased it open. The sun had yet to top the horizon and spill over the crowns of the skyscrapers. For the moment, nothing stirred, nothing moved in front of Selene's apartment. Lights remained off in the buildings surrounding the little dress shop and its basement apartment. One by one the streetlights blinked off.

Still weak, but getting stronger, Gryph slipped out the door, up the stairs and eased into the gloom. Years of blending into obscurity had refined his skills at disappearing.

Rounding the corner of the building, he paused and listened. The rumble of an engine grew louder until a dark motorcycle turned onto the street and slowed in front of the dress shop. Two people got off.

He risked being seen or caught, but he had to know if the rider or the passenger was Selene.

Both riders pulled off their helmets. The driver's long, inky-black hair slipped free and fell to her shoulders, the streetlight shining down on it, giving it a blue glow. The second rider struggled with the strap beneath her chin.

Gryph held his breath as she finally loosened the strap and lifted the helmet up and over her head. Long, chocolate-brown hair slipped free and fell in a dark cloud, tumbling down her back. Selene, with her brown hair and deep, brown-black eyes, stood beside the motorcycle.

The driver pulled a gun from a holster beneath her black leather jacket, released the clip, checked her ammunition and then slammed it back into the handle.

Selene laid a hand on the woman's arm. "Brigid, that's not necessary."

"I'd ball up some fire, but I don't want to burn your place down."

"He wasn't the killer. Whoever it was had an enmity, an evil about him that was palpable. I never sensed that with Gryph."

"So his name is Gryph, is it?" The woman with the coal-black hair and ice-blue eyes held out her hand, palm up. "Give me the keys."

Selene dug in her pocket and handed over the keys. "He's not a monster."

"Could have fooled me."

"He's different," Selene insisted.

"I'd say. How many people do you know who look like him? He's a freak and he killed a woman tonight."

Gryph ground his back teeth. *I didn't kill anyone*, he wanted to shout aloud, but he held his tongue.

As the black-haired woman descended the stairs to the basement apartment, Selene turned in his direction. She stared straight at him, as if she could see into the shadows.

His eyesight, keen in the dark, both from experience at moving in the blackness of the underworld and from the inner lion's nocturnal nature, could see the worry lines etched into her brow. He inched backward, ready to run.

A soft sensation brushed across his senses as if someone

reassured him that it was okay. At the same time it gave him a gentle mental push, urging him to leave.

Headlights filled the street as an SUV turned the corner and came to a stop behind the motorcycle.

The redhead who'd helped Selene get him down the stairs climbed out of the driver's seat and a man unfolded from the passenger side. A blonde and a brunette emerged from the back doors.

"Is he still here?" the redhead called out.

"About to find out," said the black-haired woman with the key in her hand.

"I tell you, he wouldn't hurt anyone," Selene insisted.

"You saw what he did to that girl in the hospital. We all saw the bruises on your arms. He's dangerous."

"He didn't kill her and he didn't mean to hurt me."

Guilt squeezed Gryph's chest so hard he couldn't breathe. He'd hurt her when all she'd tried to do was help him. Balthazar had been right all those years. The only place for him was below the surface. Up until the past five years, he'd lived his life in the underworld, where the misfits and freaks existed judgment-free, and where he wouldn't be unleashed to hurt innocents. Amassing a fortune and building a business didn't make him any more human.

"You say he didn't hurt her, but the victim had the forensic artist draw a picture of her attacker, which happened to match your guest from what you say." The redhead nodded to the woman at the bottom of the steps. "Sounds pretty damning to me. Let's check out your monster."

The woman at Selene's door unlocked it and pushed it open, her gun held in front of her. A light went on inside the apartment. She disappeared inside. A few moments later, she called out, "He's gone."

It was time to go. Gryph turned to leave. His night vision temporarily compromised by the headlights, he didn't see the soda can until he nudged it with his bare foot. The can skittered across concrete, making a metallic grating sound that echoed against the buildings in the alley.

"What was that?" the man who'd arrived in the SUV said from the top of the stairs.

"Probably the wind," Selene said.

Gryph stood poised to run, out of sight of the group standing near Selene's apartment.

"I'll check it out," the man said.

Gryph took off, aiming for the corner of the building at the end of the alley. If he could get there before the man rounded the side of Selene's building, he could lose him in the maze of downtown structures.

Channeling his inner beast to give him speed and strength, he ran, reaching the corner as a shout rang out.

"Stop or I'll shoot!"

He didn't slow, didn't stop, just ran as fast as his feet could carry him. At the end of another building, he flew around the corner, crossed the street and ducked around another structure.

Before long, he was several blocks away, the sound of pursuit long disappeared.

Careful to ensure he wasn't being followed, he entered a back alley, swung wide around a large trash bin and a stack of decaying pallets, and stopped in front of a solid steel door. He dug his fingers into a chink in one of the bricks beside it and unearthed a key that fit the door.

With practiced efficiency, he twisted the key in the lock. The door opened inward, revealing stairs that led into a basement. Replacing the key in the chinked-out space, he entered, closing the door behind him. On quiet feet, he moved through the darkness, descending to the basement floor.

One of the oldest buildings in downtown Chicago, it had access to the tunnel system beneath the city. Built in the early nineteen hundreds, city planners had hoped the tunnels, with their narrow-gauge rail cars, would allow quick and efficient transportation of cargo to and from the buildings downtown, freeing some of the congestion of the streets above. The plan failed, but the tunnels remained, for the most part. Some had collapsed, others had been filled in when skyscrapers had been built on top of them. The labyrinth provided a warm, safe haven from weather and prying eyes to the inhabitants who called it home.

Having been abandoned as a small baby, unable to fend for himself, Gryph had known no other domicile. If not for the benevolence of Balthazar, he'd have perished in the harsh Chicago streets, unwanted, unloved and unprotected. When he'd discovered a good living in day trading five years ago, he'd accumulated enough wealth to own his own building downtown and he dared to move closer to the light.

Like many who had been forgotten, shunned or thrown away, like himself, he'd lived his life in the shadows of the city, rarely venturing out. Even in his own building, he rarely stepped outside, preferring to limit contact with humans to avoid any mishaps or triggering his inner beast to appear.

Balthazar warned him about the surface dwellers and their lack of compassion or understanding of anything strange or unusual. His adoptive father taught him to sense the rise of his inner beast and control the urge to morph into his animal form. As a child, spikes in emotion had thrown him into animal form.

At those times, for his own protection and the protection of the others in his care, Balthazar had confined Gryph to a cage, letting him out when he'd returned to human form. Those times had marked him deeply. He'd hated the cage and everything it stood for and vowed never to be caged again.

Kindhearted yet firm, Balthazar had taken him into the Lair, brought him up as his own son. The older man collected strays like him, bringing them into the fold, helping them to assimilate into a life in the shadows, finding useful work for them, from running street cleaners to servicing office buildings at night when everyone else slept.

Balthazar raised Gryph and another lost boy who'd been the child of a crack addict with no other family to call her own or to claim the child. Broke, homeless and strung out, his mother had holed up in the basement of a building. When the maintenance super had discovered her temporary lodgings, she'd tied her baby to her back and hidden beneath a trap door, clinging to a ladder to avoid being evicted. She'd descended the metal ladder until her feet touched the bottom of the well.

A light glowing at the end of a long tunnel led her to the center of the underworld city. Balthazar had taken her in, offering food and shelter for her and the baby as long a she resisted the lure of her addiction and promised to keep the community secret.

Not long afterward, her hunger for drugs drove her back to the surface. She never came back.

The baby named Lucas came to live with Balthazar and Gryph when Gryph was eight.

Balthazar, a college professor in his former life amongst the humans, had taught Gryph and Lucas to read and write, instilling in Gryph a love of classic literature and the arts. Determined to give them all the educational advantages of the surface dwellers, he'd set up a computer lab in the Lair, running ethernet cables from above to allow them to learn about the world in the light.

Though he'd never traveled outside the city limits of Chicago, Gryph could name all the countries on earth. He'd learned about finance and day trading, becoming quite good at following the news and anticipating market

changes. Using seed money he'd earned cleaning buildings after sundown, he'd amassed a small fortune he kept
stashed in banks stateside and abroad. Five years ago, he'd
come out of the darkness to buy the building he now lived
and worked in.

He'd dreamed of one day visiting other countries.

For now, his home was in the basement of his office
building with a shaft that led to the maze of passages beneath the city.

He worked his way to the center of the Lair, passing old
Joe Lowenstein, fast asleep in his cubby, blankets tucked
up to his chin to ward off the chill and damp of the underworld. Joe had been a chemist until he'd been severely
scarred in a chemical accident. Half his face melted off,
blind in one eye and his right arm completely useless, he
now made a living carving beautiful figurines out of wood,
with his good hand and a vise grip Balthazar had appropri-
ated from an abandoned workshop. Each finished figure
sold in an upscale art gallery on 35th Street for thousands
of dollars. Still Joe slept in the cubby, his money accumu-
lating in a bank.

He rolled over, his good eye opening. "Gryph? That
you?" Joe's voice was as mottled as his face, gravelly to
the point of almost being unintelligible.

"Go back to sleep, Joe," Gryph whispered.

"Trouble's brewin'," Joe rasped.

"How so?"

"Some say it's you." Joe rubbed a hand across his
scarred cheeks. "Don't know what they're talkin' about.
Balthazar will know."

"I'm headed there now. Thanks for the heads-up."
Gryph continued toward the forgotten city's center, the
hairs on the back of his neck spiked, the inner beast clawing at his insides to be released to attack the tension in
the air.

A small gathering ringed the entrance to the rooms he, Balthazar and Lucas had called home for so long. It was nothing more than a former storage area beneath the city, where supplies had been kept. It consisted of four large compartments. Gryph, Lucas and Balthazar each claimed one as his own and the fourth was a common area they still gathered in to share the events of their days or nights when time permitted. Balthazar had refused to move in with Gryph in his building nearer the surface, claiming he preferred the darkness to the light after all these years.

Now Balthazar stood at the entrance, his voice ringing out over the angry shouts of the small crowd. "Keep calm, people. I'm sure there's some kind of misunderstanding."

"What if he leads them down here?" someone asked.

Balthazar held up his hand. "He wouldn't. He's much too smart and cautious to let that happen. Please, go to your homes. Let me talk to Gryphon. I'm sure he can clear it all up."

"Clear up what?" Gryph strode across the wide, open space where the old tracks had switched and turned down the long tunnels leading to the ends of the old city. He clutched his cloak around him, to hide the tattered remains of his clothing beneath.

"There he is!" a woman shouted. "What have you done? What kind of monster are you to attack a defenseless woman?"

"I've done nothing." Gryph stood straight, his shoulders thrown back. "I'm no more a monster than any of you."

"You killed a surface dweller." Raymond Henning, a man with the ability to blend into the surroundings as easily as a chameleon, shook his fist at Gryph. "We all took an oath when we came to live here. No one hurts anyone. Now that you've let your beast kill, it will crave more bloodshed."

"I didn't kill anyone, and I don't crave blood," Gryph

said, his voice urgent but calm. These were his people. Most of the money he earned through his day trading and businesses went to providing food and comfort for them. He'd only ever told Balthazar, whom he'd sworn to secrecy.

"How soon before they start a city-wide manhunt for you?" A young woman with blue and green fish scales on her neck and face pulled a scarf up over her head, her eyes darting around the group. "They'll find us and drag us back into the light, or worse, exterminate us."

"Will any of us be safe if the authorities discover what we have built down here?" Raymond asked.

"No!" shouted a mutant man with a bulbous blob completely covering the entire left side of his face spoke up. "We're doomed. The authorities will track him here. They can't have a killer on the loose in Chicago. It's bad for tourism. They had an eyewitness, they know his face, and they won't stop until they string him up for the woman's murder."

"I won't lead the authorities down here. I'm careful to preserve what we have. It's as much my home as yours. You all know me." He waved a hand at Raymond. "Raymond, didn't I lead you here when you'd passed out drunk in an alley and given up hope?"

Raymond frowned. "Yeah, but—"

Gryph continued, "Tara, when you first came to the Lair, didn't I show you around the maze of tunnels until you were comfortable on your own?"

The furry woman nodded. "You did."

"Many of you have known me my whole life. Have I ever hurt anyone?"

Many in the crowd muttered no.

Gryph lowered his voice and said softly, "I wouldn't condemn the people I love to exposure to those who don't understand us."

Lucas, who had long dark hair, draped an arm over

Gryph's shoulder. "That's right. You all know Gryph. He's a good man. He might not be able to control his beast, but he'd give his life for any one of you."

Gryph frowned at his brother. "I have control."

Lucas's mouth twisted. "Of course you do, even when you're angry, right?" He clapped his hand on Gryph's back. "Always the hero who could do no wrong." Though he smiled, Lucas's lip pulled back on one side in almost a sneer.

Gryph stared at his brother whose hand on his shoulder was tight, his fingers digging in.

Balthazar held up his hands. "You heard the man, he didn't kill the surface dweller. Go home and get some sleep. Everything will be better by morning."

Reluctantly, the crowd of misfits dispersed, muttering and grumbling as they trudged to their makeshift rooms constructed of abandoned pieces of plywood or cardboard in offshoots of the derelict rail tunnels.

Not long ago, Balthazar had worked with a handful of people to tap in to the electrical grid of the buildings, reactivating the lighting system in select tunnels so that they wouldn't have to live in total darkness. For safety's sake, everyone was required to have a stash of emergency flashlights. Every inhabitant knew that when city workers descended into the underground tunnels, they had to make themselves scarce. If they were discovered, the good surface-dwelling citizens of Chicago would force them to the surface, where they'd be pitied and treated as freaks.

"Where have you been?" Balthazar asked as he led Gryph and Lucas into his chambers.

"Recovering." Gryph whipped the cape off his shoulders exposing his naked chest and the bandage Selene had carefully applied.

Balthazar's lips pressed into a thin line. He peeled back

the bandages and examined the ragged scabs over Gryph's shoulder. "Who did this?"

"Question might not be who, but what?" Lucas said. "Looks like an animal attack. Did you do this to yourself?"

Gryph cast a tired glance at Lucas. "What reason would I have to attack myself?" he asked, then turned to Balthazar. "The woman was attacked by a large black wolf. I got to her as he was ripping into her."

Balthazar's brow lowered into a *V.* "Wolf, you say?"

"Since when have there been wolves in downtown Chicago?" Gryph asked. "I thought they stayed well north. Could they be shifters?"

"Are you sure that's what it was?" Lucas lifted the tattered shirt. "You didn't black out when you transformed?"

"I didn't black out," Gryph assured him.

"Were you unconscious at all last night?" Balthazar asked.

Gryph hesitated. "Yes. After I made sure the woman would be okay, I left her for the emergency medical technicians and got away before they could see my face."

"But not before the woman saw yours." Balthazar walked to a bookshelf and selected a brown leather journal. "Unfortunately, the victim was able to describe you in sufficient detail for a sketch artist to draw a reasonable likeness of you in your half-shifted state. And equally unfortunate, the news publicized it. Did anyone else see you? Did you pass anyone while you were running?"

Again Gryph hesitated. "No." The lie came hard to him. But he didn't want any of the otherkin to seek out Selene or the other woman and consider them threats to the Lair's existence. The two women had helped him when he might have died of his wounds or from exposure to the potentially toxic river water. The fewer people who knew he'd spent time in Selene's apartment, the better. He hoped that she wouldn't tell the police he'd been there. If she did, it might hit the news and the inhabitants of the underworld would once again see it on their televisions, even in the depths of the tunnels.

Yes, cable television was another improvement, along with internet connection, that Balthazar had been adamant about bringing to the people who lived below Chicago. Because of his desire to bring technology to the underworld, Balthazar had opened up an entire world of learning to Gryph and Lucas.

Balthazar checked Gryph's wound and bandaging. "Since when did you learn about poultices, son?"

Lucas's pale gray eyes narrowed, watchfully.

"I've been studying the internet for holistic cures. It was one of the remedies."

"Made of what?" Lucas leaned close and sniffed. "Some kind of herb and mud?"

"Something like that." Gryph strode into his old room and dug a shirt out of the dresser, his gaze lingering on the world map tacked to the wall.

"Traveling among the humans is dangerous. You risk your life and anonymity each time you walk among them." Balthazar held up a hand. "I know you've been doing it for the past five years, but this was exactly what I feared might happen." Balthazar stood in the entrance to his room. "Last night you thought you had control of your beast, yet you still transformed."

Gryph stiffened. "What else was I supposed to do? I couldn't let him kill her."

"Indeed, but by transforming and showing yourself as such, you've made yourself a target."

"No one in my office knows."

"But the woman you saved saw you with your face half man and half lion."

"I saw the drawing on the television. They won't link it

ball is over. Perhaps, in the meantime, the police will find the animal responsible for Miss Grant's attack and death."

If the animal was a shifter, there had to be others in the city. Gryphon would put out feelers among his staff.

All his life he'd held on to the dream of traveling to other countries. After the previous night, he was certain he couldn't risk getting too far from his haven beneath the city. Where else would he go if his inner beast emerged unbidden? Where would he hide if his secret was unleashed?

"Son," Balthazar said, "none of this would be an issue if you hadn't transformed."

"I had to transform to save the woman," Gryph said.

"And her attacker came after you." Balthazar spoke like it was a statement instead of a question.

Gryph nodded, his thoughts processing the information and coming up with what lay at the back of his mind during his escape to the Lair. "It had to be a shifter."

"Why do you say that?"

"How else could it have entered the hospital without being detected to finish the job it started? A wolf can't open doors without hands."

"Are you sure it was the same person or creature who attacked the woman in the first place?"

"Why would anyone come back to smother her unless he wanted to make sure she didn't expose the true nature of the animal that attacked her?"

Chapter 6

"Chicago Police Department and animal control have issued a warning for citizens and guests to be on the lookout for a man fitting the forensic artist's rendition of the murder victim's attacker. What more proof do you need?" Brigid drummed her fingers on the bistro table at the local delicatessen, where she'd insisted Selene meet her and Deme.

Selene's salad remained untouched on the plate in front of her. She hadn't had much of an appetite since Gryph had disappeared. If only she knew where to look for him, she could set her mind at ease and quit worrying about his wounds and whether he'd healed properly.

Unlike her siblings, she understood why he'd left. The television in her kitchen had been on when she'd gone inside her apartment. He had to have seen the report on the news about the attack on the victim in the hospital.

He'd been there when she and Brigid rode up on the motorcycle. Selene felt his presence and had sensed him in the shadows at the corner of her building. While her sisters figured his absence confirmed his guilt, Selene knew he couldn't have been the one to attack the woman in the hospital. He'd barely been able to stand when they'd left. When Cal had gone after him, she'd held her breath, praying to the goddess that he would escape. Injured like he was, he might not have been so lucky. Cal was one of

Chicago Police Department's best, was in good shape and hadn't lost several pints of blood in a vicious attack.

"Cal said he just disappeared. One minute he ran down an alley and the next, he was gone. The doors into the buildings on either side had been locked. Unless he had a key to one of them, he couldn't have gotten in."

Yeah, he'd disappeared, after stirring up such intense feelings inside her. How far would they have gone had he not been injured? Could she have stopped herself from making love to the man?

"Selene?" Deme stopped in the middle of her conjecture. "Are you even listening to me?"

"Yes." Selene blinked, her cheeks burning. "What was it you said?"

"Is it possible that we have more shifters in the city?" Deme asked.

Selene glanced from Deme to Brigid. "Shifters? As in half man, half animal?"

"Yes." Brigid leaned forward. "If the stranger you had in your apartment could look like a man one moment and a lion the next, who's to say there aren't other kinds of shifters roaming the streets?"

"Seems reasonable." Selene wasn't sure where the conversation was going.

Brigid dug her smartphone out of her pocket and tapped the screen. "We know whatever attacked Amanda in the parking garage wasn't human."

"Right," Deme agreed. "The scratches and bite marks could only have been a large animal."

Brigid's thumbs flying over the keypad, she continued talking with her head down. "Whoever entered the hospital and Amanda's room was human. An animal would have certainly been noticed well before making it to her door."

Deme nodded. "Undoubtedly."

Brigid's brows drew together. "At least human at the time he entered the hospital, killed the girl and escaped."

"What do you mean?"

Brigid glanced up. "Amanda was attacked by an animal on the street."

"Agreed," Selene said. "Gryph said it was a wolf."

"Though an animal supposedly attacked her, a human thought it important enough to finish her off, right?"

"Right." Brigid glanced up. "I just got word that the surveillance video showed a man dressed in scrubs with a stolen ID entered her room with a chart. Walked right past the guard we had posted. It was shortly afterward that they found her and informed us.

"Unfortunately, before she died, the description she gave of her attacker was that of a lion with a man's face." Brigid laid a hand over Selene's. "Honey, it's a pretty damning eyewitness account."

"On the video, what did the man look like?" Selene demanded.

Brigid shook her head. "Couldn't tell from the video. He was wearing a surgical mask."

"Gryph said it was a wolf that attacked Amanda in the alley, and I believe him. I don't know who the man was who came in the hospital to kill her, but it wasn't Gryph."

"He could have left your apartment right after you did, come to the hospital, waited for us to leave Amanda's room and sneaked in to kill her."

"I'm telling you, he wouldn't have killed her," Selene insisted.

"If he didn't come to the hospital to kill her, why did he leave your apartment and make a run for it? Why not hang around and tell his side of the story?"

"With a description circulating on the television, knowing I'd seen him like…like that, he had to feel like it was run, or be sent to jail for a crime he didn't commit."

"If it was a wolf, we could have a lot more shifters in the city than any of us can imagine. If they can look human, there's no telling who they are or where we should look to find them." Brigid tipped her head toward the man seated at the table beside them, and she leaned close to whisper, "The guy in the seat beside you could be a shifter and we'd never know until he shifted in front of us."

Deme and Selene both looked left at the same time. The man had lifted a large hoagie to his lips and was just about to take a bite when their gazes met.

He frowned, the frown turning into a glare as he turned his chair, put his back to them and bit into the sandwich.

"Who would know more?"

"We could go to a library and research the news reports," Deme offered. "Or check through the police files of all the reports passed to the special investigations team."

"Or we can go to Byron Crownover." Brigid shoved her phone across the table, the screen displaying an internet page identifying strange and unusual happenings in Chicago.

"Who is Byron Crownover?" Selene leaned over the screen and read the title—Chicago's Secret Inhabitants. "What's this about?"

"We've had loads of calls about strange happenings reported to the police department, from sightings of pumas on the streets to a huge bird flying past the Willis Tower with the wings of a hawk and the face and body of a man."

Deme snorted. "Sounds like the people who report being abducted by alien creatures."

"I know." Brigid leaned forward. "But we know from our experience battling the Chimera beneath the Colyer-Fenton College campus, that otherkin exist."

Selene shivered. She and her sisters had nearly been killed trying to save Aurai, the youngest, from the creature who'd taken up residence in the tunnels deep beneath the city.

"Question is—" Deme leaned closer to the phone "—what kind of shifters and how many live here in the city?"

"We need to contact Byron. He's the area expert, although some suspect he's a kook. But if he's got statistics on where the sightings occur most often, that might narrow our search down to a specific location."

Deme pushed her chair back. "Let's talk to Byron. Where do we find him?"

"He's an anthropology professor at Colyer-Fenton College."

Selene's lips twisted. "Why does that not surprise me?"

"Haven't we suffered enough at that place?" Deme asked.

"I'm just glad Aurai is finished with her studies there. The place still gives me the creeps." Selene's badass sister Brigid shivered.

They'd all come so close to dying trying to rescue Aurai from the Chimera's clutches. Before that time, Selene had assumed the creature with three heads—a lion, a goat and a snake—had been nothing but a Greek myth. The reality was even more frightening than she could ever have imagined.

"I'm coming with you." Selene stood.

"Shouldn't you be minding your shop?" Brigid asked.

Selene gathered her purse, determined to go with her sisters. "I closed it for the day."

"What about the planning for the Women's Aid Organization charity ball? Weren't you supposed to meet with them at five o'clock?" Deme glanced at her watch. "You have fifteen minutes if you still want to make it."

Selene clapped a hand to her mouth, torn between her obligations to the charitable event and going after information that could help them find out who was responsible for a woman's tragic death. "Damn. I forgot all about that. It seems so inconsequential compared to finding Amanda's killer." And proving Gryph wasn't the one to do it.

"I know, but for some of us, life goes on. And the children will benefit from the money raised." Deme patted Selene's arm. "Let Brigid and me do our jobs and you do yours."

"I want to find the killer just as much as you do." Selene straightened. "Even more so."

Brigid's eyes narrowed. "What's so special about this man you rescued that has you so protective of him?"

"Nothing." Selene looked away. "I just don't like to see the wrong man accused of such a horrific crime."

Brigid and Deme both stared at her for long moments. The intensity of their glances made Selene squirm.

"Something tells me there's more to it than that," Brigid said.

Unfortunately, there was, and damned if Selene was going to tell her sisters. Not when she didn't know what to make of the feelings she had for a man she'd crawled into bed with after only knowing him for a few hours. "I'd better get to my meeting." She turned and almost ran out of the deli.

Deme's hand on her arm stopped her. "Be careful, Selene. Falling for the wrong man could be painful."

"Especially if he's a killer," Brigid said, her voice tight and edgy.

Her sisters' words hit a little too close to home and left Selene wondering what she'd gotten into by rescuing a man-lion. She couldn't regret her actions. Gryph was worth saving. She knew that in her heart. "He's not a killer." Selene lifted her chin, squaring her shoulders. "And I'm not falling for a man I've only met once."

Once outside the deli, Selene checked the calendar on her smartphone and headed for the downtown building of

GL Enterprises, where she was to meet with the Women's Aid Organization. She hoped the meeting wouldn't last long because she wanted to spend some time on her own, searching for her mysterious houseguest.

Gryph returned to his apartment beneath his corporate headquarters, redressed his wound and then crawled into his king-size bed and slept until mid-afternoon the next day. Not until he felt someone watching him did he awaken, then he jerked to a sitting position, his pulse slamming through his veins.

He stared at the man sitting with his legs crossed elegantly in a chair beside him. It took a moment for his eyes to focus and his brain to engage before he relaxed. "Sneaking into a man's bedroom can get a body killed."

"I didn't sneak. I knocked on the door, but you didn't answer, so I let myself in to wait." Lucas stared at Gryph's wound. "Thought you'd never wake up. How's the shoulder?"

"Fine." Gryph shoved a hand through his thick hair, pushing it away from his face. He flexed, a stab of pain shooting through his sore shoulder. "What are you doing here?"

"Father asked me to check on you."

"Tell him I'm okay, and not to worry." Gryph flung the sheet back and rose, naked from the bed.

"Many of the inhabitants of the Lair have been pounding at his door. They're afraid."

Gryph stepped into a pair of sweats and pulled them up over his legs and hips, cinching the drawstring. "Tell him I'll stay clear of the Lair until this all dies down."

"Some are calling for you to turn yourself in to the authorities."

Gryph's brow furrowed. "I haven't done anything." He

to Gryphon Leone. The features weren't specific enough. She concentrated on the animal."

Balthazar nodded. "True enough. In the meantime, you're better off taking a leave of absence. Tell your office staff you'll be out of the country."

Already shaking his head, Gryph stepped forward. "I can't."

"What is so important you can't lay low for a few weeks until the furor dies down?"

"The charity ball for the children."

Balthazar's lips formed a thin line. "The charity ball. Why do you have to be there?" Balthazar's eyes narrowed. "Can't you just spend the money and let someone else take the reins on planning?"

"My company is sponsoring it. The money raised will go to the homeless children of Chicago. I've helped sponsor it for the past three. This year, GL Enterprises is the main sponsor. The Women's Aid Organization is demanding that the head of GL Enterprises needs to attend the ball to show his support."

Lucas chuckled. "My brother, a home-grown Chicago celebrity. A wanted man in more ways than one."

"Believe me, I'd let them handle all of it, but they said our donations have dwindled and the public wants to know the man sponsoring the ball is fully committed. They're afraid I'm Mafia or something—you know, dirty money."

"That's right, father, the philanthropic Gryphon needs to put in an appearance, to set the old biddies' minds at ease."

"You can't risk it," Balthazar insisted. "If you transform during the ball, you'll have the entire city on you so fast you won't have a chance to escape."

"The children need me."

"They need you alive. Not dead."

"I'll keep my exposure to a minimum. At least until the

strode through the apartment to the room containing his workout equipment and stepped up on the treadmill.

Lucas followed. "The picture of you is everywhere. If you turn yourself in, they won't have to worry about being discovered."

Gryph started walking, then adjusted the settings to a steep incline and broke into a jog. "I'm not turning myself in." Every time his heels hit, it jolted his shoulder, reminding him of the attack that had cost a woman her life and almost his own. "I need to be free to find the animal responsible for that woman's murder."

Lucas leaned against the wall, crossing his arms. "Aren't you afraid you'll cross paths with the police working the case?"

"They can't find me from the picture they have unless I change in front of them. I have no intention of providing that opportunity."

"Are you certain no one saw you?"

He hesitated for a moment before responding. "Yes. No one saw me but the victim."

"The inhabitants of the Lair know you. Aren't you afraid one of them will turn you in?"

"I have to trust them. I have no other choice. I can't change who I am or where I've come from." And he would never completely blend into the world of the surface dwellers. It couldn't happen. Not when he had so much to lose and could potentially harm a human. "You're lucky." He glanced at his brother.

"How do you figure?"

"You are human."

His brows rose. "Your point?"

"You can live anywhere you want and you don't have to worry about changing or hurting others. You have choices in your life."

"And you don't?" Lucas pushed away from the wall.

"No one will call you a freak. You're a good-looking guy with a great future ahead of you." And he could love anyone he wanted—otherkin or human.

An image of Selene's dark brown hair splayed out across his skin, the residual warmth of her leg draped over his and her breasts pressed against his side, made him miss a step and he almost fell off the treadmill. He grabbed the rail, sending stabbing pain through his shoulder. The pain brought him back to reality. He couldn't be with a surface dweller. Although he'd established a tentative place in society, maintaining a certain level of anonymity was required to keep from exposing his true nature.

Lucas nodded toward the healing wound. "That's quite an injury you have there. How'd you manage to get away after you were attacked?"

Gryph snorted. "I threw myself into the river."

"I'm surprised you didn't drown."

"I managed to pull myself out."

"But you were gone quite a while. You had to be freezing."

"I managed."

"Did someone help you?"

"I'd rather not talk about it."

Lucas's eyes narrowed. "Ah, it must have been a woman."

Gryph hit the stop button on the treadmill and climbed down. "I have a meeting to attend. Don't you have to be at work?"

"I'm on a sales call."

"Not if you're with me." Gryph stepped around his brother and returned to his bedroom, shedding his sweats and tennis shoes as he went. "I have a business to run, I'm sure you can find your way out as easily as you found your way in. Tell Father I'll steer clear of the Lair for the time being." He stepped into his shower and turned the spray on cool.

Silence reigned as Gryph let the water wash down his body. His wound stung, but was healing nicely. The poultice Selene had used had done the trick.

Selene.

What a mess. She'd saved his life, going above and beyond the role of nurse to keep him warm when he'd nearly gone into shock.

Trouble was, he couldn't get her scent or the feel of her body against his off his mind. Even now, his groin tightened, blood flowing south. He twisted the water controls to ice-cold and forced himself to think of something else until he had his body under control, then stepped out of the shower.

He dried off, wrapped a towel around his waist and left his bedroom for the kitchen and a cup of coffee.

"Mr. Leone, you have an appointment with Althea Washburn of the Women's Aid Organization in ten minutes." Marge Reingan, his executive assistant, held out a clipboard with several papers on it. "Sign here." She handed him a pen.

"What am I signing?"

"A letter authorizing the purchase of the building on Wacker."

He scribbled his signature.

Marge flipped a page. "And here." She pointed to a line on the page.

Gryph signed. "I guess you heard about the attack?"

She nodded.

"Do you think I should turn myself in?"

"Not if you didn't do it." She took the pen from him. "Besides, too many people depend on your generosity. What would happen to them?"

"Balthazar can manage my assets."

"Not like you do. He has no desire to rejoin the surface dwellers."

"I've always wondered why. As a human, he could blend in easily."

"Not all who live in the Lair are otherkin."

He smiled at Marge. "Like you?"

She nodded, the gray hairs standing out more in the overhead lighting. "It's a safe haven to many."

"I know and I wouldn't want anyone to be displaced by my elimination. That's why I have Balthazar on my accounts. If anything should happen to me—" and it almost had "—he will have access to the money from my corporation. He can continue to support the inhabitants of the Lair."

"Why do you let them continue to think Balthazar provides for them when it's the money you make that helps them survive?"

"I owe my life to Balthazar. He took me in when my own mother couldn't take care of me."

Marge nodded. "He has a big heart."

"He's taken in a lot of strays, like me, Lucas and just about everyone in the Lair."

"Many of us wouldn't be alive today if not for him."

"Exactly." His chest swelling, Gryph remembered the many times Balthazar had played with him in the tunnels, how he'd taught him to read and write. Balthazar had been responsible for getting them connected to the internet and online for distance learning. He wanted every person in the Lair to have a chance to provide for themselves should they choose to live amongst the surface dwellers. "Balthazar deserves the credit."

Marge tucked the clipboard against her chest. "Do you want me to cancel your meeting with Mrs. Washburn?"

"No, I'll see her."

"Are you sure that's a good idea?"

"The drawing that's circulating doesn't look enough like my human form to present a danger." His only danger lay in the hands of the woman who'd rescued him. He could only pray she wouldn't turn him in.

Marge's gaze went to the wound on his shoulder. "Did the animal that killed the woman do that?"

He nodded.

"What was it?" she asked.

"I suspect it was a wolf shifter." He paused, waiting for her response to his announcement.

She didn't even blink. "My husband, God rest his soul, was a member of a pack that lived on the edge of the city. I can put out some feelers, if you'd like."

He'd known, but didn't want to ask for her help. Since her husband's death, she'd had no connection with the wolves. "Thank you, Marge. I'd appreciate that." He nodded toward the door. "In the meantime, I'll get dressed and see you up in the office."

"Whatever you do, don't let anyone take you to jail." Her lips formed a thin line. "Shifters don't do well in captivity. My husband's cousin was jailed for stealing. He didn't last long behind bars. Captivity made him crazy."

"I'll bear that in mind." He had no intention of spending time in jail. Metal bars gave him the hives. But if he wanted to clear the air, he had to do something to find the murderer.

Marge spun and headed for the elevator, then stopped and faced him as she waited for the door to slide open. "Oh, and, Mr. Leone, I believe you didn't hurt that girl."

"I'm glad someone does." He smiled.

"A more troubling concern is that whoever did could strike again."

He nodded. "I know." All the more reason to do something before it happened again. "Stall Mrs. Washburn. I'll be up in five minutes."

"Yes, sir."

"And, Marge. Anything you can find out about the shifter packs…"

"I'll get right on it." The elevator door slid open and she stepped inside, turning to face him.

"Hey, Marge." He held a hand over the closing door, forcing it back.

"Sir?"

"What was it like for you, as a human, to be married to a shifter?"

Her gaze drifted to the far wall, her mouth softening. "Like a woman in love. What he was didn't matter. It was *who* he was that I fell in love with." Her attention returned to him. "Why do you ask?"

"No reason." He let go of the door.

This time, Marge put her hand out to stop it from closing. "Gryphon, you know I love you like a son. Okay, a grandson." She cupped his chin. "Life is way too short to squander a chance at love. If you fall in love with someone, look at what you have in common, and don't focus on your differences."

They exchanged glances, then the door closed, leaving Gryph alone.

Marge had been with him since he'd moved closer to the surface. She'd lived among surface dwellers in her youth and part of the time after she'd met and married her husband, Tom.

When Tom had come down with a brain tumor, she'd moved him to the Lair to live out the remainder of his days so he wouldn't be judged if he shifted without warning.

After his death, Marge had gone to work helping Balthazar raise Gryph and Lucas. When Gryph's success in day trading had grown to the point he had to invest what he was making in other businesses, he'd moved closer to the surface and taken Marge with him, giving her an apartment in his building. One with floor-to-ceiling windows to let in as much light as possible. He knew she loved the sun. And he loved her like the grandmother he'd never known.

What he hadn't expected was that she was a wizard at managing his office and his schedule, and her compact frame was every bit a match to stand up to unwanted visitors.

Gryph hurriedly dressed in a business suit, shirt and tie, hating the constriction around his throat. The suit was his cover. He glanced into the mirror, his skin smooth with no sign of the fine hairs that appeared when he shifted. No one would recognize him in the drawing being circulated. No one but Selene and the other woman who'd helped him into her apartment.

With a deep breath, he stepped into the elevator that whisked him to the top floor of the building. No amount of rationalization could erase the sense of foreboding that went with him.

Chapter 7

"It was nice of GL to offer his conference room for our planning efforts, don't you think?" Mrs. Washburn said.

"Indeed. That and his funding." Mrs. Stockton laughed. "Without it, we'd have had to have the ball in some squalid concert hall instead of at a grand hotel. We've already sold out of tickets and the finest of Chicago society will be in attendance."

"Isn't the ball open to the public?" Selene dared to ask. Surrounded by the matrons of Chicago's wealthiest, she was outnumbered and feeling out of place. Perhaps she wasn't right for the costume-planning portion of this particular event, except she had the most popular dress shop in downtown Chicago and she knew her unique clothing and designs suited the fairy theme the ladies had chosen for this year's charity ball.

Mrs. Washburn's brows rose as she directed a stare down her nose at Selene. "Yes, but who can afford the price of the tickets? Only the most connected."

"And isn't that as it should be?" Mrs. Stockton said. "We want high-dollar contributors to come and give lots of lovely money."

"For the children," Selene reminded them.

"Of course." Mrs. Washburn tapped the paper in front of her. "How are the costumes coming?"

On the spot, Selene straightened. "I pick up the completed fairy costumes after our meeting is over."

"You can have the servants' costumes delivered directly to the hotel, and the Women's Aid Organization's dresses delivered to my house, please."

"Shall I schedule a seamstress to do any last-minute adjustments?"

"No, no." Mrs. Washburn waved her hand. "I'm sure none of us have changed measurements significantly in the past two weeks." She eyed the others in the room, as if sizing them up. "With the ball only days away, it would be foolish to scramble at the last minute."

"Very well." Selene nodded. "Whom do I submit my bill to?"

"Leave it with the man at the front desk on your way out of the building. Security will ensure it gets to GL for payment."

Selene exited, glad to be out of the room of stuffy women, full of themselves and what their husbands made. She would love to go to the charity ball, if only to see her dress designs on display, but she couldn't afford the ten-thousand-dollar ticket price and really didn't want to be stuck with a lot of Chicago's elite snobs, like the elusive GL of GL Enterprises.

Outside the conference room, she waited in front of the elevator. She could hear the car rising up the shaft. As it grew closer, her pulse quickened, her breathing growing shallower. If she wasn't going crazy, she could swear the person inside the elevator was the man she'd rescued from the side of the river. She could sense his presence.

She punched the button several times, but the car didn't stop at her floor. Instead, it continued upward toward the roof of the building.

It had to be him. Selene spun back toward the conference room and burst through the door. "Who owns this building?"

Mrs. Washburn frowned at the interruption. "GL, of course."

"Of GL Enterprises. One of the richest men in the city of Chicago," Mrs. Stockton added.

"What does he look like?" Selene demanded.

"Not many of us have actually had the pleasure of meeting the man. He prefers his privacy."

"However, I have." Mrs. Washburn straightened, lifting her nose to the ceiling. "Why do you ask?"

Her heart beating against her ribs, Selene backed out of the room. "No reason. Excuse me. I apologize for disrupting your meeting."

As she closed the door between her and the ladies, she heard Mrs. Washburn say, "Silly girl. Are you certain she's the best for the costumes?"

"With the ball only a couple of days away, you're asking now?" The other woman laughed. "We'll have to make do."

The woman's words hurt. She'd put a lot of time and effort into the design, planning and construction of the costumes. Not to mention fronting the effort with her own hard-earned funds. If they backed out now, she'd be out thousands of dollars and she still had to pay the seamstresses.

"She came highly recommended—" Mrs. Stockton said.

Selene retreated to the elevator and punched the up button. When the car opened, she stepped in and glanced at the control panel. The penthouse suite had its own button and a key card slot beside it. The only way she'd get into that suite was with a card, or if she accompanied a person with a card.

She hit the button for the lobby and rode the car to ground level.

At the desk, she paused in front of the security guard.

"I'd like to see GL." She frowned, ashamed to admit she didn't know what GL stood for. If she had to guess, the G stood for Gryph.

Her stomach fluttered. Surely this couldn't be only a coincidence. How serendipitous could it be to have a meeting in a building Gryph owned?

She shook her head. Was she thinking right? Gryph, the man she'd found shivering beside the river, half-dead and wounded, was a multimillionaire? A member of Chicago's elite? A man of great wealth and assets? If that was the case, why had she found him wounded by the river?

Unless he'd been wounded by the attacker that killed the woman or…the woman he'd killed.

Her mouth tightening, Selene waited for the guard on duty to respond.

"I'm sorry, he's not available for meetings."

Selene turned away, disappointment and frustration bubbling up inside her. She could walk away and never know if the man passing her in the elevator shaft had been Gryph or she could stay and try again to get to the penthouse. Full of determination and not willing to take no for an answer, she pushed guilt aside and turned back to the guard. Instead of reading his thoughts, she stared into his eyes and said, "You want to take me to GL."

"I do?" The man chuckled, shaking his head. "'Fraid not."

Selene gathered a deep breath, focused all her energy into her next words. "You will take me to GL."

The security guard tipped his chin downward, his gaze clouding. He shook his head and pinched the bridge of his nose. "Let me see if he's in."

She maintained her focus, as if applying steady pressure to get a ball rolling. "He's in."

His hand left the phone and he stood. "If you'll follow me, I'll take you up to meet with GL."

"Thank you." Selene stepped into the elevator and waited for the guard to slide his card into the slot and punch the penthouse button.

"You don't need to go with me," she said.

The guard smiled politely and stepped out of the elevator, saying, "I don't need to go with you."

The door slid closed and Selene was on her way up to the penthouse, guilt, elation and a wicked sense of power flooding her. She'd manipulated the security guard's mind. A thrill shivered across her skin. She'd never done that before. Able to sense thoughts and emotions, she'd never attempted to plant ideas in another person's brain. Until now. Had she pushed the boundaries of right and wrong?

The elevator rocketed to the top. The closer she got, the more certain she was that she'd find Gryph. She could sense his presence, feel his emotions, and knew without a doubt it was him. As the elevator slowed, her feet grew cold, her nerve slipping down the shaft. Though she'd found him irresistible in bed, he might not have been as taken. Not that she was going after him to finish what they'd started. She told herself she only wanted answers. Nothing more.

As the elevator doors slid open to reveal an opulent suite of offices, Selene shrank against the back wall, suddenly afraid of his reaction to seeing her. Would he be angry that she'd found him? Would he deny having ever set eyes on her? Would he call security and have her thrown out?

An older woman rose from behind a large mahogany desk. "Are you lost?" she asked, stepping forward.

"N-no." The elevator doors started to close, sparking life into Selene's limbs, she stepped through into the office suite. "No, I'm not lost," she said with more conviction. "I'm here to see GL."

"I don't have any appointments scheduled on the calendar for him." She stood in front of Selene, her small stature no less intimidating.

When Selene couldn't come up with a reason why she was there without an appointment, she clamped down on her bottom lip.

"I see. Perhaps I should call security." The older woman backed toward her desk and lifted the phone.

"No." Selene stepped forward and focused on the woman, channeling her thoughts toward her.

The older woman frowned and pressed her fingers to her temples. "I'll just call…" She glanced up at Selene, her eyes narrowing, the irises flashing a deep red.

A stabbing pain ripped through her own temples and her mental push slammed back into her, making her stagger backward and hit the closed elevator doors.

What the hell? Selene pressed her fingers against her throbbing temples, but refused to give up. "Please. I need to see your boss. I need to know—"

"Marge, I hear voices out there. What's going on?" A tall man in a black suit stepped through the doorway to the adjoining office. His tawny blond hair, thick and full, was combed back from his forehead and hung down to the top of his collar.

"Gryph." Selene's knees wobbled at the startling pushback from the seemingly gentle Marge, and from seeing the man she'd been thinking about nonstop since she'd found him by the river.

"I was about to call security to escort this woman out of the building." The older woman lifted the phone on her desk.

"No." Gryph held out his hand. "I'll deal with her." His gaze never left Selene's. "Please, come into my office."

Marge stared from her to him and set the phone back in the cradle.

"Aren't you supposed to run an errand or something?"

Gryph turned to Marge as Selene gave the other woman a wide berth and slipped by him into his office.

Selene caught the older woman's frown and the dark red that flared in her eyes. What the hell had just happened? She'd never had someone slam her thoughts back at her. Nor had she run in to anyone whose eyes could change from plain gray to bloodred in a heartbeat.

"I guess that means you want me to disappear." Marge rolled her eyes. "Just say so." She grumbled as she gathered her purse from a desk drawer. When she straightened, a small smile played at the corner of her lips. She patted Gryph's face. "I hope you remember what I said." She turned toward Selene and poked a finger at her, her smile fading. "Hurt him, and you'll answer to me." Her back to Gryph, her eyes flared red again, then she stepped up to the elevator, the door slid open and she disappeared inside.

"What did she say that you're supposed to remember?" Selene asked, a shiver shaking her.

"Nothing." Gryph closed the door to the office and stood silent, staring down at her.

Selene's stomach turned cartwheels and her gaze focused on his mouth. Her tongue slipped across to moisten her suddenly dry lips. She wanted him to take her into his arms so badly, she could practically taste him. *Kiss me.*

In one smooth movement, he gathered her into his arms and crushed her lips with a breath-stealing kiss that rocked Selene all the way to her core. She ran her hands up his chest and curled them around his neck, pressing her body as close to his as was possible with her clothes still on.

He cradled the back of her head as he deepened the kiss, his tongue sliding past her teeth to stroke hers in a long sensuous caress. His free hand slipped down her back to cup her bottom, pressing her pelvis against the growing ridge beneath the fly of his trousers.

When he finally set her back on her feet, he was breathing hard and so was she.

"I shouldn't have done that," he said.

"Why not?"

"I'm not the man for you. You have to understand."

A horrible thought insinuated itself into her mind. What if her longing had pressured him to kiss her? And now that he'd done it, he was regretting it.

Her knees shaking, afraid she'd gone too far by following him up to his office and possibly pushing thoughts into his mind, she opened her mouth to apologize but what came out was "You left without saying goodbye."

He leaned his forehead against hers. "I had to. I couldn't let you be accused of harboring a murderer."

"You didn't—"

His finger pressed against her lips, warm and gentle. "I know, but the sketch they're circulating is pretty damning. You and the redhead who helped me into your apartment were the only humans who could identify me and place me close to the scene of the crime."

"I wouldn't have turned you in." She shook her head. "And my sister…" Selene bit her lip. "I'd like to think she wouldn't have, either."

"I couldn't bank on it. I don't know you well enough." He smoothed the hair back from her face. "And I couldn't count on your sister's silence. When everyone showed up at your place, I knew it was time for me to leave."

"Those were my sisters."

"And the guy?"

"My sister's fiancé." Selene's lips quirked. "He's a cop. And two of my sisters are consultants for the Chicago PD."

Gryph pushed a hand through his thick hair. "Wow. I believe I'm in up to my eyeballs in trouble. Are they going to show up any minute to rescue you from me?"

Selene shook her head. "They don't know I'm here.

They think I'm at a meeting for a charity ball. Which I was until I...found you." She'd been about to tell him that she'd sensed him.

His thumb brushed across her lips and he bent to sweep his mouth across where his thumb had been. "And will you tell them where you found me?"

"No," she whispered into his mouth. "At least not until we find out who killed the woman."

"And then?"

"If you want me to." Right then she didn't want to tell anyone she was with him. That way she could have Gryph all to herself. Maybe she'd rekindle those feelings he'd inspired, the hot, lush lust she'd never before experienced in any other man's arms. She hadn't been able to push him out of her thoughts since she'd discovered him.

"I haven't stopped thinking about you," he whispered against her lips.

If he hadn't been so close, the heat of his body spreading fire through her veins, she might have paused to consider his words mirroring her own thoughts. But she couldn't think past his lips sliding across hers in a slow, intense attack on her senses.

Coarse hands slipped the strap of her dress over her shoulder and his mouth trailed kisses down the column of her throat to the curve of her neck and across her bared shoulder.

Urgent need drove her to shove his jacket over his shoulders.

He shrugged free and let it drop to the floor.

Selene fumbled with the buttons on his shirt until she had them all loose down to where the tail disappeared into the waistband of his trousers. She yanked it free, finishing the job, and the shirt joined the jacket on the floor.

Gryph's hands found the zipper on the back of her dress and slid it down to the base of her spine.

Without hesitation, she stepped back and slid the straps down her arms. The dress fell, leaving her standing in front of him in a white lacy demi bra and matching white thong panties.

Gryph's gaze raked across her from the tip of her head, caressing her all the way to the apex of her thighs. His golden eyes flashed.

A cool air-conditioned draft brushed across her skin and made her pause for a moment, heat rising up into her cheeks. She raised her hands to cover her breasts. "I'm sorry. I didn't come to seduce you."

He chuckled, lifted her hand and drew her close. "I'm beginning to get a complex. I thought *I* was seducing *you*."

Selene's gaze shifted to the wound on his shoulder and she frowned. "You'd never know you'd been injured so badly such a short time ago."

"Thanks to the magic in that poultice, I'm well on the way to recovery."

Selene stiffened at the reference to magic. Did he know that she was a witch? Did she dare tell him about her ability to sense emotions, sometimes read minds and now push thoughts into others' heads? He should know so that he could make a rational decision about where they were going with whatever it was raging between them. "About the poultice…" Her hands landed on his bare chest, his muscles flexed and all her logic flew out the window.

"Hmm?" Gryph nuzzled her neck, kissing a path down to the swell of her breast.

Intense pleasure washed over her in a tsunami of sensations, rendering her incapable of breathing properly. Her fingers skimmed across his chest, testing the strength and hardness of the muscles beneath the smooth skin.

His hands slipped down her back and grazed the rounded curve of her buttocks. Then he scooped her up, wrapping her legs around his waist, walking her across the room to the huge black desk in the center of the room. Gray light shone through the floor-to-ceiling windows from a storm-laden sky, the clouds dimming the vastness of the Chicago skyline, making the atmosphere more tempestuous, as well as intimate.

One hand balancing her against him, Gryph swept his other hand across the surface of his desk, sending papers and pens flying across the room. Then he settled her bottom on the cool, hard surface, laying her back until she was sprawled across the middle, her legs dangling over the side.

Her body was on fire, her mind caught in the blaze, unable to generate coherent thoughts. Selene rode a wave of lust so powerful she wanted nothing more than to be naked, with Gryph between her legs, riding her hard and fast.

The man-beast bent over her, pushing aside the bra's cup to take a beaded nipple between his teeth and biting gently. He swiped a raspy tongue over the taut nub.

Selene arched her back, pressing closer to his magical mouth.

He wrapped his lips around the taut bud and sucked, drawing it deep into his mouth. His hand slid down over her belly, angling toward the tuft of curls covering her sex.

Selene stilled in anticipation of his fingers finding and stroking her there.

Releasing her breast, he seared a path to the other breast, pushing aside the bra to shower equal attention on the opposite side, then continued his storm of passion across her torso and down to join his hand, sliding between her swollen folds.

Selene moaned, her body writhing against the wooden desk. She wanted more, wanted him inside her, filling her, stretching her channel with the huge member she'd born witness to when she'd undressed him.

Gryph parted her folds and, with one long finger,

stroked the small strip of flesh packed with the most sensitive nerve endings in her body.

The force of sensations made her moan, her thighs spreading, welcoming him in. A wash of liquid coated her channel, warm, wet and ready to accept him.

Her fingers joined his and guided them to her aching entrance.

One long finger entered her, then another and another until he had all four fingers easing in and out of her.

It wasn't enough. "Please," she said, her voice raspy with her need. "I want you inside me."

His hand froze for a fraction of a second, then he ripped her panties down her legs and tossed them across the room.

Selene sat up and reached for his belt buckle, while he pulled his wallet from his back pocket and removed a small foil packet. He tore the edge with his teeth and removed the condom.

Selene unbuckled his belt and eased his zipper down. His cock sprang free into her hand, long, thick and hard. Her tummy tightened and her breasts tingled as she gauged his length and girth. Praise the goddess, he was big.

"Are you sure?" he asked, holding back. "What if I'm too big. What if I change?"

Her hands circled him, caressing him from tip to base, reveling in the feel of steel encased in velvet. "I'll take my chances."

His jaw was tight, his breathing ragged. "I don't want to hurt you."

"You won't." She gripped his arm with one hand. "Please," she pleaded, past caring that she begged, anxious to feel all of him inside her. She held out her hand for the condom.

He placed it in her open palm and threaded his fingers through her hair, his gaze capturing hers, the hunger in his eyes so real it burned through her.

Before she rolled the prophylactic over him, she scooted off the desk, dropped to her knees and ran her tongue across the rounded head, poking into the small hole, oozing come. Smooth and musky, he tasted good. Selene flicked the sides, running her tongue the length of him all the way down to the base.

His fingers dug into her scalp, pressing her down over him.

She took him into her mouth, swallowing him until the tip of his member bumped the back of her throat.

He withdrew and she grasped his buttocks, dug her nails into his flesh and pulled him back in, loving the taste, texture and feel of him in her mouth. The intimacy of the moment sparked a desire so powerful she lost herself to it.

He pumped in out until his body jerked to a stop and he yanked free of her lips. In one smooth motion, he had her seated on the desk again, his hands caressing her thighs, spreading them wider. "Tell me no, and it stops here."

She slipped the condom over his cock and guided it to her entrance.

With a low growl rumbling inside his chest, Gryph draped her legs over his sinuous arms and eased inside of her.

Selene struggled to breathe as his length and thickness seemed to push the air from her lungs.

He backed off a little until the muscles of her channel contracted around him, urging him closer. He leaned over her, sliding even deeper as he took one of her nipples between his teeth and bit down. The slight pain made her gasp. She caught his head in her hands and pressed his mouth down over her.

He moved in an out, slowly, at first. As the heat built, his body tensed and his movements became more fervent, ardent and all-consuming.

Rising to the edge, her thoughts jumbled, her being an

inferno of lust. She forgot to breathe, forgot where she was, that the windows bared her to the sky and that she'd only known this man for a day.

He rammed into her, slamming hard, his thrusts deep, his grip on her ass bruising.

But she didn't want him to stop. She tightened her legs around his waist and rode the passion, wishing he'd thrust harder, rougher. Maybe even let out some of the animal inside him.

Tiny hairs sprang from his skin, his grunts became more guttural and primitive. As he reached his climax, he threw back his head and roared, his face covered in sweat and tawny hairs.

The large brawny fingers digging into her buttocks grew sharper, the extending claws scraping the flesh.

As the pain and pleasure mixed to fling her over the edge, Selene cried out, rocked by the most powerful orgasm she'd ever experienced. She locked her ankles around his waist and held on until they both returned to earth.

She was the first to take a deep breath and let it out on a sigh. Her legs slid down over his hips and dangled over the edge of the desk. She was shaking and spent.

Gryph's fingers loosened, the sharp pain receding as he let go of her bottom. Her skin felt warm and sticky against the desk.

When Gryph raised his hands, he stared at his fingertips, his eyes widening. "Oh, dear God." He rolled her onto her stomach, his hands smoothing over her rounded bottom. "My God, you're bleeding, and I did that." He backed away, leaving her on the desk.

Selene pushed to her feet and faced him. "I wanted it."

"This can't be." He shook his head, backing farther away, mentally as well as physically. "This can't happen again."

She crossed to stand in front of him, naked and feeling thoroughly satiated, but afraid he'd make good on his promise. "Gryph, they are only scratches." She glanced over her shoulder. "See? They've already stopped bleeding."

He stared down at his hands, the claws having receded, leaving only dried blood on his fingers. "I hurt you."

She cupped his face, her thumb brushing across his lips like he'd done at the beginning. "I wanted you. The pain only made my climax better."

"Making love shouldn't hurt."

"For me, it made it even more intense, more sensual." She smiled. "If we were to make love again, I'd want it the same."

"What if I went too far?" He shook his head. "I can't risk it. This ends now." Grabbing her wrists, he shoved her hands away from him. "Get dressed, I'm taking you home."

Selene could feel his anger and fear and she wanted to reassure him that everything was okay. She'd never been more attracted to another individual or more satisfied with sex than what she'd experienced with him.

The solid line of his jaw, the tightness of his lips and the way his brow furrowed made her clamp down on her words and gather her clothing.

She dressed quickly, her body still tingling in the aftermath of mind-blowing sex, her bottom still burning.

By the time she was clothed, she was ablaze with desire all over again.

Gryph stood at the elevator door, his back to her. "Are you ready?"

Selene walked around to stand in front of him. "I am."

"Then let's go. The sooner you're out of my life, the better for both of us."

Selene stepped into the elevator and leaned her back against the wall, her arms crossed over her chest, her thoughts warring. On one hand, she didn't want this to be the end. But the more she reflected, the more convinced she was that her thoughts and desires had pushed their way into Gryph's mind, causing him to transform. He'd been fine and remained in his human form until the point at which she'd wished he'd let go of the animal inside.

Which begged the question: Had he really wanted to make love to her, or had she overlaid his common sense with her own needs and desires?

Gryph took her to the garage level of the building and exited onto a large open area with only a couple of vehicles taking up the space—a sleek silver Ferrari convertible with the top down and what appeared to be an armor-plated, foreign-model SUV that could be as comfortable on a red carpet as a battlefield. He waved a hand toward the latter.

Selene slid into the passenger seat and waited while he closed the door.

Gryph took the wheel and drove toward a closed over-head door. As he approached, the door slid upward and he drove through and out into the Chicago dusk that had arrived early due to the low-hanging clouds.

Selene sat with her hands in her lap, her insides still simmering from making love. She wanted to say something, but the solid granite of his jaw didn't bode well for conversation.

All too soon, he approached her shop building and came to a halt at the curb.

When he started to get out, she laid a hand on his arm. "I can open my own door."

He ignored her, dropped to the ground and rounded the SUV before she could locate the door handle. The door opened for her and he held out his hand.

She laid hers in his and that spark of desire engaged and sent a flash of desire through her that made her ache all over again.

When she was safely on the ground, he didn't let go of her hand, instead drawing her into his embrace.

"I don't know what it is about you," he growled. "But I'm finding it impossible to resist."

She smiled up at him, her hand resting on his chest. "Then don't." Whether he was feeling that way himself, or she was putting the thought into his head, Selene didn't want to know. All she wanted was to feel his lips against hers.

Gryph lowered his head, claiming her mouth in a long, hard kiss.

Selene melted against him, her body merging with his. As her hands snaked up to entwine around his neck, an angry darkness pierced the veil of lust surrounding her and Gryph, sending a shard of razor-sharp pain through her head.

Selene gasped and broke the kiss.

If not for Gryph's arms around her, she'd have fallen to her knees.

"What is it?"

"I don't know." She struggled to remain upright and forced a wobbly smile to her lips. "I must be tired."

"Let me help you inside."

"No." She shook her head, fumbling for the keys in her purse. "I'll be fine. I just need something to eat and a chance to rest."

"I'm staying."

"I thought you couldn't get rid of me soon enough."

"You're not well. I can't leave you like this."

"You don't have to bother. My sisters are supposed to be by soon."

He hesitated. "Then I'll stay until they get here."

"And risk being recognized by Deme?" Selene inhaled and let out a slow, cleansing breath. "I'm fine. Really."

She stepped out of his arms, ignoring the wicked darkness pushing against her subconscious.

Gryph reached into his wallet and pulled out a business card. "If you need me for anything, that's my cell phone number. Call me." He placed the card in her hand and curled her fingers around it.

Selene wanted to hand it back to him. To tell him she didn't need it or him. That he'd been right when he said what they'd done had been wrong and shouldn't be repeated. She wanted to say she agreed with him, but it would all be a lie. What had happened between them had been so very natural and…right. She pocketed the card and turned away before she broke down and cried, or worse, begged him to take her into his arms and hold her until the evil went away.

Obviously reluctant to leave, Gryph remained standing on the sidewalk until Selene descended the stairs and unlocked her door. With a wave, she entered her apartment, shut the door and collapsed against the wood paneling, waiting for the sound of Gryph's vehicle leaving before she let herself slide to the floor, trembling.

Something heinous and hateful had been watching them kiss and hadn't liked it one bit. Its antagonism had been so palpable, it had sapped the energy from her body. The last time she'd felt something this strong, this life-depleting, she'd been at the hospital near the evil that had killed Amanda.

Chapter 8

If Gryph could have flogged himself for what he'd done, he would have. Seeing Selene's punctured skin, blood oozing from the wounds, had been the cold bucket of ice water he'd needed to douse his passion and bring him back to the stark reality he'd known all his life—he couldn't be with a human.

He was a danger to her. Yes, she'd wanted him as badly as he'd wanted her, but *he* had to end it. He could never forgive himself if he caused her harm.

Slamming his foot to the accelerator, he sped back to his apartment in the basement of the GL Enterprises building. Once inside he flung his keys against the wall, stripped his jacket from his shoulders and sent it in the same direction. Rage ripped through him, making hairs spring forth from his skin. He need to run, to get outside in the darkness and charge through the countryside, roaring. But a lion couldn't be so obvious. A wolf could get away with being seen. A lion would be hunted down and shot, deemed unnatural to the area, and a danger to the human population.

And wasn't that what he was? A danger to humans?

He entered his workout room and stepped up to a large punching bag suspended from the ceiling. Channeling his anger and the beast within, he rammed his bare fist into the canvas, not even wincing at the pain in his knuckles and his sore shoulder—the shoulder *Selene* had nursed back to health.

Her scent still lingered against his skin, the image of her lying naked on his desk seared into his memory.

What good did it do to think about her? He couldn't be with her without wanting to make love to her. And God forbid he made love to her again, and hurt her like he'd already done.

He slammed his hand into the bag, again and again, until his knuckles were bruised and raw. Then he hit it again, welcoming the pain.

"Shouldn't you be using gloves?" Marge's voice forced him to stop.

"I thought you were gone for the day," he said without turning to glance in her direction.

"I did, but I'm back with someone you should talk to."

Gryph slowly turned to face her.

"Gryphon Leone, meet my brother-in-law's son, Rafe Cain, leader of the Kenyon pack from the north side of Chicago."

Gryph extended a bruised hand.

Rafe's gaze narrowed, and his nose twitched as if he was sizing up Gryph's scent and sincerity. Finally, he took the hand and gave it a firm shake. "Marge tells me the woman killed last night was attacked by a wolf."

"Initially, that's right."

Rafe tipped his head, eyeing the healing wound on Gryph's shoulder. "He do that?"

"Yes."

"Shifter?" Rafe asked.

Gryph's heartbeat stuttered and then pushed on. "I am."

Rafe's lips twitched and he sniffed the air. "Lion?"

After a long moment, Gryph nodded his acknowledgment. He hadn't told anyone outside the Lair of his affliction. It felt oddly liberating to admit what he was to a fellow shifter and stranger.

"Thought so." Rafe grinned. "But I really wanted to know if you thought the wolf was a shifter."

If the situation hadn't been so dire, Gryph would have laughed at himself. He had to be reminded that the world wasn't out to expose him for the lion shifter he was. "He managed to get inside the hospital to finish what he'd started. I don't think a wolf could do that without being noticed."

The leader of the wolf pack nodded. "I asked around and I'd stake my reputation that it wasn't one of ours."

"And you came all the way from the north side to tell me that?"

Rafe's mouth twisted. "No."

Gryph waited. Whatever Rafe had to say might prove to be a link to this case that would help them solve it.

"There's a pack on the southwest side of Chicago that call themselves the Devil's Disciples. As part of the initiation rites, they have to attack influential targets."

"To kill?"

A frown dented Rafe's brow. "That's what had me stumped. The pack doesn't usually kill women. They usually go for the offspring of some rich or influential bastard. And they don't kill."

"What *do* they do?"

"They bite or scratch them deep enough to draw blood."

"And you think they went too far with Amanda?" Gryph shook his head. "As far as I know, she's not from a rich or influential family."

"The Disciples don't go for women and don't kill unless in gang warfare. They turn their targets."

"As in make the human a shifter?" Gryph blew out his breath. "Wow. That means there's a growing population of shifters in the city."

Rafe nodded. "The rich are keeping it on the down low. They don't want their status to be impugned by the knowledge they have tainted bloodlines."

"Why did I not know this?" He turned to Marge.

She shrugged. "It's the first I've heard of it."

"It started about six months ago. Their alpha male was murdered by a fresh turn who took over and started the initiation rites."

"Southwest Chicago, huh?"

"Warehouse area, Archer Heights district. They congregate at night at this pool hall." Rafe handed Gryph a slip of paper with the address. "I'd go with you, but that would start a gang war I'm not ready to commit my pack to."

"No," Gryph said. "It's best I handle this alone."

"After nine is the best time to catch a large number of them."

Gryph stared at the address, then glanced at the clock on the wall. Evening had turned to night and he had an hour to kill until nine. He stuck out his hand. "Thanks for the information."

"Don't mention it." Rafe gripped his hand hard. "Really. Don't mention it. You didn't get this information from me. I wouldn't have passed it on if I didn't think it was important to find and stop the shifter who killed the woman. If word gets out to the general population that there are shifters in the city, the humans will go on an extermination hunt."

"Understood."

Marge showed Rafe to the exit and returned a few minutes later. "Are you going there?"

"I am."

"Without backup?" Marge planted her fists on her narrow hips.

"Who would I take?"

"How about some of the misfits you support in the Lair?"

"Most of them are women, children and broken-down men. They wouldn't be of any use standing up to a gang of young shifters."

His assistant clucked her tongue. "You're going to get yourself killed."

"As long as I stop whoever killed Amanda from taking another life."

Marge frowned. "If it's all the same to you, I like my job, and I'd like to keep it."

Gryph wrapped an arm around her shoulders. "I'll keep that in mind."

Marge hugged him around his waist and stared up at him. "What happened with your woman?"

Gryph stiffened. "She's not my woman."

She harrumphed. "Is that your way of avoiding an answer?"

"There are some things that don't bear discussing."

"She ditched you?" Marge's back straightened like a ramrod. "Say the word and I'll scratch her eyes out."

Gryph frowned down at Marge. "You say that like you mean it."

Marge crossed her arms and stood with her feet slightly apart, like a militant grandmother. "I do."

"Well, it wasn't *her* ditching *me*." He shoved a hand through his hair. "I ditched her."

Marge took a step back so that she could face him head-on. "You like this girl?"

Gryph turned toward the punching bag, flexing his sore knuckles. "Too much."

"Then what's stopping you from seeing her again?"

"There's been a BOLO, be on the look out, issued on me, for one. And then there's the other thing I can't just clear up with a phone call."

"What other thing?"

"The beast."

Marge snorted. "It's a part of you. Has she seen it?"

He nodded. "Partially."

"And she didn't run screaming?"

He'd been delirious with pain and infection, but she'd stayed right there with him, even when he'd roared and half changed. "No."

"That's a good sign." Marge nodded approvingly. "She's not afraid."

"Yeah." He slugged the bag again, regretting it as soon as his knuckles hit canvass. "I'm afraid of what the beast will do to her."

"Your beast doesn't control you, Gryphon." Marge laid a hand on his arm. "*You* control *it*."

He stared at her small older hand. "And if I can't?"

"There's no question about it."

"I can't risk her life to prove I can control my beast. There are…situations…that bring it out."

"Hot-and-heavy sex?" Marge grinned. "I'm old, not dead. My husband always half turned in the middle of making love to me. He even bit me a time or two."

The image of Marge and her husband getting naked in the sheets wasn't one Gryph wanted permanently imprinted in his head. "What did you do?"

"I bit him back."

"Did he draw blood?"

"Not much. It was more of a scratch."

"And you didn't turn?"

"Takes more than a scratch. You have to exchange a little blood."

"Assuming shifting to a lion is similar to wolf-shifting, what if I scratch her and mix my blood with hers?"

"Have you ever thought she might want the opportunity to decide if she's willing to risk it?"

"No." Gryph headed for the door. "She's a happy,

healthy and well-adjusted human. I won't subject her to the kind of life I lead."

"Who said she's all that? Do you really know who or what she is?" Marge shook a fist at him and walked toward him. "And what's wrong with your life?"

"I'm hiding in plain sight. I don't travel. Chicago is the center of my world."

"And why is that?" She held up her hand. "And don't tell me because of the beast. You have the most control of any shifter I've ever known."

He shook his head. "Not always."

"You do, when it counts."

"Don't you understand?" He grabbed Marge's arms. "I scratched her. My claws came out and sank into her skin. I drew blood." His heart squeezed so hard in his chest, he dropped his grip on Marge and pressed a hand to the pain. "I can't risk it."

"Fine." Marge rubbed her arms. "Go through your life sad and lonely, and miss out on everything love has to offer. It's your choice." She backed toward the door. "I'm going to my apartment, putting my feet up and watching *CSI*."

"Marge."

Gryph's voice stopped her from punching the elevator button. "You gonna yell at me some more?"

"No." He crossed the room and pulled the woman into a gentle hug. "Thanks. You always know how to bring me down off the ceiling."

"Wouldn't have to, if you'd just use your head, not your…" She glanced at his crotch. "You know." She pushed the button and the doors slid open. Once inside, she looked back at him. "And don't think your pretty little girlfriend is all so human. She might have a secret or two she's keeping from you." The elevator door slid closed.

"Huh?" Gryph lunged for the button and pressed it, but the car had already gone.

What the hell did Marge mean by her parting comment? Selene was human. Wasn't she?

Selene stepped out of the shower, feeling clean and refreshed. The oppressive evil had abated and her world had righted itself.

Well, almost. Her thighs still had a delicious ache and the wounds on her fanny stung every time she sat down, a continuous reminder of the intensity of the passion they'd shared on Gryph's office desk.

No amount of cold water in the shower had cooled her desire. How she wished she'd invited Gryph to come in. But he'd been so bipolar in how he'd treated her. One minute he'd been anxious to leave her with the promise to never see her again, the next he'd volunteered to stay until he was sure she was okay. She sensed he really wanted to be with her, but was afraid he was bad for her. The claw marks had been the clincher for him.

So be it. She didn't need him, or his warm caresses, or the raspy tongue licking the insides of her thighs. No, sir.

She checked her cell phone, half hoping he'd called, changing his mind. Disappointment filled her as she noted two calls from Deme, not Gryph.

She played the voice-mail message, her hand tightening.

"Selene, they've taken Amanda to the Cook County morgue. We've located Professor Crownover and he's asked to see the body. Meet us at the morgue at nine o'clock."

Selene rushed into her bedroom and dove into her dress pockets, her pulse speeding until her fingers touched the slick gray card Gryph had given her. Standing with her hair wrapped in a towel and another wrapped around her middle, she debated calling Gryph and asking him to meet them at the morgue. He had a right to know whatever Crownover had to say.

Then again, if there was big news to come out of the meeting, she could relay the information to him. She'd already interrupted his life and busy millionaire schedule enough by dropping in on him with a surprise visit.

She set the card on her nightstand and hurriedly dressed. Twice she almost lifted the phone and called him.

Dressed in jeans, T-shirt and a black leather jacket, her wet hair combed back and secured in a ponytail, she lifted the card from the nightstand, stuck it into her back pocket and headed for the door to her apartment.

Her hand paused on the doorknob and she reached out with her thoughts, searching for the evil she'd felt earlier.

A lingering thickness hung in the air as if the evil hovered, waiting to manifest itself in something more solid, more physical. A faint warning tremor rippled across her.

Selene grabbed the long, black flashlight she kept beside the door in case of emergency. It was solid and heavy, like the ones cops used as a light or a billy club, depending on what was needed at the time.

Armed, in a fashion, she stepped out the door and rounded the building to the driveway at the side, climbing into her compact Prius.

She drove away without incident; the farther from her apartment she went, the less she felt the disturbing and disconcerting feeling of being watched.

At the morgue, she climbed out of her car and entered the building. A night watchman checked her driver's license and led her back to one of the autopsy rooms, where tables stood in a line like a factory waiting for parts to be assembled. Or in this case, to be dissembled.

At the far end of the room, Deme, Brigid, Gina and Aurai stood with Cal, a man in a white lab coat and another man in a brown tweed jacket. They were gathered near a table with a body on it.

As Selene neared, she recognized the woman on the stainless-steel surface as Amanda Grant. Her body had been stripped and she lay on her belly, her long blond hair pulled away from the back of her neck, exposing the bruising and skin trauma of puncture wounds.

Deme glanced up. "Selene, good. I'm glad you're here. You'll want to hear what the professor has to say."

The man in the brown tweed jacket barely acknowledged her, his attention on the woman's body as he pointed with a scalpel to the wounds at the back of the woman's neck.

"As I was saying, these bite marks are from a large canine. A very large dog or a wolf, to be more specific."

"You're sure about that?" Selene asked.

"I've examined cattle killed by wolves on numerous occasions. Although they usually attack the hindquarters, the spacing between the canine teeth is narrower on a wolf than on a lion. The lion's is noticeably broader. Most likely a wolf attacked this woman. And it had to be a really big wolf."

"Professor, have you heard of wolves of this size in downtown Chicago before?" Brigid asked.

The professor nodded to the ME and stepped back. "Perhaps we should move this discussion outside the morgue so that the medical examiner can finish his work and get home before midnight."

Selene, her sisters and Cal left the autopsy room and stepped out in front of the morgue with the professor before they spoke again.

"I didn't want to say anything to alarm the ME." The professor removed a handkerchief from his pocket and wiped his hands on it, then dragged it over his face. "I've been studying wolf sightings in Chicago for the past five years, tracking the locations and documenting the time, size and colors reported."

"Sightings?" Brigid asked. "How many?"

"Over three hundred, and counting. The trend has become more frequent over the past year." He waved toward the parking lot. "If you'll follow me, I'll show you what I mean on my laptop."

The group gathered around the professor's older model Cadillac as he pulled his laptop from a case, set it on the hood of his vehicle and booted the system.

When the screen came up, he punched several keys and a map filled the display with red flags marking different locations on the Chicago city map. Many overlapped each other.

"All these were wolf sightings?" Selene asked.

"Those were just the *reported* sightings."

"Why don't we hear about it in the news?" Aurai touched the screen. "Look at all of them."

"The mayor is keeping it low-key. As long as no one had sustained injuries from a wolf attack, he didn't want to alarm the citizens."

"Until last night." Selene's fists tightened. "There seems to be a concentration of sightings in the southwest part of the city."

"Right. In the Archer Heights district. I've set up surveillance there several times. Some of the sightings were added from my own observations."

"So there really are wolves in the city?" Selene's heart soared. "And it wasn't a lion that attacked her? You're positive?"

"I saw the picture posted on the news, like everyone else. Just looking at the picture, I can tell you her attacker wasn't whatever she described. The facial structure was all wrong. Frankly I don't know what that was she had the forensic artist draw. Maybe some hallucination."

Selene knew, but she kept the information to herself.

Brigid pointed to the computer. "Can we get a copy of your data?"

"Sure," the professor said. "Got a flash drive?"

"As a matter of fact, I keep one on my keychain." Deme handed over her keychain, the professor plugged the storage device in and downloaded the information and removed the thumb drive.

Deme took her keys and held out her hand to the man. "Thank you for coming out so late at night, Professor."

"Let me know if there's anything else I can do. I have a daughter about Amanda's age. I'd hate to think there was a man-eating wolf roaming the streets close to where she lives on the northeast side."

"We'll let you know," Brigid assured him.

The professor closed his laptop, climbed into his Cadillac and drove away.

"So, what now?" Selene asked.

"I don't know about you, but—" Deme pocketed her keychain with the flash drive "—I'm headed to Archer Heights to see if I can catch me a killer." She spun toward her SUV.

Selene held up her hand and said in a clear and firm voice, "Hold on."

Her sisters and Cal all turned toward her.

"You heard the professor. Amanda was killed by a wolf. Just like Gryph said."

"Yeah, so?" Brigid frowned. "Your point?"

"You all agree then that Gryph didn't do it?"

Deme nodded. "I'd go as far as saying we're ninety-nine percent sure."

"Close enough." Selene took a deep breath. "I found him."

"Your wounded stranger?" Aurai laid her hand on Selene's arm, her eyes sparkling her excitement. "Where?"

"Doesn't matter where. I think he deserves to know about the professor's research. His life and reputation are on the line for trying to help."

Brigid shrugged. "Then call him. Cal, Deme and I are heading for Archer Heights."

"I'm going with them," Gina said.

"And me," Aurai added.

Selene smiled. "Guess we're all going. Who's driving?"

"Me." Deme pulled her keys from her pocket and headed across the parking lot for her SUV. "I can take most of us."

"I'll follow on my bike." Brigid straddled her Harley and glanced at Selene. "You riding with me?"

"Yeah. Just as soon as I place this call." She strode away for privacy, then punched the numbers on the keypad and hit Call. She held her breath, her pulse beating so hard it reverberated against her eardrums.

"Selene?" Gryph's deep, gravelly voice spread over her like warm melted chocolate.

"We're headed for Archer Heights. We think the killer may be there."

"Wait. I got the same information."

Selene glanced across at Deme. "From what source?"

"I can't say, but I have the address of a pool hall where we might start our search. I've mapped out the area. It's mostly warehouses and low-income housing. We should meet somewhere else and form a plan before we go charging in. The locals might not be so ready to answer questions otherwise."

"Good point."

"Where are you?"

"With my sisters at Cook County morgue."

"I'm less than a mile from you. Stay there. I'm coming." He hesitated. "That is, if you sisters aren't going to shoot me as soon as they see me."

A smile curled Selene's lips. "I'll make sure they don't."
When he rang off, Selene rejoined her sisters.

"Ready?" Brigid revved the engine on her Harley.

Shaking her head, Selene told them what she'd learned.
"Gryph got a tip on the Archer Heights area and, even better, an address of a pool hall where we might get some answers. He's on his way."

"Good," Brigid said. "I have a few questions for him
when he gets here."

Selene lifted her phone like a weapon. "If you even
think about shooting him or taking him in for questioning. I'll tell him not to come."

Brigid's eyes narrowed. "Fine. But he better not hurt
you, or all bets off."

For a long moment, Selene stared at her sister, torn.
She trusted her sisters with her life, but could she trust
them with Gryph's? Finally, she sighed. "He wants us to
wait here."

"The longer we wait the bigger chance of the attacker
going after another victim."

"We don't know that. Archer Heights is a big area, are
you going to cover the entire district?"

"She's right." Deme crossed her arms. "If this Gryph
guy has a specific address, it could save us a lot of time."

"We need him," Selene said. "We'll wait." And pray her
sisters didn't harm him.

Chapter 9

Within minutes of Selene's call, Gryphon pulled up in the armor-plated SUV he'd driven Selene home in. He dropped down and crossed to her.

The redhead Selene had identified as one of her sisters and another woman with jet-black hair stepped in front of him, before he reached her.

A growl rumbled up his throat and he fought to keep it from emerging. "I'm not going to hurt her. I came to help find the animal that killed Amanda."

"These two rude women are my sisters, Deme and Brigid." Selene stepped around them and stood beside Gryph, facing the women. "The other two are Gina and Aurai, also my sisters. And the cop is Cal Black. Sisters, this is Gryph." Her cheeks reddened and she glanced up at him. "I'm sorry, I don't know your last name." She'd made love to him, but there were a lot of things she didn't know about him. And a lot he didn't know about her.

"Leone. Gryphon Leone." Gryph's chest swelled at her show of faith as she stood with him in front of her sisters. The heat from her body ignited those embers he'd thought banked by a few hours' separation, reminding him of how beautiful her pale skin was against the black surface of his office desk.

The sandy-haired sister stepped up beside Brigid, the raven-haired one. "*The* Gryphon Leone?"

Gryph cringed. He preferred to maintain his anonymity. That others outside his corporation knew of him always baffled him. Why would they care? He wasn't his business.

"You know him?" Brigid asked.

"I don't *know* him," Gina said. "But I've *heard* about him. I contracted to clean the built-in aquariums in his corporate headquarters. He's one of the richest men in Chicago."

"By the goddess, we have a celebrity among us." Aurai chuckled. "And one of the hardest to get a picture of. The media would kill to get an interview with him." She covered her mouth. "Sorry, I didn't mean to infer someone in the media would have killed Amanda to get an interview with you, Mr. Leone."

"Please, excuse my ignorance." Deme's voice dripped sarcasm. "I'm not up on the rich and famous."

"Maybe not, Deme." Gina faced her sister. "But you've heard of GL Enterprises, haven't you?"

"Who hasn't?" Deme's eyes widened. "You mean to tell me we rescued the owner of GL Enterprises?"

Gryph nodded.

Selene's lips quirked on the corners.

Brigid wasn't laughing. "Rich or not, we know it was you Amanda drew the picture of."

Gryph's mouth firmed into a straight line. "Mine was the last face she saw. I was leaving the theater when I heard her scream. I found her *after* the wolf had already attacked. I fought him off, or he'd have finished the job then." He touched his shoulder where the wolf had bit him, the pain still all too memorable. "I stayed with her as long as I could until I heard the ambulance. I didn't attack her."

"The ME and a forensic anthropologist said that based on the bite marks, she was attacked from behind," Selene said, filling him in on what the professor had said about the bite being from a large dog or wolf.

"A shifter," he said.

"You know?" Aurai asked.

Brigid laughed. "Hell, *he's* a shifter. I'd guess he'd know if there were others in the city."

"Not necessarily," Gryph responded. "I shift to the form of a lion. I haven't had much contact with many wolves. However, I know they exist."

"And how many lion shifters are there in the city?" Deme asked.

His chin lifted. "I'm the only one I know of."

"You say you know an address of a place in Archer Heights we can start looking?" Brigid asked.

"I have an address of a pool hall where a gang of wolf shifters has been known to hang out."

"Where'd you get it?" Deme asked.

Gryph shook his head. "Sorry, I can't say."

Brigid crossed her arms and glared at him. "Why should we trust you?"

His lips quirked. "Do you have any better ideas?"

"No." Brigid's arms fell to her sides. "Let's look at it."

He pulled out his smartphone and brought up the map location, clicking on the satellite image that displayed the roofs of homes, businesses and warehouses.

"We can't all go barging into the pool hall demanding answers," Cal said.

"You're not leaving me behind," Selene said.

"Or us," Gina added as she nodded to Aurai.

"Some of us can stay in the vehicle outside the building in case we need to make a quick getaway." Deme stared around the group, her gaze landing on Aurai and Gina. "You two will be in the vehicle, at the ready, if we need a bit of sister persuasion."

The two of them nodded, and Gina glanced at the sky and sniffed. "If we're lucky, it'll rain."

Aurai draped an arm across Gina's shoulder. "We can make our own luck with a little help." She winked.

Selene shot what seemed like a nervous glance at Gryph.

His eyes narrowed. "I don't like the idea of any of you going in. It's a wolves' den, not an ice-cream parlor."

Cal chuckled. "You don't know much about the Chattox sisters, do you?"

He shook his head. "It's not safe. If they choose to attack, they'll outnumber us."

"I have my gun." Cal patted the weapon beneath his black leather jacket. "But it's nothing compared to their talents."

"Deme and I can handle anything thrown our way. We've walked into worse situations." Brigid turned to Selene. "Although I don't like the idea of Selene going in, we could use her skills."

"What skills? What do you mean?" Gryph asked.

"Nothing." Selene glared at her black-haired sister. "And don't worry, I'm going in."

"You'll stay in the SUV with Gina and Aurai," Gryph insisted.

Gina laid a hand on Gryph's arm. "Trust her, she can be our best asset inside."

"I'll be okay," Selene said softly. "I know what to do."

"Those are some of the roughest neighborhoods in the city," Gryph argued. "The humans are more like animals."

Gina grinned. "We can hope the animals are more human."

"Look, Gryph, we can be one of the most formidable opponents anyone will ever meet." Deme glanced around the circle. "Right?"

"Right!" Selene and the rest of her sisters all answered as one.

Brigid clapped a hand on Gryph's back. "Guess we're

going to the pool hall. Unless you think it's too dangerous. You can stay here until we come back."

He glared at Brigid.

"Cheer up." Cal checked his firearm. "They're a force to be reckoned with."

"I'm beginning to realize that."

"We'll stop two blocks short of the warehouse and let Brigid, Cal and Deme go in first."

Deme pulled a kerchief from her back pocket, tucked her hair back behind her ears and tied the cloth like a do-rag, securing the knots at the back of her head.

She'd transformed from classy detective in a black leather jacket to a thug in seconds.

Brigid, in her kick-ass black leather chaps and well-worn black Harley jacket, already fit the part. She climbed onto her motorcycle and revved the engine. "Selene, you can't go in like that, get dirty or something."

"These are my best jeans."

"Exactly. Roll in the mud or something." Brigid's gaze skimmed across the neatly pressed line down the front. "They're too new, and switch shirts with Aurai. That white T-shirt will get you killed. You look like a high-school prep."

Selene's cheeks bloomed bright red. "We can change in the SUV."

"Just don't get yourself killed." Aurai grinned, running her hands over her shirt. "It's one of my favorite Smashing Pumpkins T-shirts."

"Nice to know where I rank." Selene hugged her sister. "What are we going in?"

"You're riding with me." Gryph wasn't giving her any other choices. He didn't like that she was going at all. At least if she was with him, he could provide some kind of protection.

"Aurai and I will ride with Deme and Cal," Gina said.

They made plans and synchronized their watches.

Aurai and Selene stepped into Deme's SUV and exchanged shirts, mussing Selene's hair to give her a tougher, more badass look. When she emerged, wearing Aurai's stilettos, her chin high, sunglasses shading her brown eyes and bright red lipstick slashed across her full, luscious lips, Gryph wanted to skip the pool hall and take her straight to his apartment, where his king-size bed would be a lot more comfortable than the top of his desk. He'd make love to her until the sun rose the next day.

She strutted by him, running a finger across his chest. "Ready?"

His cock twitched. Yeah, he was ready.

Aurai giggled. "What a tease."

Brigid roared out of the morgue parking lot, leading the way to Archer Heights.

Before long, Gryph was driving past the pool hall. Several men leaned against the outside wall, smoking cigarettes. A couple of girls in tight jeans and strategically torn jean jackets hung on the arms of two of the men. Motorcycles, tricked-out cars and junkers lined the parking lot and rock music vibrated through the walls of the dilapidated building.

Gryph didn't even slow. He drove past an old bottling company warehouse, turned on the next street and pulled in behind a guard shack. The huge warehouse was surrounded by a chain-link fence, the gate chained and locked.

"Aren't you afraid someone will steal your car?" Selene asked.

"I have insurance."

"I hope you have life insurance. We might need it by the look of that pool hall."

Gryph turned in his seat and captured her hand. "I don't want you to go in."

She squeezed his hand. "I have to do this. They need me, and I need to help find Amanda's killer."

"Stay here. Let me handle it."

Her gentle smile made his insides flutter. "Between me and my sisters, we can handle anything that's thrown our way. We've been in worse situations than a little pool hall."

"Those are shifters in there. If they are anywhere as big as the one that attacked Amanda, they will dominate you and your sisters by sheer size and strength."

Again her smile sent blood rushing straight south. "There are things you don't know about us and that I don't have time to explain. We have to get in there. Deme and Brigid need me."

"I don't like it."

"So noted."

Gryph slid out of the vehicle and rounded the hood to open the door for her. Grasping her around her middle, he lowered her to the ground, sliding her body down the length of his, rubbing her pelvis over the hard ridge beneath his jeans. "We could call this off and go back to my place."

"I thought making love to me was a big mistake." She traced a finger in a swirling pattern across his chest. "Change your mind?"

"I still think it's a mistake, but I'd rather risk me hurting you than that gang of wolves in the pool hall."

"See? You're beginning to make more sense."

"So you'll go with me?"

"No." She stepped back. "You see, I have skills my sisters don't."

"Like?"

She bit her lip and stared to the far right. "I can read people."

Gryph studied her face. Selene wasn't meeting his

eyes. Something about what she'd said didn't ring completely true.

"We don't have time to discuss it. Just know, I can tell when it's time to leave, before it's too late."

"I hope so, because we'll be surrounded." He grabbed her hand and guided her past the guard shack to the sidewalk. They rounded the corner two blocks away.

"Brigid just entered."

"How can you tell?"

"I know." She gazed ahead toward the pool hall, where a dingy neon light hung over the door. "Deme and Cal are inside."

"How do you know?" He squinted. "I have good night vision. It's one of the perks of being part lion. But from here, I can't distinguish who's going in or out of the building."

"Trust me." She pushed her sunglasses up on her nose and put a little more sway in her walk, slipping his arm over her shoulders. "Let's get inside and find us a killer."

Gryph gritted his teeth and went along with the plan. As they neared the pool hall, the men leaning against the building straightened, eyes narrowing, nostrils twitching.

Oh, yeah. They looked like humans, but something about the way their nostrils flared made Gryph think these could be some of the wolf shifters Rafe had said would be here and the whole area reeked of dog.

Without slowing, he tucked Selene close against his side and entered the building.

The guys on the outside followed them inside.

His gut told him things were about to get sticky.

As soon as they stepped through the door, Selene could sense the tension rising in the room. All eyes angled toward Gryph.

They knew he wasn't human and he was on wolf turf.

Perhaps having Gryph along wasn't such a good idea. Humans were expected. She and her sisters might have been better off coming in sans the men. Most men assumed women were helpless and didn't consider them a threat.

Selene could feel the first prickles of hair rising on the backs of the necks of the wolf shifters in the room. A low rumbling built in some of their chests. Too low to be heard over the music, but she sensed it, nonetheless.

Cal and Deme sat at one end of the bar, talking to the bartender. The bartender's lips were moving and his eyes were shifting around the room as if he was afraid of talking to the two.

Brigid stood beside one of the pool tables, observing a game and chugging a mug of beer.

Selene steered Gryph to a table in a shadowy corner and sat, glad for the glasses so that she could browse the room without being too obvious. The tabletop was sticky and the room smelled of old cigarettes and spilled alcohol.

Selene was in no hurry to order drinks she had no intention of drinking. She focused on the thoughts and mental images of the patrons of the pool hall.

Two tattooed men racked the balls on the pool table close to where Brigid stood. They were sizing her up and debating whether or not to let her in on the game.

Selene almost laughed out loud when her kick-ass sister dropped her keys on the floor and bent to retrieve them, hiking her ass in their direction, displaying the smooth curve in the tight jeans beneath her leather chaps.

The men's temperatures rose and a wave of lust flowed over Selene's senses. Two seconds later, they invited Brigid to play a round.

Selene shifted her focus to the bar, where Cal and Deme leaned toward the bartender, their faces purposely relaxed. Inside they were tense. Whatever the man behind the bar was telling them had their full attention.

"I'm going to the bar to order drinks and ask questions." As Gryph started to rise, a scuffle broke out by the pool table.

A third man had joined Brigid and her two pool players, his attitude and vibes shooting off anger and aggression. The man grabbed for Brigid.

The two men she'd been playing with stepped between her and the interloper, spun him and slammed him against the wall, knocking the cue rack over. The man slithered to the floor, a knot the size of a quarter rising on his forehead.

The bartender shouted, "Take it outside."

The two men picked the guy up, dusted him off and shoved him toward the door. He swayed, steadied and then staggered out the door.

A heavyset waitress, who was wearing a T-shirt with the words Waiting for Mr. Right written across her ample breasts in faded and peeling letters, stopped by their table. "What can I getcha?"

"Information." Gryph slid a one-hundred-dollar bill into the woman's hand.

She stared at the bill, then tucked it into her pocket. "For that kind of money, I'd give you the combination to the safe in the back room."

"I don't want the combination."

Selene didn't sense any animosity from the woman. She was tired from working two jobs, her feet hurt and she wanted the night to end so that she could get four hours sleep before she started all over again. An image of a small boy wove through her thoughts.

"Which one of the people in this bar is the Devil's Disciples pack leader?" Gryph asked, keeping his voice low and conversational, adding a little louder, "We'll have two beers."

Immediately the woman's back stiffened and her hands

shook. Fear replaced exhaustion. "Don't know what you're talking about."

"She's lying," Selene said softly. "And she's frightened."

"There's another one hundred dollars in it for you if you point him out," Gryph said.

She backed away. "I got a kid. I don't want no trouble."

"I'm not asking you do anything but point."

She looked left then right. "He's not here."

"Is there a second in command?" Gryph asked.

She leaned over the table and wiped a dirty rag over the surface. "In the corner at the pool table. The tattoo with the upside-down cross."

Gryph slid another bill into her hand.

The woman hurried away, looking back toward the man beside Brigid with the upside-down cross tattoo on his upper arm.

Selene closed her eyes and sent a warning nudge to her sister.

Brigid gave an almost imperceptible nod and lifted her pool cue to take the shot.

A few moments later, the waitress returned with their two beers and a big burly man with tattoos covering his arms followed.

The waitress set the beers on the table and scurried away, keeping her gaze averted from Gryph and Selene.

The woman was cringing inwardly and envisioning an escape route from the crowded bar, anticipating a fight, as if she'd seen many fights before.

The man who'd followed the waitress moved closer, his arms crossing over his massive chest. "We don't serve the likes of your kind here." Every gaze swung toward him.

Trapped in his seat, with the big guy threatening him, Gryph smiled and leaned back. "And what *kind* would that be?"

Though his words were casual and drawn out, as if he

didn't have a care in the world, he was revving up beneath the surface, ready to react to any threat.

Selene could sense the animal inside waking and flexing, preparing to spring, and she marveled at his self-control.

The pack member snarled, canines extending enough to let Gryph know he recognized a shifter when he saw one. "You better leave."

Gryph tapped the bottle in front of him "My girl and I haven't finished our beer."

In a lightning move, the man swiped his tree-trunk-sized arm across the table and the full bottles of beer crashed to the floor. "Looks to me like you're finished now."

Selene jumped, but managed not to squeal. The animosity emanating from the man could only be described as primal. One animal defending his territory against another, the wolf beneath his skin fighting to get out, barely leashed.

Gryph shrugged out of his jacket, folded it neatly and laid it across Selene's lap. "I'll leave when I'm ready."

Her breath lodged in her throat, Selene whispered, "Gryph, don't."

"I'm not starting anything, babe." He patted her hand, then glanced at the guy standing over him, his eyes narrowing.

Selene sent a silent push to her sisters. *Get out. The shit's about to hit the fan.*

Several other men closed ranks behind the tattooed man standing in front of Gryph, all shrugging out of their jackets.

Selene felt the wolves shift a few seconds before it happened, and the tiny hairs springing out of the men's skin almost made her itch.

She touched Gryph's leg and gave him an urgent nudge with her mind. *Shift. Now.*

He leaned over and kissed her cheek, whispering, "Get out while I distract them." Then he lunged from his seat in a flying tackle, hit the man in the gut, sending him crashing backward into the others. All of them landed in a pile on the floor, giving Gryph enough time to transform—the change was almost instantaneous, from man to lion.

He roared, dropped to all fours and pounced on the downed men even as they shifted into wolves. One by one, they were sent flying with a powerful swipe of his massive paw.

With three wolves in front closing in on him, Gryph didn't see the two who'd been playing pool with Brigid shift and spring toward him.

Brigid balled up a fist of flames and flung it at one of them, catching his fur on fire. The wolf howled, dropped and rolled, the scent of singed hair filling the room.

The other wolf bunched his muscles as he prepared to leap, but Selene hit him hard with a mental slap, making him stagger and fall on his face. He lurched to his feet, shook his head and would have leaped into the fray, but vines that snaked out from an ivy growing along a ledge wrapped around all four legs and pulled tight, like in a calf-roping contest. The wolf fell hard on his side and struggled to break free.

More wolves gathered until a dozen circled Gryph. A brief yip from the leader and all of them lunged at once.

If all the wolves ripped into Gryph, he wouldn't make it. What he needed was something like a force field, a wall between him and the enemy.

Fear for Gryph made Selene concentrate her telepathic abilities on him, a chant in her mind calling forth the influence of the goddess. A swell of power built inside her, around her, encompassing the space around Gryph, building an invisible barrier that prevented the wolves from reaching him, but it was more in their minds than grounded in reality.

Wolves charged toward Gryph and, at the last moment, skidded to a halt, their minds refusing to let them cross the invisible line.

Snarling and snapping at the air, they remained back, pacing, waiting for the moment they could pass through a barrier they could not see, but most certainly felt.

Deme dropped from her stool on the bar and raised her hands, sending a twist of vines at the wolf who'd yipped the attack signal, trussing him up like a pig for slaughter. In moments, he transformed back to his human form, the upside-down cross tattoo easily discernible in the dim lighting of the pool hall.

The other wolves backed away, growling.

Selene sent thoughts of fleeing to them. Some shook their heads, backed toward the door and ran. Others glared at her, seeming to know she'd been the one to put the thoughts into their minds.

The tattooed man fought against his bindings. "What do you want with us?"

Gryph allowed himself to transform back to almost human form, retaining enough of his animal to still appear fierce, but not enough he couldn't be understood. "Which one of your pack killed Amanda Grant?"

The wolf on the ground at his feet shook his head and spat on the floor beside Gryph's feet. "You're barking up the wrong tree."

"Lion's don't bark." Gryph's animal came out enough for him to slam a giant paw on the man's chest and he growled against the guy's face, his canines, wickedly long and sharp, pressing into the skin.

Selene shivered, glad Gryph was on their side.

The man flinched. "It wasn't us. Whoever it was went

rogue. He's acting on his own. He's not part of the Devil's Disciples."

"You're known for turning humans. Do all the humans you turn join your pack?"

"No."

Selene prodded the man's mind, but couldn't get beyond the image of another wolf. One that had held off his pack in a daring standoff. "He knows who it might be."

Gryph roared and bounced his paw on the man's chest for effect. "Who did it?"

"I wouldn't tell you, even if I knew." He growled, his snout elongating, wicked teeth bared, the effect frightening even with the man securely tied in vines. "You can't fight off the entire pack. You won't get out of here alive."

Selene couldn't help glancing toward the door, half expecting an army of wolves to step through.

Gryph transformed into full lion and opened his jaws wide, his teeth gleaming in the darkness. He dropped his head fast, his teeth connecting with the man's throat, without breaking the skin.

"You better tell him what you know. He's not very good at holding back his beast," Selene warned him.

"Go ahead," the man on the floor snarled. "Kill me."

Gryph roared again.

Selene willed him to spare the man. He might be useful.

The lights in the building blinked out, the music from the sound system died with the lights, leaving the room pitch-black and eerily quiet except for the snarling wolves, and shifting feet and furniture as people and animals shuffled in the darkness.

Then the sound of wind wailed at the building and the pinging of something hard hitting the roof sent a shiver of dread through Selene.

She sensed the urgency in her sisters outside, a silent call to hurry it up, things were getting bad. "Time to go."

Chapter 10

Gryph, his paw firmly planted on the leader's chest, shot a glance toward Selene, blinking to focus his catlike night vision. *How do you know?* he thought.

"I just do." She stood with wide eyes, apparently unable to see the wolves, *knowing* they were creeping closer to her.

Gryph growled low in his throat, a warning to the animals taking advantage of the darkness to press in for the attack.

A flame flared in Brigid's hand, forming a bright glowing circle around her body.

What the hell? For the first time, Gryph noticed the woman had fire in her hands and wasn't burning.

Selene's mouth tipped upward in a lopsided smile. "Brigid likes to play with fire."

"Think that's cool?" Brigid dug her free hand into her jacket pocket. "Get a load of these." She pulled out what appeared to be tiny creatures, tossing them into the air. Soon, the little buggers flew around the room, giving off bursts of fire like fireflies blinking, only with real flames, creating a strobe-like effect over the room and its occupants.

The night couldn't get stranger. Having lived in the Lair most of his life, Gryph knew other animals, magical beings and mythical creatures existed, but he'd never known one to pack fire in her fist like a softball.

Red eyes gleamed in the shadows, the wolves of the pack inching closer, snapping at the fire-belching, flying animals when they came too close and singed their fur.

Already outnumbered eight-to-one, Gryph had to get Selene and her sisters out of the pool hall before the rest of the wolf pack surrounded the building, if they hadn't already.

"Come on, let's go." Gryph, returning to half man, half beast, grabbed their captive from the floor and dragged him out the door.

Selene scrambled after him.

As soon as he emerged into the open, a gale-force wind nearly knocked him off his feet. Pellets of hail rained down on him, stinging against his fur-covered skin. What the hell had happened to the weather? The forecast had been for a clear and cool evening.

Then he saw it, and had to do a double take. A small, tightly wrapped tornado spun in front of him, grabbing up any loose objects, spinning them into the twister and flinging them outward.

On the other side of the funnel cloud stood Deme's SUV, which was supposed to have been parked a couple blocks away. Aurai perched on the running board, her arms raised into the air, as if directing the chaos like a symphony conductor.

First the vine-throwing Deme, then the fire-wielding Brigid, now this... What *were* these women?

Witches. The answer came like a whisper in his mind. One moment he was wondering, the next he knew.

He glanced back at Selene, her body hunched low to remain standing, her gaze shooting to his at that exact moment.

"You, too?" he asked, his words whipped away by the blast.

Again she nodded, as if she heard him, even in the din from the storm.

When they got out of this mess, they sure as hell were going to have a conversation.

In the meantime, a pack of wolves stood in the street, leaning into the wind. Each time the wolves tried to make a dash for the door, hail pounded on them, driving them back. Gina stood on the ground beside Aurai, her hair twisting and dancing around her face.

"Get him to the SUV," Selene called out over the howling of wind and wolves. "My sisters will hold them off."

"Anything else I should know about you?" Gryph snapped, feeling the fool for thinking Selene defenseless.

Selene gave him an apologetic look, squinting as her hair lashed across her face. "I didn't mention that my sisters and I have special talents?"

"Yeah, but I thought you meant self-defense skills, not—" he waved a hand "—this."

"I'd say it's all about self-defense." Selene stepped out into the street, the tornado moving enough to allow her to pass behind it.

The shifter he had in his grip struggled against the restraining vines, his wolf snout jutting out of his human face, grabbing and tearing at the bonds. He jerked hard, ripping through enough to free his arms and lunge at Gryph with razor-sharp teeth.

Gryph dropped him in time to miss being slashed by vicious canines. The man rolled away, ripping at the vines around his legs, his body shifting into wolf form. Gryph dove for him, snagging a leg before he could make a run for it.

Deme, Brigid and Cal backed out of the pool hall at that moment, followed by the flying fire-breathing things.

Cal had drawn his weapon, ready to shoot anyone following them. When they cleared the door, Gryph shouted to Deme, "A little help here."

The wolf twisted and snapped at him.

Gryph let go of one leg and grabbed another to avoid being ripped to shreds.

Deme spun toward Gryph, whipped her hands into the air and, despite the storm raging around her, had their prisoner's four legs bound together so tightly, he toppled over in a snarling heap.

The wolves in the street howled, leaping forward, only to be slapped back by the twister. Several wolves burst through the door.

Brigid was ready with a ball of fire in each palm. As quickly as she launched a ball, another appeared in her hand. She twirled the balls, daring any wolf to make a play for her or any of her sisters.

Once Deme had their prisoner secure, she lassoed the pool hall door and jerked it shut, tying it with heavy vines, blocking the remaining pack members from exiting that direction. "We don't have much time before they'll be coming out the back."

The fireflies flew over the pack of wolves, spitting flames into their fur. Two of them got too close to the funnel cloud and were sucked up inside.

"Damn. Sorry," Brigid called out to the trapped creatures.

Gryph, still in a halfway state, dragged the angry wolf shifter along with him and stuffed him into the backseat of the SUV. Then he turned to help the others.

Wolves raced around the side of the building, joined the other members of the pack and closed ranks in a semicircle around them.

The tornado spun to the ground and disappeared as if it were a balloon that a child had let all the air out of.

"I couldn't hold it any longer," Aurai said.

"We've got it now," Gina called out, raising her hands to the sky. Brigid, Deme, Gina, Aurai and Selene joined hands. Cal stood on one side while Gryph stood on the other, wondering how they'd get out of this mess intact.

Gryph stepped out in front of the sisters and called back over his shoulder. "I can hold them off for a few minutes while you all get into the SUV and make a run for it." He let his inner beast loose, shifted into full lion and dropped to all four paws.

"I'll stay, as well." Cal raised his gun and aimed at the closest wolf. "Go."

"I'm not leaving you." Selene stepped up beside Gryph and put a hand on his shaggy shoulder.

"We're all in this together," Deme said.

Behind them, the SUV door slammed shut.

Gryph looked back in time to see their prisoner in human form, leaning over the steering wheel as he shifted into Drive and hit the accelerator, leaving a streak of rubber on the pavement as he shot forward.

"Hey, that's my car!" Deme started to run after him, but Cal snagged her arm.

"It's just a vehicle."

"Yeah, but it was mine." Deme glared after the retreating SUV.

Tattoo man hadn't gone a block before a commercial semi tractor-trailer rig appeared out of nowhere and broadsided the SUV so hard, it flew through the air. The SUV crashed through a fence and slammed into a building upside down, the roof crushed beneath.

Then the rig barreled toward them, engine revving, a gigantic bull plowing through a ring of amateur matadors.

Wolves scattered as they leaped over each other to get out of the way of the oncoming vehicle.

Aurai and Gina dove one direction, rolling out of the way. Brigid, Cal and Deme dove in the other direction.

Selene stood firm, her gaze on the oncoming monster of a truck, like a deer in the headlights.

Fear shot through Gryph. Fear for Selene. Still in lion form, he rammed into her, knocking her off her feet and out of the way of the truck. He barely cleared the wheels as the killer truck blew by.

Selene jumped to her feet as the sisters regrouped. "Run! Now! While they're still scattered." She led the way to Gryph's vehicle. He and Cal followed, bringing up the rear as the wolves regrouped and started after them.

Selene reached the vehicle first and slid in behind the wheel. The others piled in. Brigid, Cal and Gryph stood guard.

Cal climbed in, the windows down, his gun aimed out at the advancing pack.

"Get in," Selene yelled.

Gryph roared one last time, wanting to attack, not run. But if he wanted to stay alive long enough to figure out who had killed Amanda Grant and now the second in command of the Devil's Disciples, he had to retreat.

Selene pulled up beside him, leaned across the passenger seat and pushed open the door.

Gryph leaped in, the change coming over him slowly, his human side fighting back the lion defending his pride.

Selene hit the accelerator with all the force of a race car driver and sped away from the wolf pack.

After only a block, Brigid yelled, "Whoa! Stop!"

Selene slammed her foot on the brake, throwing everyone forward.

Gryph flung out his arms to keep his head from crashing into the windshield.

"What?" Selene shot a glance at the side mirror.

"My bike." Before Selene had come to a complete stop,

Brigid shoved the door open and leaped out of the vehicle. "I wouldn't hang around here for long. See you at the station." With a quick nod toward their rear, she dove behind a bush and rode out on her Harley, leaning low over the handlebars as she sped away from the glowing fire of Deme's burning vehicle.

Selene followed, driving fast.

Gryph kept watch out the side mirror, hoping the members of the Disciples weren't following. Soon the wolves dropped back.

Before all the hair on his body receded, Gryph leaned over the seat. "Deme, if you'd hand me the duffel bag at your feet, I'll get dressed."

"I don't know. I was enjoying the scenery." She grinned, then reached down and came up with a gym bag, handing it across the seat. "Smart to keep spares handy. Does this happen to you often?"

"No." He gritted his teeth. He'd never turned in public. Balthazar had kept him in the tunnels until he'd matured enough to control his changes. He'd sneaked out on occasion as a young teen, but he hadn't officially been allowed to go topside until Balthazar was sure he could handle any situation without changing.

He was almost certain Balthazar hadn't considered a situation like being surrounded by a pack of wolf shifters with nothing but witches and an armed detective to help bail him out.

Selene kept her gaze on the road, slipping up onto the expressway as Gryph shoved his legs into the sweatpants he'd kept in the gym bag, never really expecting to have to use them.

His jacket lay over the console. Despite having to beat a hasty retreat from the pool hall, Selene had held on to it and made sure it came with them. Without his fur, the jacket was welcome. He slipped his arms into it and leaned back. "Who wants to fill me in?"

By the time they pulled into the parking lot of the police station, Deme had called 911 to report the fire, and Brigid was waiting on her motorcycle.

Selene cringed, realizing there was no keeping the truth from Gryph. Much as she'd liked being with him, once he knew what she was able to do, he'd probably never want to see her again.

"Witches, huh?" Gryph asked as he dropped down out of the SUV.

"Yeah." Selene glanced across at him as she pulled the key fob from the ignition and tossed it to him. She was quick to add, "We don't always use our...skills. Only when we need to."

"Some of those magic tricks your sisters pulled made shifting look tame."

"I wouldn't say that." Selene smiled across at him. "You're superstrong and ferocious when you've shifted. Not that you aren't strong in human form." Her cheeks heated at the memory of him thrusting into her, his taut muscles glistening in the natural lighting from his office windows. "Every gift has its advantages and drawbacks."

"Don't I know it." He turned toward her. "Let me get it all straight in case some of those so-called gifts are used on me. Deme, you, can throw vines."

"I have the ability to influence all things relative to earth." Deme slid out of the SUV and dropped to the ground.

"Not only can she throw vines, she can create a pretty convincing earthquake," Aurai said.

"Among other things," Selene added.

"Good to know." Gryph shoved a hand through his

tawny hair. "I'll have to take out earthquake insurance. Never thought I'd need it in Chicago."

"Aurai can influence wind and weather," Selene offered, hoping he'd forget to ask her where her talent lay.

Aurai grinned as she climbed down out of the backseat. "My weather, plus Gina's ability to channel water, made the hail storm pretty handy, don't you think?"

Gryph nodded. "Gina's got water, and Brigid's pyrotechnics were pretty spectacular." Gryph got out of the vehicle and stood beside the others. "And what were those bugs she let loose?"

Aurai's smile brightened. "Not bugs. Miniature dragons."

"Fire-slinging, fire-breathing dragonflies and tornado tossing. What's that leave you?" Gryph stared across at Selene as she joined them in front of the building.

"Selene has the gift of spirit," Brigid said as she climbed off her motorcycle. "She's telepathic."

"She can read minds and feelings of the living and sometimes the dead."

"I can't read all minds. And usually it's more a sense of what the person is feeling." She studied his face, looking for any sign of revulsion and finding none.

His eyes narrowed. "Is that how you found me down by the river?"

"Some thoughts come to me louder than others. I couldn't ignore yours that night."

"So you knew I hadn't attacked Amanda?"

"That's what she kept telling us," Cal said.

Selene nodded. "I didn't exactly read it in your mind. It's more like I sensed it. Again, some thoughts and feelings are more prominent than others."

"Cal, Brigid and I have to report in to the lieutenant." Deme motioned toward the building. "You want to continue this discussion inside?"

"If it's all the same to you, I'd rather not." Gryph's gaze captured Selene's. "The less people know about my...other side, the better."

"We understand." Aurai touched his arm. "For the most part, we like to blend in."

"With mad skills like you all have, that has to be hard."

Brigid shrugged. "We get 'em out and brush them off when we have to."

Gina patted Gryph's back. "Your secret's safe with us."

"Unless you hurt one of us." Brigid's eyes narrowed.

Gryph half expected fire to shoot out of her eyes and burn him for even standing close to Selene. He raised his hands. "Message heard, loud and clear."

Selene glared at Brigid and hooked Gryph's arm. "Can you drop me at my place?"

"Do the rest of you need rides home?"

"That's right." Deme's lips pressed together. "I don't have wheels."

"The lieutenant should authorize a vehicle from the motor pool," Cal said. "We're working a case."

"Think the department will cover the replacement cost of my SUV?"

"If not, your insurance will. It was stolen."

"By a shifter." Deme crossed her arms. "I'm still trying to figure out how to explain stolen, run into and flipped over with a guy still inside."

Cal pulled her against him and kissed her lips. "You don't."

Aurai raised her hand. "I'll ride in the cop car."

"It's unmarked and doesn't have all the whiz-bang stuff the patrol cars have," Deme warned.

"I don't care. I've always wanted to ride in back." She held out her wrists. "Wanna cuff me?"

Deme swatted at her.

Gina rolled her eyes. "I don't know what she's thinking."

Brigid laughed. "Too many erotic romance novels."

"Tattletale," Aurai said, pouting.

"I'll go with Brigid," Gina said. "I could use a little more wind in my hair."

That would leave Selene riding alone with Gryph. Her stomach tightened and her heartbeat kicked up a notch. "Will the lieutenant need statements from us about what happened at the pool hall?"

Deme frowned. "Come to think of it, you never told us whether you read anything in the leader's mind."

"I didn't get much. When you asked him if they'd turned a human that could have gone rogue, I got an image of a pitch-black wolf with green eyes."

"Most of the wolves at the pool hall were gray or brown."

"Think the black wolf was the one who attacked the woman?"

"I'll check with the crime scene investigators," Cal said. "Maybe they recovered black wolf hairs at the scene of the crime."

"If it was a black wolf shifter, how do we find him?" Deme asked. "We can't just line up all the seemingly human men in the city and tell them to shift and see what we get."

"I felt him when he showed up at the hospital. When he smothered Amanda," Selene said. "And I've felt him again since."

"When?" Gryph demanded.

Selene looked away, refusing to meet Gryph's gaze. "When you dropped me off at my apartment earlier today."

Gryph frowned. "When you weren't feeling well?"

"Which means he knows where you live." Gryph's lips pressed together. "Damn."

"I don't like it, Selene," Deme said. "Anywhere else?"

"I felt him again when the truck tried to run us over."

Her brow furrowed. "I tried to read his mind, but it was as if he knew, and pushed back."

"And almost made roadkill out of you." Gryph gripped her shoulders. "Promise me you'll let us know the next time you sense his presence."

She nodded, the intensity in Gryph's expression making her very aware of the warmth of his hands on her arms. His jacket swung open, revealing his muscular chest, reminding her of what it felt like to run her hands across his taut skin.

His nostrils flared and his fingers tightened.

"You should stay with one of us tonight," Brigid said.

"Yeah," Aurai agreed. "He finished off Amanda to keep her from talking and ran down the Devil's Disciples dude. If the killer knows you can sense him, he might target you."

"And he knows where you live," Gina pointed out.

Selene shook her head. "I'll be fine in my own place. I have locks on my doors."

"What about when you open your store?" Gina persisted.

"Close it for the next few days," Brigid ordered.

Selene laughed. "I can't close my store for long, or I'll go out of business. And I can't hide in my apartment, I have places to go and people depending on me for the charity ball."

"I'll hire someone else to take care of things," Gryph announced.

"No way." She moved out of Gryph's hands. "I've worked too hard coming up with the costumes for the waitstaff. If you take it away from me, how will I pay the suppliers?"

"*I'll* pay them."

"No, this is a chance for me to get my name and my work seen." Selene crossed her arms over her chest. "I'm not going into hiding because of what *might* happen. It might *not* happen and I will have missed this chance."

Aurai leaned close to Gryph. "You're not going to convince her now. When she gets that look, she's planted her heels in the dirt and she's not going to let you change her mind."

Selene rolled her eyes. "I can hear everything you're saying, Aurai. I'm right here, and I'm not running scared."

"We don't want you to end up like Amanda." Gina slipped an arm around her waist. "You said he pushed back when you tried to read him. What if he attacks you?"

"You can't throw fireballs." Brigid spun a ball of fire in her palm.

"And you don't have the ability to tie him up." Deme stood with her fists on her hips. "What will you do to defend yourself?"

"I have a brain, you know." Selene glanced at her feet, wanting the conversation to end so that she could get home to bed. "I'll think of something."

"That wolf had to be huge and heavy, Selene," Cal said. "How is your brain going to fight him off? It could be like throwing a BB at a fence post. You might hit it, but it's not going to have any effect. You have to go after an animal that large with an elephant gun and blow it out of the water."

"I can handle it without an elephant gun," Selene said quietly.

"What aren't you telling us?" Brigid's eyes narrowed. "Was that you holding back the wolves attacking Gryph in the pool hall? By the goddess, when did you learn how to do that?"

Selene's cheeks burned. "It just happened."

"You did that?" Deme grinned. "I wondered why they couldn't get to Gryph."

"How?" Gina asked.

Gryph's frown deepened. "What are you talking about?"

Selene shrugged, not wanting to make a big deal out of it. Talking about her abilities only made it more apparent that she had some control over others' minds. How soon would it be before Gryph realized she might have the ability to control his thoughts and feelings? Thus the reason for her to stay out of relationships she really cared about. And for some reason, she felt this one had the potential to be one of those. "I can't explain it and, if it's all the same to you, I'd like to go home and get some rest. It's been a stressful night, as it is." To Deme, she added, "Let me know what you learn, if anything, from the lieutenant."

Deme gripped her hand. "Will do."

"Don't try being a hero," Gina added. "We're your sisters. We're in this together."

"Yeah." Aurai extended her other hand to Gina. Soon all the Chattox sisters stood in a circle and, as one, chanted:

"Feel the power,
Free our hearts,
Find our way
Be the one.
With the strength of the earth,
With the rising of the wind,
With the calm of the water,
With the intensity of fire,
With the freedom of spirit,
The goddess is within us.
She is power.
We are her.
We are one.
Blessed be."

They broke apart and Selene joined Gryph. "I'm ready."
It wasn't until they got into his SUV that he sat back

against the seat and stared across at her. "Maybe you can fill me in on everything."

She looked away. "You heard it all from my sisters."

"I'd like to hear the part about your controlling a pack of wolves with your mind."

Selene lowered her eyelids and sent a silent prayer to the goddess to help her let this man go. There was no other way.

Chapter 11

Gryph drove away from Selene's sisters, the moon shining bright in the sky. So many thoughts churned in his head with one rising to the top. "Let me get this straight. You can read minds?"

Selene sighed. "Sometimes. If the thought is prominent in the person's mind, sometimes I can hear their thoughts word-for-word. More often, it's a feeling, emotion or sense."

"Can you read my thoughts right now?"

"I can sense you're angry and that you have a lot on your mind. Images are flashing through of the wolves, the truck and the interior of the pool hall."

"And what do you see about you?"

Her cheeks reddened and she glanced at her hands, twisting in her lap. "I sense confusion."

"Anything else?"

"Anger...and...lust." She stared out the window, her chest rising and falling with shorter, ragged breaths. Her reflection was one of a woman torn by honesty and longing.

Gryph almost pulled to the side of the road and took her into his arms. Instead, he shifted his gaze back to the road in front of him. "I'm not sure I like having someone in my head." His fingers tightened on the wheel. "Granted, if you hadn't sensed my distress the night I went for a swim in the river, I'd most likely be dead. But this mind read-ing and maneuvering is another thing entirely. Is that how you manipulated the wolves attacking me?"

"Something like that. I didn't even know I could stop those wolves. It just…happened."

"Nothing just *happens* like that. What were you feeling at the time? Was it like a buildup of emotions that mani-fests itself in a type of force field?"

"I don't know." She pinched the bridge of her nose. "Could we not talk about this?"

He bit back the questions spilling into his head and nodded. For the next few minutes he sat in silence, going over everything that had happened over the past forty-eight hours.

The attack on Amanda, Selene showing up to save him, the intense thought he'd had right before the leader of the wolf pack had transformed from human to animal. In his head, he'd felt the urge to change. As though someone told him to change.

When he pulled up in front of Selene's building, Gryph shifted into Park and stared at the storefront with the pretty sign and dainty vintage and designer clothing display in the window.

Selene reached for the door handle.

He grabbed her hand before she could get out and held on with a firm grip. "Why didn't you tell me?"

She twisted her wrist, trying to slip out of his grasp. "It's not something you announce to strangers."

"Okay, I get why you didn't tell me, at first. Same rea-son I keep my inner beast secret. But later, you might have given me a hint."

She quit struggling and stared at where his hand held her wrist. After a long pause she said, "I was afraid."

"That I'd be angry?"

She glanced up. "Well, you are, aren't you?"

"Only because you didn't bother to tell me you could be reading my mind and pushing thoughts into my head." He released her hand.

Selene didn't get out right away. "I know. I should have told you. But I didn't expect things to go as fast or as far as they did. I expected to walk away from you before then."

"Instead, we made love in my office." His jaw tightened, a muscle twitching in the hardness. "Did we because *you* wanted to, or because *I* wanted to?"

She flipped her hair back. "That's why I didn't tell you. *I* wanted to and I was afraid *you* might not want to as much as I did. For all I know, I could have pushed the thought into your mind. I'm sorry. It's just that I wanted you, so very badly." Her head dipped again, her gaze shifting away from his. She turned and scrambled for the door handle, missing several times before she found it and jerked it hard to open.

Gryph was out of the SUV and around the front to her side before she could drop to the ground and run. He reached for her waist and slid her down the front of his body, sure to let her know the effect she was having on him. Slowly, he settled her on her feet, his hands resting on her waist. "Are you pushing thoughts into my head now?"

"I don't know," she whispered.

With his thumb, he brushed a stray hair across her cheek. He was so close he could smell her fragrance, a mix of herbal shampoo and shay-butter body lotion. He wanted to taste her, to feel her skin against his. "What are you thinking?"

She chewed her bottom lip before answering. "That I should go inside, and you should go home."

He bent his head, his lips hovering over hers, so close he could feel her breath. "Is that all?"

Her gaze shifted to his lips. "No," she whispered.

The brush of air across his mouth was almost his undoing. His fingers tightened on her hips. "I have the sudden urge to kiss you."

Her brow furrowed. "You see? That's exactly why you should leave and never come back." She pressed her hands against his chest in a weak attempt to push him away.

He caught her fingers in his, bent and pressed his lips to her fingertips. "No, I want that kiss." His mouth slipped across hers, a feathery brush at first, then he was crushing her in his arms, holding her so close, their bodies melded together.

She opened to him, her mouth parting.

His tongue thrust against her, darting and tangling in a warm wet dance, making his blood turn to molten lava, pushing hard through his veins, flowing south to the hard evidence of his lust.

Selene moaned into his mouth, her fingers digging into his shirt, dragging him impossibly closer, her leg circling behind his, her crotch riding his thigh.

Gryph broke off the kiss long enough to say, "Your key."

Selene fumbled in her jeans pocket, and then handed him the key to her apartment. He scooped her into his arms and carried her down the short flight of stairs to her basement home, dropping her to her feet in order to unlock the door.

As Gryph reached for the doorknob, Selene grabbed his wrist. "Wait." Her tone was soft, but intense.

That concentrated nudge of danger rippled through him. He recognized it as the same feeling he'd had just before the wolf leader transformed. He stared down at Selene.

Her brow furrowed and her eyes narrowed as she nudged the door with her fingertips, jerking them back as if they'd been burned. The door swung open without resistance, the doorjamb splintered, the lock broken. "He was here."

Gryph shoved her behind him. "Stay here."

Her hand touched his back. "He's not inside. I can't sense him."

"Fair enough." He turned to face her. "Humor me, and let me check things out before you go inside."

She nodded, shrinking against the walls of the alcove, hidden in the shadows from the streetlights above.

Gryph allowed his inner beast to rise to the surface, just enough to give him good night vision and increase his auditory and olfactory senses. If Selene was wrong, and the intruder was still there, he needed to be ready to defend himself.

Once inside the apartment, he slipped from one room to the next, checking beneath the bed, in the closets and behind the shower curtain. As small as the apartment was, it didn't take long. When he returned to the living room, Selene stood in the doorway and flicked on the light switch.

A soft glow filled the room, chasing away the shadows, revealing a room that appeared to be untouched, other than the shattered doorjamb.

"Is anything missing or out of place?" Gryph asked.

Selene walked silently around the room, touching picture frames, lifting items from tabletops. She entered her bedroom, her frown deepening. "He was in here the longest." Opening the closet, she ran her hands across the clothes, pausing as her fingers touched a gown she'd designed and sewn herself for the upcoming charity ball.

"Are you sure it was Amanda's killer?"

She nodded, a shiver shaking her from her shoulders all the way down her spine.

Gryph sensed her unease, the fear and anger over having had her personal space violated. His heart aching for her, he hooked her arm and turned her to face him, brushing a strand of hair from her face. "Your sisters were right. You're not staying here tonight."

"It's my home." Her gaze skimmed across the furnishings, the artwork on the wall, the candles lining the tabletops.

"Yeah, but it's just a place. And if he's been here once, he knows where you live, and there's a chance he'll return. You can't stay here."

Her body stiffened. "I won't be frightened away."

"Think through this. Your doorjamb is busted, you don't have a way to lock him out, or anyone else for that matter. Not that locks stopped him this time. If you stay here, you're setting yourself up for attack."

She stared at the door, another shiver rattling across her body, vibrating against his grip on her arm. "I can stay with Deme."

"You'll stay with me."

"No!" She jerked free of his hand. "I'll be fine at Deme's place."

"She might not be there yet."

She glanced around as if in a daze. "I'll call. And if she's not home, I'll go to Brigid's."

Gryph's jaw tightened. "Are you afraid to stay with me?"

"Yes." She gazed into his eyes. "Aren't you afraid I'll manipulate your mind—make you do things you had no intention of doing?"

His lips twitched upward. "Like making love to you? I can see where that would be a hardship. Look, if it bothers you that much, I'll sleep on the couch, you can have my bed and I'll resist any urges, yours or mine, to make love to you."

"What if *I* can't?"

"I guess that's the chance we'll have to take." He spun her around and gave her a gentle shove toward the bedroom. "Get whatever you need for tonight and tomorrow. And hurry, I want to make a stop before we settle in for the night."

"All the more reason for me to stay with my sisters. I don't want to be a burden."

"Says the woman who rescued me. Seems to me, I owe you one for saving my life."

She shrugged. "I'd have done it for anyone hurt."

"You're stalling. I want to get there before everyone is asleep."

"Where are you taking me?"

"My place first, and then to where I grew up."

Selene hurried through her bedroom and bathroom, throwing clothing, panties and toiletries into a small duffel bag, her heart skipping beats every time she thought about where they were going. Gryph wanted to take her where he grew up. Curiosity pushed her to move faster.

"Do you happen to have a hammer and nails?" he called out.

"In the kitchen pantry." Within five minutes, she had everything she needed for a night in Gryph's apartment, including a condom. She dug in her stash for another, and another. Her body flushed with warmth. Not that she intended to use them. But a woman never knew when desire would outweigh caution.

Her lower abdomen clenched and lust washed over her like butter melting over a hot potato, sliding into every crevice.

Finally, she emerged from the bedroom, her cheeks flushed, her insides trembling in anticipation of the night to come. She sensed that Gryph didn't share his life easily, and that he was going to show her where he'd grown up was something big.

He'd found the hammer and nails she kept and stood waiting by her damaged front door.

As she passed him, she could sense his body tightening.

She prayed to the goddess it wasn't her thoughts creating his automatic response.

Gryph checked outside and then caught her arm before he let her exit. "You don't sense him?"

She shook her head. "No."

Once outside, the night air feathered across her skin, raising gooseflesh and cooling her rising passion. Selene wrapped her arms around herself, as the city that had been her home and sanctuary felt less welcoming and safe.

Gryph's warm hand on the small of her back chased away some of her hesitation and she let him guide her to his SUV.

Once settled in the passenger seat, she expected him to take her to the suburbs. Instead he drove her to GL Enterprises' corporate headquarters.

"You grew up in your headquarters building?"

He shook his head, his lips thinning. "Not hardly." But he didn't give her more than that. After parking in his secure access parking place in the underground garage, he led her into the building and into an elevator that required an access card and his thumbprint to open the door. They were whisked downward, into the basement, the air growing cooler the lower they descended.

Again, she wrapped her arms around herself to ward off the chill and Gryph didn't offer to wrap her in his warm embrace.

He stood beside her, but he might as well have been somewhere else. The lower they went the colder, more distant and unapproachable he became.

"Why are we going into the basement of your building? I don't get it."

"You will, soon enough." His tone was flat, emotionless.

Selene waited for the elevator to come to a stop and the doors to open. When they did, she expected to see the inner workings of what it took to keep a huge building operational, from pipes and electrical equipment to plumbing and air ducts.

What greeted her was white marble floors, opulent decor and artwork worthy of a museum, in an open, well-lit foyer to what appeared to be a spacious apartment.

"Do you live here?" Selene asked.

He nodded. "This is my home."

She walked out of the elevator onto the smooth marble, her footsteps echoing against the walls. "And you grew up here?"

"No." He hooked her elbow and led her through the foyer, down a long hallway, past a sitting room, a library and a dining room to the back of the apartment and a room equipped with commercial-grade, exercise and weight-training equipment.

Gryph slid a hand across what appeared to be a poster of a world-famous boxer. The poster shifted to the side, revealing a panel beneath with a keypad and retinal scanner. He leaned forward, lining up his eye with the scanner. A beam of light fanned out over his eye, then a soft click sounded, motors engaged and a door slid open, revealing a spiral staircase leading even deeper into the bowels of Chicago.

When Gryph turned toward her, Selene shivered and stepped backward. He held out his hand. "Come with me."

She shook her head. "The only place I know lower than the basement of a Chicago building is the tunnels beneath the city. Been there, didn't like what I found."

"You want to see where I grew up?"

She nodded, bracing herself for what he was about to say, knowing it before the words left his lips.

"I grew up in the tunnels."

"Blessed be." Selene pressed a hand to her chest.

Gryph's hand fell to his side. "I take it you're familiar with the tunnels?"

She nodded. "My sisters and I had an...altercation with a very dangerous...opponent in the tunnels not long ago. We almost lost Aurai to it."

Raising his hand again, he gave her a half smile. "Must have been in one of the lesser-used tunnels. Let me show you mine."

His gaze begged for her trust.

Selene placed her hand in his.

Gryph grabbed a flashlight from a recharger that was plugged into the wall and switched on the beam, the light barely penetrating the inky blackness below. Then he led the way down the long, winding spiral steps. By the time they reached the bottom, Selene was disoriented and dizzy. Like the tunnels beneath Aurai's college in another part of the city, the rails were rusted and dusty, abandoned equipment lay scattered along the way.

"You lived down here?" Appalled at the desolation, darkness and creepy atmosphere, her heart went out to the young Gryph.

"Not right here, but close." With his fingers wrapped around hers, he stepped over the rails and led her through the maze of tunnels, turning left, then right and back to the left. Just when she thought she couldn't get more confused, soft lights appeared high on the walls, sending a golden glow down over the tracks.

Ahead, beneath one of the bulbs lay a stack of cardboard boxes and a bundle of rags, leaning against a wall.

Gryph stopped in front of the rags. "Good evening, Joe."

The rags shifted and a face, tortured by burns, peered up out of them—one eye seemed almost fused shut by scar tissue.

Selene pressed a hand to her mouth to keep from crying out.

"Gryph, what brings you back to the Lair so soon?" Joe said, his voice coarse and scratchy.

"I came to speak with Balthazar," Gryph said.

The old man nodded, his gaze shifting to Selene, who'd been standing in Gryph's shadow. When the man saw her, he ducked his head and pulled the ragged blanket up around his mutilated face.

Gryph ignored his withdrawal and pulled Selene into the light. "This is Selene."

"A surface dweller." The man spat at the floor by Selene's feet. "What's she doing down here? You know the danger."

"I know," Gryph said quietly. "Let's just say she's special. Not like the rest."

The man's head came halfway up, his brows rising. "Like us?"

Gryph nodded. "Like us."

Joe stared at Selene.

Selene wanted him to feel safe with her and projected that thought toward the man.

Joe's eyes narrowed and his brow furrowed toward the bridge of his nose. Slowly, his head dipped in a nod. "Yup. She's special all right. But watch her. We don't want folks followin' her down here."

"I promise to keep your home a secret, Mr....Joe." Selene held out her hand.

Joe thrust out his right arm. Where his right hand should have been was now a scarred stump. Immediately, he yanked it back and held out his normal, left hand.

Selene took it and squeezed his fingers. "Nice to meet you."

He grunted, but squeezed her fingers.

Gryph urged her to continue down the tunnel toward a light at the end.

A soft tapping sounded behind her, and Selene turned.

Joe used a stick to tap against a metal pipe. He seemed to be tapping a pattern.

Selene wondered if it was Morse code and, if so, who would he be sending it to down here? She shrugged and pushed to stay up with Gryph's longer strides.

As they reached the end of the tunnel, the underground opened into a cavern-like room, where rails crossed, switched and multiplied, disappearing into other dark tunnels. Bulbs cast a soft, warm light from the ceiling down onto the tracks and box-like structures against the walls. Some walls had doors built into them that were painted in bright, cheerful colors.

The box structures were made of plywood, also painted, but with flowers lining the bases like so many gardens with daisies and roses in bloom.

"What is this place?" Selene asked in a hushed whisper. "It's beautiful."

Giggles erupted from a shadowy corner.

Selene spun to face a battered, small railcar, standing against one wall, abandoned decades ago. "Did you hear that?" she whispered.

Gryph chuckled. "It's just the fairies who inhabit the underworld. Pay them no mind." He winked at Selene, let go of her hand and walked lightly toward the railcar. When he got close enough, he dove behind the heavy metal cars and came up with his hands clutching the scruffs of two children's necks. "It's not nice to spy on people," he admonished the two. "And why are you two up so late?"

"Mrs. Martin said we could stay up, since we did so well at our studies this week."

"Well, then come say hello." He turned the children toward Selene.

"What…" Selene clamped down on her tongue to keep from blurting out inane questions of the two catlike creatures who giggled like normal children and struggled half-heartedly to get loose of his grip.

"Let us down, Gryph," the little girl pleaded.

Gryph frowned mightily. "Not unless you promise to greet our guest politely."

"I promise," the girl agreed.

"Being polite is for sissies," the little boy grumbled.

"Nevertheless, you will greet her, and make it nice." Gryph's voice was stern, but gentle. Not until he set the two kids on their feet in front of Selene did she get a good look at the pair.

Both looked almost normal. The girl wore a worn pink dress and had long golden blond hair flowing in wavy locks down her back. The boy's hair was shaggy, hanging in his golden eyes. Each had two arms, two legs and two ears. But that's where normal ended. The children were uniformly covered in short, fine hairs, like the sleek pelt of a cat. Two beautiful, tawny cats.

Chapter 12

What kind of place was this, buried beneath the streets of Chicago? Selene stared at the tawny, fur-covered girl, unable to look away. She was mesmerizingly beautiful as well as strange.

The little girl dropped a quaint curtsy. "I'm Jillian. Nice to meet you."

The boy stuffed his hands into faded blue-jeans pockets and stared at his feet until the girl beside him poked her elbow into his side.

"I'm Jack," he said.

Gryph touched the boy's shoulder. "And?"

The boy scuffed his worn tennis shoe on the uneven surface, then glared up at Selene. "You're a surface dweller. Are you going to rat us out? 'Cause if you are, I'll kill you." He ducked to the side, but not fast enough to escape Gryph.

The big man snatched him up and held the wiggling child until the boy went still. Then Gryph set him on his feet, maintaining one hand on his narrow shoulder. "Want to try that again?"

"Well, she is, isn't she?" Jack said, glaring at Selene mutinously.

"I'm not going to bring anyone down here." Selene held up her hand like a person in court. "I promise. And a witch's promise is sacred."

Jack's frown slowly eased up. "A witch?"

Selene nodded.

"But you don't have warts," Jillian observed. "And you're not ugly."

"Not all witches have warts or are ugly."

"Will you turn Jack into a rabbit?"

Selene laughed. "I'm not that kind of witch."

"What kind of witch are you?"

Selene thought hard, trying to think of a way to explain what she could do with her powers. "The kind that tries to see things that cannot be seen?"

Jillian's little face screwed up and she thought about what Selene said. "Like dreams?"

"Yes, like dreams." Selene smiled at Jack. "So is it okay if I visit today?"

"I guess."

"Jack…" Gryph squeezed the boy's shoulder.

"I'm Jack." He stuck out his hand. "Nice to meet you."

Selene took his hand with a serious expression. "I'm Selene. Pleased to meet you, Jack."

With the pleasantries over, Jack turned to Gryph. "Will you push us on the merry-go-round?"

Jillian looked up at him with soulful golden eyes. "Please, Gryph?"

"I need to speak to Balthazar first."

"Then hurry." Jack turned Gryph toward a doorway and gave him a shove from behind.

"Pushy little fairies, aren't you?" Gryph ruffled Jack's hair and bent to Jillian. "I'll be there in five minutes."

"Yay!" The two children scampered away.

Selene's heart warmed at how gentle the big man was with the small children. Then another thought occurred to her. Were they his?

Gryph leaned close and whispered, "No, they aren't mine."

Her cheeks heating, Selene wondered if Gryph had read her mind.

"We're two different creatures. I shape-shift. Jack and Jillian are like that always." He straightened, his gaze following the little girl and boy. "But if anything ever happened to Mrs. Martin, the woman who adopted them, I'd raise them as my own. They're wonderful children."

Selene smiled. "Yes, they are." Her heart went out to them. She and her sisters had grown up knowing they were different than other children. Physically, they looked the same. These children, with their beautiful fur, would be teased and tormented by *normal* children in the world above. Surface dwellers.

"Are there more?"

"Like Jack and Jillian?" Gryph shrugged. "Not that we've seen so far. But there are other inhabitants of the Lair with equally unusual characteristics."

"Like Joe?"

"His were scars from an industrial accident."

"And the others?"

"Are a mix of scars or accidents of birth...abnormalities by surface dwellers' standards." He gripped her elbow in his strong hand. "Come, I want you to meet Balthazar."

"Someone looking for me?" A deep, rich voice with a faint British accent called out, the sound filling the still air of the cavernous space.

Selene spun to face an older man with shaggy white hair, wearing a worn, wool jacket with patches on the elbows. Wire-frame glasses perched on the end of his nose as his gaze skimmed over Selene.

Gryph's lips lifted in a smile. "Father." He engulfed the man, who was stooped with age, in a bear hug.

Father? Selene stared at the older man, trying to see in him traces of Gryph and finding no similarities whatsoever.

Balthazar patted Gryph's back. "Back so soon?"

Gryph's smile faded. "There's been more trouble."

"So much trouble you would forget to introduce me to your beautiful lady-friend?" Balthazar held out his hands to Selene.

Selene immediately trusted the man, placing her hands in his. He had an aura of serenity that made her comfortable with him from the moment her hands touched his. "I'm Selene Chattox. It's nice to meet you."

The gray-haired man waved toward a doorway that was painted a sleek antique blue. "Come inside."

With his hand on Selene's arm, Gryph led her through the door and into what once must have been a kind of warehouse, but was now an open, high-ceilinged room with soft rugs covering a concrete floor and walls painted in shades of cream and the warm gold of wheat. Prints of famous paintings from the ages decorated the walls and antique furniture graced the living areas. There were lamps glowing on tables and track lighting hung from the ceiling. On several walls, murals had been painted of French doors and windows, overlooking lush gardens filled with sunshine, roses and gerbera daisies. The paintings were beautiful and looked almost real, as if you could step through the doors into a garden.

Selene was struck by the beauty and the light and the airiness of this underground abode.

"Do you like my home?" Balthazar asked.

"It's stunning."

"I fill it with all the things I love. I have a library with all the classics in multiple languages and many contemporary works."

"I'd love to see it."

"Gryph can show you, while I prepare a pot of tea."

Gryph shook his head. "Father, we don't have time."

"Nonsense. You both look flustered. A bit of tea will

calm you so that you can sleep. Show your young lady the library. I'll bring the tea there."

Selene wanted to contradict the older gentleman and tell him that she was not Gryph's lady. But she bit down on her lip and kept her words and thoughts to herself.

Balthazar entered an open kitchen area as Gryph led Selene toward another doorway.

As they stepped into the room, Selene was overwhelmed by the rich reds and golds of the furnishings, and the mahogany bookshelves that stretched to a twelve-foot ceiling and were lined with leather-bound, hardback and paperback novels. A thick Persian carpet filled most of the floor space and a large mahogany desk dominated the room, with a leather sofa placed in front of it.

"This room is amazing," Selene whispered.

"Balthazar encouraged us to read from the moment we could started talking."

"We?" Selene wanted to know more about this enigmatic man.

"My brother and I."

"You have a brother?"

He glanced down at her. "I do."

Selene shook her head. "A father, a brother… Are there any more people in your family I should know about?"

His lips tightened. "That's all of us. And the others who live in the Lair are like my extended family. We look to each other for support."

"Why is it people—surface dwellers—haven't discovered the Lair? I would think the people who've come to explore the underground tunnels would have come across all of you by now."

"We've sealed off most entrances, hidden those that we use and manage to discourage entry by those curious enough to dig beneath Chicago's glitzy surface."

"And Balthazar? I'm sorry, but you two don't look anything alike? Is he like you? A shifter?"

"Balthazar is not my biological father. I've never seen or met either of my parents. My mother left me with Balthazar when I was an infant. She couldn't handle raising me, knowing I was a monster. Balthazar accepted me and raised me. I owe my existence to him."

Selene's heart squeezed. "You and your brother were abandoned?" A woman had to be either heartless or desperate to leave her child.

"My brother came to the Lair with his mother when he was not quite two years old. I was eight at the time. From what I recall, they were homeless, his mother had been an addict, abused and stalked by her former boyfriend and in need of a place to hide out and get clean. Other than the trauma of an unhealthy situation, they were normal. When Lucas's mother couldn't shake the addiction, she disappeared back to the surface, leaving Lucas behind. Balthazar opened our home to him."

"Does Balthazar do that often?"

"Do what?"

"Take in strays?"

Gryph chuckled. "It's who he is."

"How many people live in the Lair?"

"Last count, around forty."

"Forty?" Selene stepped back. "That many?"

"Those who can, work on the surface."

"If they're that…different, how do they get jobs?"

"Balthazar has connections and, as you know, I have businesses."

"You employ them?"

"I try to accommodate as many as possible. It's not always a fit."

Selene let her brows inch upward. "You can't have cat people working for GL Enterprises?"

His mouth tightened. "I'd hire them all, but many don't want to work during daylight hours, where they will be seen, and I don't have as many night-shift opportunities."

"What do you think of my library?" Balthazar entered carrying a silver tray with a silver teapot and cups. "You're lucky—Mrs. Martin brought by scones this morning." He set the tray on the edge of the desk. "Gryphon will you be so good as to fetch the tray of scones from the kitchen?"

Gryph frowned. "Father, we have to discuss an urgent matter."

"Certainly." His father nodded. "After you retrieve the scones."

Gryph's chest rose and fell on a silent sigh and he left the room.

Selene stood in the middle of the Persian carpet, not sure what to say. The entire setting, the underworld society, this home beneath the city—everything was so unusual she struggled to take it all in.

Balthazar poured a cup of tea and turned to hand it to her. "Gryphon has always been a blessing to me and the other inhabitants of the Lair."

She accepted the cup and sipped carefully before asking, "How so?"

"He was the one who got permanent electricity wired into the homes within the Lair. I managed to get internet here, but he insisted on high-speed access for all those who desired it, wanting our children to take online coursework to enhance their homeschooling, and so that they could learn about the world above from the relative safety of their homes here."

"I don't completely understand. They are people like the rest of the world. They should be allowed to live in peace on the surface." But she knew even as she spoke the words what life on the surface would be like. She'd been bullied as a child when she'd been in public schools.

"You know their reasons. Fear of rejection. Past experiences." Balthazar's shoulders rose and fell. "Has Gryphon told you about how his mother abandoned him?"

Selene nodded.

"It was more than that. She was a young college coed when she was raped by a monster."

"That's terrible. Did they ever catch the man?"

"Maybe you don't understand that when I say she was raped by a monster, it was a true monster, not just a man with evil in his soul."

"Oh." Selene's eyes widened. "Oh."

Balthazar nodded. "You see, Gryphon's mother was human. Her rapist was not. We're not certain what it was, but once Gryphon started shifting, even as early as two months old, she knew she couldn't provide for him and keep him safe from people who would exploit him and turn him into a science experiment.

"Though she loved her baby, she didn't have the strength or the resources to support him in a private environment, where he would be protected from the ridicule, poking and prodding of people trying to understand what exactly he was.

"I found her outside a church, near one of our hidden entrances. She was bent over a basket, crying softly, tucking blankets around her baby."

"Gryph." Selene's eyes welled with tears, her heart filled with the ache of despair Gryph's mother must have felt to come to the conclusion that only by abandoning her baby could he get the care that he needed.

"She told me her story and how she couldn't keep him in a world that wouldn't understand. She begged me to take good care of him and that she loved him, but couldn't be a part-time parent. When she gave up custody, she didn't want him to come looking for her. I never told him who she was."

"And you took him in."

Balthazar nodded. "He was a fighter then and now. As a toddler, he nearly ripped off my arm."

"Sweet goddess," Selene exclaimed.

"Don't worry. He's learned to control his beast. Now he only calls on the animal inside when danger is present. He would rip anyone apart who tried to hurt someone he loves." Balthazar glanced down at Selene, his gaze softening.

Selene's face heated. "Gryph and I just met," she muttered. She refused to consider their urgent lovemaking as anything more than lust.

"Really, Father, don't fill Selene with tales of monsters and demons," Gryph said as he returned.

"Are there demons in the Lair?" Selene asked.

Gryph chuckled. "No, but there are monsters."

"Only in the eyes of people who won't understand."

"Don't scare her more. I need her to go with me to D'na Ileana."

"The gypsy." Balthazar set his teacup on the desk. "You remember the dangers?"

With dip of his head, Gryph stared hard at his adoptive father. "The animal who attacked the woman outside the theater was a wolf shifter. When we went to question the Devil's Disciples—"

Balthazar reached out and gripped Gryph's arm. "You went into Disciple territory?"

Gryph nodded and the hint of a smile curved his lips. "And lived to tell." Beneath his breath, he added, "Barely."

Balthazar turned and paced away, coming back to stand in front of Gryph. "When you confront a pack, you take your life into your own hands." Balthazar glanced at Selene. "And you? Were you with him?"

"Yes, sir," Selene responded, feeling like a recalcitrant

child. "With the help of my sisters, we managed to get away."

"Very fortunate, indeed." He crossed his arms over his chest. "And why must you visit the gypsy?"

"We need to find the rogue werewolf threatening the city." Gryph stepped forward. "Unless you know where we can find him, D'na Ileana may be our only hope."

Balthazar shook his head. "I've only heard rumors of the wolf. Remember, the gypsy sees the future," Gryph's adoptive father said, "not necessarily individuals."

Gryph's eyes narrowed, his jaw tightening. "If she can see where he'll strike next, we can be there."

Selena smiled, now that she understood why Gryph had brought her with him. "We could stop him before he kills again." They might get ahead of the killer and catch him before he harms another. "Where is this gypsy?"

"Deep in the darkest tunnel," Balthazar said.

Like spider legs crawling across her arm, Selena's skin tingled. "I take it where she lives isn't as nice as this place?"

"No," Both Gryph and Balthazar said at once.

"And there are other creatures who live in the maze of tunnels we don't want to anger along the way," Gryph added.

Her knees suddenly shaking, Selena asked, "Would one happen to be a Chimera?"

Balthazar shook his head. "There was legend of such, but none of the inhabitants of the Lair have come across one."

Selene bit down on her tongue. She and her sisters had fought a mighty battle against a Chimera in the tunnels beneath Colyer-Fenton College in another part of the city.

Selene needed to know what the stakes were, how difficult it would be to get to D'na Ileana. "What do we have to aware of?"

Balthazar counted off on his fingers. "Old rusty machinery, possible sinkholes, crumbling bracing and a nasty old troll who threatens to eat you if you pass through his tunnel."

"Don't worry." Gryph's lips twitched. "He has no teeth."

"Let me guess," Selene said. "Although he has no teeth, he's strong enough to grind my bones to mush?"

Gryph shrugged. "He's big, but I won't let him hurt you. He's slow and not very bright."

"Anything else?" Selene asked, though she wasn't sure she wanted the answer.

"We might run into Kobaloi."

"And that is…?"

"Spritely creatures who like to deceive people and lead them into danger." Gryph pushed a hand through his tawny mane. "As a child, I followed one who'd disguised itself as a firefly. I almost fell into a sinkhole. If I hadn't shifted at the last minute, I might still be at the bottom of that hole. I believe the drop fell all the way to the reservoir deep beneath the city."

A huge tremor shook Selene and she was afraid to ask, but had to know… "Is D'na Ileana somewhere near this Kobaloi and that sinkhole?"

"Unfortunately, yes." Gryph drew in a long breath. "I shouldn't have brought you. But I thought—"

"I might be able to see what the gypsy sees?" Selene pushed aside her fear of the dark and dangerous tunnels that had nearly been the death of her and her sisters. "If this helps us find the one responsible for that woman's death, we should get going. The sooner, the better."

"You'll need a flashlight." Balthazar reached for one in a recharging unit plugged into the wall. "You think she's up for the journey?" he asked Gryph as he handed the light to Selene.

Gryph's lips curled upward at the corners. "Absolutely."

Selene's heart swelled at the confidence Gryph had in her. After the episode at the bar, she'd been more shaken than she cared to admit.

She'd always considered herself the weak link among her sisters. Not anymore. She'd just begun to realize the extent of her powers.

And what could be worse than battling an evil Chimera, or a pool hall full of angry werewolves?

Chapter 13

Gryph stopped to play with Jack and Jillian for a brief moment, then promised he'd be back when he had more time.

"Oh, don't go, Gryph. You hardly visit us anymore," Jillian cried.

Being a busy businessman meant staying at the office more than he preferred and the relationships he cared about had suffered. The ones with the man who'd raised him as a son, his brother, Lucas, and the people of the Lair had all taken a hit lately.

"I promise. I'll be back to play soon." Gryph grabbed Selene's hand and headed back the way they'd come.

Jack ran ahead of them. "Can I go where you're going? Are you going to the surface? When can I go? Are the people up there as mean as everyone says? Why can't we live in the light?"

"Not everyone is mean who lives on the surface." Gryph rubbed the boy's head. "Selene is from the surface and she's not mean."

"Only when I haven't had my morning coffee." She smiled down at the boy.

Jillian raced up behind them. "Are you taking Jack? May I come, too?"

Gryph stopped, blocking the way ahead. "You two have

to stay here. It's not safe where we're going. Besides it's way past your bedtime."

Jack puffed out his chest. "I'm strong and brave. I've gone all the way to the sinkhole on my own. And I can stay up very late and never get tired."

Gryph gave the boy a stern look. "You should never go that far without an adult. You know the tunnels can be tricky. You could get lost."

"But I didn't and I looked down into the sinkhole, and I could see all the way to China."

"Could not," Jillian said. "It was just a dark hole."

Gryph gripped her arms, his pulse pounding at the thought of these small children teetering on the edge of the sinkhole's abyss. "You went with him?"

Contrite, Jillian nodded, her eyes round. "Yes, sir."

Squatting in front of the two children, Gryph stared hard at them. "Promise me you will not go back to the sinkhole without an adult."

"Ah, Gryph." Jack rolled his eyes. "It was easy."

"And you probably didn't run in to any Kobaloi."

Jillian shook her head. "No, we didn't. Jack said he saw a light, but I didn't."

"Promise." Gryph stared from Jack to Jillian and back to Jack, the older of the two kids.

Jack ducked his chin and scuffed his sneaker on the ground in front of him. "I promise."

"I promise, Gryph. I didn't want to go anyway." Jillian flung her arms around Gryph's neck. "I'll be good."

"Thank you." Gryph stood, with Jillian on his arm. He hugged her tight, then set her on her feet and touched Jack's shoulder. "You have to protect your little sister. She's younger and smaller and needs a big brother to make sure she doesn't get into trouble."

"I didn't want her taggin' along, but she always does." The boy glared at his sister.

Jillian crossed her arms. "I don't, either."

"Enough. You two stay in the Lair. Selene and I have an errand to run and can't be worried about two hooligans following us through the tunnels." He turned them around, gave them a pat and sent them on their way. "Go back home to bed."

"Are they always so precocious?" Selene smiled after the children.

The twinkle in her deep brown eyes made Gryph look again. "You're beautiful when you smile."

"Thanks." Her lids closed over her eyes, hiding the shine. "And you're good with children." She straightened and looked him in the eye. "We should be going. The wolf could be planning another attack as we speak."

"Right." Gryph took her empty hand, liking the feel of it in his. Smaller, more delicate, yet strong. She'd surprised him in the pool hall. He'd never known someone who could stop an attack by thinking it.

One thing he'd learned in the Lair was that there were all kinds of people and creatures living on or beneath the surface. He shouldn't have been surprised.

Wanting to get their meeting with D'na Ileana over with, he hurried through the tunnel, wishing he could shift to his lion form. He was much more sure-footed on all four feet.

"You should make the change," Selene suggested, her warm voice echoing softly off the cool brick walls.

He slowed and shot a glance her way. "Were you reading my mind?"

She shook her head. "No, but if I had the ability to shift, I would. You'd be able to see better in the dark and four feet are steadier than two."

He hesitated, knowing he would be in a better position to protect her as a lion, but not willing to shift when he had to lose his clothes in order to do it unrestrained. Finally, he nodded. "Okay, but only halfway. Enough to see better in the dark and sniff out trouble ahead of time." He stopped in the middle of the rail track they'd been walking along, slipped out of his leather jacket and handed it to her, his hands tugging the T-shirt from the waistband of his jeans.

Her gaze followed as he lifted the shirt up over his head.

Gryph's pulse quickened and jumped into overdrive when her tongue came out to moisten pretty pink lips. "Stop that."

She glanced up, her gaze meeting his. "Stop what?"

He reached out and ran his thumb over her bottom lip. "That."

She swayed, her hand reaching toward his naked chest. "Do you want me to take that?"

He wanted her to take him, all right. Instead, he handed her the jacket and shirt, and then grasped her hands in his. "When we get close to D'na Ileana's we can't lose focus."

Her knuckles rested on his naked chest. "Unfortunately, I'm completely focused." Her voice was low and gravelly and so damned sexy.

Gryph dragged her closer, his hands circling to the small of her back and downward to cup the curve of her bottom. "What is it about you that makes me forget everything?"

"I could say the same." Her mouth was so close, her breath warm against his chin.

Before he could think through his actions, question his sanity, he lowered his head and claimed her lips. At first tender, the animal inside surged and demanded more. The gentle kiss hardened, changing with the flash of molten blood coursing through his veins. He crushed her to him, lifting her legs to wrap around his middle.

Selene dropped the items in her arms, the flashlight clattering against the metal tracks, the beam flickering, then shining down the rail into the pitch-black. She intertwined her arms around the back of his head and deepened her connection, her tongue lashing out, thrusting through his lips and teeth to tangle with his.

He ground the ridge of his erection against the apex of her thighs, not satisfied to mimic the motions of making love, wanting all of her now, against the cool brick walls of the tunnel.

Out of the corner of his vision, Gryph saw the glimmer of a pinprick of light. At first he ignored it, unable to drag his lips from the sorceress consuming him. When it twinkled again, then again, he slowly came back to his senses and broke the mind-numbing kiss, resting his forehead against hers. "Now is not the time, nor the place."

As her legs slid down his sides, he eased her to the ground. She was breathing hard, her hands resting against his chest. "You're right. We need to move."

"And if I'm not mistaken, one of the Kobaloi have found us."

Selene jerked her head to the right, staring into the darkness. "I thought I felt something else here with us."

"Watch," he whispered, gathering her into the curve of his arm.

A moment of silence passed and the flash of light recurred—it was like a firefly, only bigger.

"Did you—"

She gasped and pointed. "There!"

He nodded. "Don't try to follow it. They're known to be mesmerizing."

"But it's so pretty."

"When you live in the darkness, you tend to appreciate anything that gives light. Except the Kobaloi. Now that they know we're here, they won't leave us alone." He gathered the clothing and flashlight she'd dropped and handed them to her. Then he concentrated all his control on transforming just enough to allow him the nocturnal advantages of the lion. Fine hairs sprouted from his skin and his muscles bulged, stretching, changing. He willed his metamorphosis to slow and stop before he dropped to all fours.

His night vision sharpened and he could smell the sticky sweet scent of the Kobaloi ahead in the tunnel. Unfortunately, he and Selene had to pass the Kobaloi and the sinkhole before they reached Ileana's cave, carved out of the oldest tunnel in the maze beneath Chicago.

"Hold my hand and whatever happens, do not let go," he said, his voice coarse, almost the growling rumble of a lion. He held out his hairy hand, not quite human, nor lion.

She stared at it for a brief moment.

Gryph didn't realize he held his breath until she placed her hand in his. The air rushed from his lungs and he curled his thick fingers around her thin, hairless ones. That she would place her trust in a beast made him want to prove to her that he could protect her. That he wasn't just an animal.

He continued on, leading her away from the relative safety of the Lair and into the darkness and danger of the outer tunnels inhabited by all manners of creatures less human, and less benevolent, than himself.

As he neared a turn, he slowed, trying to remember exactly where the sinkhole was. He sensed it was close and could smell the water of the reservoir beneath the city. Gryph rounded the corner.

The single Kobaloi was joined by another, and another, until there were three small blinking lights farther along the tunnel, luring them with their cheerful promise of illumination in the darkness.

Selene stepped up beside Gryph. "Oh, look, now there are three." She started forward, eagerly continuing the journey.

Gryph's hand tightened on hers, jerking her back.

Her foot slipped on loose gravel and she fell, nearly jerking him off his feet. He braced himself, her hand slipping through the fur on his.

"Help!" she cried, shining the flashlight beam into the black abyss of the sinkhole below her dangling feet.

Willing his fur to recede, he laid back on the track, pulling her body up and over his. For a long moment, she lay on top of him, breathing hard. She released the flashlight and it clattered against metal, settling on the ground beside him. Her fingers curled into the hairs on his chest as if she was afraid to let go, lest she slip back into the hole.

"Are you all right?" he growled.

"I think so," she said, her breath warm on his body. Selene made no move to roll off him, still clinging to him like a lifeline.

He closed his eyes briefly, liking the feel of her body on his, her soft curves pressed into the hardness of his muscles, her legs tangled with his. If only the train rail wasn't digging into his back and the Kobaloi weren't waiting to tempt them into more danger.

"I should have remembered exactly where the hole was."

She laughed shakily. "And you were right about the Kobaloi. They're like the dragonflies my sister keeps. Always looking for trouble." Finally, she leaned up, her hands pressing against him, and glanced over her shoulder at the hole that had almost taken her. A shiver rippled across her body. "I shouldn't have been so careless. Are there any more sinkholes we should be worried about?"

"I haven't been deep in the tunnels for years."

When she moved to get up, his hands reached out to grasp her face, dragging her down to his, which was distorted into that of half lion, half man. "I want to kiss you."

"Then why don't you?"

"I'm not myself."

"I think you are." She cupped his face and leaned down, pressing her lips against his mouth. "Your fur tickles me," she whispered before her tongue slid between his lips and slipped along the length of his. When her head came up, she smiled. "And your tongue is raspier."

"I'm sorry."

"Don't be. I think it's very sexy and could be a definite asset in other areas." She winked and rolled carefully to the side.

If he was not mistaken, the color in her cheeks had darkened to a deep rosy hue.

She grabbed the flashlight and stood well away from the hole, refusing to lock gazes with him.

Gryph climbed to his feet.

"How do we get around it?" Her beam circled the edges of the hole, then shone down into the center, barely penetrating the blackness. Another shiver shook her body.

Gryph slipped an arm around her waist. "We should go back."

"No." She stood straighter. "If the gypsy can help us, we need to get to her."

"She might not be willing."

"Then we'll convince her." Selene pointed the light toward the far left of the sinkhole. "I believe there's a ledge along the side."

"If my memory serves me right, it's wide enough for a person to traverse and there are pipes above to hold on to for balance." He held out his hand. "Stay close. I'm not sure how sturdy the sides will be. They could have sloughed off since my last visit."

"Reassuring." Selene gaze moved ahead. "Let's do this." She aimed the light at the nearest edge of the hole.

Gryph inched his way around to the left, gripped a pipe secured to the ceiling above and sidestepped with his back to the wall.

Selene followed his lead, juggling her flashlight and

reaching for the pipe overhead. She was too short to grab it and held even tighter to Gryph's fingers.

The Kobaloi danced in the air on the other side of the sinkhole as if laughing. If Gryph wasn't mistaken, they moved closer each time he glanced up.

"Those things don't bite, do they?" Selene's whisper was like a shout in the complete silence of the tunnel.

"No. They're like a pesky mosquito. They irritate." When they were only halfway around the hole, one daring Kobaloi darted across and buzzed Gryph's face, the flutter of its wings causing him to blink. His foot slipped and he clung to the pipe above him.

"Gryph!" Selene pulled hard on his hand to keep him from dropping into the gaping maw.

He regained his balance and chuckled. "Like I said, irritating."

The Kobaloi flickered past Selene's nose. "No kidding."

Gryph continued on, swatting at the Kobaloi, careful not to lose his balance again. If he fell, he'd take Selene with him. And if she didn't fall to her death, she could be lost in the tunnel and have to face the troll on her own.

No, he didn't have time or the desire to disappear into a black abyss. It could be only a short drop, or all the way into the reservoir. As dark as the hole was, even his excellent nocturnal vision couldn't see down into it very far.

Finally, he stepped onto solid ground past the hole and into the tunnel on the other side. He helped Selene the last couple steps and continued on.

"How much farther?"

"Not too far. Try to keep the noise down. The troll will be nearby. He guards the entrance to her cave."

"Oh, goody." Selene swatted at the three Kobaloi hovering around her face. Now that she had time to examine them, she realized they had tiny little humanoid bodies with wicked gargoyle faces. And they didn't want to let up their attack on them. "I think these little buggers must work for the gypsy, as well."

"Could be. I've only run across them in this tunnel."

"Wait just a moment. Let me try something." She stopped in the middle of the old rail tracks and closed her eyes.

After a moment or two, the three Kobaloi stopped their frenzied fluttering and backed away.

Gryph shook his head. Amazed. "What did you do?"

"I let them know we weren't there to harm the gypsy and that we only wanted information."

"That's it?"

She shrugged. "I'm glad they were receptive. Not all creatures are."

"I just hope that if we run across the troll, he's as easily persuaded."

"You and me both." Selene shined the light down the tunnel, the beam only reaching five feet ahead of them. "I like the lighting you had installed in the Lair."

"The people of the Lair should live in light."

"Then why don't they move to the surface?"

"Many of them would like nothing better. But they also want to live their lives free of the kind of torment some have been subjected to on the surface."

"Why can't people accept others for who they are inside instead of what they look like?"

"Unfortunately, it's part of nature. Birds are attracted to the most beautiful of their species. Some animals shun those of their kind that aren't strong or appealing. It's survival of the prettiest, strongest, most genetically sound."

A resonant thumping sound broke into their whispered words. Gryph raised his hand and stepped in front of Selene, urging her back against the tunnel wall. "Shh."

"What?" Selene asked.

"I heard something," he said softly, pressing a finger to his lips. "Turn out the light."

She hesitated. "Will you be able to see?"

"Yes."

She hit the off switch and the light blinked out. Only the Kobaloi provided any kind of illumination, but it was barely enough to surround them and not sufficient to see anything coming.

Selene rested a hand on Gryph's arm. "I can sense it."

"The troll?" he asked.

"I'm not sure, but it's confused and angry and headed this way."

The thumping grew louder and the ground beneath them shook.

"When it gets closer, be ready to flash the light in his eyes. It will blind him temporarily and give us the chance to run past him. Trolls are generally slow," Gryph said, his voice barely a whisper. "Once you blind him, keep the beam focused on his face."

"Can he see in the dark?"

"As well as I can." Gryph touched her arm. "There he is."

"I don't see him."

Thumping became loud pounding against the ground, vibrating up through Gryph's feet into his body.

"Now."

Selene fumbled with the flashlight beside him and the beam flashed into the tunnel ahead, filling it with light and bouncing off the giant form of the troll.

"Run." He grabbed her hand and raced straight for the troll, praying they could get around him before the creature's eyes adjusted to the bright light.

Selene's heart beat frantically against her ribs as she ran, tripping and stumbling over the rails and discarded debris in the tunnel. The closer she came to the troll, the stronger her panic mingled with the fear and anger of the troll.

His huge bulky body stooped beneath the ceiling, filling a majority of the narrow tunnel. He shouted, swinging his beefy arms right and left.

Gryph waited for the troll to swing away from them, then practically jerked her arm out of the socket dragging her past the creature.

Once past, Selene's light no longer blinded the troll. He spun, knocking his shoulders against the tunnel walls, roared and thundered after them.

Selene ran, her feet flying over equipment left behind. A few steps ahead, Gryph stopped. "Keep going."

"What are you going to do?" She slowed as she passed him. "You can't fight him. He's huge."

"I'm not going to." As soon as Selene ran past him, Gryph pushed a big rotting crate into the middle of the tracks, turned and continued to run. "Go!"

Selene turned and ran, tripped over a rail and fell, hitting her forehead on the hard metal track. Pain shot through her temples. The flashlight's beam dimmed where it lay on the ground just out of her reach.

"Selene!" Gryph dropped down beside her at the same time the troll crashed through the wooden crate and reduced it to splintered kindling.

Selene tried to rise, to get to her feet and run, but her head spun every time she lifted it.

Gryph leaped to his feet, changed the rest of the way into his most ferocious form and leaped at the troll.

The troll swung a club-sized arm, backhanding Gryph, sending him flying through the air. He slammed into the brick wall of the tunnel's interior and slid to the ground. Shaking himself off, he scrambled to his feet as the troll threw a ham-hock-sized fist at him.

Gryph dodged the blow and sprang to the troll's side and onto his back, sinking his teeth into the giant's neck.

With an eardrum-shattering roar, the troll reached over his head, snagged Gryph by his mane and threw him down the tunnel.

Selene shook her head and pushed to her hands and knees, forcing back the gray cloud. She reached for the only weapon she could find, the flashlight. Heavy at one end, she balanced the lighter end in her hand.

When the troll started toward Gryph, Selene went after him, tiptoeing so as not to alert him to her presence.

Ahead of the troll, Gryph staggered to his feet. He spotted Selene as she raised the flashlight over her head.

"No!" he yelled.

The troll ground to a stop and braced to turn around and look behind him. Only he didn't get that far.

Selene wielded the flashlight like a baseball bat, aiming for the back of the troll's thick skull. She nailed the swing, connecting with his head.

Her arms jolted and vibrated with the force of her swing. The glass over the bulb cracked, but the metal remained intact. And a good thing, because the blow didn't fell the troll. However, it made him angrier.

He spun on clumsy feet, swatting at the back of his neck as if the flashlight had impacted him as nothing more than an irritating bee sting. The troll spotted her, his heavy brows dropping low over his eyes. Then he snarled and snorted through his nose like a bull in a bullfighting ring.

"Uh-oh." Selene stared down at the flashlight in her hands, debating, for a split second, whether it would help to hit him again. It wasn't going to be the weapon she'd hoped for. Perhaps it was time to run. She turned and sprinted back the way she'd come.

A lion's roar echoed through the tunnels.

Selene shot a glance over her shoulder. The troll had switched direction and was headed back toward Gryph.

"Oh, no you don't." Selene stared at the troll's back, concentrating all her effort, all her inner strength, and even called on the power of her sisters to help her stop the troll before he ground Gryph into mush.

The troll's steps faltered, but he didn't stop and just plowed forward, like a runaway train on a downhill slope, picking up speed as he lumbered on.

"Stop!" A woman's voice sounded in Selene's head. She glanced around, but the answering echo never reverberated against the tunnel walls.

The troll skidded to a stop and stared past Gryph to a shadowy figure in a flowing skirt, standing in the middle of the track.

Selene moved closer, despite the danger of being within range of the troll's mighty hands. She sensed the troll was being controlled by this creature in the darkness. As she stepped past the giant, he grunted and tightened his fists. But he stood so still it was as if he was cemented to the floor.

Who are you? Selene wondered.

I am who you seek.

Gryph, his body slipping back into human form, stood and glanced over his shoulder. "D'na Ileana." He turned fully and bowed.

"What brings you to disturb my sentries and privacy?"

The Kobaloi flitted around her head and landed in the thick, flowing hair that piled high on her head and tumbled down her back in long loose jet-black curls.

"We need to see the future," Gryph said.

"I do not tell fortunes anymore. Go away." Her words were for Gryph, but her gaze remained on Selene.

Selene returned her gaze with a steadfast one of her own. *We need your help. Lives are at stake.*

"Please," Selene begged aloud. "We need to know where a wolf will try to kill again. We have to catch him before he takes another innocent life."

The gypsy's gaze ran the length of Selene and her lip curled in a snarl. "Why should I care?"

"Your gifts come with responsibility to help others."

"And you share your gifts?"

Selene nodded. "I do."

"More fool you."

"D'na Ileana, will you help us?" Gryph asked.

Ileana's lips curled upward, her gaze zeroing in on Gryph.

Selene blinked, and in that short moment, Ileana had closed the four yards distance between herself and Gryph. How she'd moved so fast, Selene didn't know. She suspected Ileana was more than a simple fortune-teller.

The gypsy ran a long fingernail down Gryph's jawline. "I will help you, my dear Gryphon." She drew a line down his bare chest to the waistband of his tattered trousers, which had been ripped by his instant shift into his lion form and back again. "What will you give me in return?"

"What do you want?" he asked.

Her gaze shot to Selene and back to him. "A night alone with you." Her ruby lips trailed along the curve of his muscled shoulder.

Selene's hackles rose and she stiffened, ready to rip the gypsy apart.

The other woman cast a sly glance her way. "You wouldn't mind, would you?"

Selene wanted to scream and scratch her eyes out. But she had no hold on Gryph. He wasn't hers to claim. If he wanted to give the gypsy a night in the sack, he could. Never mind they'd made love less than twenty-four hours ago.

"No." Gryph caught the gypsy's hand and held it in his fur-covered one. "I'm not here to trade sexual favors."

The gypsy tsked. "Such a shame. It's been a long time since I've had a worthy bed partner."

"Find someone else."

"Very well. I will help you, if it is in my power to do so." She glanced at Selene. "But why did you not ask the witch to help you?"

Gryph didn't glance Selene's way, his jaw tight, the muscle beneath the skin twitching with his effort to control his anger. "She cannot see into the future. You can."

"Then why bring her along? She is of no use to you." Ileana leaned into his body. "Which brings us back to me and you. I'll make your body sing."

"Enough. Time is running out. We have to find the wolf responsible for a woman's death before he strikes again."

"I cannot see the present. Only the near future."

"Then tell me where he'll strike again in the near future so that I might catch him before he succeeds in killing another innocent."

"Follow me." Ileana turned, the length of her colorful skirt swirling around her ankles.

Gryph followed D'na Ileana and Selene brought up the rear, not liking that they would be at the gypsy's mercy once inside her home.

Selene shot a glance at the troll. The giant creature glared down at her, his gaze following her every move as she entered the door leading into the dark depths of the cave.

Selene hoped they'd be able to leave unharmed. If they happened to anger the gypsy, would she sic the troll on them as they left?

Chapter 14

Gryph had been inside D'na Ileana's cave only once before. He'd been in his early twenties when he'd come with Balthazar, seeking information about the whereabouts of Jack and Jillian's mother, who'd disappeared a day earlier, leaving her small children with Mrs. Martin.

Ileana had seen Rebecca Miller huddled on a street in the cold, her body wrapped in newspapers and cardboard. Her descriptions hadn't been detailed enough to find the woman in time to save her from hypothermia or the ups and downs of her mental condition. Rebecca had been bipolar and completely incapable of dealing with small unusual children like Jack and Jillian.

By stepping out of the Lair into the blasting cold of a Chicago winter, she'd resigned herself to death.

Between Mrs. Martin and Balthazar, the children had grown up pretty normal for who and what they were. Better off in the Lair than on the surface, where, at the least, children their own age would have harangued them for being so very different. Worse, scientists would have poked, prodded and examined them to discover how this cross-species mutation could have occurred.

They were getting the best education possible under Balthazar's tutelage and when they were old enough, they could study at any college that would provide courses via the internet.

Ileana had been distraught when her future prediction hadn't led to finding Rebecca until too late. She'd withdrawn deeper into her cave and refused to join the people of the Lair for company or even celebrations.

Too caught up in building an empire and enough wealth to care for his extended family in the Lair, Gryph hadn't been back to visit the gypsy. Balthazar made an annual trek into the tunnels to check on her and make sure she was okay and wanted for nothing. She'd chosen to reject any of Gryph's improvements, preferring to live in the near dark, using more primitive means to chase back the shadows.

As they stepped into Ileana's cave, Selene switched off the flashlight. Candles burned on every flat surface, casting soft, warm circles of flickering light, calming in their quiet intensity. By the items scattered around the interior of the gypsy's home, it was clear she had a way of accessing the surface to acquire things. How she acquired them was her business.

Ileana pointed to a round wrought-iron bistro-style table with a dark red tablecloth draped over it. "Sit," she ordered.

Selene perched on one of the two mismatched chairs and Gryph sat across from her in the other.

Ileana dragged a cushioned straight-back wooden chair up between them. "Tell me about the wolf," she said.

Gryph explained what had happened on the streets of Chicago and in the hospital.

All the while Ileana remained silent, studying Gryph, then Selene.

"We need to find the wolf before he hurts another," Gryph said, ending his tale.

Ileana's eyes closed and her head tipped back slightly as if she basked in a warm ray of light.

Gryph glanced across at Selene. Her gaze was on him. She blinked and refocused on Ileana.

The gypsy swayed gently from side to side, a low hum

rising up her throat. The more she swayed the faster she moved, until she was rocking back and forth, the humming turning to a distressed keening.

Gryph's pulse quickened.

Selene's brows drew together, her eyes narrowing. "I can't see what she's seeing," she said.

She reached out to touch the gypsy's arm.

Ileana screamed, a bright flash blinded Gryph's mind and the next thing he knew both women toppled out of their chairs, crashing to the floor.

Pain shot through the back of Selene's head where she hit the hard stone of the cave's floor. She lay for a moment, her head spinning with images, trying to make sense of them all.

"Damn you," Ileana stormed. "You shouldn't have come." She pushed to her knees, her long dark tresses hanging in her face, her eyes wide and wild. "Leave." She waved toward the doorway. "Go away!" She turned her focus on Gryph. "You shouldn't have brought her here. She'll die. They'll all die. Mark my words, hurry, before there's nothing you can do. Nothing." She buried her face in her hands and rocked back and forth, wailing.

Selene rolled over and pushed to a sitting position, her vision blurring.

Gryph kneeled on the floor beside her. "Are you okay?"

"Yes. No." She shook her head, as, one by one, the images shifted, bringing into focus the most prevalent and urgent.

She gripped Gryph's arm and her heart seemed to stop beating for a second, then leaped ahead, pounding so hard, her pulse banged against her eardrums. "We have to get back."

"Back where?"

Selene didn't wait to answer, she grabbed her flashlight

from where it had landed on the floor, lurched to her feet and staggered toward the door.

Gryph ran after her. "Where?"

"The Lair!" Ileana screamed. "It's too late." She resumed her rocking and keening. "It's too late."

Selene burst through the doorway into the tunnel.

The troll stood as sentry to the gypsy's abode.

When she passed him, all he did was grunt. He did nothing to stop her or Gryph, who emerged on her heels.

Selene ran back the way they'd come, careless of the rails, the abandoned equipment and debris littering her path. She fell, dropped the flashlight, scraped her hands and knees, but got up and ran some more.

"Selene, wait!" Gryph called out.

She couldn't. She had to get to the Lair before…before…

A flash of tawny fur dashed beside her. Gryph, half changed, stood in her path, blocking her from going any farther, forcing her to stop.

Tears streamed from her eyes. "We have to get back."

"Why?" His growling, deep voice demanded an answer.

"They're coming." She tried to push around him.

His furry hand on her arm halted her movement. "Who is coming?"

"The authorities. They'll find the people, they'll drag them to the surface and expose them to the world."

"You saw this?"

"Yes!" She fought to free her wrist. "We have to get back and warn them. There isn't much time, the police are on their way. They're going to shoot anything that moves." She gulped back a sob. "Including Jack and Jillian."

His lion-man mouth tightened, the long incisors flashing in the beam of her flashlight. "Let me lead the way."

She nodded and took his hand, and they ran together. As they approached the sinkhole, Gryph slowed and edged to one side, holding tight to the pipe overhead and to her hand.

Frustrated by how slowly they had to move past the obstacle, Selene bit down on her lip and forced herself to focus on putting one foot in front of the other.

Midway across the abyss, Gryph's foot slipped.

Selene held tight to his hand, leaning hard against the wall to keep him balanced and to avoid being pulled into the dark depths.

"Thanks." He pushed on to emerge on the other side.

As soon as they'd passed the gaping hole, they ran again. Thirty minutes later, they emerged into the Lair.

Gryph ran to the center of the track switch, where a pole held up an old bell with a rope dangling from the middle. He rang it three times and moved to the side. In moments several men emerged from buildings, wearing pajamas, rubbing their eyes.

A large man whose face was normal and human on one side and more ape than human on the other, stepped forward. "What's wrong, Gryph?"

Gryph stared hard into the other man's eyes. "Nelson, help me evacuate the Lair. We may only have minutes before surface dwellers arrive bearing arms."

"Why?" Nelson asked.

"It doesn't matter why, just get everyone out. Now!" Gryph ran to the nearest doorway and banged.

"Keep your pants on." An elderly lady emerged. "Where's the fire?"

"Mrs. Martin, it's a Code Red."

"Oh, dear." She pressed her knuckles to her lips.

"This is not a drill. Surface dwellers are on their way down. We have to get out before we're destroyed.

"Oh, dear." Her eyes widened. "Oh, dear! The children."

Gryph gripped her arm. "Where are Jillian and Jack?"

"I don't know. They were out playing and didn't come in when I called. I must have lost track of time. Where could they have gotten to?"

"Pack only your essentials, hide what you can and retreat into the tunnels."

She pulled back. "I can't leave without the children."

"You can and will. I'll find them." Gryph frowned down at her. "I promise, I'll take care of them. We'll find them, Mrs. Martin." He gripped her elbow. "Now, go to the shelter. Hurry."

She flapped her hands, looking right and left. "I need to pack up my belongings."

"No, you need to go."

"Now," Selene insisted.

"But who will take care of hiding my home? What if they destroy it?"

"I'll hide it. If they find it and destroy it, we'll build again."

"They need to hurry," Selene whispered.

"I'm too old to start over. What if I get lost?"

Despite the urgency, Gryph hugged the older woman. "You're younger than you think." He turned her toward a woman hurrying by, carrying a tote stuffed full of clothes, books, yarn and knitting needles. "Please, Mrs. Martin, go with Jen Cramer. She'll make sure you take the right tunnels."

Jen Cramer, a woman with the glittering scales of a colorful fish glowing in the lights along her neck and face, overheard her name. She detoured to hook Mrs. Martin's arm and steered her down a tunnel, shining a flashlight into the darkness.

Mothers gathered their children and herded them after the disappearing Jen Cramer and Mrs. Martin.

Gryph ran to the doorway into Balthazar's home and flung it open. "Father!" He ran inside, Selene on his heels. "Father!"

No one answered.

"Father!" Gryph called out, searching from room to

room. When they turned up empty, he ran for the doorway, hustling Selene with him. Once outside Balthazar's home, he pressed a brick on the wall and a panel slid in place, covering the doorway. He pressed another brick, extinguishing the overhead lights and those leading down the main tunnels.

Flashlights blinked on and men pushed heavy metal sliding doors over the otherwise normal wooden doorways. When they were in place, the panels blended into the tunnel walls, with a facade of old brick the same color and texture as the old tunnel walls.

By the time the last door was covered, Selene couldn't tell what was real and what was facade, allaying some of Selene's fear of the Lair's detection.

The sound of men shouting reached Selene's ears and her anxiety level pitched upward. "It's them." She stared at one of the dark tunnels. A light glowed far into the darkness. "They're almost here."

"Come, I think I know where Jillian and Jack might have gone to play."

Gryph led the way toward one of the half-dozen tunnels leading out of the Lair. They slipped into the darkness as the light from the other tunnel grew brighter.

Selene followed, glancing behind her every step she took.

"Turn off the flashlight."

A ripple of fear tightened her belly.

"Trust me," he said.

The crunch of dozens of feet on the gravel floor made her hit the button on her flashlight before they were seen.

Gryph grabbed her hand and continued down the tunnel until they rounded a bend in the tracks. Only then did he stop and turn back to see what was going on.

Over a dozen SWAT team members filled the Lair, semiautomatic rifles at the ready, headlamps shining from their helmets, the red of laser sights bouncing off the dull gray of the tunnel walls.

She could hear a dozen thoughts streaming through her head, as tension and adrenaline raged through each of the men. "Someone tipped them off," she whispered. "They think Amanda's killer is hiding out in the tunnels."

"You can read their minds?" Gryph asked.

"A little. And that's the overall impression I'm getting," Selene said. "Whoever tipped them off told them to be ready. The suspect is considered very dangerous. They're loaded for bear, and were told to shoot anything that moves."

His hand tightened on hers. "We have to find the children."

Selene let him lead her away from the little bit of light filtering through the tunnel from the SWAT team headlamps.

They moved slowly. Selene carefully placed her feet, afraid to make a noise, but unable to see anything. She prayed Gryph could see well enough to guide them to the children. If Jack and Jillian returned to the Lair while the SWAT team was there…

It didn't bear thinking about. The men wouldn't know what they were and would shoot first, clean up the mess later.

Her heart lodged in her throat, Selene sent out a fervent message to the children to stay hidden where they were. Gryph was coming to find them.

A shout from the tunnel behind her made Selene jump. She tripped over the rail and fell to her knees. Her extinguished flashlight banged against the metal tracks, the sound echoing against the tunnel walls.

"I heard something over here," a voice called out. Light shone at the corner they'd left behind, growing stronger.

"Run." Gryph hauled her to her feet and dragged her along behind him, racing over the uneven ground.

Struggling to keep up, Selene did her best, her lungs burning, her heartbeat banging against her chest. Another turn and the darkness consumed them yet again.

Gryph came to a halt and grabbed the flashlight from Selene's fingers.

A soft click sounded then he flicked the switch. Red light glowed from the flashlight, illuminating what was in front of them enough that Selene could make out a stack of pallets, an old bucket railcar that had probably been used to haul coal beneath the city. Behind all this, two small furry faces peered out, eyes wide.

Relieved they'd found the children, Selene didn't have time to waste.

Gryph dragged her back behind the stack of wooden pallets, where the little girl and little boy crouched. Gryph dropped to his belly and pulled Selene down with him, switching off the light as the SWAT team rounded the corner, their headlamps glowing brightly. Three men stood with their hands on the triggers of their wicked-looking weapons, the red laser sight tracking through the tunnel until it landed on the pallets and railcar.

Jillian shrank against her, so scared, Selene had difficulty telling where the child's thoughts ended and hers began. As the adult, Selene couldn't let fear take control.

The men approached, their headlamp beams swaying right, then left.

Selene's arm slipped around Jillian, tightening enough to be reassuring.

At one point, one of them nudged the pallets with the tip of his rifle.

Jack, who was beside Gryph, let out a soft gasp, masked by the scuffling of the boots.

Selene stared hard at the three headlamps, the men's

faces barely visible in the shadows. She concentrated on projecting her thoughts, not certain it would work. These men were focused, on a mission. If she could make her thoughts theirs, they had a chance. *The suspect is not here. There is nothing of interest in this tunnel.*

The more she thought it, the more her head hurt, until she thought it might explode.

Finally, one of the men touched his empty hand to his temple and shook his head. "There's nothing of interest in this tunnel. The suspect isn't here."

One by one the other two agreed and backed away from the pile of debris behind which the man they were searching for lay.

As soon as the SWAT team members backtracked around the corner of the tunnel, Selene let go of the thought and lay her cheek against the back of her hand, her body and mind drained.

For twenty or thirty minutes more Selene, Gryph, Jillian and Jack lay still, listening to the sounds of footsteps and voices echoing from the Lair. Nothing indicated the team had found anything that would show Gryph had been there.

Too far away now to read their minds, Selene contented herself with soothing the two children. Jillian's furry body snuggled up to hers. After a while the little girl fell asleep from inactivity.

Selene wasn't sure how long they'd been there. Finally, Gryph stirred and whispered, "I'm going to check things out."

"No." She reached out where she'd last seen him, touching his arm.

"I need you to watch out for the children. Keep them safe. Stay here—don't make a sound until I give the all clear."

She knew it was the right thing to do, but she didn't like

the idea of him getting caught in the crosshairs. "I'm not the one they're looking for. Wouldn't it be better if I went?"

"I'm going to shift. I move quietly on all fours."

Not happy, but aware of how important it was to the people of the Lair to maintain their secret existence, Selene bit down on her tongue and let him go.

The *shoosh* of clothing falling to the ground was followed by complete silence.

Selene counted to three hundred, waiting for whatever all-clear sign Gryph would give. She'd about given up when the tunnel lights flickered on.

At first blinded by the glare, she blinked several times.

Jack was up and running toward the Lair before she could stop him. Jillian stirred beside her, yawning. "Is it over?" she asked.

"I suppose so," Selene responded. "The lights are back on."

Jillian rubbed her eyes and sat up. "That's the all-clear sign. We can go home now."

Selene climbed to her feet and stepped around the pallet and railcar.

Jillian slipped her furry hand into hers and led the way back to the Lair.

The inhabitants returned, one by one or in groups, carrying what few belongings they'd escaped with and talking in low, hushed tones.

With Jack coming to a stop beside him, Gryph stood at the open doorway to Balthazar's home, wearing trousers and a clean white shirt. He was buttoning the cuffs. "I was about to come get you."

"Thankfully, it wasn't necessary. My capable helpers knew what the all-clear sign was, and got me back here safely." She ran her hand across Jillian's smooth golden hair. "You all act as if you've run this drill before."

"Quite a few times. The people of the Lair like things

the way they are. They've gone to a lot of trouble to keep their secret for the past thirty years."

"I'm impressed."

Mrs. Martin emerged with Jen Cramer. Her worried frown cleared as soon as she spied Jillian and Jack. She opened her arms and the little girl and boy ran into them, hugging her tightly.

Balthazar emerged from one of the tunnels, hurrying through the throng of people, talking softly, reassuringly. When he reached the door to his home, where Gryph stood, he raised his hand above the crowd. "If I may have you attention, please."

The talking ceased and all eyes turned to their leader.

"I know you all are worried about the return of the police. And rightly so. Our emergency procedures are in place for that very reason. As you can see, the protocol served us well. I ask that we all remain aware and diligent in assessing outside contacts to insure no one leads others into the Lair. Rest assured I will look into the construction of additional barriers to close off little-used tunnels and installing more early warning devices so that we can evacuate sooner should this happen again. In the meantime, you can all go home."

When Balthazar finished, he turned toward Gryph and Selene. "From what I gathered as I hid in the tunnel, the SWAT team was looking for Amanda's killer, and apparently they know something about our little community. This is the first time we've had an actual breach. People are scared."

Hell, Selene was scared down to the depths of her soul.

"They blame us." Gryph's mouth closed in a tight line.

"Did you get what you needed from the gypsy?" Balthazar asked.

Gryph nodded. "I think so."

"You know I love you, but right now there are so many

more people at risk than you. Come inside and tell me all you learned. Then you and your friend must leave."

"I understand." Gryph took Selene's hand and led her into Balthazar's home.

Now that she had time to breathe and think back through what had happened, her thoughts whirled.

She'd seen what was going to happen with the SWAT team, but getting back to the Lair before they did precluded an all-out attack. Though D'na Ileana could see the future, it was only one *possible* future.

It gave Selene hope. Because the other image was of a huge attack by a pack of wolves, led by one big black wolf with green eyes. In that attack, she, her sisters and Gryph were all killed.

Chapter 15

Balthazar insisted on Gryph and Selene taking tea and wouldn't let them talk until they'd settled in chairs with their teacups in hand. "Now, tell me what happened with D'na Ileana."

The images Selene had seen when she'd touched Ileana's arm shot through her mind like balls in a pinball machine, each bouncing off other ones in a disjointed pattern.

Gryph filled in Balthazar about what he knew, Kobaloi, the troll and even D'na Ileana's reluctance to reveal their future. His gaze stayed her, warming Selene with his concern at the same time it chilled her with the possible outcome of what she'd seen in Ileana's prediction.

"We haven't had time to discuss anything. Apparently Ileana predicted the SWAT team raid."

"Apparently?" Balthazar's brows rose.

Gryph turned to Selene. "What did you see?"

"It wasn't so much what I saw as the overwhelming feeling that troops were on their way to raid the Lair."

Balthazar's brows descended. "All who are aware of our little community are sworn to secrecy. The only way the police could know about us is if they followed someone here."

Selene shook her head. She didn't want to contradict the older man. In her heart, she knew there was a traitor among the people of the Lair, she just wasn't sure who it was. Whoever it might be wasn't there. She hadn't sensed sinister thoughts from any of the evacuees. Only surprise and concern. "The thoughts and images I gathered from the SWAT team leader were that they'd received a tip to check out the tunnels beneath the city. Not just a tip, but also an entry location and direction once down under."

Balthazar's face darkened. "Who would have told?"

Selene shook her head. "I don't know, and I didn't get a name out of my eavesdropping on the SWAT leader's mind."

"Did you get anything else out of your connection with Ileana?" Gryph asked. "What happened when you touched her? Whatever it was knocked both of you out of your seats. It must have been something big."

Her chest tightened and the air left her lungs, the fog of a faint threatened to steal the light from her vision. It took several moments of concentration to sort through the overwhelming flood of images that moment had brought with it. "All I know is that what Ileana sees is what *could* happen. Today I sensed the SWAT team raiding the Lair and all the people being herded to the surface. Because we were here before the police, we altered that possible outcome."

"That's an interesting hypothesis and a good one to know. However, you avoided my question." Gryph pinned her with his stare. "What else did you see?"

Selene paced faster, refusing to meet Gryph's gaze. "Vague images, situations, scenarios."

Suddenly Gryph was standing in front of her. "What images, situations, scenarios? Whatever they are, we can handle them together."

"That's just it. We *are* together in the images I got from Ileana. You, me, my sisters. And we're all killed." Selene threw her hands in the air. "We were surrounded by wolves. And they were led by a big black wolf with bright green eyes."

Gryph gripped her arms. "Did you recognize any of the wolves as those from the pool hall?"

Selene shook her head. "No. But that doesn't mean it couldn't be one of them."

"What about the surroundings?" His fingers tightened. "Do you have an image of where we were?"

She shook her head, straining her memory to clarify the image. "All I got was the glare of bright lighting and… diamonds. A lot of diamonds, maybe crystals, sparkling everywhere I turned. Other than that, it's all pretty much a blur."

"Indoors or outdoors?" Balthazar asked.

Selene frowned. "Inside."

"That narrows it down." Gryph's lips twisted. "Not really, but it's a start."

"I'm sorry. I wasn't prepared to see you or me die. The whole scene was bad. Bloody. Horrible." Selene pinched the bridge of her nose. "I wasn't prepared."

Gryph's hands smoothed down her arms. "You did good."

"I wish I'd done better. I wish I'd seen the scenario where we won the fight."

"We asked for what our killer would do next. At least he won't be targeting another woman."

"No." Her heart rose to clog her throat and her eyes burned. "He'll be targeting you, me and my sisters."

Gryph's lips curled. "Now we know what to expect and we have a fighting chance."

"I hope so." Selene had the uncontrollable urge to get out of the tunnels and up into the open air of the city. "If it's all right with you, I'd like to get some sleep. I'm sure I'll be better able to handle a full-scale attack when I've had a few hours of sleep."

Balthazar rested a hand on Gryph's shoulder. "Take her home. We could all do with some sleep."

Selene's heart hurt with Balthazar's words. She couldn't go home. Her apartment had been breached. Gryph's plan was to take her to his home. The thought of being alone with him had her torn. On the one hand, she didn't want to be alone. Not after all that had happened. On the other hand, she didn't want to be alone with Gryph and the inevitable outcome of falling into bed with the handsome shifter. At the moment, their destinies were entwined and pretty shaky.

Her blood pounded through her veins—fear of SWAT team raids or trolls having nothing to do with it. Images of their naked bodies lying against the sheets pushed to the forefront of her mind.

Tension built inside her as Gryph led her back the way they'd originally entered the Lair, in what felt like a lifetime ago.

Once they emerged into his basement apartment, Selene was wound up tighter than a drawn bowstring.

"I should go stay the night with my sister Brigid." She headed straight for the door, without waiting for his response.

Before she reached for the knob, a hand on her shoulder stopped her, sealing her fate.

"You're not going to your sister's." Gryph growled low in his throat.

The sound sent fingers of lightning shooting across her nerves, angling toward her core. "You can't keep me here like a prisoner." The image of being bound was positively titillating and she almost groaned.

"You know you want to stay," he said, his golden gaze mesmerizing in its intensity.

"So now you're the mind reader?"

"I study body language. And yours is telling me you

want this." Gryph leaned close, captured the back of her neck in his big hand and bent to claim her lips.

"I don't want—" she began.

Gryph swallowed her words, slipping his tongue inside her mouth, sliding it against hers in a warm, wet assault she couldn't resist.

Her arms circled his neck and her calf curled around the back of his. Whatever words she might have said flew from her mind as his kiss stole her thoughts and her will to resist.

Without breaking their kiss, Gryph scooped her into his arms and carried her through the apartment to the bedroom, where he set her on her feet and slowly peeled the layers of clothing off her. First her jacket. He unzipped it and pushed it over her shoulders, letting it slide down her back to drop to the floor.

He tugged the shirt from the waistband of her jeans and lifted it up over her torso.

Selene raised her arms and the shirt came off and was tossed to the side. In her bra and jeans, she could feel the stress of the encounter with Ileana leaving her to be replaced by a different kind of tension. One that began at her center and radiated outward.

She reached for the button on her jeans, only to have her hand brushed aside.

Gryph flicked the button loose and dragged the zipper down, parting the edges. He slipped his hand inside the jeans and her panties to cup her sex, a finger sliding between her folds.

Selene sucked in an unsteady breath, aching to be naked and lying in the sheets with this man. "Too slow," she said and grabbed his T-shirt, ripped it up over his head and tossed it aside. While he pushed her jeans over her hips, she yanked the button loose on his and pushed them down over his bulging thighs.

In a few frenzied movements, they were rid of their jeans and shoes.

Gryph scooped her up again and laid her across the shiny gold-and-black satin duvet.

The fabric felt cool against Selene's feverish skin, but did nothing to temper the torrid heat burgeoning inside as Gryph stood beside the bed, gorgeous, naked and danger-ous, his golden eyes sultry and dark. "You're beautiful."

"You're not so bad yourself," she said, her voice low and gravelly. She leaned up, grabbed his hand and drew him onto the bed beside her, amazed at her own hunger and eagerness to consummate their shared desire in what promised to be a fiery conclusion to a very long night. With no windows to let the sunlight in, Selene couldn't tell if it was night or day and really didn't care. All her focus centered on this man-beast and what he was about to do to her and with her.

Her channel slicked in anticipation, her heartbeat rac-ing, blood pounding through her veins as she trailed a hand across his broad chest and down his ribs to the hot, stiff member jutting upward, thick and proud. She wrapped her fingers around him, sliding them slowly up and down the velvety smoothness.

He captured the back of her neck and leaned over her, his lips descending on hers, the force of his assault press-ing her into the mattress. Then his hand skimmed down her throat, over one shoulder and across a breast to tweak the distended nipple.

Selene arched her back, pressing into his hand.

With his large capable hand, he cupped the breast, roll-ing the peaked tip between his thumb and forefinger. He broke the seal of their lips and feathered kisses down the column of her throat to the swell of her breast, replacing his fingers with his tongue. At first stroking across the bud with a strangely rough tongue, he made the tip even tighter, then he sucked it into his mouth, pulling hard on it, unleashing a lust so powerful Selene squirmed.

Her legs fell open, her hand guiding his cock to her opening. "Please."

"Patience," Gryph whispered, blowing a warm stream of air across her damp breast. Then he blazed a trail of kisses and nips down her torso to the apex of her thighs, parting her legs to settle between them.

Selene lay back against the comforter, her breath caught in her lungs, waiting for the moment.

With care and calculation, he parted her folds and touched the tip of his coarse tongue to the bundle of electric nerves, setting off an explosion of sensations that had Selene rocking her hips high above the mattress.

He chuckled. "Like that?"

"By the goddess, yes!" she screamed, her fingers threading into his tawny hair, pulling him back to the goal for more of the same.

Flicking her again, he treated her to long, sexy strokes that left her gasping, her knees tightening around his ears and her world coming apart with an explosion of brightly colored fireworks.

Spasms of electrical shocks racked her body until she was begging him, "Please, come inside me. Now!" Selene tugged on his hair, urging him to climb up her body.

Gryph lapped once more then rolled off her and reached into his nightstand for a condom.

"Let me," Selene said, her voice strained, her body poised for what came next, her anticipation even more pronounced after he'd brought her to an earth-shattering orgasm. It wasn't enough. She wanted more.

With shaking hands, she tore open the packet, slipped the rubber over his member and rolled it down the sides, loving how thick and hard he was, imagining what he'd feel like buried inside her.

Then he was between her legs, where he pushed her knees up, pressed his cock against her opening and paused.

Selene almost came unglued. She wrapped her legs around his waist and dug her heels into his buttocks, urging him into her.

He held back. "There is no way we're going to die anytime soon."

"You bring that up now?" she wailed.

"Damn right. I won't let it happen." He stared down into her eyes, his cock nudging against her wetness. "We have far too much to live for." With those words, he drove into her, stretching her inside, filling her with a fullness she'd never experienced before him. It went beyond lust to a sense of coming home.

Then Gryph moved in a steady, pounding rhythm, driving into her, again and again.

She dropped her heels to the mattress and met him thrust for thrust, loving how deep and fierce his movements were, craving more with each stroke.

Once again, she rocketed to the crest and soared into the atmosphere.

At that moment, Gryph sank deep and held it there, his member twitching, throbbing, hot and thick inside her.

When Selene finally returned to earth, she lay spent, satiated and complete.

Gryph rolled over, taking her with him, without breaking their intimate connection, his shaft still hard inside her.

Her eyelids drifted closed, her body relaxing in the safety of Gryph's arms.

"Sleep," he said, his breath warm on her cheek as he brushed strands of hair from her face.

Exhausted from all the events of the past few days, Selene let the worry of what might happen soon fade from her mind. She basked in the afterglow of the best sex she'd ever had and she slipped into warm, blessed oblivion.

Gryph lay on his side with Selene nestled in the crook of his arm and marveled at the strength and resilience of this witch who'd stormed into his world, saved his life and refused to sit on the sidelines when the odds were stacked against them. What troubled Gryph was the anguish he'd seen in her face after she'd experienced Ileana's view of what the future had in store for him, herself and her sisters. He didn't want this woman to die. She had so much to offer, so much to give, and a life worth living. And he wanted to be a part of it.

Thinking back to her description of the place the attack would take place, he tried to picture it himself—lots of light, stars, diamonds. Was she referring to a sunrise on Lake Michigan when the angle of the sun makes the water look like it's coated in diamonds? No. She'd mentioned that it was inside. Was there a place bright with lights that sparkled like diamonds? In a city the size of Chicago, that could be just about anywhere. The hotels had rooms with high ceilings and great lighting. Maybe.

Dread threatened to take the joy out of what he'd just shared with Selene. Somehow he had to figure it out and come up with a plan to stack the odds in their favor. If they were to be attacked by wolves, they had to have their plan in place to defend themselves. Surely even witches with the incredible talents of the Chattox sisters couldn't keep up with an overwhelming numbers of wolves. Ileana's vision proved that. One potential outcome was for the six of them to die.

Gryph's arm tightened around Selene's shoulders and he stared down at her face, her creamy cheek pale against his golden tanned arm. Her dark brown hair splayed out across the sheets in rich, luxurious waves. He had such a feeling of belonging, he couldn't imagine her with anyone else.

When had she come to mean so much to him? And how could he ask her to be a part of his life when he wasn't free to be who he was in public? She deserved to find love with someone who wasn't a monster like him. If he wasn't so caught up in his own desires, he'd let her go. Let her live her life without the challenge he faced on a daily basis—namely, hiding his true identity. If the public learned what he was, the empire he'd built would crumble. And he refused to take Selene down with him.

In that moment, he chose to let time stand still. He didn't want to let her go—he wanted to hold her and protect her from whatever horrible event Ileana had predicted. Until they lived through that—overcoming their enemies—he was going to stick to her like a fly on flypaper.

He drifted into a restless sleep, plagued with horrific dreams of rabid wolves surrounding Selene, cutting her off from him and her sisters. As they edged nearer, Gryph tapped into his inner beast, his muscles expanding, changing, morphing into his alter ego, the massive lion that could rip off a man's head in a single swipe of his paw. As he landed on all fours, he let out a roar and stalked toward the wolf pack, squaring off with the leader, a jet-black wolf with bright green eyes.

With a sparkling gleam in its eyes, it lunged. Not at Gryph, but at Selene, knocking her onto her back, pinning her against the floor.

Gryph leaped at the wolf, too late to stop its wicked canines from slashing into Selene's throat, ripping away flesh.

With the force of a Mack truck, Gryph hit the black wolf. The two of them rolled across the ground, teeth flashing, claws tearing into fur.

Gryph suffered a vicious bite to his shoulder, his muscles seizing. With renewed anger, he bit into the wolf's neck, severing the carotid artery. The wolf staggered, blood pouring from the open wound. He stumbled and crashed to the ground, facedown, blood forming a thick copper-scented pool beneath him.

Gryph turned to Selene and gathered her in his arms. She lay as still as death, her skin cool, her eyes open and vacant.

"No!" he cried in his dream. "No!"

A hand shook his shoulder. "Gryph. Wake up." Again someone shook him. "Gryph! Wake up."

He blinked his eyes open and stared into the dark chocolate of Selene's bright irises. He sat up and gripped her arms, the soft skin reassuring him that she was not a figment of his imagination. Then he noticed the deep cuts on her arms and neck. "Good Lord, Selene, what happened?"

She smiled softly at him. "You were having a bad dream."

Gryph recoiled, horrified. "I did that, didn't I?"

Chapter 16

Selene raised her hands. "They're just scratches."

"I could have killed you."

"No, you wouldn't have," she said, though the look in his sleep-glazed eyes had been murderous when he'd pinned her to the mattress, roaring in his half-human form.

Gryph left the bed, grabbed trousers from the closet and slid his legs into them. By the time he returned, his face had changed completely back to his human form, worry and self-reproach etching lines into his forehead.

Selene sat up, letting the sheet fall down around her waist, exposing her breasts. "Please, Gryph, lie down. We can pick up where we left off before we went to sleep."

"Are you insane?" He ran his hand through his hair. "I almost killed you."

She shrugged, both breasts bobbing with the slight movement. "I'm okay."

"No, you're not." He scooped her into his arms, the sheet falling to the floor. "We're going to clean up those wounds before they get infected, then I'm taking you to your sisters."

She wrapped her arms around his neck, pressing her breasts to his chest. "I don't want to go to my sisters. I want to stay here with you."

"Tough. It's not up for discussion."

Selene, unused to flirting with men, tried her best interpretation of a vamp. "Can't we just stay here and make love? Or don't you want me?" She tightened her hold around his neck and nibbled the corner of his lip. "Please, Gryph. I mean it. I'm okay."

Without another word, he carried her to the bathroom, set her naked bottom on the cool granite countertop and rummaged in a cabinet for a first-aid kit.

When he advanced on her with a wet washcloth, she held up her hand. "I can take care of it myself."

He growled. "Move your hands."

For a moment, she contemplated defying him, but the stern hardness of his jaw told her he was in no mood to argue.

Selene tipped her chin up, exposing the long line of her neck.

Gryph gently applied the clean, damp cloth to her torn skin. Though it stung a little, it was the water trickling down her neck that captured her attention. It rolled across the swell of her breast to drip down the valley between, skirting past her belly button to be captured in her mound of curls.

Lust flared like a spark to dry kindling, sending her blood speeding through her veins. She captured his hand and dragged it, cloth and all, over her breasts and down the same path as the drop of water.

His nostrils flared, his hand gripping the cloth so tightly, his knuckles turned white. When she reached the juncture of her thighs, his hand stilled and his breathing grew more labored.

"I can't stop myself," he groaned through gritted teeth.

His words were like a cold slap in her face, a wake-up call to reality. "What did you say?"

"I don't want to hurt you again, but I can't make myself stop this insanity."

"You won't hurt me." Part of her wanted him to continue

on and make mad, passionate love to her. The other side of her didn't want to admit what was happening.

"I...can't...control...the beast," he said, his hand moving lower. "Why can't I stop?"

"Because I want it." Pushing aside the nudge of guilt, Selene took the cloth from his fingers and set it aside, urging his hand to take the place of the fabric, to slide through the curls to the folds beneath.

Gryph closed his eyes, his hand cupping her sex, a single finger dipping into her warmth. "You tempt me, witch."

She knew she did more than that and couldn't bring herself to stop. Instead, she wrapped her legs around his waist, tightening to pull him closer, trapping his hand between them.

The hard ridge of his cock pushed against his knuckles, pressing his finger deeper. She lifted his other hand and laid it over her breast.

"This is wrong." He squeezed the flesh between his fingers. Once, twice, his finger pumped in and out of her. When his gaze shifted back to the scratches on her arm, his lips thinned.

Selene wanted him so badly it hurt her to realize she was manipulating him into making love to her. He obviously didn't want it to happen. Her mental push was forcing him into it.

What kind of witch was she? The cool, calculating, dark witch without a conscience?

No way.

With a great deal of effort, she tamped down her base urge to fall back into the bed with this man-beast.

As soon as she backed off her own longing, Gryph's finger left her channel and he unhooked her ankles from behind his back. "You need to clean those scratches yourself."

"Why?" Selene scooted off the counter and stood before him, fighting an inner battle to subdue her lust.

Gryph backed out of the bathroom. "I won't touch you again. I can't risk it. It's too dangerous."

"That's too bad. I was willing to take the risk." She reached up, sliding her body against his one last time.

His eyes glazed with desire.

Damn, she was doing it again. How could she get out of his head, if she couldn't get out of her own?

He captured her wrists in his big hands and held her away. "No, Selene. The risk isn't worth it."

"Maybe it is to me," she whispered, her cheeks heated, disappointment and sadness filling her. "Okay, then." When he let go of her, she let her arms fall to her sides. Pushing her shoulders back, she didn't try to hide her nakedness. If anything, she wanted him to see her, to know what he was giving up. "If we're done here, I have a job to do." With the ball only a day away, she had a dozen things to check on. It had to go off without a hitch or her reputation as a designer and clothier would take a huge hit.

His gaze raked over her. "I'll have my assistant bring you fresh clothing, and my driver can take you to whichever sister you want to stay with."

"Don't bother." She marched past him, purposely rubbing her hip against his thigh. "I can call a taxi."

"With the wolf out there, it's not safe. I insist," he said behind her.

Selene ignored him and snatched her clothing from the floor, where it had landed in their frenzy to get naked earlier. By focusing on her work, she was able to push her longing to the side, apply antiseptic and bandages to her wounds and dress in record time, knowing the sooner she left Gryph's apartment the better off both of them would be. When she was ready, she went in search of Gryph, stopping long enough to place a call to Aurai.

"Selene, where have you been?" Aurai demanded.

"It's a long story," she answered. "Could you pick me up?"

"Where?"

"At the GL Enterprises building."

A long pause met her request. "You were with him all night and half the day?"

Selene closed her eyes and counted to ten to maintain her patience. "Yes. Now, are you going to come get me, or do I need to call a cab?"

"We'll be there in ten minutes."

"We?" Selene gripped the phone harder. "What do you mean *we*?"

The phone had gone dead. Great. The *we* Aurai mentioned could be another sister or all of them, and she wasn't ready to face her entire family. Not yet.

Selene wandered through the spacious apartment to the kitchen, where the scent of coffee filled the air, reviving her.

Gryph stood at the gas stove, wearing a crisp white, long-sleeved shirt and a tie, looking naturally gorgeous, vibrant and more distant than ever. "Do you like eggs?"

Saddened by his remoteness, Selene resisted pouting, something she never thought she'd do but wanted to at that point. "No, thank you. I'm not hungry."

"You haven't eaten anything in at least twenty-four hours." He sighed. "Look, I'm sorry I was so short with you. I just don't want to hurt you."

Bread popped out of a toaster on the counter. Selene's stomach rumbled despite her claim that she wasn't hungry. She decided it was foolish to refuse his offer. "I'll have a slice of toast, if you have enough."

Gryph's brows dipped, then smoothed. "Fine." He placed two pieces of toast on a small plate and set it on the bar. "Have a seat."

Selene settled on a cushioned bar stool and studied Gryph over a mug of coffee. "I'm sorry."

He glanced over his shoulder as he cracked eggs into a small skillet. "For what?"

"Pushing thoughts into your head."

"I'm beginning to recognize when you do that. And believe me when I say, it wasn't all you." He adjusted the heat on the stove and opened the refrigerator. "For your information, I didn't stop because you wanted me to stop. I stopped because I didn't want to hurt you again." He set a jar of strawberry preserves in front of her and stared into her eyes. "My desire to keep you unharmed trumped the desire to make love to you."

As much as she wanted to believe him, Selene couldn't. She feared her telepathic abilities were growing stronger each day.

He brought his eggs to the bar and sat beside her.

Selene chewed the toast dry, if for no other reason than to give her an excuse not to talk. She found herself wishing she wasn't a witch with the ability to influence others. Instead of choking down her food, they'd be rocking the bedsprings. Maybe. She wondered if Gryph truly found her desirable, not just because she planted the thought. Then there was his reluctance to hurt her.

"You think too much." The man of her thoughts took her plate of half-eaten toast, piled it on his empty plate and stood. "If you're ready, I'll take you to one of your sister's houses."

"I'm going back to my shop. I have work to do."

"I can't leave you there alone."

"It's still daylight and my shop can't remain closed forever. I'll lose customers and ultimately my business. Besides, I have a gala to prepare for and no one will attack me in broad daylight."

"You can't be certain."

"I'll take my chances. Besides, I need to arrange for someone to fix my door and locks."

His lips pressing together, he walked past her and laid the dirty dishes in the sink before facing her again. "At least inform your sisters."

"Done. Aurai's on her way. I won't need you to take me."

"Good. And I've already arranged to have your door repaired. The contractor will have a key there for you."

"Then we're done here," she said with finality. Hollowness settled in her belly as she headed for the elevator. Before she reached it, an alarm went off, the sound reverberating through Gryph's apartment. Her heart pounded as she glanced around for the source of the noise. "What's that?"

Gryph raced across the room and snatched the bell-shaped antique phone from the wall and pressed it to his ear. "What happened?"

Selene closed the distance between them, the worry on Gryph's face drawing her nearer.

"When?" He listened, his face growing tighter, grimmer. "I'm on my way." Gryph slammed the phone on its hook. "Jillian's missing."

"Little Jillian?" Selene ran after him. "I'm coming with you."

"Your sister will be here to pick you up. We don't need your help." He hit the switch on the wall, stripping out of his shirt as the door slid back. His chest bare, his hand on the top rail, he glanced back at her. "Go."

His words hit her in the gut, knocking the air from her lungs. Gryph started down the long spiral staircase leading down into the tunnels. He was gone, a little girl was missing and Selene stood staring at the empty staircase, her heart on its way into the bowels of the city with Gryph.

She stepped back and the panel started to slide over the opening. Before the hidden door could close, Selene jammed a fifteen-pound weight into the gap, bracing it open. She couldn't stand back and pretend she didn't care. Jillian was missing and Gryph needed all the help he could get to find her.

A buzzing sound penetrated her thoughts as she stepped over the threshold and onto the metal stairs. It jerked her back to the workout room. "Mr. Leone, you have guests," a voice called out.

Aurai.

Selene followed the sound to an intercom mounted on the wall, found the talk switch, poked it and said, "Send them down."

"I'm sorry, only Mr. Leone has authority to send people into his private quarters."

"Mr. Leone is otherwise occupied," Selene said. Then she closed her eyes and tried again. "You will send them down." This time, she focused on the guard's thoughts, wiping out his orders to defend the private sanctuary of his employer, replacing it with the order to allow the sisters to enter.

"Sending them down" was the guard's response.

Minutes later, the elevator doors opened and all four of her sisters piled out.

"What's going on?" Brigid asked.

"Where's Gryph?" Deme demanded.

"Why are you still here?" Aurai queried.

"Are you okay?" Gina placed a hand on Selene's arm.

Selene fought the urge to cry, knowing there wasn't time to give in to her emotions. "I don't have much time to explain, so listen carefully." She told them of the community of people living in the tunnels below the city and how Gryph had been raised among them. "He feels responsible for them and now one of the children has gone missing. We have to help."

Gina clapped her hands together. "Then let's go."

"How do we get down there?" Brigid asked.

"Follow me." Selene led them to the exercise room, where the panel remained open, jammed on the barbell.

Deme stepped over the weight and stood at the top, her hand on the rail, a frown denting her brow. "I remember the last time we went below."

"To save me from the Chimera." Aurai started to push past Deme. "If there's a little girl down there, lost in that maze of tunnels, we can't just stand around and talk about the past."

"Let me go first," Selene said. "I know the way to the Lair. We can spread out from there."

"Wait." Deme blocked the staircase. "We need a protection spell."

Selene shook her head, a sense of doom urging her to follow Gryph. "We don't have time."

"We *make* time," Deme insisted, her eyes narrowed. She reached out one hand to take Selene's and the other to take Aurai's.

She led off, the others chiming in on the chant they knew so well:

"Feel the power.
Free our hearts.
Find our way.
Be the one.
With the strength of the earth,
With the rising of the wind,
With the calm of the water,
With the intensity of fire,
With the freedom of spirit."

Deme, still holding tight to her sisters' hands continued, "Should evil dwell within this place, banish it with the power of earth."

She nodded toward Brigid.

Brigid picked up the chant. "Banish it with the power of fire."

She turned to Aurai, who said, "Banish it with the power of wind."

Aurai turned to Gina. "Banish it with the power of water."

All her sisters turned to Selene, who added, "Banish it with the power of spirit."

Together they ended with:

"So sayeth, so let it be.
The goddess is within us.
She is power.
We are her.
We are one.
Blessed be."

Once the chant ended, Selene plucked a flashlight from the charger on the wall. Each of her sisters grabbed one, as well. Then she descended into the darkness once again, a chill slithering down the length of her spine.

Gryph arrived at Balthazar's door, half transformed, his sense of smell and eyesight heightened, ready to do what it took to retrieve the child and bring her home safely.

Balthazar was waiting for him, holding a sheet of paper in his hand. "I don't understand."

"What don't you understand? Show me."

He held out the paper with a tear in the top of it. On it typed in block letters were the words "The days of the Lair are at an end."

"Who gave you this?" Gryph demanded.

"It was stuck to my door with these." Balthazar held up a small stuffed bunny and an elaborate knife with brushed silver scrollwork and an emerald set in the silver.

Gryph grabbed the bunny. "I gave this to Jillian."

Balthazar nodded, his old, lined face pale. "I know."

"Where's Jack?"

"With Mrs. Martin. He was beside himself and quite upset."

"What happened?"

"From what I gathered, they were playing hide-and-seek in the south tunnel when Jack heard Jillian scream, and then nothing. He ran to find her, but she was gone. He searched for a few minutes, calling out her name, hoping she was playing the game still. When she didn't respond, he came running back, straight to me. He was the one to find the note on my door."

"No one saw who put it there?"

Balthazar shook his head. "No. Most of the people of the Lair were inside their homes or gone to the surface for food or to work."

"Someone was bold enough to stick that on your door during daytime hours?" Gryph shook his head. "It has to be someone amongst us. Someone we all know for him to slip in like that."

"No one saw anything."

"Where's Jack now?"

"He wanted to go back out and search for his sister, but I have Mrs. Martin keeping a tight leash on him. It's bad enough one of them is missing."

Gryph nodded. "Who else knows?"

"I haven't alerted the rest of the folks of the Lair. I wanted your take on it. When they realize there is a traitor among us, no one will feel safe again. At the same time, the longer we wait to find Jillian's abductor, the less chance we'll be successful."

"I'm here, now. We need volunteers to search the tunnels."

"There aren't enough folks around."

"Then we bring in more."

"You know the rules."

"Look, rules were meant to be broken and finding Jillian is the best reason I can think of." He glanced back the way he'd come. "I'm going for help. I'll be back as soon as I can."

"Hurry."

To move quicker, Gryph changed into lion form and sped back to the staircase leading up into his apartment. Halfway up, he spied a beam from a flashlight. He slowed his ascent and willed his change back halfway to human, all in a matter of seconds. His trousers shredded and his shoes were lost in the tunnel. Barefoot, he continued upward to meet the person with the flashlight coming down.

Even before he saw her, he knew it was Selene. When she spotted him, she stopped, her eyes widening. "I couldn't stand by and do nothing. And I brought—"

"Us." Brigid leaned over Selene's shoulder. "If you'd told me I'd come willingly back into the tunnels yesterday, I'd have called you a big fat liar and singed you with a fireball."

Gryph's gaze captured Selene's. "I'm glad you came."

Selene touched his arm. "We came to help."

Gryph smiled. "I was coming to ask you if there was some spell you could use to help find her."

Selene nodded. "I might be able to help you with that."

"Can you sense her thoughts?"

"Selene found a child lost in a big department store once," Aurai offered.

Gryph took Selene's hand. "Do you think you can find Jillian?"

"All we can do is try." She glanced over her shoulder at her sisters on the stairs above. "Do you mind if my sisters know about…"

"The Lair?" He shook his head. "I've always trusted

my instincts and they're telling me to trust you and your sisters."

Deme added, "The most important thing right now is to find the child."

"Come." Gryph led the way to the Lair.

A small crowd gathered around Balthazar's home.

Gryph introduced the sisters and explained, "They're here to help find Jillian."

A pale woman with jet-black hair and a streak of white at her temple shook her fist. "We don't need surface dwellers helping us."

Gryph raised his hand. "Please, Layla, give them a chance. They have special talents we hope will help us find Jillian faster."

"Please, bring back Jillian." Mrs. Martin sobbed, holding Jack against her side.

The boy's eyes were red-rimmed and his bottom lip trembled. "He took her and I couldn't save her."

Gryph bent to eye level with Jack. "Did you see him?"

Jack shook his head. "No, but I think I heard something. I should have stopped him." Tears trickled down the boy's face.

Selene kneeled beside him, her resolve strengthening. "We'll get her back."

Jack flung his arms around her neck and cried—his tears, his fear and images of dark tunnels flitted through Selene's mind.

When Jack had calmed, Selene handed him over to Mrs. Martin and stood back.

Gryph took charge, assigning certain tunnels to the few able-bodied adult inhabitants who were available and sent them on their way.

Then he turned to Selene and her sisters. "What can I do to help?"

"I'll need something of Jillian's," Selene answered.

He pulled a stuffed bunny from his back pocket and handed it to her. "This is her favorite toy."

Selene held it in her hand and closed her eyes. Images filled her mind of a happy Jillian holding the stuffed animal, having tea with it and sleeping peacefully in her bed, the bunny tucked under her arm.

"Sisters," Selene declared.

All four of her sisters gathered close, reaching out to touch her. Then together, they chanted:

"Goddess of the sun, earth and the moon,
Show us the way to bring the lost home.
So we pray, so mote it be.
With the strength of the earth,
With the rising of the wind,
With the calm of the water,
With the intensity of fire,
With the freedom of spirit,
Blessed be."

Her sisters dropped hands and stepped away from Selene, watching for her next move.

At first, she balked, her mind a blank, nothing surfacing to tell her where to find the girl. A jolt of fear made her close her eyes again and focus. She couldn't fall apart now. Not when a little girl needed her.

Selene clutched the bunny, absorbing the aura of the girl still clinging to the fake fur. An image flitted across her consciousness, one of crumbling walls and dust choking the already dark tunnels. Something was banging, hammering, pounding.

Selene raised her hands to her ears, the pounding beating against her eardrums.

Gryph touched her arm. "What is it?"

"The noise," she whispered. "It's loud, it's loud like a

jackhammer, beating against concrete and the dust—"
She coughed, trying to clear her lungs. "So dark. Alone.
Rocks falling around my feet." Then a hand reached out
of the darkness, a pale hand with a light coat of fur covered in a dust.

Help me, a tiny voice cried, the sound reverberating
with the pounding in her head.

Selene reached out to take the hand, but it popped out
of sight like a balloon with a pin stuck into it.

She opened her eyes and stared down, expecting to see
the rocks, hoping to see the hand, but all she saw were her
tennis shoes and jeans. Not the choking, dusty darkness
or the girl.

Hurry. The whisper of a voice raised gooseflesh on her
skin. "Hurry," Selene echoed. "We have to hurry."

"Which way?" Deme asked.

Selene didn't answer, her feet already moving, carrying her where, she didn't know. All she did know was that
Jillian was in danger, the walls around her crumbling. If
they didn't reach her soon, she'd be buried alive.

Chapter 17

Gryph ran to keep up with Selene, her sisters not far behind. She'd taken the tunnel leading toward the sinkhole. If he didn't catch her soon, she'd fall to her death in the reservoir beneath the city.

When they arrived at the turn in the tunnel that would have led her to the sinkhole, the troll and D'na Ileana, she continued straight, her flashlight bouncing light off the walls, her breathing growing more labored.

The dust grew thicker the farther along they went until Selene slowed to pull her shirt up over her nose. Then she ran on, the beam of her flashlight barely penetrating the swirling dust filling the tunnel.

A distant pounding reached them. If he wasn't mistaken, this section of the tunnels had been declared off-limits to the inhabitants of the Lair long ago. The walls were breaking up, water leakage from the older city streets above ate away at the mortar between the bricks and weakened the support beams.

Gryph racked his memory for where they were in relation to the city above. He recalled a construction site in downtown Chicago.

Oh, hell. His company was tearing down an old hotel that had fallen into a terrible state of disrepair. Even the historical society had deemed it unsalvageable. He'd hired a demolition team to take the building down. They were due to set off explosions to implode the building in place. His assistant had marked the day on his calendar in case he wanted to be present for the event.

It was as clear in his mind now as if he read the calendar all over again. Today was the scheduled date. There would be police barricades set up for several blocks surrounding the building, but none in the tunnels. Most people thought the tunnels too deep to worry about, and uninhabited. Just like the folks of the Lair liked it. He'd informed Balthazar to keep people away from the forbidden zone.

If Selene's abilities were taking them directly to Jillian, there was a good possibility this was all a trap.

It didn't matter. They couldn't stop now, not when a little girl's life was at stake. At the very least, the sisters should know what they were up against.

Gryph caught up with Selene, grabbed her and pulled her to a stop. "Wait."

"No time." Selene sucked in air. "Jillian's in danger."

"I know." When she tried to pull away, he tightened his grip.

Her sisters stopped behind him, breathing hard into their shirts to keep from inhaling all the dust.

Gryph spoke loud enough to be heard by all five of them. "The noise you were hearing is from the surface. They're preparing a building for demolition. They're going to set off explosives today."

"Damn." Selene's eyes rounded and glanced from him to her sisters. "I'll go in alone. You should all stay here."

"Like hell." Brigid sucked in a lungful of dust and coughed.

"I agree," Gina said. "You can't continue on your own." Aurai nodded. "It's all or none."

"A child wouldn't have wandered this far," Selene said. "Whoever did this wanted someone to come after her."

Gryph's jaw tightened. "It smells like a trap."

"Who are they trying to catch?"

"Me," Gryph said. "I can't let you all go in after the girl. We could be up against more than collapsing tunnels and debris."

"You won't find her without me." Selene touched his arm. "Not in time to save her and possibly yourself."

Where her fingers rested on his arm, warmth spread throughout his body. At least he knew she cared and that grounded him, giving him hope.

"I have to go. Jillian's fate is my responsibility. Someone is using her to get to me." His hands clenched into fists. "I mean to find him, and when I do, I'll kill him."

"*After* we get Jillian out." Selene started forward, moving as quickly as she could with limited visibility. Her flashlight beam only lit two feet ahead. Navigating over old rails, crumbled bricks and debris became increasingly difficult.

When they arrived at a junction, Selene stopped, closing her eyes.

Gryph and her sisters waited silently, the sounds of collapsing rubble and dripping water the only noises. The pounding had stilled.

Selene opened her eyes and stared at the ceiling. "They're about to set off the charges."

"We don't have time. We have to get out of here," Deme said.

"Not without Jillian." Selene turned left and took off at a run, tripping and stumbling as she went.

Gryph forced the change, dropping down on all fours, and ran ahead of Selene, his vision no better than hers with all the dust, but he was more sure-footed on four feet instead of two.

At another junction, not far from the previous one, he paused and listened. Was that a whimper? He glanced back as a fuzzy light pushed through the murky passage. Then he ran in the direction he'd heard the sound coming from.

He hadn't gone ten yards when he practically tripped over Jillian, lying on the rail tracks, her arms duct-taped to her sides, her legs bound together in tape, as well, a rag tied around her eyes. She was sobbing quietly, coughing every time she took in a breath of air.

As Gryph came to a halt, Jillian grew still. "Hello? Who's there? Please, help me."

Gryph changed back to human, his skin and muscles stretching, reshaping until he could stand. "It's me— Gryph."

Her sobbing began anew. "I knew you'd come. I knew."

Gently, he pulled the rag off her eyes and extended a sharp claw to slice through the tape on her legs and around her arms.

Selene and her sisters reached him as he gathered Jillian into his arms. "We have to get out of here."

"Now," Selene agreed. "They've begun the countdown. Even if they want to stop, they can't."

"Move!" Gryph followed the sisters down the long tunnels. On their way back, they didn't have the directional pull that had led them to Jillian. Twice they hesitated at junctions, until Gryph pushed past them and followed his feline sense of smell, clouded by the fog of dust.

"Get down, everyone! Cover your heads and brace yourselves," Selene called out and dropped to her belly. "The charges are about to go off."

Gryph lowered Jillian to the ground and between him and Selene, they covered her body with theirs.

Several rumbling booms shook the earth as, one after the other, the charges above went off. Bricks fell from the ceiling, crashing on and around them.

Gryph used his body and hands to cover Selene and Jillian, protecting them from the debris as it fell. Several large bricks pummeled his back, the pain nothing compared to the thought of losing Jillian or Selene.

As soon as the resonant booming stopped and the earth stilled again, he was on his feet.

"We have to move fast. The second round of explosives will go off in ten seconds." Selene staggered, helped Jillian up into Gryph's arms. Together, they ran back the way they'd come.

The second round of charges went off, pitching Gryph forward. He turned and hit the ground on his back, quickly rolling over to cover Jillian's body.

Selene stumbled to her belly beside him, her flashlight gripped in her hand but shedding so little light in the gloom as to be ineffective.

A brick fell with a soft thud.

Selene grunted beside him.

"Are you okay?" he said as more shaking loosened additional bricks.

"Yes." With her hand over her head and neck, she shined the light back toward her sisters. "Deme?"

"I'm still with the living." She called out, "Aurai?"

"I'm okay. Might have a shiner tomorrow, but I'll be okay, if this doesn't get any worse."

"Gina, Brigid?" Deme continued.

"I'm good," Gina said.

Brigid moaned. "I think I sprained my wrist, but I'll live."

"Are they done?" Aurai asked, her disembodied voice seeming to hover in the murk. She'd climbed to her feet and was shining her light upward. "If not, we could be in a heap of trouble. Get a load of that ceiling."

Selene glanced up. The beam barely penetrated the dust cloud filling the tunnel. They were all covered in a fine layer of dust, appearing like so many ghosts.

Another string of rumbling booms shimmied the earth.

"Get down, Aurai!" Deme shouted as loosened bricks gave way.

Gina swept her hands in the air, directing a wall of stagnant water over their heads, knocking the bricks to the side.

Deme followed with a movement that wove a tight web of vines covering the remaining masonry, stabilizing it long enough for them to get out from under the collapsing tunnel.

Gryph stood, clutching Jillian to his chest. He hunched over her as a stray piece of brick found its way through the blanket of vegetation and bounced off his shoulder. "We need to keep moving. If the falling bricks don't hurt us, breathing the dust will."

"We're right behind you." Selene touched her hand to his back as they moved single-file over the rails and fallen bricks.

He liked knowing she was there. Her compassion for a child, almost a stranger to her, captured Gryph's heart and refused to let go.

The farther they moved away from the demolition site, the easier it was to see, and soon they left the thickest dust behind and were able to breathe more freely.

When they emerged into the switching station that was the Lair, a crowd gathered around them.

Mrs. Martin reached out for Jillian, but the little girl wasn't ready to let go of Gryph. She hugged his neck so tightly, he was afraid he might choke yet again.

When she finally loosened up enough to lean back and look into his face, her tears were making trails through the dust on her cheeks. "You saved me." She kissed his dirty face.

"Not me…" He turned to Selene and pulled her into the curve of his arm. "Selene was the one who led us to you."

Jillian tipped out of his arms into Selene's. "Thank you."

Selene chuckled and held the child, her own tears trickling, making mud tracks down her face. "I'm just glad I could help."

Mrs. Martin engulfed Selene and Gryph in a bear hug.

Gryph handed Jillian off to Mrs. Martin and stepped up to Balthazar's door, where the older man stood, regarding the dispersing crowd, his face grim. "Who would do that to a child?"

"It had to be someone we know," Gryph said. "Someone familiar with the tunnels and what's going on at the surface."

"But, why?"

The why baffled Gryph, as well. "It has something to do with me." Who had he angered so much so that he'd use a child to get to him?

"Why do you think that?"

"Why else would he leave the note on *your* door?"

Balthazar rubbed his chin. "He could have been targeting me."

Shaking his head, Gryph said, "No. He took Jillian to the forbidden zone. The very area I warned you would be unsafe while demolition and construction is going on at the surface. It's one of the construction sites *my* company is responsible for. He did it deliberately to get me there at that exact time, knowing the demolition team would blow the building today. He knew *I'd* go and *you* would stay here to keep the people calm." He stared out at the emptying space. "I don't know who did it, but I intend to find out."

"It has to be someone who knows the people of the Lair and your business on the surface. Someone privy to your warning to stay clear of the forbidden zone."

His back stiffening, Gryph stared out at the junction station that had been his home since before he was old enough to remember. Though he'd thought it before, it was clear, now. "It's one of our own."

* * *

Selene stood with her sisters as the people of the Lair thanked them for helping rescue Jillian. The whole time, her head hurt and she had difficulty forcing a smile.

At first she thought the pain an aftereffect of breathing too much dust. But the longer it persisted, the more convinced she was that it was something else. Something evil and so angry it created a darkness that threatened to cloud her mind. She glanced around, trying to figure out where it was coming from. Her gaze was drawn to the mouth of one of the unlit tunnels. Something moved in the shadows. Or at least she thought something moved. She stepped toward it, but a hand gripped her arm.

"Selene, are you okay?" Aurai leaned close. "You're shaking." She lifted one of Selene's hands. "And your hands are so cold."

Deme, Brigid and Gina gathered around, each of them examining her as if she was under a microscope.

The pressure of hatred increased at her temples. With as much conviction as she could muster, she said, "I'm fine." Her focus was drawn once again to the dark tunnel.

"Let's get you home and into the shower. Then you can take a long, much-needed nap."

Selene wanted to push away from her sisters and investigate the tunnel, but her siblings weren't going to take no for an answer, and after all they'd just been through, Selene didn't want to alarm them.

Before she knew it, they were hustling her back toward the tunnel they'd navigated from the stairs to the Lair.

Gryph fell in step beside her and took over, letting her lean on his arm. "Did that brick hit you harder than I thought? I can have a doctor pay a house call."

"No, no, I'm okay, really. It's just a bruise and barely hurts."

"Then why are you so quiet and weak?" He stopped, bringing her and her sisters to an abrupt halt.

"I..." She glanced back over her shoulder. The evil presence, filled with so much hatred that she'd sensed before, was gone. She straightened, her strength returning. "I felt something...but now it's gone."

Gryph gripped her arm and pulled her to a stop. "What did you feel?"

She shrugged. "Anger. Hatred." Selene grimaced. "Malevolence."

"Should I check the tunnel?" Gryph turned to do that.

Selene grabbed his arm. "No. Whatever it was is long gone. I need to get home and check on a few things before it gets any later."

"If you're worried about the charity ball, don't. I can have anyone you need sent to assist you."

"I don't need help. I just need to be back at my home."

Gryph hesitated a moment longer and then led them up the steps into his apartment.

Brigid tapped her fist into the punching bag hanging from the ceiling in the exercise room. "Quite a place you have here, Mr. Leone."

"Call me Gryph." He shrugged. "It's okay."

"Who drove?" Selene asked.

"I did," Deme responded. "Ready?"

"I am." Selene headed for the elevator, without turning back. After all that had happened between her and Gryph, the angry presence in the tunnel and with her sisters there in Gryph's apartment with them, their parting could be nothing but awkward.

As she stepped into the elevator car, Gryph's hand reached out and stopped her. "Selene, promise me you'll stay with your sisters."

She stared into his deep golden eyes, the electricity crackling between them.

"Don't worry, Gryph. One of us will be with her at all times," Deme said.

Gryph didn't let go of Selene's arm, his gaze never left hers.

"I promise," she whispered, her glance dropping to his lips, the urge to kiss him more than she could hide.

His hand slipped to the back of her head. "I'm going to kiss you, but not because *you* want me to, which I know you do. I'm going to kiss you because *I* want to."

Despite the dust, the muddy tear tracks and dirty hair, his lips claimed hers, bearing down on her mouth, the pressure soft at first then increasing in its intensity.

Selene leaned into him, all will to resist gone. She wanted him, and to hell with her reservations. She couldn't get enough of him and didn't want the kiss to ever end.

Someone cleared her throat behind Selene.

"You want us to wait in the car?" Brigid asked.

Selene pushed away from Gryph and brushed her dust-caked hair back from her face. "No, I'm ready." He let go of her arm and she stepped out of the doorway and back into the elevator. The doors closed and the car rose.

"Want to tell us what's going on between you two?" Gina asked.

What was going on and where would it go? Selene wasn't sure herself. She touched a hand to her lips and shook her head. "No."

Gryph showered, dressed in jeans and a T-shirt and hurried back down into the tunnels. Whoever was causing him problems, threatening the people he loved, would pay.

Jillian had been the pawn in this latest game. Amanda had only lived long enough to identify Gryph as her attacker. The killer had finished her off after she'd had the police forensics artist draw a sketch of him. Almost being run over by a truck at the pool hall hadn't seemed like an attack by the Devil's Disciples, either.

Since the attack on Amanda, the more recent attacks had hit closer to home. Closer to Gryph, making it more personal. And when he entered the Lair, he went directly to Balthazar's house. Balthazar had been his father, his mentor and the man he went to whenever he had a question or problem he couldn't resolve himself. Now was no different. In fact it was even more important. The people around him were in danger for just being around him. It had to stop.

He entered without knocking, Balthazar's home was just as much his as when he was a child. Voices sounded from the den on the opposite side of the home. Gryph followed.

"Gryph, I'm glad you came back." Balthazar waved toward the man standing behind him and stepped aside.

His brother, Lucas, sat at the table, his lip curled up on one side. "I understand I missed all the excitement."

The anger Gryph had held in check bubbled up and spilled over. "Damn it! This isn't a game. Someone is targeting me and the people around me for some very sick reason."

"And yet you always manage to come up smelling like a rose." Lucas grinned. "My big brother, the hero."

"I'd rather none of these things were happening. There's a dead woman and a terrified child who suffered because of me." Gryph paced the length of the den, across a red-and-gold Persian rug, without seeing the beautiful Victorian antiques Balthazar had collected over the years.

The room was a warm study in the culture and taste of a bygone era, a contradiction to the gloom and darkness of the tunnels, where it was located.

"Why would someone want to hurt these people? What have *they* done to deserve it?"

"Come, brother." Lucas rose from the table and draped

an arm around his shoulders. "You've conquered every obstacle in your rise to power. Surely a little mystery won't stump you for long."

Gryph shook the arm from his shoulder, his jaw clenched so hard it twitched. "I *will* find the one responsible."

"Now you're talking." Lucas grinned. "That's the self-assured brother I know and love. It's that certainty that has made you the man you are today. The rich philanthropist that gives all his wealth to the needy."

Gryph stared at his brother. Had there been a thread of contempt in his tone? "Is there something bothering you, Lucas?"

"Of course not. My life is just the way I like it."

Gryph had spent a considerable amount of time counseling Lucas on college and course work that would help him land a good job that would pay for the things he loved, like fast cars and expensive restaurants.

So far Lucas had been as human as any of the surface dwellers. Regrettably, he'd been raised in the Lair with little connection with the world above until he was a teen, venturing to street level at night when no one was looking. He'd fallen in with a gang of miscreants who'd rather deal in drugs than do an honest day's work. "Have you finished those online college courses I helped you sign up for?"

"I'm working on it. You and Father won't have to put up with me much longer."

"We don't *put up with you*. You're family. And a degree will go a long way toward building a career."

"With you as my role model, how can I go wrong?" Lucas smiled, which looked more like a sneer. "Now, if you'll excuse me, I have to go to work."

"You might check in on occasion," Balthazar said. "Things haven't been right lately and people are getting scared."

"Of what? That their safe little hiding place isn't so safe anymore?" Lucas shook his head. "We can't hide forever. Sooner or later, the world will know we exist."

Gryph knew it was only a matter of time, but the folks living in the Lair didn't want to be exposed any sooner than they had to be. The surface dwellers tended to be cruel when it came to people who were different on the outside.

What they didn't know was that while they might look very different on the outside, they were all the same on the inside, with emotions, fears and desires that transcended gender and species. An image of Selene filled his consciousness and his desire spiked and was immediately squelched as another thought hit him.

If he was the target of all that was happening, and the people around him were the collateral damage, Selene could be caught in the crossfire. He couldn't let that happen. Gryph left the Lair and headed back to his apartment. There was only one way to ensure Selene's safety.

Chapter 18

Back at her shop, Selene and her sisters took turns in the shower, then scrambled through Selene's closet for clean clothes. Then they crowded in the store with her, hovering like a bunch of mother hens. "I don't need five baby-sitters. You all can go home," she said, more irritably than she'd intended.

"We made a promise to have someone with you at all times," Deme said.

Aurai slipped her arm around Selene's waist and hugged her close. "If there's any chance someone might target you, he'll have to go through one or all of us."

"If you're trying to scare me," Selene grumbled, "it's working."

"Be serious, Selene." Brigid tossed a fireball in her palm. "We won't let what happened to Aurai, happen to you."

Selene gave her flame-throwing sister a pointed look. "We defeated the Chimera. The chances are pretty slim that there's another lurking beneath the city."

"That might be true. But this family sticks together." Gina stuck her hand in the center of the circle of sisters. "No witch left behind."

Brigid, Deme and Aurai covered Gina's hand with ones of their own.

Selene sighed and laid her hand over top for a brief

show of force, then dropped it to her side. "I appreciate your concern, but right now, I could use a little *alone* time to gather my thoughts."

"And think about the dreamy Gryphon Leone?" Aurai grinned. "He's very handsome without his shirt, what with all those lovely muscles and those six-pack abs." She fanned herself with her hand. "How does the rest of him stack up?"

"Aurai!" Selene's cheeks burned. "That's not something we discuss."

"Don't be such a prude, Selene." Aurai planted a fist on her hip. "I'm twenty-one and not a virgin. We all know you and the shifter are doing the nasty."

Her cheeks on fire, Selene turned away and punched the button on the shop's answering machine.

Selene had no fewer than fifteen messages from the combined forces of Mrs. Stockton and Mrs. Washburn. Each woman demanded to know why the costumes hadn't been delivered to the hotel with the charity ball only a day away.

"Damn." Selene clapped a hand to her forehead.

"What's wrong?"

"In all the excitement, I forgot to deliver the costumes. They were supposed to be at the hotel yesterday afternoon."

"We can deliver them," Gina offered.

Selene shook her head. "Deme, you and Brigid have a murderer to find. I would think your time would be better served out beating the streets to find the black wolf."

Brigid's cell phone buzzed and she glanced down at the display screen. "Speak of the devil, it's the boss." She punched the talk button, turned and walked a few steps away.

"We can't leave you alone," Deme said softly, but in that firm tone of an oldest sister used to giving orders.

"Even if we can't all stay, at least one of us will be with you at all times."

Selene knew they were hanging around because they cared. "Thanks."

Brigid ended her call and turned back to the group. "Well, Deme, that was our cue. The lieutenant got a tip on a secret meeting location of an unnamed wolf pack. We're to meet Cal at the station and go from there back to Archer Heights."

Deme gave Selene a stern look. "Stay with one of your sisters. Having backup isn't a sign of weakness."

"Tell me about it." Brigid snorted. "Deme saved my ass on our last assignment against that telepathic demon who tried to get me into his car. If she hadn't been there, who knows what he'd have done."

Selene nodded. "I get it. I'll keep a backup. Now go. We need to find that wolf before he attacks again. Call me if you need me to help with the investigation. And don't forget, I need help tomorrow night getting the waitstaff ready for the charity ball."

"We won't forget," Deme said over her shoulder as she followed Brigid out.

Gina and Aurai stuck to Selene like glue. They rode with her to the seamstress's shop to collect the costumes and back to Selene's to unpack and check over each garment. She ended up pulling five costumes of the hundred for rework. She and her sisters delivered the rest to the hotel in ten boxes.

When they returned to Selene's apartment, all three women flopped into chairs, exhausted.

"I think I could sleep for days," Aurai said, yawning into her palm.

"Nothing like fighting wolves and escaping a tunnel collapse to get your blood humming." Gina leaned her head back, closing her eyes. "But I think delivering costumes wore me out even more." She tipped her head up and stared at Selene. "How do you do it?"

"How do you clean fish tanks all the time?" Selene shivered. "All that slime and fish poop gives me the heebie-jeebies."

Gina shrugged. "I love the finished product—clean water and happy fish."

"Same here. I like the finished product of beautifully dressed people."

"Speaking of beautifully dressed people…" Gina's eyes narrowed. "What are you wearing to the ball? Are you keeping your gown a surprise or something?"

Selene blinked. "I haven't got a gown because I'm not attending the ball. You know how expensive the tickets are."

"Let me get this straight…" Aurai's brows rose. "You don't get in free for all the work you've done?"

"I'm getting paid for my work. That's enough for me. Besides, the ticket money goes to a children's charity. It's a good cause."

"Oh, come on, admit it," Gina said. "You'd love to go to that ball."

"Think of the hundreds of yards of expensive fabric and gowns made by the world's top designers," Aurai continued, painting a picture with her words. "Sparkling jewels, gorgeous hairstyles, the crème de la crème of Chicago society decked out in their finest. A ball fit for royalty." She swung out her arm with dramatic flourish.

Selene had dreamed about attending, imagining the beauty of the decorations and the people dressed in their finest. It would be truly magical. But even with the money she'd make with the fairy costumes she'd designed for the staff, she couldn't afford to plunk down thousands for a ticket. "It's just a ball. They're only people. I have no interest in going," she lied.

"Aren't you in the least interested in seeing Gryphon in a tux?" Aurai's sly smile didn't fool Selene a bit. The girl was digging for information.

Again, Selene felt it necessary to lie. "No."

"Oh, come on, can't you imagine all those fabulous muscles contained in a tailored black tux." Aurai smacked her lips. "Yum."

Hell, yeah, she'd imagined Gryph in a tux. But she'd seen him in a whole lot less, leaning over her in the bed, making love to her until she cried out. Heat spread down her neck into her chest and lower, pooling between her legs.

As tired as she was, Selene pushed out of her chair and paced the floor. Sure, like any woman who loved fashion and beautiful clothes, she'd dreamed of attending a beautiful ball with music, dancing and men dressed in tuxedoes.

But this was different. Gryph was sponsoring the event and he hadn't invited her or expressed a desire for her to be there. It was a charity event he would barely tolerate and at which he'd probably make a five-minute appearance. Why should she want to be there with the backbiting society matrons picking apart every woman's outfit and hairstyle like the fashion police of Chicago? "Besides, I'm sure it's too late to purchase a ticket anyway."

"Ah ha!" Aurai sat up straight and pointed a finger at Selene. "I *knew* you wanted to go." She pulled her smart phone out of her pocket and clicked buttons.

Selene frowned. "What are you doing?"

"Going online to find a ticket for you," she said in a matter-of-fact tone.

"Oh, no you don't." Selene snatched the phone from her hands.

Aurai lunged for it.

Gina plucked the phone from Selene's hand and swung away. "Here's the website."

Aurai wrapped Selene in a hug, trapping her arms against her sides.

Selene struggled to free herself. "Let go. I'm not going to the ball. There are more important things to be concerned about."

Ignoring her protests, Aurai asked, "Any tickets left?"

A long pause and Gina looked up, her lips turning down on the corners. "Sold out."

Aurai released Selene.

"See?" Selene stepped away from her sister, hiding her disappointment. "It wasn't meant to be."

Not as convinced she should give up, Aurai touched a finger to her chin. "We have to think of a way to get her in."

"I'm not going."

Aurai grinned at Gina. "She doth protest too much, methinks."

"Me, too."

Selene rolled her eyes then pinched the bridge of her nose to force back the growing headache. "I need rest. To-morrow is a busy day. I have five costumes to alter and deliver, and I want to be in the staff area before it starts to make sure everything fits and looks right." And maybe she'd catch a glimpse of Gryph. Selene glanced at her wristwatch and swallowed a groan. She hadn't been with him for all of six hours and she was counting the minutes until she saw him again.

Damn. She had a business, a home and her sisters. She didn't need the complication of falling for a man, much less falling for a man who wasn't human.

Gina's eyes narrowed. "Are you in love with him?"

Damn. Was everyone becoming a mind reader? Selene shook her head. "No, no, I'm not. Other than an animal attraction—no pun intended—he's not my type."

"You mean your type isn't tall, broad-shouldered and gorgeous?"

"Look, I'm not in the market for happily ever after."

"So, you're in the market for miserable and lonely?"

"Of course not. I'm not miserable, and I'm not lonely."

"Then why have you been checking the time ever since we left the Lair?"

Her cheeks burned and the heat spread down her neck. "I'm not watching the clock." Unable to stop herself, she glanced at her watch again. This time she did groan. "Okay, so I'm clock-watching. The ball isn't very far off. I'm tense, keyed-up and second-guessing my work."

Gina snorted. "Yeah."

"Honey..." Aurai crossed her arms over her chest, her lips twisting into a wry grin. "You're wondering when Gryph will walk through that door, sweep you off your feet and kiss you like there's not gonna be a tomorrow."

"No, I'm not." Though the thought made her knees weak. She had to admit she was disappointed he hadn't come by to check on her. The sun had set and still he hadn't dropped in or called. "I'm going to get a shower and go to bed."

"I call dibs on the couch," Gina said.

Aurai shrugged. "Fine. I'll take the chaise. I feel decadent when I sit on it." The piece was in a rose-and-burgundy red fabric, an antique from a 1930s boudoir. Selene had found it scuffed and torn in a flea market. She'd brought it home and lovingly restored it to its former glory.

"You two do whatever makes you happy. Good night."

Selene grabbed clean underwear and her favorite, worn nightgown and headed down the hallway to the only bathroom, closing the door behind her.

As she stripped out of her clothing, she couldn't help thinking about Gryph. Standing naked in front of the tub, she touched her fingers to her breasts, imagining Gryph's hands there instead of her own. So sensitized by her imagination, her nipples tightened into hard little buds. The least little flick set off electrical charges, bursting along her skin and sending a rush of liquid lust to her core.

She stepped beneath the shower's spray and let the water wash down her chest to the mound of curls over her sex. A soft moan left her throat.

"Are you all right in there?" Gina asked.

Selene raised hands to her taut nipples and said, "Yes." More than all right, she was well on her way to one-handed sex. It would be every bit as good as the real deal she'd shared with Gryph.

Yeah, right.

"Let us know if you need anything," Gina called out.

She needed something, all right—a man. And not just any man. Gryphon Leone was the only man who knew exactly how to scratch her itch. But he had too much on his mind to think about her. Lives depended on him. Sex was only a distraction.

She built a foaming lather with the bar of soap and slid her hands down over her breasts, plumping them in the warm water, continuing the descent to her nether regions. Her channel clenched in anticipation. If only her hands weren't so soft. If only they were the big coarse hands of a man who did more than push paper for a living.

She parted her folds and stroked herself with the tip of her finger, sending shards of sensations shooting across her nerves, lighting a fire deep in her core. Her breath caught in her throat and she stroked again. She wished Gryph was there. He was so much better at this. But in a pinch...

Dipping a finger into her channel, she swirled it around, testing how wet and ready she was.

For what? Her battery-powered pleasure device? Who was she kidding? Nothing was better than the real thing.

Yet, she'd been as guilty about pushing Gryph away as he'd been. By the goddess, she wanted him!

She rinsed the suds and lathered her hair with the sweet scented shampoo, scrubbing hard as if to wash the man out of her head before she ducked under the water.

A scraping sound penetrated the blast of water in her ears. She pulled back out of the water to listen.

At the same time, big rough hands slipped around her belly and pulled her back against a hard, muscular body.

She tensed, sucked in enough air to scream.

"Shh. It's me," Gryph whispered against her ear.

Leaning into him she let go of the tension of the day, reveling in a different kind of tautness blossoming in her belly and spreading outward. She reached behind her and grasped his buttocks, pressing him into her, his member nudging her behind.

"How did you avoid the gauntlet of my sisters?"

"What gauntlet? The minute I arrived, they disappeared."

"Some protection they were."

"They did tell me to call them if you needed anything. Do you want me to call them?" He nibbled her earlobe then trailed kisses along the curve of her neck.

"No."

"Do you want me to leave?"

"No."

"What do you want, Selene?"

She curled her fingers around his and pushed them lower, to cup her sex. "This." With her hands guiding him, she pushed one of his big fingers into her channel. "Touch me."

"My pleasure." With one finger sliding into her folds, the other rising up to cup her breast, Gryph had her complete attention.

"Holy hell, I missed you," he breathed against her skin.

"Ditto," she rasped as he flicked that highly sensitive bundle of nerves and sent her body and mind shooting skyward.

"How much?" he asked, his rough tongue sliding down her shoulder, his teeth nipping along the way.

"Enough." She turned, pressed against him, chest to chest, wrapped her arms around his neck and drew his head down until her breath mingled with his. "What took you so long?" She claimed his lips.

Laughter rumbled up his chest, dying off before it could escape his throat. He lifted her, pushing her up against the cold shower tiles, circling her legs around his waist. Nothing could cool the heat raging inside her.

Selene locked her ankles, her wet entrance rubbing against his erection. "What's taking you so long now?"

He grasped her face in his hands and then kissed her long and hard, his hips rocking against hers, yet he refused to penetrate. When he tore his lips from hers he spoke in a low growl. "Promise me…"

"Anything."

"Stop me when I get too rough." He held her motionless, his gaze glued to hers.

Selene could tell by the intensity of his expression, this meant a lot to him. She laid a hand against his cheek and brushed a kiss across his lips. "I promise."

With her gathered in his arms, he swiped the curtain aside and grabbed a foil pack from the counter. Water sprayed out on the floor.

Selene didn't care, desperate for him to slide the condom over his engorged manhood and enter her in one long powerful thrust. She ached to feel him deep inside, filling her, stretching her, making her scream with desire.

With painfully slow movements, he took his time, centering then rolling the prophylactic down.

With a tight huff, she brushed his hands aside and finished the job.

His laughter echoed against the bathroom walls, but he didn't prolong her torture, entering her like she wanted, fast and hard, driving deep, her back banging against the wall. That little bit of pain, coupled with his intense hammering, rocketed her to the edge of reason.

She dug her fingers into his shoulders and screamed out his name as her body shook with the force of her release.

Gryph rammed into her once more and held, his face tight, half-morphed into the beast. When he came back to earth, he looked down at his hands, his claws extended, digging into her buttocks, trickles of blood dripping into the shower's spray.

"Damn!" He lifted her off him and set her on her feet, turning her so that he could assess the damage, his heart squeezing hard in his chest. "You promised to stop me."

She tried to hide the puncture wounds. "They're just scratches."

"I did that."

"Yeah, and that was the best sex I've ever experienced." She reached up to cup his face, a face he knew would be half man, half beast.

Gryph knocked her hand away, regretting his anger as soon as he let loose. "I'm sorry." He stepped out of the tub onto the bath mat and reached for his clothing. "I keep saying never again, but then I can't seem to keep my hands off you."

"Then don't." She climbed out and stood in front of him, pressing a finger to his lips. "I enjoyed every moment. And if I'm not imagining it, so did you."

"I don't enjoy hurting you."

"You didn't."

"For the love of heaven, woman, you're bleeding!" He

jammed his feet into his jeans and flung his shirt over his shoulder. "I'll understand if you want me to leave. Aurai said call her if you wanted her to come back tonight."

"Don't make me call her." Selene reached out with her mind. He could feel her strong pull. "Stay." She leaned into him, her hands circling his neck.

He shook his head, and dragged her arms down to her sides. "I shouldn't. Every time we make love, I hurt you."

Selene's jaw firmed. "It's okay."

"No, it's not. I don't want to." He brushed a thumb across her lips and bent to kiss her.

His phone buzzed from where he'd left it on the counter. Ignoring it, he deepened the kiss. But it buzzed again. Finally, Gryph lifted his head and stared down at Selene. "Hold that thought." Then he reached for his phone. Two text messages glowed on the screen.

The first from the lieutenant at the police department. "Got a lead on the black wolf. Call me."

Gryph's heartbeat ratcheted up and his jaw tightened. A lead on the black wolf was what he'd needed, but he didn't want Selene involved.

Selene wrapped her arms around his waist and laid her cheek against his back. "What is it?"

"I'm needed at the office."

Her arms tightened. "Now?"

He turned in her arms and pressed a kiss against her soft brown hair. "'Fraid so."

"Sure it can't wait?" she asked, her hands splaying out across his back and sinking lower.

Gryph captured her arms and pulled them away from him. "As much as I'd like to stay, I have to go. Duty calls."

"Then I'll come with you."

"No. You have a gala to prepare for."

Her lips firmed. "If I didn't, I'd go with you."

As he dressed, Gryph shot a glance at her. "I'll call Aurai and have her come stay with you."

"I'm okay on my own."

"I'd feel better if she came."

"I'd feel better if you stayed." She wrapped her arms around his waist and buried her face against his chest. "I wish you didn't have to go."

"Me, too." He kissed her one last time. "But I have to."

He hurried out the door and up the stairs to the street above. Night had enveloped the city in darkness, broken up by streetlights dotting every other corner. Neon lights blinked to life, advertising beer and vacancies.

Gryphon's heart throbbed with a heaviness he couldn't dispel. Reluctant to leave Selene unaccompanied, he called Aurai.

She answered with a bright "Hello."

"It's Gryph."

"Oh. Everything all right?"

"Can you stay with Selene tonight?"

"Of course," she answered. "You two have a fight?"

His hand tightened around his cell phone. "No. I want to find the black wolf."

"So you're going to join Deme, Brigid and Cal?"

"Why?" he asked, his curiosity peaked. "Where did they go?"

"Somewhere in Archer Heights. The lieutenant got a tip that the black wolf had been spotted with a pack of rogues. They went to investigate."

"Without backup?"

"I don't know. They left Gina and I in charge of being Selene's backup until you showed up."

"Why didn't they call me before they left?"

"Ha!" Her bark of laughter grated on Gryph's nerves. "You seemed to have other things on your mind."

He ignored her innuendo, focusing on what needed to

be done versus what he wanted to do. "Do you know the exact location your sisters were headed?"

"No. And I don't understand why they didn't take all of us sisters. We're stronger together."

Gryph figured he'd only seen the tip of the iceberg that was the power of the five witches. "Are you good with staying with Selene?"

"I'd rather be out looking for the black wolf," Aurai admitted. "But if Selene needs me, I'm there."

"She needs you."

Aurai sighed. "Okay. I'll be there in a few minutes."

Gryph clicked the off button and walked to the end of the block, keeping to the shadows. He wouldn't leave until Aurai arrived.

While he waited, he checked in with the lieutenant and got the same information he had passed on to Cal, Deme and Brigid.

"Deme said you were a big help the other night," the lieutenant said. "They could use your assistance again, tonight."

He assured him he'd be on it as soon as he was sure Selene was safe.

As he leaned against a brick building, his gaze returned to the apartment where Selene lived. Why couldn't he control his inner beast? All his life, he'd worked hard to know the signs, to suppress the animal when it rose to the surface. With Selene, he lost all sense of time and presence. He became one with her, forgetting who and what he was.

And each time, he'd drawn blood.

Aurai arrived, parking against the curb in front of the building.

Gryph remained in the shadows until Aurai made it safely into the apartment. Then he stripped off his shirt and shoes and let his beast free.

On all fours, he ran through the streets, avoiding people,

staying in the deepest shadows, out of sight. He ran until he could run no more, clearing his thoughts, grounding himself in what must be.

When he looked up to see where he was, he found himself in Archer Heights, several blocks over from the pool hall they'd barely escaped from the other night. For thirty minutes, he ran through the streets, checking any suspicious locations until he came to a group of warehouses surrounded by a run-down chain-link fence.

Slipping through the darkness, moving from shadow to shadow, he inched closer, recognizing the scent of wolves.

After studying the building for a full fifteen minutes, he located all the sentries. Wolves stood at each corner, two on the roof and one near a door at the rear of the building.

Keeping back and downwind to remain undetected, Gryph wondered what was going on inside that required guards and so many standing watch.

About the time he decided to move in, the door opened and several wolves strutted out, and then broke into a run.

Five or six men dressed in jeans and dark shirts emerged, looking back over their shoulders. The men mounted motorcycles and raced away from the building.

Gryph thought that was all of them, but then a woman in a short sexy dress and killer heels stepped out of the building and held the door.

Moments later, a large black wolf exited, head up. He paused for a moment, sniffing the air, his head moving slowly in a 180-degree turn until it stopped, his nose pointed directly at Gryph.

The hackles rose on the scruff of Gryph's neck, his muscles bunching, ready to defend his position.

After a long moment staring in Gryph's direction, the black wolf's shoulders gave what could only be considered a shrug and he turned toward the female, following her to a limousine. Again, she held the door for him. He jumped in and she climbed in beside him.

The limousine left the warehouse through an open gate, headed north.

A shiny new SUV burst from a side street. Gryph recognized Deme in the driver's seat and he leaped into the middle of the road, blocking its path, roaring so loud the sound echoed off the buildings.

The SUV screeched to a halt and Cal and Brigid dropped out, Deme remaining behind the wheel.

Cal pointed a nine-millimeter pistol at Gryph.

Brigid held a fireball in her hand, cocked and ready to throw. "You better be Gryph or you're going to get a mouthful of fire from one angry witch. I nearly wet my pants."

As proof, Gryph partially transformed to human.

Deme jerked her head and shouted, "Get in."

Cal claimed shotgun, Brigid held the back door open.

Gryph jumped in and Brigid slid in next to him.

Deme slammed her foot to the accelerator and sped after the limousine, taking a corner so fast, Brigid was thrown against him.

Brigid righted herself, a frown denting her brows. "I don't know if I'll ever get used to sitting so close to a lion shifter."

Within seconds, Gryph completed his change to human. "Better?"

She nodded. "Much." She smirked. "Though I don't know what's more disturbing. Sitting next to a changeling or a hot-bodied, naked male. I see why Selene is smitten."

Deme raced to the end of the street, where it T-junctioned, and let the SUV drift halfway past the stop sign. Everyone glanced in both directions.

The limousine was a quarter of a mile to the south,

turning onto a street Gryph knew to ramp up onto the expressway.

"Hurry. If they get on the expressway too far ahead of us, we might miss what exit they take."

Deme gunned it, turning the wheel hard to the right. The back end of the SUV fishtailed and straightened before the tires got enough traction to propel the vehicle forward.

With the limousine turning farther ahead, Gryph could only hold his breath and pray they didn't lose it.

As they neared the turn the limousine had made, the SUV was rammed from behind, jolting them forward.

A black sedan with dark tinted windows slid up beside them and swerved over, broadsiding their vehicle.

"Hey!" Deme yelled. "I just got issued this SUV."

"Yeah, but now you're pissed off. What are you gonna do?" Brigid prompted as she crawled across Gryph to hit the button that slid the window downward. "I know what I'm gonna do." She balled up a flame and slung it like a professional baseball pitcher, straight at the windshield. The fireball landed and scattered, making no difference to the driver, who slammed into them again, throwing Brigid back onto her side of the vehicle.

The passenger seat window lowered and a deadly look-ing rifle barrel poked out.

"They have guns!" Gryph shouted.

Deme swerved toward the attacking vehicle, slamming into the passenger door.

The gunman ducked backward, the rifle barrel disap-pearing for a moment.

Gryph knew it wouldn't be for long. He rolled his win-dow all the way down and, using his great balance as a feline, crawled out on the edge of the window, holding on to the oh-shit handle. When the rifle barrel poked out again, Deme jerked her steering wheel, aiming the SUV at the side of the sedan.

Gryph seized his opportunity and leaped across the small gap, grabbed the top of the other vehicle and held on as the driver jerked back and forth in an attempt to dislodge him. It only made him angrier and even more determined to bring the vehicle to a halt. The gunman leaned out, trying to get a bead on the half man, half cat clinging to the roof.

Grabbing the barrel of the weapon, Gryph yanked it out of the gunman's hands, threw it to the street and sank his claws into the man's arm, dragging him halfway out of the vehicle.

The man screamed in pain, his face elongating, his nose stretching into that of a wolf.

Before he could fully transition, Gryph jerked him the rest of the way out of the car and dropped him to the pavement.

He rolled into the path of the vehicle still trailing them, causing the driver to slam on his brakes too late to avoid the body.

The car hit the shifter and bumped over him before it came to a halt straddling the limp form. Another gunman leaned out the passenger seat window aiming at Gryph, who was still clinging to the rooftop.

A bullet pinged into the metal roof near his hand. Another shattered the back windshield.

The driver continued to swerve back and forth as they neared the ramp to the expressway. The limousine had pulled way ahead, cleared the ramp and shot into the ever-present Chicago traffic.

Deme rammed the sedan with the heavier SUV, forcing the car up on a sidewalk, headed straight for a telephone pole.

Gryph saw it and leaped to the side at the last minute, hit the ground and rolled to his feet as metal crashed into wood.

Deme brought the SUV to a halt and all three passengers jumped out.

"You okay?" Deme asked.

Gryph straightened and dusted himself off before going back to the vehicle wrapped around the pole.

"Quite the acrobat." Brigid chuckled as she caught up to him. "Kind of handy to have around, ya know?"

"Deme, call for an ambulance and also have them run the license plate while we check for survivors and take care of the tail vehicle," Cal ordered.

Gryph glanced into the vehicle—the people inside weren't moving. A driver, and a passenger in the backseat. The vehicle that had run over the gunman wasn't going anywhere and the occupants were bailing.

Gryph roared, dropped to all four paws and ran after them, catching the slowest man, letting the others go. They'd lost heart in shooting him, preferring to sacrifice one of their own to guarantee their escape.

Gryph pounced on the slowest man, slamming him face-first into the pavement. When the man tried to get up, he planted a foot in the middle of his back and applied enough pressure to keep him immobile.

Cal and Brigid gathered around in time to see the man's attempt to shift into a wolf.

Leaning close to the man's ear, Gryph growled—a low, dangerous sound. "I wouldn't do that, if I were you."

The man's transformation receded and he lay still. "What do you want?"

"To know why you tried to kill us?"

He snorted and refused to answer.

"Perhaps you need a little persuasion." Gryph grabbed the man's arm and yanked it up the middle of his back.

His captive grunted, sweat popping out on his forehead, but refused to enlighten them.

"Let me give it a shot." Brigid dropped to her haunches.

"Do you know what it feels like to have your flesh burn until it melts off your body? Every nerve in your body screaming for it to stop?" She twisted her wrist and brought up a ball of wicked-looking flame.

The man's eyes widened and his face paled.

"Maybe I'll just go for the eyes and burn them out of your head." Brigid gave him an evil grin and moved the ball of fire so close the heat turned his cheeks red.

"No! Please, don't!" The man squirmed and bucked in an attempt to throw Gryph off his back.

Gryph leaned harder on the arm until the man almost passed out.

"Okay, okay! I'll talk!" He lay with his face pressed into the asphalt, his eyes on the fireball. "Want do you want to know?"

"Who's in charge?"

"Black Wolf."

"That's it? That's all you've got for me?" Gryph tightened up on the arm. "His name."

"That's what he calls himself. I swear," the man cried.

"Where can I find him?"

"We don't find *him*, he finds *us*."

"That limousine has to park somewhere."

"It's rented."

Gryph glanced up at Deme. "Did anyone get the license plate?"

Deme shook her head. "Got away too fast."

"Someone has to know how to get in touch with Black Wolf." Gryph growled. "A second in command? The woman? Who are they? My patience is wearing very thin."

"Brayden. Brayden Sellers is his second, now. Miriam Crestley is the woman. They arrange for his transportation. Ask them."

"If you know anything else, now's the time to tell. And

if you're lying to us—" Gryph dropped his voice into a menacing whisper "—we'll kill you."

The man closed his eyes, his body shaking. "It doesn't matter. They'll kill me anyway for what I just told you."

Gryph let go of the man's arm and straightened. "Then get out of here. Get out of town. Just don't let me catch you anywhere near Archer Heights or Black Wolf again."

Deme was on the phone with the lieutenant, relaying the names and the location of the wrecked car and the dead man. When she hung up, she tipped her head toward the SUV. "Let's go. We have an address. And, Gryph, Cal's gym bag is on the floorboard."

Cal chuckled. "There's a pair of sweatpants in it."

Gryph left the informant lying in the middle of the street, barely feeling sorry for the shifter who'd tried to kill him. He should never have fallen into the group of rogue werewolves to begin with.

The team climbed into the SUV. Gryph found the bag and the pants, pulling them up over his naked legs. They headed to an area Gryph was familiar with. Lincoln Park, filled with some of the most luxurious homes in the city and on top of some of the oldest tunnels. The homes here were as old as the money.

"Why are we here?" he asked.

"Miriam Crestley lives here. Or at least her father and mother do," Deme said. "She's the daughter of a man whose family helped establish Chicago."

"I'm sure they'll be pleased to know who their daughter is hanging out with."

They parked in front of a stately white stone mansion with towering oaks and lush landscaping. Deme turned to the others. "Let me and Cal handle this."

Without a shirt and shoes, Gryph was more than willing to take a backseat to this part of the investigation.

When Cal and Deme returned, they were both frowning.

"Thomas Crestley said that Miriam is staying with her boyfriend in a loft in the Gold Coast area. He wasn't sure where. He did, however, say that she was expected to be at the charity ball, and suggested we talk to her there."

"Did the lieutenant have an address for Brayden Sellers?"

"No. Seems the address on his license is old and he's moved around since."

"Damn. We're back to square one."

"No, we have tomorrow night at the ball to corner Miriam," Brigid argued. "*If* we had tickets to get in."

"I can get tickets. How many do you need? Three?" Gryph asked.

"Yes," Deme said.

"No. We need six." Brigid gave Deme a sharp glare.

Deme cleared her throat. "Right. We need six."

"Okay. I'll have a courier send them over in the morning." Gryph leaned back in his seat, tired to the bone. They had been so close to finding out the identity of Black Wolf.

"Do you want me to drop you off at Selene's?" Deme asked.

He wanted to go back to Selene's. But he couldn't risk it. "No. Take me to my building. Please."

Brigid crossed her arms. "I thought you liked my sister."

"I do. But that's beside the point."

Deme pulled up to the GL Enterprises building and Gryph hopped out, thankful the interrogation was over and he could get on with his life…without the complication of falling for a witch with four very concerned and nosy sisters. He slammed the door and walked away.

If only it was easy to walk away from Selene.

Chapter 19

"Get up, we have a lot to do today and no time to waste."

Aurai's cheerful voice blasted Selene out of a lovely dream where she and Gryph were making love on the tropical island of St. Croix, away from the noise and traffic of Chicago, surrounded by sun and sand.

She'd been there once to visit Deme when she'd been working as a private investigator. The climate was idyllic, the beach clean and beautiful and the sun so bright it could blind you and you wouldn't care.

Selene raised her arm to shield her eyes from the overhead light. "I don't have to be up until eight."

"Honey, it's nine."

"What?" Selene sat up straight, flinging back the covers. "Why did you let me oversleep?"

"You were smiling and moaning. It must have been a pretty good dream. Were you with Gryph?"

"No." Selene's cheeks heated with her lie and she regretted it immediately. "Yes."

"Is he as good in bed as he looks like he'd be?" Aurai lifted one of the pillows and plumped it.

Selene's thighs clenched, her body warming to the memory of him inside her. "Yes."

Crushing the pillow to her chest, Aurai sighed. "I hope I find someone that makes me look that dreamy."

"Yeah, well, it's not all roses and sunshine." Selene climbed out of bed.

"Why not?" Her sister followed her through to the bathroom.

"Do you mind?" Selene shut the door and leaned her forehead against it, tears pooling in her eyes when she thought about how quickly Gryph had run out the door last night. And she'd been the one to worry about influencing him—using her powers to make him want to stay. Apparently he had enough willpower to resist. He probably wasn't that into her.

"So you like him, huh?" Aurai said through the door.

Selene moaned and refused to answer, going through her morning routine, relieving herself, then climbing into the tub for a stimulatingly cool shower that did nothing to quench the embers burning low in her belly. With Gryph on her mind, she couldn't eliminate thoughts of him down the drain with mere water.

She washed her hair, applied conditioner and rinsed, then turned off the water, grateful for that little bit of time she'd had without having to answer her sister's questions. Wrapping a towel around her body, she left the bathroom and entered her bedroom.

Aurai stood with her eyes shining, a smile spread across her face and something in her hand.

"Why the silly grin?" Selene wasn't in the mood for happiness. Not when she'd been rejected by the only man she'd found interesting in a very long time. Interesting *hell*. Possibly the only man she'd *ever* found so intensely attractive and captivating.

Aurai squealed and hopped up and down. "We're going to the ball!"

Selene frowned. "I know we're going to the ball, preferably early enough to get the staff ready in their costumes."

"No, silly. We're going to the charity ball as guests."
She waved two tickets in Selene's face, her hand shaking.

Selene had to grab it to make her stay still.

"How can that be? These tickets are worth ten-thousand
dollars each."

"That's right." Aurai grinned. "And there were two of
them."

"This must be a mistake." She turned them over.
"Where did you get these?"

"A courier just delivered them in this." Aurai handed
her an envelope.

Her stomach fluttered and her pulse kicked into panic
mode as she turned the packet over and read the return
address. GL Enterprises. Her heart beat faster then settled
like a lump of lead in her belly. "I'm not going."

"What?" Aurai stared at her like she'd grown two heads.
"You most certainly are."

"You take my ticket. Invite a friend." She handed the
ticket to Aurai. "I'm not one of Chicago's elite."

"Neither am I. But we have tickets." Her sister held
up her hands. "We're *both* going, and I won't take no for
an answer." Aurai marched to Selene's closet and riffled
through her dresses. "Don't you have a ball gown you
can wear?"

"I don't go to balls. Why would I keep a ball gown in
my closet?" Selene shook her head. "I'm not going. I don't
have a dress. I don't have time to shop, and it wouldn't matter if I did. I couldn't afford the kind of dress they wear."

Aurai faced her, a frown pulling her brows together.

"Look, Gina just texted me that she, Deme, Brigid and
Cal all received tickets this morning, courtesy of GL Enterprises. We're all going, so you can't back out."

Selene's heart beat faster and her palms grew clammy.
To be seen in a ball gown, dressed to the nines in the company of the man she feared she was already in love with

would be too much like Cinderella going to meet Prince Charming. It was too surreal. She couldn't go.

"Don't even think it." Aurai shook her finger. "You're going. We'll find a dress for you and you'll be absolutely the prettiest girl at the ball."

"While a killer roams the streets." Selene snorted. "Seems kind of frivolous."

Aurai planted her fists on her hips, looking so much like their mother, it made Selene's heart hurt. "Who's to say that killer won't be at the ball tonight. With all those people there, someone would make a prime target. You and I both know Deme and Brigid will be close by, if not there. You also know our powers work better when we're all together. Gina said as much. We all need to go to support each other."

Damned if Aurai didn't have a point. Still, Selene didn't bother arguing. With five costumes to oversee the alterations of and a store to open, she had her work cut out for her. She didn't have time to shop for a dress and she was getting too close to Gryph. Now would be a good time to back off, play it cool. Not see him. Especially if he was to show up in a tuxedo, so handsome he was sure to melt her heart.

No. She didn't want to see Gryph.

Liar.

Truth was, she wanted to see him more than she could stand.

Selene worked with the seamstress and customers needing last-minute alterations, waited on customers and cleaned her shop through the morning and afternoon. She had Gina deliver the costumes to the hotel on her way to one of her jobs cleaning aquariums for a law firm near the hotel.

By keeping busy, Selene had little time to think about

Gryph, the killer or anything else, until two hours before she was due to be at the hotel. Funny how the world continued to turn, even after the loss of one woman's life.

Selene had promised the waitstaff she'd be on hand for any last-minute adjustments to their costumes and come hell or collapsing buildings, she'd be there.

Gina arrived five minutes before closing, carrying five long garment bags. "I figured you wouldn't have time to go shopping and Aurai wouldn't have time to stop by her apartment. So, I did, and brought several of her gowns for us to choose from."

"Oh, thank goodness." Aurai hurried to take some of the bags from her sister. "We have just enough time to go through the dresses, run a quick iron over them, do our hair and get to the hotel if we hurry."

Selene waved a hand over her calculator. "You two have fun. I'm still working."

"Come on, Selene," Gina said. "We need to get ready for the ball."

Selene stuck to her guns, refusing to consider Gryph, the tickets and the ball. Even though they'd been on her mind all day long. "It seems so frivolous to go to a ball when there's a killer out on the street."

"I was just getting to that," Gina said. "Deme, Brigid, Cal and Gryph almost caught up to the black wolf last night."

"What?" Selene glanced at her phone to see if there were any messages she'd missed. "I didn't get a call, no one let me know."

"He got away."

So after Gryph had left her place he'd gone on the hunt. Selene pinched the bridge of her nose. "Why didn't anyone tell me?"

Gina hefted the dresses in her arms, glancing around the shop. "Well, they weren't going to call anyone in the middle of the night. And I guess they've been busy chasing down leads all day. I just got a call from Deme a little while ago."

"Any progress?"

"They discovered the name of a woman who was seen with the wolf. She's supposed to be at the ball tonight. That's why we all got tickets. Gryph made it happen."

With a glance at the clock and down at her receipts and ledger, Selene muttered, "I wonder if I have time to call Deme for an update on the investigation."

"You can talk to her at the ball, she'll be there with Cal and Brigid." Gina hung the dresses on a hook on the wall. "Now hurry up, we have to get dressed."

"I'm dressed in what I'm going in."

Gina glanced at Aurai.

Their youngest sister shrugged. "You know how stubborn she can be."

"*She* is still in the same room." Selene gave them her best schoolmarm glare. "And I'm not stubborn. I'll be at the hotel, I'm just not going in to the ball other than to make sure my costumes fit."

Gina let go of a long steady breath, and then removed the garment bags from each, one at a time.

Despite her protestations, Selene couldn't help glancing at them, her heart twisting as Gina unveiled each dress. Aurai had been right. Selene had been the dreamer, imagining herself the scullery maid turned princess for the ball, and falling in love with a handsome prince. Only life didn't turn out that way. She was falling in love with a shifter. He was afraid of hurting her, and she was afraid of manipulating him with her psychic abilities to stay with her.

Secretly she was glad that so far he couldn't be pushed by her thoughts. But she'd lain awake all night wishing he was lying beside her, his arms wrapped around her, holding her close.

Selene shook away the mental images, prepared her receipts and locked her cash register. She was headed for the door to lock it when a delivery van pulled up outside.

"I don't have time for this," she muttered.

Aurai hung the dress she'd chosen on the hook and turned. "Do you want me to get it?"

"No, I'm here. I'll handle it." She opened the door as the deliveryman stepped down from the truck carrying a large box.

The sender's address read Mira Bella.

"I don't remember ordering anything from Mira Bella."

Shoving the pen and an electronic pad toward her, the delivery driver asked, "Are you Selene Chattox?"

"Yes."

"Then this box is for you. Sign here."

Selene scribbled her name and handed the device back to the man, who then shoved the box into her hands and left before she could protest again.

"What is it?" Gina leaned over her shoulder.

"I don't know."

"Oh, it's from Mira Bella!" Aurai clapped her hands, her eyes sparkling. "Only the most exclusive designer couture in Chicago."

"I know, but why did they send me a box."

"Open it and find out," Gina suggested.

Selene laid the box on the counter and slit the tape holding it together with a letter opener. Lifting the lid, a layer of tissue paper rose with it and fluttered to the ground, revealing a dress of exquisite lace and shear fabric that was the pale blue-green of glacier ice.

Her breath hitched in her throat, Selene lifted the gown out of the box and layers of glacier-ice taffeta and feather-soft gossamer curled around her legs, drifting across the floor like clouds.

"It's the most beautiful gown I've ever seen," Aurai whispered.

A small card fell from the folds and Gina bent to pick it up. "It's definitely for you."

"Selene" was written across the envelope in bold strokes. She handed the dress to Aurai, who held it as if it was magic and might disappear if she blinked her eyes.

The card read "Please come to the ball" with the initials GL scrawled beneath.

"That's it?" She turned the card over. What did she expect? A declaration of love?

Well, she wasn't getting it. Nor did she want it. He was a rich, influential recluse who happened to shift into a lion whenever he felt like it, and sometimes when he got carried away.

Her body tingled at the remembered feel of his catlike tongue laving the inside of her thigh and flicking her special nubbin of tightly packed nerves. Instantly, her insides were awash with desire.

She was a witch with the ability to push thoughts, read some minds and, on occasion, throw up a force field of sorts. Why did she think she needed him? They had nothing in common.

Nothing but mind-blowing sex.

Okay there was that. And he had gone to a great deal of trouble to choose a gown for her that suited her to perfection. She couldn't have come up with a better selection.

"Try it on." Aurai shoved the dress into Selene's hands.

The only reason she agreed was to answer the burning question: What were the chances he'd get the right size?

She locked the shop door and descended the back stairs into her apartment, her sisters on her heels.

"Just because I try this dress on doesn't mean I'm going to the ball." She said the words aloud to keep firm in her stance, though her resolve was definitely crumbling.

Laying the dress over her bed, she stripped out of the broomstick skirt and peasant blouse she'd thrown on that morning.

"Lose the bra, too," Aurai insisted. The bodice was sheer in all the right places with thick lace of the same glacier ice hue as the rest of the dress strategically layered over the breast area.

Selene unhooked her bra and, wearing only a pair of bikini panties, she stepped into the dress and pulled it up over her hips and torso.

Aurai zipped the back to just above the curve of her bottom, the back neckline plunging low, bearing so much skin, Selene felt positively naked.

"Sweet goddess, it's…" Gina began.

"Perfect," Aurai proclaimed on a sigh. "Look for yourself."

Aurai angled her in front of the full-length mirror hanging on her closet door.

Selene gasped. Was that really her? She looked so… surreal…almost ethereal, as if she was otherworldly. And more of her skin showed through the sheer bodice than she'd ever exposed in public when not on a beach.

If the dress wasn't so incredibly beautiful, it might be considered obscene.

Gina stood with her mouth open and her eyes wide. "Wow."

"No kidding, wow." Aurai took charge. "Get out of the dress and let's do your makeup and hair. You can't be seen in a dress like that without the face and hair to match.

"I'm not going," Selene muttered, although much less convincing this time.

Gina and Aurai glared at her, Gina speaking first. "Like hell you're not."

"It would be an absolute crime to let that dress go to waste," Aurai said.

"Then you wear it." Selene slipped the zip down and stepped out of, feeling as thought she'd lost part of herself in the process.

Aurai shook her head. "I'm shorter. The dress would drag and be ruined."

When Selene turned to Gina, her sister held up her hand. "It's not my color. Face it, Selene, it was made for you."

"Don't be silly." Selene stood in her underwear staring at a dress that practically called to her, trying to come up with any other excuse she could possibly live with. When it came right down to it, she *wanted* to wear that dress.

For Gryph.

Maybe he'd changed his mind. Or maybe he *would* if he saw her in a dress fit for a fairy princess.

"Come on, into the bathroom." Gina handed her a button-up blouse to wear while they applied makeup to her cheeks and eyes. Once they were satisfied with her makeup, Aurai swept Selene's hair up on the sides and let it fall in long, loose ringlets down her back, the rich brown shining in the lights from the mirror.

Selene stared into the looking glass feeling more like Alice having fallen down the rabbit hole. "That doesn't even look like me."

"Oh, honey, it does, and better." Aurai hugged her and applied her own makeup in a hurry, brushing her long blond hair back on one side and draping it over the opposite shoulder in loose waves.

Gina combed her straight hair back from her face and secured it in a sexy messy bun at her nape.

Selene smiled in the mirror at Gina and Aurai. "I have such beautiful sisters."

"If only you could see yourself as we do." Aurai flapped her hands. "Now, get into your dress, we have to catch a cab or we'll be late."

"Don't forget, I promised I'd help with the last-minute adjustments to the costumes." As Selene shoved her keys, driver's license and some cash into a slim silver clutch, her cell phone chirped with a text message from the event coordinator at the hotel.

Costumes are perfect, no need to come early.

Well, then, she was stuck in the dress, with no excuse to sneak in through the back of the ballroom.

Gina held up her cell phone. "Ready for me to call a cab?"

The buzzer on her apartment door rang.

"Another delivery?" Selene headed for the door, but Aurai beat her to it and peered through the peephole. "There's a man in a suit out there."

"Open the door and see what he wants."

Aurai opened the door.

"Pardon me, ma'am. Mr. Leone sent the limousine to collect you and your sisters and take you all to the charity ball."

Aurai squealed and hugged Gina. "We're going to the ball!"

Selene frowned. "What *didn't* he remember?"

"Please, Selene, stop looking the gift horse in the mouth." Gina rolled her eyes as she walked past her and up the stairs to the street, like a society debutante.

"Come." Aurai hooked her arm. "Our chariot awaits."

With a resigned sigh and a rising sense of anticipation, Selene stepped out of her apartment, gathered her skirt and climbed the steps. As she slid into the plush leather seats, a stabbing pain shot through her temples like a searing poker and a flash of another's anger overwhelmed her thoughts with its intensity.

She pressed her fingers to her temple and closed her eyes.

Aurai touched her arm. "Something wrong?"

The limo slid into traffic, leaving her street and the pressure of that someone else's powerful malice behind.

"I don't know. For a moment, I felt something. But now it's gone."

Aurai hugged her. "Hopefully, it will stay gone through the ball."

Selene stared out the window, trying to see into the shadows. Who had been watching them? And why? She prayed to the goddess whoever it was didn't follow them to the ball.

Gryph paced the floor of the penthouse suite on the top floor of the downtown Chicago hotel. The ball had begun over an hour ago. He'd had his bodyguard call no less than six times to the detail at the door, and still the limousine carrying the Chattox sisters had not arrived. He paced once more across the expensive carpet, arriving at the door, ready to hit the streets and look for them.

As he reached for the doorknob, the phone in his pocket vibrated.

He scrambled for it and read the incoming text message.

Chattox sisters have arrived.

The air rushed out of his lungs. He grabbed his tuxedo jacket and hurried for the elevator.

He punched the button that would whisk him straight to the ballroom level. Gryph counted the floor numbers, willing them to go by faster. The soft ping announcing his arrival at his destination couldn't come fast enough.

At last he stepped out of the elevator and into the ballroom's hallway, inhaling a mixture of the most expensive perfumes and colognes, none of which smelled as good as Selene's fresh, natural scent.

If someone had told him ten years ago that he'd be hosting a highly publicized event with thousands of people in attendance and that he'd actually make an appearance, he'd have laughed in his face. Now, he eagerly entered the ballroom teeming with the richest people of Chicago, dressed in their finest, not at all worried about shifting at an awkward moment and scaring these people out of their minds.

No, he worried more about where Selene was and if she would actually show up to the event after he'd run out on her.

His hands were clammy and his beast paced internally, anxious to see her as much as his human self.

Then a waft of her essence filtered through all the other warring aromas from the buffet of finger foods to the layers of hair spray used in each coiffure.

Was it her? He lifted his nose and inhaled deeply.

Yes.

Across the crowded floor, she practically floated into the room, the light from the crystal chandeliers glancing off her beautiful, rich brown hair, her eyes sparkling brighter than the diamonds in his breast pocket. And the dress fit her to perfection, just as he'd known it would, the delicate pale lace and filmy layers clinging to her curves. She turned around to say something to Deme behind her and Gryph's breath lodged in his throat.

He hadn't realized just how revealing the back of the dress was, dipping low enough to tempt a saint into naughty thoughts, hoping for a glimpse of the crevice between her buttocks.

His member jerked to attention, swelling beneath the soft folds of his tuxedo trousers. To hell with the ball. He wanted to spirit her away to the top of the hotel and make sweet love to her with the starlight shining through the floor-to-ceiling windows, moonlight the only thing covering her pale skin.

An older woman with blue-white hair and a pinkish gray gown stepped into his path.

He tried to go around her, but she moved to block him.

"Mr. Leone, may I have a word with you?"

Gryph dragged his gaze away from the beautiful Selene and looked down at the woman, who was vaguely familiar to him. "I'm sorry, who are you?"

She sniffed, her nose climbing a bit higher. "Mrs. Stockton. One of the organizers of this illustrious event."

"Oh, yes. I remember. You and your partner did a wonderful job pulling it together." Again he tried to step around her.

Her hand snaked out, snagging his elbow. "Yes, well, thank you. There is one other thing we need from you."

"My assistant will see to your needs. I really must go."

"Mr. Leone, your assistant cannot perform the function of giving the main speech and leading off the dancing. Only the sponsor of this event has that responsibility. And that, sir, is you."

He stared across the room where Selene had been standing and didn't see her. He frowned down at Mrs. Stockton. "What did you say?"

Her brow puckered. "It's time to make the speech thanking all the contributors and to lead off the first dance."

"I'm sorry. I thought I'd made myself clear. I don't give speeches."

"I suggest you make an exception. After all, it's tradition."

He opened his mouth to tell her what she could do with her traditions, but the orchestra in the corner played an introductory tune and the room grew silent, all gazes on him.

Damn.

A hotel employee appeared beside him and held out a microphone, clicking the on button.

Never having given a speech in public, Gryph stared

down at the mic for a long moment then up into the eyes of the woman he'd been searching for in the crowds.

Selene stood ten feet in front of him, an absolute vision. Gryph was afraid to blink lest she disappear.

She smiled at him and nodded toward him.

Mrs. Stockton took the proffered microphone, and tapped it before saying. "Ladies and gentlemen, it's my pleasure to introduce your host and sponsor for this event, Mr. Gryphon Leone." Then she placed the microphone in his hand and stood back.

Though he'd rather go talk to Selene, Gryph lifted the mic to his lips. A dozen flashbulbs went off, blinking like so many strobes, blinding him and making it impossible for him to see Selene. "Thank you all for attending the annual Children's Charity Ball. Your contributions will help the children of Chicago live better lives. I'm not one for long speeches so, if the orchestra will play, we should dance." He handed the mic to the appalled Mrs. Stockton, pushed through the reporters and strode across the floor to the only woman he cared to see in the roomful of people.

He bowed and held out his hand, a spark of apprehension assailing him when she hesitated to take it.

Then she smiled up at him, took his hand and stepped into his arms, moving with his steps to the swelling strains of a beautiful waltz.

For the first minute, they were alone in the middle of the dance floor, floating around the room. Even as others joined them, Gryph could only see Selene.

They moved in silent unison, him leading, her following, effortlessly as if their bodies were in tune with each other.

As the song ended and another began, he led her off the floor and to the refreshments table, handing her a glass of champagne.

"Thank you for coming."

"Why did you invite us as guests? We could have waited in the wings in case you needed us. Those tickets cost a small fortune."

He waved his hand. "The money isn't important. I wanted to see you again."

Her heart warmed. "And the dress?" She sipped her champagne, pinning him with her stare over the rim of the glass.

"I knew you wouldn't have time to shop, and when I saw it, I knew it was meant for you."

"Thank you. It's perfect." She sucked in a breath and let it out before saying, "Gryph, every time we've been together, you've claimed it was a mistake. Why do you keep coming back? Why do you do nice things for me when you know it'll only make me want to be with you more?"

"Because, saying I shouldn't see you and following through has proven harder than I anticipated."

"That makes two of us." Her face softened. "So, what are we going to do about it?"

"I don't want to hurt you."

"You haven't so far."

He frowned. "What if I go too far?"

"I'll take my chances."

"I'm not willing to risk it."

"Then why did you invite me here?"

"One: I wanted to see you again. Two, I think the black wolf might show up, or at least the woman who has been reported with him. And though I didn't want to involve you, I need you and your sisters to help me find him."

"Fair enough. Maybe once we nail the black wolf, you and I could figure out our situation?"

He nodded.

Before he could say anything more, Deme and Cal stepped up beside her.

"She's here," Cal said.

"Who's here?" Selene asked.

"Miriam Crestley." Brigid joined them from behind Deme and Cal, Aurai and Gina close behind. "The woman we saw with Black Wolf last night."

"Where?" Gryph stared over their heads, his gaze scanning the crowd.

"By the entrance." Cal glanced that way. "And she's with a man."

"You think he's the shifter?" Selene asked.

"I don't know, but he has black hair."

"So do about fifty people in the ballroom. It could be a coincidence," Aurai offered.

"True." Cal stared around the room. "But I don't believe in coincidence."

Gryph's jaw hardened. "Neither do I."

"Well, we can't all converge on them at once." Brigid flexed her hand sans the usual fireball.

"Why not?" Selene asked.

"If they get spooked, they might bolt," Deme said. "Like they did last night."

Cal led the way. "It's our job, let Deme, Brigid and I handle it." Deme and Brigid fell in step with him.

"We've got your back," Gina called out. "The rest of us can circle around."

"Gina and I can cover the door." Aurai, dressed in a soft rose-colored gown, looked no less bold than a soldier headed into battle.

"They could be dangerous," Deme warned. "If they make a run for it, don't do anything that will get you hurt, or that will hurt the guests."

Gina nodded. "Got it."

Cal clapped his hands once. "Then let's go."

Gryph grabbed Selene's elbow. "Stay with me."

"Wouldn't it be better if we spread out?" She tugged at

her arm, but he refused to release her. He wanted to know where she was in case things got dicey.

"Humor me, will ya?"

"You want me, and you don't. Make up your mind. You're making my head hurt," she muttered, pressing her fingers to her temples, but she didn't pull away as she let him lead her around the huge ballroom.

The closer they moved toward the entrance, the more Selene's feet dragged and her shoulders hunched.

Gryph came to a halt. "What's wrong?"

"I can feel…"

"Feel what?"

"Anger, resentment…so strong. Like…" She looked up, her eyes wide. "Like I did the other night. When I could feel someone watching us."

Gryph looked around, searching each face for one that stuck out as malevolent, dangerous and sinister. People laughed, talked and went on about the business of enjoying the ball, unaware of something menacing among them.

Then he spotted the girl. Blond hair piled high. A black dress slit up to her hip. Several men stood in front of her escort, blocking Gryph's view.

"He's here," Selene said softly, her head coming up, her stricken gaze straight ahead.

The crowd parted, revealing the man next to Miriam. A man Gryph recognized immediately.

His brother.

"What the hell is Lucas doing here?" He marched forward, wanting answers.

Selene gripped his arm. "That man, you know him?"

"Yes, he's my brother, Lucas."

Selene pressed her hand to her chest. "Oh, no."

"What?" Gryph was torn between the look on Selene's face and demanding to know why his brother had come to the ball with a woman who'd been consorting with the wolf who'd killed Amanda Grant.

He took another step, practically dragging Selene along with him.

"Gryph, he's not…"

"Not what?" He didn't slow, didn't stop when her hand squeezed his arm.

"Don't go there, Gryph. He's dangerous."

"If that's the case, then I want to know why."

Gryph stopped in front of Miriam and Lucas. "Why are you here?" he said, keeping his voice low to avoid disturbing the people around them.

Lucas waved a hand. "I have just as much of a right to attend this event as anyone who's paid good money to be here. It *is* a public event, is it not?"

"Why are you here with her?" Gryph nodded toward Miriam.

"Please, *dear* brother." Lucas's arm circled the woman's waist, dragging her against his side. "Miss Crestley is my date."

"And she was seen last night with a black wolf shifter. One we suspect killed Amanda Grant."

"Have you taken up spying?" Lucas's brows rose high on his forehead.

"I have since a shifter has taken to killing innocents. This woman is known to consort with a possible killer."

Miriam Crestley laughed, the sound harsh in Gryph's ears. "Lucas, darling. You didn't tell me your brother was so old fashioned. So now I'm a consort?" She laughed again.

Gryph's eyes narrowed into slits as his gaze shifted from the woman back to his brother. "I take it you knew she was hanging out with the black wolf." His gut clenched as it became clear. "Oh, brother, please tell me you're not involved with him, too."

Anger radiated from Lucas like a heat wave, his green eyes darkening to black, then red. "Since when do you care who I'm with?"

"I've always cared." Gryph laid a hand on his brother's arm.

Lucas shook it off. "You've been very busy making a fortune to squander on people who are too useless to live. The Lair should be destroyed. It's outlived its purpose."

Gryph stared back, refusing to back down. "What are you talking about?"

"It's time for the people of Chicago to know of the other creatures who walk among us." He snapped his fingers.

The doors burst open at the end of the ballroom and at the emergency exits on each side and wolves of all shapes, colors and sizes entered the ballroom.

Panic ensued with women screaming and people rushing toward the exits only to be stopped by a growling wolves. The crowd was herded into a huddle of scared humans at the center of the floor.

Gryph refused to break eye contact with his brother. "It was you all along."

"Took you long enough to figure it out." Lucas's lip curled up on one side. "You're not as smart as Father gives you credit for."

"I trusted you. I saw no need to suspect a man who I'd considered family."

"You left me in that sewer of a Lair." Lucas poked a finger into Gryph's chest. "But while you were topside making a name for yourself, I was struggling to find myself. When I was bitten and turned, it came to me. I needed to make a name of my own."

"We're brothers."

Lucas waved his hand at the wolves. "*These* are my brothers.

Holding Selene behind him, shielding her body with

his, he warned, "This can only end badly. These guests don't deserve to be frightened and your pack will only die."

"So be it." Lucas's face changed so quickly Gryph wasn't prepared. His brother lashed out at him with wicked teeth, ripping into his arm.

Lucas's beast burst out, his muscles and sinews ripping through the tuxedo, shredding it beyond repair. He swiped a giant paw at the animal he'd called brother. No more. This creature was cruel, inhuman, had killed innocents and was now out for blood. His blood.

At first, the anger pressing against Selene's mind worked to cripple her, to weaken her in a way she didn't know how to fight.

She could only watch as Gryph, fully transformed, lunged at Lucas, hitting him hard and knocking him on his back. They rolled toward the crowd of frightened people.

Screams filled the air. Men and women fell, trying to escape the ferocious battle between them. Wolves snapped at the guests, ripping through tuxedos and expensive gowns.

The woman who'd come with Lucas sneered at Selene. "You're all going to die. These people are so fake, pretentious and backstabbing. They deserve it."

"They do a lot of good for the children this charity supports."

"Only for the recognition they get, not because they're altruistic or give a damn about anyone but themselves."

"Right or wrong, it takes all kinds to make things work."

"Not all kinds. Our kind is shunned. But not anymore. And I might as well start with you." Miriam's face stretched, her nose elongating into the snout of a wolf.

Before she could fully transform, Selene shoved the woman backward so hard, she landed on her butt on the hardwood flooring and slid several feet away.

Selene turned and ran toward her sisters, who were trapped in the middle of the screaming humans.

Behind her Miriam growled.

Selene wouldn't make it to safety. She had to defend herself or die trying.

She ground to a stop, turned and focused all her thoughts on stopping Miriam.

Transformed into a white wolf, Miriam launched herself at Selene.

"Selene, look out!" Aurai cried, having worked her way to the edge of the crowd.

Selene could see her sister in her peripheral vision, but didn't acknowledge her, refusing to back down or let Miriam win.

The she-wolf flew through the air. A hair's breadth from Selene's face, she crashed in midair, sliding to the ground in an unconscious heap.

The room went wild. Wolves leaped at the guests, snarling and tearing at them with razor-sharp teeth.

Deme spun a web of vines from a nearby pot, throwing it over a group of six wolves, immobilizing them long enough for Selene to send out a thought for the crowd to part and allow Deme, Brigid, Aurai and Gina to stumble their way free.

With her sisters gathered around her, Selene concentrated on putting a halt to the madness, sending one thought after another into the minds of the crazed wolves.

At first they disregarded her push. Gina blasted their eyes with stinging spray from the lovely water fountain set up specifically for the event. Deme's clinging vines tangled around their feet and sent them sprawling and Brigid singed the hair and whiskers on more than a dozen. The wolves' fanatical attack waned, their strength draining in response to Selene's suggestions that they were tired and would never win this fight.

When Selene thought they had a good handle on most of them, she broke away from her sisters and went in search of Gryph and Lucas. The door into the garden gaped wide open. Selene could sense a powerful struggle taking place among the manicured bushes and flower beds.

Gryph had Lucas pinned to the ground. No matter how much the big wolf struggled, he couldn't work his way loose of the massive lion.

Slowly Lucas returned to human form, his struggles abating.

Gryph half changed, still pressing his weight into his brother. "Give up, Lucas. You're not going to win."

"I can't let you win. Not again. You always win."

"This is not a contest of who should win or lose. We are brothers."

"Father loved you more."

"Father loves all the people of the Lair."

"No. He loved your mother and he swore he'd take care of you and never reveal her secret. All because he loved her and wanted her to have a decent life."

"You're wrong."

"Ask him."

"Lucas, you're my brother, whether by blood or not doesn't matter."

"You'll never be my brother." Lucas turned his face away from Gryph, refusing to look him in the eye.

Selene could sense the loss and hurt in Gryph and wanted to go to him as he rose to stand on two feet. She could also feel the anger still churning in Lucas, and a sudden shift to an eruption of uncontrollable hatred.

"Gryph, look out!" Selene ran toward Gryph.

Lucas sprang to his feet, hit Gryph in the midsection and knocked him on his back, morphed into a wolf and lunged for Gryph's throat.

Selene threw herself at Lucas, wrapping her arms

around his hairy neck and squeezing with all her might, physically and mentally.

Lucas fought her, stretching his lethal jaws toward Gryph's throat. Unable to reach his goal, Lucas rolled over, taking Selene with him, shaking loose of her hold.

Then he attacked her.

She threw her arm over her face, the wolf's teeth tearing into her flesh.

No sooner had he bitten her, he was flung across the room with the mighty sweep of Gryph's big paw.

Lucas slammed into the wall headfirst with a loud thud and a snap. He lay still at an awkward angle, his eyes open, his body returning to human.

Gryph gave him no more than a glance before he dropped down beside Selene. "You're bleeding."

"Now, that's a real scratch." She laughed shakily, her eyes filling with tears. "I'm sorry."

"For what?"

"Your brother."

"You don't have to be sorry." He removed the tattered remains of his jacket and ripped what was left of his shirt into long strips, making quick work of applying a pressure bandage to the torn skin of her arm. His tuxedo trousers hung around his waist, shredded during his transformation from man to beast. He didn't care. "I need to get you to a hospital."

"No. You have guests to help. My sisters—"

"Can help the guests." He lifted her in his arms and held her tightly against his battered body.

Selene didn't have the strength to argue, just leaned her face against his furry chest and sighed. "This is where I want to be."

"And where I want you to be," he whispered against her hair.

"Then why fight it?" She wasn't sure she spoke the words out loud or in her mind.

"I surrender."

A smile curved her lips and her eyelids slid downward. The loss of blood and the strain of fighting to protect the ones she loved had taken their toll. In the warmth of Gryph's arms, the black wolf dead and no longer a threat, his minions scattering to the winds, Selene succumbed to darkness.

Chapter 20

Emts from all over the city converged on the hotel, treating the wounded and sedating the hysterical. Gryph left the hotel in the back of the ambulance with Selene, her sisters promising to wrap things up and meet him at the hospital.

All the way to the trauma center Gryph had too much time to think and imagine the worst. Selene had slipped into unconsciousness and had yet to wake up. She'd been injured worse than he first thought. The bite had ripped several veins and she was bleeding tremendously. Her loss of so much blood scared Gryph more than anything he'd encountered in his entire life. Gryph pressed Selene's hand to his cheek, praying to every god he'd ever had need to pray to that Selene would live. She had saved him from the river and captured his heart with her warmth and understanding of his family in the Lair. She aroused in him a desire so rare and beautiful he could not imagine living life without her in it. And as soon as she awakened, he'd tell her. If she'd have him, he'd do his best to quell his beast and be gentle with her the rest of their lives.

The EMTs unloaded the gurney at the hospital and wheeled Selene into a room. When Gryph followed, a nurse blocked his path. "You'll need to stay in the waiting room."

He wanted to roar and tell the woman to get the hell out of his way.

But she smiled and laid a hand on his arm. "Trust us and let us do our jobs. She's in good hands."

Gryph backed into the waiting room and paced.

Within minutes, the rest of the Chattox sisters arrived, explaining that Cal had remained behind to help sort through the mess of guests and shifters, identifying those who'd changed back into their human form before they mixed with the guests and could escape.

"How's our girl?" Brigid asked, peering through the window of the swinging door leading to the back.

"I don't know. She wasn't conscious going in." Gryph spun and walked to the end of the room and back. "I should have done more. I should have seen it, suspected him. I should have known it was Lucas."

"We heard the black wolf was your brother." Aurai laid a hand on his arm. "I'm sorry."

Gryph shook her hand off and closed his eyes, the image of Lucas lying against the wall not nearly as painful as Selene slipping away in his arms. "He might have killed her."

"The doctors will save her," Deme said.

"We have to believe." Gina took Deme's hand and held her hand out to Brigid. The sisters came together in a circle, each holding a hand.

Gryph stood on the outside, wishing he could add to their power to save their sister.

Aurai broke the chain and extended her hand to him. "Come."

Gryph took it, and Brigid's, and stood with them as they chanted:

"Feel the power.
Free our hearts.
Save our sister.
Bring her home.
With the strength of the earth,

With the rising of the wind,
With the calm of the water,
With the intensity of fire,
With the freedom of spirit,
The goddess is within us.
She is power.
We are her.
We are one
Blessed be."

Something swelled inside him, lifting his spirit, giving him the confidence to face what would be, and the whole-hearted belief that Selene would be all right.

After a moment of silence, they dropped hands and stepped back.

Gryph walked toward the exit and out into the hallway and almost ran into Balthazar.

He gripped the man's arms, his heart squeezing so hard in his chest he could barely breathe. "Father, I'm sorry."

Balthazar raised his hand. "I know. Word travels fast in the underground. Lucas is dead." For a moment his lips pressed into a tight line, his eyes filling with weary tears. "I'm sorry it came to this. I knew I was losing him, I just didn't realize how badly."

Gryph hugged the man who'd raised him his entire life, who'd shown him more love and care than most biological fathers ever did. This man had opened his home and his heart equally to Lucas.

Gryph stood back from his adoptive father. "What I don't understand is why he was so angry with me. Why he thought I was the favored son."

"Probably because he knew you weren't abandoned like he was. You see, his mother didn't love him. Wanted nothing to do with him."

"So? My mother didn't want me, either."

"No, that isn't true. I told you long ago that your mother brought you to me when you were an infant. She loved you and didn't want you to be exposed to the ridicule and hatred of living your life among humans who wouldn't understand when you shifted to lion and back. And in the early years, you did, without warning. Even as an infant.

"When your mother was raped, her parents threatened to cut her off if she didn't abort you. She told her parents she had, but hid her pregnancy from them. When she gave birth in her apartment, she knew the moment you came out, your condition would be impossible to hide.

"She loved you, but to ensure you lived a happier life, she gave you to me, knowing I could raise you better than she could and in a place that would accept you for who and what you were."

"Why didn't she come to live among us?"

"She wanted to, but she was prone to depression and living in the tunnels wouldn't have been conducive to a happy life for her."

"But she never came to visit."

"We thought it best that you not be tempted by the surface until you had your beast under control."

"And when I did attain that goal?" Gryph prompted, trying to grasp what his father was saying.

Balthazar shrugged. "It was just easier."

"Is she—"

"Still alive?" Balthazar nodded. "And she'd like very much to meet you."

Gryph's stomach churned, his palms were sweaty and his beast surged, threatening to unfurl. "When?"

Balthazar patted his arm. "Soon. In the meantime, we need to make sure no harm comes to your little witch."

"She's not mine."

"Then convince her."

"How?"

"Trust your instincts."

"I'm dangerous. I can't control my beast when I'm with her."

"Give her the choice," Balthazar said softly.

Footsteps rang out in the hallway and Gryph turned.

A man in blue scrubs pushed a surgical mask down from his face. "Are you all with Miss Chattox?"

The sisters filed out of the waiting room to join Gryph and Balthazar.

"We're her sisters," Deme said. "How is she?"

"She'll live. It was a nasty wound, severing several veins, but we were able to stop the flow of blood and stitch her back together. You can go in to see her once she's settled in her room. She should be ready to go home tomorrow, if she has someone who'll stay with her."

"She does," Deme assured the doctor. Once he'd left, she held out her hands to her sisters and they gathered in a tight hug, opening their family embrace to Gryph and Balthazar, who gladly accepted.

A nurse found them in the waiting room and led them to the floor and room where they'd moved Selene.

They gathered around Selene's sleeping form, hooked up to monitors and an IV.

Gryph's chest hurt and the scent of antiseptic made him want to vomit. Selene looked so small and helpless against the clean white sheets.

"She probably won't wake until morning," the nurse was saying. "You all might as well get some rest."

"I'm staying," Gryph informed her.

The nurse's gaze ran his length. "Someone put your tux through a blender, sir? You might want to go home, shower and change. You don't want to frighten our patient."

For the first time since he'd left the hotel, Gryph glanced down at his tattered clothing. It didn't matter. "I'm staying."

Her nose wrinkled and she crossed her arms over her chest. "Are you family?"

Deme, Brigid, Aurai and Gina all answered as one, "Yes!"

The nurse relaxed. "Then I guess you're staying. I'll get a spare pillow and blanket and see if I can't find a shirt."

"That won't be necessary," Gryph assured her.

The woman shook her head. "If I want the nurses to do their jobs and not duck in every five minutes to stare, I'll be finding you a shirt and you will by golly wear it!"

Gryph smiled. "Thank you."

The woman snorted. "That's more like it."

"I'm for that shower and fresh clothing the nurse suggested," Deme said. She touched a hand to Selene's pale cheek. "Be safe, sister." Then she pressed a kiss to her sister's forehead.

The others followed suit.

Deme stopped in front of Gryph. "I'll only be gone for an hour. Call me if she wakes or if you need anything."

"I will."

Brigid faced Gryph. "You're all right for a shifter." She glanced back at her sister lying in the bed. "Selene could do worse," she said, her voice gruff. She touched his arm. "Point is, I trust you to look out for her."

"Thank you."

Gina and Aurai both kissed Selene and turned to leave.

Aurai was at the door when she spun and ran back to Gryph, throwing her arms around him. "Thanks for saving her. We couldn't live without Selene."

Acceptance from the tight-knit family of sisters warmed Gryph's insides, making his chest swell. He hoped he could live up to their expectations and protect their sister from any threats. He'd almost lost her this time. If she gave him a chance, he'd sure as hell do a better job the next time.

Balthazar was the last to leave, laying a hand on Gryph's shoulder. "She's special."

"Yes, she is."

"And so are you. You're as human as anyone, where it counts." His father pressed a hand to his chest.

Gryph nodded. Animals came in all forms, both physical and mental. He prayed he could be the man and beast Selene deserved.

When everyone left but him, he settled in the chair beside Selene and held her hand through the night, praying the bite of the wolf didn't impact her and if it had, that she'd be up for the challenge.

No matter the outcome, he'd accept her for who she was. Because he loved her.

Chapter 21

Selene pulled herself out of the gray fog clouding her brain and opened her eyes to sunshine streaming through the open curtain. She blinked and stared around at the sterile walls and surroundings before she realized she was in a hospital.

"About time you woke up." Deme leaned over the bed and brushed a strand of hair out of her face.

"How long have I been asleep?"

"Just through the night. The doctor was pleased with your recovery and is sending a nurse by to brief you on your release."

"Oh." Selene glanced around the room.

"If you're looking for the others, Gina and Aurai are bringing the rental car around. Brigid is at the station with Cal filling out the mountain of paperwork that comes from an all-out attack by paranorms at a downtown grand hotel."

Selene grimaced. "How many were hurt?"

"A couple dozen, but only one death."

"Lucas?"

Deme nodded.

Selene's chest tightened. Gryph must have been devastated by his brother's betrayal. She glanced toward the door, wondering where he was.

"Gryph's not here."

"Oh."

Deme smiled. "He was here all night. I ran him home to get a shower and some presentable clothes. He was scaring the staff."

Selene's heart skipped several beats. "He was here."

"Honey, he didn't leave your side all night. The rest of us went to bed. He didn't. Looked like hell this morning."

Selene sat up, a little light-headed, and her neck and arm were sore. She stared down at the bandages and stiffened, remembering Lucas's teeth tearing into her flesh. She touched the bandages. "He bit me."

"Yes." Deme ran a brush through Selene's hair, smoothing the tangles. "The good news is that I did a little checking with the local coven. Apparently, witches are immune to werewolf bites, and it takes more than a mere scratch or bite to change a human to a wolf."

Selene let go of the tension knotting her muscles, the steady brushstrokes calming. "It's bad enough being a witch, but a shifter witch?" When Deme finished, Selene leaned back, shaking her head. "At least D'na Ileana's view of the future didn't come to pass."

"No, it didn't." Gryph's deep voice sounded from the doorway. "Her prediction didn't take into account the power of love and family."

Selene's pulse quickened, her cheeks heating. She lifted a hand to her face, wishing she'd had time to shower and apply some makeup before seeing him.

He carried a vase of red and white roses and set them on the table beside the bed. "You've got some color back in your cheeks."

"It's warm in here," she said.

"I brought you a visitor."

"Really? I'm not even dressed."

"She won't care."

"She?" Selene straightened the sheet in her lap and tugged at the hospital gown.

He turned toward door. "Dr. Richardson?"

An older woman with salt-and-pepper hair, wearing a tasteful business suit, entered the room, her steps hesitant. "Hi."

A spark of recognition teetered on the edge of Selene's memory. She stared from the woman to Gryph. "Don't I know you?"

She nodded. "I'm the president of Colyer-Fenton College, where your sister Aurai studied."

"Oh, yes. I remember now." Not only was she the president during the struggle to free Aurai, but this woman had also been a student at the college when the Chimera had first struck over thirty years ago.

Her frown deepening, Selene's glance shifted to Gryph. What had Balthazar said? Gryph's mother had been attacked by a monster.

Could she be? Her gaze swung back to Dr. Richardson. "Are you—"

"Gryphon's mother?" She held out her hand to her son.

He took it, nodding. "She is. Balthazar introduced us this morning. I wanted her to meet you."

"It's my pleasure." She held out a hand to Selene. "I regret that I wasn't strong enough to raise Gryph on my own. However, Balthazar knew what he was doing. My son is a good man."

Selene squeezed the woman's hand. "Yes, he is."

"Well, I don't want to wear you out and I have to get back to work. I just wanted to meet the woman who captured my son's heart." With tears shimmering in her eyes, she bent and gave Selene a hug. "Grab for love and hold as tightly as you can," she whispered into Selene's ear. Then she was gone, leaving Selene alone with Gryph.

Suddenly shy and at a definite disadvantage, Selene shifted in the sheets, refusing to look at Gryph, afraid she wouldn't see what she wanted to see in his expression. They'd been off again, on again and frankly, she didn't know where they stood anymore or where they were heading.

"I heard what Dr. Richardson said to you." Gryph finally broke the silence, striding across the room.

"You did?" Heat suffused Selene's cheeks and spread down her neck and onto her chest. "And?"

"I agree."

Selene's eyes narrowed. "Just so we're both on the same page...she said grab for love and hold on as tightly as you can. Is that what you heard?"

He nodded, a smile spreading across his face. "Question is, do you agree?"

Afraid of more rejection and too tired to fight about it, Selene gazed up at the man she was growing to love more with each day they were together. "Are you going to push me away again? Because I'm not sure I can handle it. A girl can only handle so much rejection before—"

He gathered her in his arms, his lips crashing down over hers.

She melted against him, recognizing this as the place she wanted to be. In his arms, with his lips on hers.

Several long, delicious minutes later, he came up for air. "I don't ever want to hurt you."

"Then don't give up on me or what we have together."

"I can't always control my beast."

"I'll help you." She smoothed a strand of his tawny hair from his forehead. "Are you sure you want to be with a witch?"

"One who can read minds and manipulate people at will?" He nodded. "I told you, I can recognize when you're doing it to me. I won't do anything I don't want to."

"Promise?"

He raised a hand. "Promise."

"Then there's only one thing left to do?" she said.

"What's that?" His arms tightened around her.

"Kiss me."

And he did.

* * * * *

MILLS & BOON

Desire

Indulge in secrets and scandal, intense drama and plenty of sizzling hot action with powerful and passionate heroes who have it all: wealth, status, good looks…everything but the right woman.

MILLS & BOON

HEROES

At Your Service

Experience all the excitement of a gripping thriller, with an intense romance at its heart. Resourceful, true-to-life women and strong, fearless men face danger and desire – a killer combination!